Some Assembly Required

The Superstars

ISBN: 154824208X

ISBN-13: 978-1548242084

To anyone who has ever looked at a book and thought, 'I wonder if I can do that?'

OTHER TITLES

By The Superstars

From The Mysterium:

Title Not Included

By Rae Bailey

Hey Kid (Coming soon)

By Jessica Grace Coleman

From Darker Times:

The Little Forest Series:

The Former World

Memento Mori

The Exalted

Carnival Masquerade

The Gloaming

The Downfall Trilogy:

The Downfall

By Hailie Drescher

From Tale Seekers:

Familiars' Calling (Coming soon)

By Mike Farren

From Templar:

Pierrot and His Mother

By The Wharfedale Poets:

Sunlight, Shadow and Sin

By Lauren K. Nixon

From The Mysterium:

Echoes of the Light

The Fox and the Fool (Coming soon)

The House of Vines (Coming soon)

ACKNOWLEDGEMENTS

Projects like this cannot happen without the support of a community of creative and practical people. Our own little group of writers and artists has grown considerably this year, following the publication of our first volume, and there are many people without whom this second anthology could not have been put together:

Firstly, no anthology could be created without the authors themselves, all of whom have stepped up to the mark, providing a wonderful variety of stories and poems every month. Thank you all for offering up your scribblings and waiting patiently for this thing to get done, and for tolerating my editing!

This year, Cynthia, Hailie, Liz and PhoenixShaman have provided some extremely cool art for the chapter headings, which got everyone excited. Thanks guys! I never get tired of seeing our stories through your eyes and clever pens!

The lovely cover was created through the creative wizardry of James at GoOnWrite.com - thanks James!

Many thanks must go to Rae, who helped immensely with the editing! Also to Hailie, M. Loftouse, Apolline Tabourot and Naveen Bhat (with his high quality written prose), who kindly looked over the front matter, acknowledgements and introduction.

Several people have contributed to our list of prompts this year, namely Gemma, Jess, Dominic Hopkins, and Lauren. Thanks must also go to Wayne Naylor, for coming up with a great title!

There are also a whole bunch of Superstars whose work isn't included in this anthology, but whom we love having around. Those members of the club who are always on hand to get discussions going, share creative ideas, read through our work and help us out of plotholes also need a big hand:

Abigail Ash, Andrew Bishop, Rebecca Cannell, Holly Crawford, Samantha Hopkins, Clare Keogh, Helen

Jeffrey-Bourne, Peter Jeffrey-Bourne, Paul Marr, Lina Martindale, Finn McClellan, Carl Mitchell, Wayne Naylor, Chris O'Brien, Sophie Phillips, and Matt Ward. Really, knowing that we have a friendly audience and in-house critics is tremendously useful!

In terms of compiling the anthology, this would not have been possible without the troubleshooting abilities of Niall Fleming, who has a way with computers that seems like an island of calm in a library of chaos.

It feels bizarre indeed to be writing a thank-you to myself, but I know if I hadn't made myself stick to curating the prompts and submissions, bouncing around the club like a crazy person and occasionally hassling people for stuff, I never would have written as much as I have these past few years. I'm also pretty pleased with how the anthology has turned out, so I'm glad I actually got around to putting it together. Yay! So, um... thanks, me!

- Lauren K. Nixon

(Curator)

Everyone involved in this project would like to thank their family and friends for their encouragement, support and patience, occasional meals and numerous cups of tea.

Picture Credits

Hailie provided the artwork for the following chapters: Take a Pebble, The Boy in the Storm, The Exit is Everything, and The Last Human Getaway.

Liz Hearson provided the artwork for the following chapters: The Lovely Perch, The Incident Pit, Nala the Impaler, and The Gorilla Murders.

Cynthia Holt provided the artwork for her own submission, Telling the Bees.

Allie Riley is a phenomenal photographer, and took the group photograph of the Superstars in the Authors section.

PhoenixShaman provided the artwork for the following chapters: Reboot Reality, Going Underground, Telling the Bees, and The Psychedelic Gnome Project.

Cover art by James at GoOnWrite.com

CONTENTS

INTRODUCTION

Welcome to the second anthology by The Superstars!

This fresh collection of stories, poems, snippets and experiments is the result of twelve months of prompts, picked at random and posted on the first day of every month between October 2015 and September 2016.

The rules are simple: prompts are posted on the first day of the month and any Superstar inspired by it will compose a piece of creative writing of any form or genre, preferably between 100 and 10,000 words, to be presented to the group for critique on the last day of the month - in whatever state it's in.

Needless to say, these rules are frequently broken!

Originally, the idea was to generate a sort of writing game where people could tell the many tiny stories that we never seem to get around to telling and improve their writing in a friendly and generally rather silly environment. These days, it's also an outlet to get something published that we can look at and remember that anything is possible, if you put your mind to it.

It has to be said that our superstars are all rather odd, which is why we get on so well, and also possibly why all the entries go in totally unexpected directions. This, quite rightly, is all part of the fun, and keeps us all on our toes. Several times we've all remarked to one another that there's only one possible way for a particular prompt to be interpreted, only to be proved entirely wrong when the submissions come in at the end of the month!

This year our offerings include the standard array of prompts, including several suggested by members of our extended writing community. One is a little different: for Going Underground, Superstars were given a line at random from the London Tube map and were asked to build a story around that line, or one of the stations from it. The Gorilla Murders was chosen in homage to one of the earliest detective stories, The Murders in the Rue Morgue, by Edgar Allan Poe.

We have Superstars, now, from all over the place, from all kinds of backgrounds. Some of us are published or self-published, some of us write professionally, some of us have never written before. Our stories and poems range as widely as we do, across love and loss, friendship and adventure, murder and magic, fantasy and family.

I think I can speak for all of us when I say we hope you enjoy reading these fragments of our imagination as much as we enjoyed putting them together!

- Lauren K. Nixon
  Curator

*

ctrl
alt
del

Reboot Reality

By G. Burton

Reboot Reality;
Stop, is it anarchy?
What about gravity?
Will it hold my reality?
Watching it bitterly,
Wondering brainlessly
At all of the bribery,
People working churlishly,
Proclaiming cockily
'Reboot Reality!'
Listening hopelessly
At all of the flippancy,
That has become the parody
Of our Rebooted Reality.

Reboot Reality

By Hailie Drescher

Cold,
Tired,
All alone.
What is it about this home?

Dark,
Empty,
Filled with dread.
Never want to leave my bed.

Restart,
Reboot,
I don't give a hoot.
Let me crawl back into bed.

It's cold,
It's dark,
I'm all alone.
Reboot,
Reboot,
Let me reboot.

No reason to get up,
No reason to leave my bed.

What I need,
And what I crave,
Is a restart,
A reboot,

To my reality.

Please,
just let me.
Let me restart,
Reboot,
My reality.

Reboot Reality

By T. J. Francis

Wake up from a dream,
Is life all that you can see?
Do you know if it is true?
Reboot my reality.

Dreams so vivid you can taste,
Life so dazed you skip through time.
Which one would you rather live?
Reboot my reality.

Truth and lies so closely bound
Chaos thrives on people's lives.
Is this somewhere I can thrive?
Reboot my reality.

I don't remember starting this,
I'm not sure if I'm writing this.
Am I here or in my dream?
Reboot my reality.

I Can Change Your Life (for £29.99)

By Philip Lickley

The Red Bicycle was the newest restaurant in town, and for a town that had practically had a street party when the Nandos had opened, this was a big deal. The opening night had been a flourish of party balloons, live acoustic music and much buzz around town. Soon the streets were awash with young couples, older couples and those singles somewhere in between, hoping to find love amongst the cocktails and food served on slates. There were selfies aplenty from the younger customers and some positive sounding buzz from the older end.

You may have picked up on my description of the food – that some was served on slates, because The Red Bicycle was a trendy restaurant. Its menus were pretentious, its décor wooden and the venue was scattered with vintage props, such as old cartwheels and nostalgically-rusted signs advertising products that stopped being sold in the 1950s. The staff weren't waiters or waitresses, they were part of the 'service team', and the bar was lined with beers known by ironic names. Even the toilets were in on the joke, the male urinals made out of metallic kegs and the women's toilets including a sofa between the cubicles. If a hipster was a restaurant, he would be The Red Bicycle.

It wasn't the opening night, though, when Niall Thomas first visited. It was a few days later, on a scouting mission to check out the venue. It was lunchtime and the place was half empty, apart from a man with a non-ironic moustache drinking what looked like Coca-Cola out of a jam jar and a gaggle of 'ladies who lunch' working their way through a platter of sandwiches. Niall found himself self-consciously walking through the trendy venue, his whatever-I-could-find wardrobe choices of checked shirt, dark blue jeans and tatty Converse feeling at odds with the décor. He could feel his top-lip quivering as if it was attempting to create an emergency moustache as a blending-in technique.

Niall, for the record, was twenty-six, with an unruly haircut and a fear that he was approaching his late twenties and was still undeniable single. So much so he feared there was a Wikipedia profile of him somewhere warning women against dating him. The closest he'd got so far to be successful on the dating circuit was downloading the Tinder app on his phone and then chickening out when it kept asking him for his location.

Niall, glancing nervously around at the metallic furniture and wooden tables decked out with candles (unlit) and fake plastic flowers (unwatered), approached the bar where a man a few years younger than him with a pencil-line moustache, grey top and braces (both on his teeth and holding up his trousers), enquired about what drink he'd like to order. Niall, wishing for something more alcoholic to steady his nerves, instead ordered a cup of tea which came to him on a metallic tray in a metallic teapot alongside what looked to be an elaborate egg-timer. Niall thanked the man, paid for his drink with a quick flash of his contactless card on the reader (ah, technology), and found a seat in a corner. There he studied the egg-timer and realised it was actually a tea-timer, with three glass receptacles containing different levels – and colours – of sand, each labelled to time a different length of brewing. Niall's lip curled, he put the timer down and poured the tea anyway. He had no interest in the science of tea boiling. Life was too short for such trivialities.

The reason Niall was performing a check on the venue was he hoped to make it his chief destination for his first date with Anya Johnstone. Anya was twenty-five and worked with a Niall at his local pub. Recently, they'd sparked up quite a friendship. Well, they'd shared a few conversations on shift over hot dishes and even hotter dishwashers, and on leaving work as they made their way down the poorly lit streets and towards their respective flats.

To say Niall was in love with Anya was a little bit of an overstatement. It had been a long time since he'd found such a connection with a human being, that was true, but love is such a strong word. He definitely enjoyed her company – she was very easy to talk to – and perhaps he lusted after her a little, but love? He wasn't sure. There was definitely more innuendo than marriage in their relationship, and much more chat over Facebook Messenger than face-to-face musings.

After several months of chatting at work and a few drinks in the pub, Niall had finally plucked up the courage to ask Anya out on a date. Except he hadn't really, instead he'd awkwardly invited her out for a meal without really mentioned the 'd' word. The conversation went something along the lines of this...

Niall, standing awkwardly at the junction where they would split nightly to go to their own homes had said, "Hey Anya, I wondered if you fancied maybe going for a bite to eat next week? I know a great place."

Anya, smiling, had replied, "Yeah sounds good," without any real commitment. "How about Friday?"

Niall, with more enthusiasm, had agreed. "Yeah, definitely."

Now Niall had managed to get a time and hopefully a place, but he was conscious that there might be a different expectation from each party about this meal. To Niall it was a date, a chance for him to finally make a better impression on Anya and hopefully move their relationship on, but he feared for Anya it was going to be little more than a friendly meal at the end of the week.

Niall took a sip of his tea – it was still pretty hot – and studied the menu, his mouth silently speaking the key headlines. "Burgers... pizzas... tortillas... salads... sandwiches..." There appeared to be a good selection of items on the menu, enough for anyone to really find something they'd like on there. He nodded and realised that The Red Bicycle was the right place for their meal: nice enough to make a good impression, not too posh as if to shout "I'VE BROUGHT YOU HERE BECAUSE I REALLY LIKE YOU AND DON'T MIND SPENDING LOTS OF CASH ON OUR MEAL AS I WANT TO GET IN YOUR PANTS EVENTUALLY, BUT NOT RIGHT NOW, DON'T BE CREEPED OUT," just in case his feelings weren't quite reciprocated.

And so Friday came, and The Red Bicycle was much busier, each table home to groups of diners. If the scene was being narrated by David Attenborough rather than the latest album from Mumford and Sons, then the naturalist would be commenting on the distinctive groups of people: the loved-up couples holding hands across the table; the awkward first dates, not entirely sure where the next bit of conversation was coming from; the older pairings comfortable enough in their own skins; and the groups of young lads and laddettes, the nosiest of all, making jokes unsuitable for repeating here. Completing the scenario were the waiters and waitresses – sorry, members of the 'service team' – buzzing around with trays of food served on plates, in boxes and on more slates, or drinks in various sizes and shapes of glasses, all in various states, some with dry ice coming off them, others on fire and others just sitting there patiently with no parlour tricks to demonstrate, other than their tasty flavours. In the corner there was also a singer with an acoustic guitar, standing in a band t-shirt, tight skinny-feet jeans and a pair of trainers, playing through a selection of hits that mainly focussed on Ed Sheeran and Sam Smith and, of course, *that* song by John Newman that it must be illegal or something not to play during a set. 'All Of Me', indeed.

As the large clock in the restaurant ticked towards eight o'clock, Niall stood outside the venue under the street-lamp, nervously checking his smartphone, flicking between the clock, Facebook, Twitter and YikYak, with a sort of nervous technological twitch. He was glad when Anya appeared just after eight, dressed in jeans, a tight red top and smart trainers. Niall smiled in her direction, trying to study her fashion choices to see if they read as casual meet-up or date. He admitted to himself that he had no real knowledge of what codes or suggestions were hidden in her clothing so instead just slipped his phone back into his jeans and smiled. Niall thrust out his hand awkwardly as if to offer a handshake; thankfully Anya helped him avoid such awkwardness by adapting his out-stretched arm as the offer of a hug and completed this new movement. Niall received said hug with difficulty, unstiffening his arm and putting it around Anya only just in time before she pulled away. He smiled once more and wordlessly gestured into the restaurant, Anya walking in with Niall following closely behind, cursing himself under his breath for his obviously awkward behaviour.

Anya and Niall entered The Red Bicycle up a flight of wooden stairs, just behind a young staff member carrying a cocktail which had a flaming element to it. Niall imagined her brain firing off electrical warning signals to her arms saying that if she dropped the drink there was a distinct possibility the whole venue would go up in flames. Niall's nervous brain jumped around jokes he probably wouldn't tell, settling on the hipster venue not being 'cool' for a long time after such an inferno.

Quickly reaching the top of the stairs, they were both greeted by a male, keen to show them to their seats, giving them a menu and a drinks menu each and gesticulating for them to sit down, which they did. Now all that was between Anya and Niall on their 'date' was a table and a candle (lit), flowers (blooming naturally) and nerves (tense). Niall watched as Anya studied the drinks menu and turned to the waiter ('service team member') and asked for a cocktail with a jokey name, but Niall missed exact which one. He instead plumped for a cold cider, and both drinks were quickly delivered to the pair by a third man with an impressive moustache, as if facial hair was some sort of requirement for the job.

The first few moments with drinks were perhaps a little more awkward than Niall would have liked, with a few snatches of conversation here and there, a couple of furtive glances and a feeling that the nature of meeting in a restaurant had somehow stifled their usually active conversations. But by the time the alcohol in the cocktail and the cider had taken effect though, the conversation was flowing like the bottle of white wine that was ordered with the starter (breads with olives and oils for Anya, pate on wholemeal toast for Niall). It was all going as smoothly as Niall's starter until a fateful moment of conversation. They had begun talking about their previous romances.

"There was this one guy," Anya said, laughing to herself, "Who was so ridiculously organised it was crazy. We couldn't go out anywhere or do anything without him having a plan, an itinerary, or something like that. It was mad. He quite literally always had to be on top of everything."

Niall laughed and that's when the joke sort of slipped out uncontrollably, like he was starting a new game called innuendo Tourette's (coming soon to Channel 5 probably).

"I bet he enjoyed being on top of you, especially."

It was almost as if that one sentence had been broadcast over the small speaker the acoustic singer was using. Niall felt like the room had suddenly gone quiet and he looked in horror towards Anya, realising what he'd said. A bead of sweat made its way down the back of his neck, making a damp journey through his shirt. He prayed she'd not really heard him or would laugh it off. He froze in horror. Anya looked away, blushing slightly. She'd noticed.

"I – I," Niall stuttered, wishing somehow he could think up some way of rescuing the situation, but he feared it was something beyond his talents. He doubted even the RAC could rescue him from this disaster. He was panicking now. He could tell. His brain had just conjured up a random metaphor about a random breakdown company. Thirty seconds had passed. Anya still hadn't spoken again or met his gaze.

"I didn't mean that, sorry, that was inappropriate,"

he muttered, before placing his fork back down on his almost finished starter and his serviette back on the table. Niall pushed his chair back quickly, almost knocking out one of the staff, who had been delivering a flaming cocktail to the next table. His visions of almost burning down the place had almost come true.

Making some muffled excuses under his breath, Niall left the table and withdrew himself to the toilets. There he fumbled with his fly, made a half-hearted attempt at using the urinal for its purpose before realising he didn't actually need to go, then retiring to the sink and staring at himself in the mirror.

"God Niall, what have you done?" he muttered to himself, but forbore any more monologuing as another gentleman came into the facilities, quickly using the urinal before promptly joining Niall at the sink space, in a very quick and swift movement. Niall felt like he hadn't really come to use the toilet but to see him, a random prophecy that came true as the man turned to him and thrust out his hand. Niall looked down at his hand then back at the man, clumsily engaging in a handshake.

"I don't usually shake the hand of other men using the gents," the man said in a gruff, Southern voice, "But since you've clearly washed your hands on this occasion I will make an exception. Anyway, enough of the small talk, let me get down to business. My name is Rory Glover and I work for a company. A company called Reboot Reality - and I believe you could use our services."

Rory appeared to pause as if to give Niall chance to take in what he'd said or reply. In either case there wasn't truly enough of a gap to do either, as Rory just continued after a minor hesitation.

"I imagine you are wondering who Reboot Reality is. You've never heard of us, right? Not many have. We're not really on Google; we don't have a Facebook page. My manager has never heard of Twitter, or Tumblr. Frankly he still thinks the Yellow Pages is a viable advertising medium, and I'm not talking about the online version.

"Basically we are a service designed to help you, others like you, people like you. To get you out of difficult situations. I was in there, on the table behind you, just enjoying one of this venue's very fine cocktails. One with Cointreau and vodka I think, in a rather unusual combination, but it was blue, and I like blue. You can tell by my tie."

Niall stood there just staring at the man, confused by the information and his fast-paced, rambling delivery. He seemed to be becoming mesmerised by his patter, and it didn't really do to be mesmerised by another man in the gent's toilet. Niall didn't swing that way.

"Anyway I saw you with that girl - lovely woman, I can see why you're taken by her. Beautiful eyes, winning smile, but most importantly a great conversationalist. Kids today don't appreciate the art of good conversation what with their swipe-here, swipe-there Tinder lifestyles, where everything is delivered now and again, now in one hundred and forty characters, don't give me a video of more than sixty seconds my brain can't take it. It wasn't like that when I was young. Granted, that was pre-computers never mind phones, when all you had to rely on was your own wits, conversation or dancing ability.

"People your age now just go for looks and then regret it afterwards when they're shacked up with some man or woman who looks like they could front a clothing campaign, but behind those good looks, pah, nothing. Emptier than my bank account after my first divorce. No conversations, no interests: boring, tedious. Once the old you-know-what wears off and it's Saturday nights on the sofa watching television instead of nights in bed enjoying positions seven through eleven they start to realise. But you've picked a good one there: bright, bubbly, friendly. And you're not bad yourself. Perhaps you need a tidy up, haircut, shave, someone to suggest Top Man not Primark, but you'll do.

"Anyway I'm rambling again. I'm from Reboot Reality and we can help with your little sexual faux pas, your inappropriate innuendo, in one easy step. Basically, and I won't bore you with the technology too much, we have created a way of helping turn back the clock, to restart those conversations which you wish you hadn't had. Let me put it another way, we can help Bill Murray your life up."

Niall looked blank.

"You know, Bill Murray."

"The voice of Garfield?"

Rory's eyes narrowed. "You could have at least picked Ghostbusters. No, Bill Murray, in Groundhog Day – reliving moments until he gets it right."

Niall continued to look blank.

"How about Eternal Sunshine of the Spotless Mind, but without all the brain washing?" (Still blank). "Oh, Jesus. Maybe something more pop cultural," he said, thinking for a moment, before inspiration hit. "Like Craig David in his 7 Days video. You remember that one? Sunday – took her for a drink on Wednesday, we were making love by Fri... oh never mind, you know in the video where he winds back the film spool and stops him from spilling the wine? Like that."

Niall continued to stare blankly, overwhelmed by the wall of words. "I actually have no idea what you're talking about."

Rory signed. "Jesus Christ, Niall. What do you kids learn about these days? Where's your pop culture? Do you not go to pub quizzes? Whatever happened to people knowing stuff?" Rob stared momentarily into the mirror. "Anyway, we can turn back the clock for you to make up for your mistakes."

"Like... time travel?" Niall asked, finally catching up with the conversation. Rory just rolled his yes.

"No, not time travel! Look at me, does it look like I travel around the place in a fucking Delorean? Do I look like Peter fucking Capaldi? Well, maybe a little. I'm a little greyer than I'd like," he mused, once more staring into the mirror. "It's more nuanced than that. Let me try and explain it to you. You know on your PC, if you fuck it up too much with porn or whatever, and you have to roll it back to a previous time, before the viruses set in? It's like that, except the world is the PC, the porn is your inability to hold down a conversation, and the roll-back service is me. Through some science research my boss funded, which even I don't fully understand and let's face it, you're only bothered if it works, not how it works, we can reboot reality – see what we did there? – and let you go back in and pick up the conversation again before your mistake. Call it a learning process where you can adjust your mistakes and make everything go much more smoothly. Get it? No time travel. No brain erasing. No slightly unconvincing CGI effects in a music video, just everyone else's reality, rebooted. You remember it all to learn from your conversational mistakes."

Niall thought about it for a moment and looked over at Rory.

"I mean, it sounds bat shit crazy, but I'll go with this for a moment. Isn't that a bit... unethical?"

Rory looked at Niall and his lip curled. "You know what, I like you. You're thinking it through. You're concerned that this is basically cheating. That you not only get two bites of the cherry, but the chance to shape the cherry into what you want. Trust me, we don't get involved in anything dodgy, this is just about conversations and social situations. We don't get involved with crime; if someone does something illegal then they're on their own. Reboot Reality have many different divisions – financial, domestic, romantic (that's me) – but it's all based around conversations. Our technology doesn't allow for anything more than resetting the world in that way. Actions have still happened, and if you commit a crime then you're held responsible for it. And trust me, it's not just men that use this service. We deal with as many women as men in this game, it's not only us that can screw up, you know?

"Though granted, for some of our female clients it's the opposite way round, restarting the conversations because they want to get away from the man, rather than get with him, but that's another conversation for another day. So, what do you think, Niall? Would you like to Reboot Reality?"

Niall considered it and nodded. "OK, I'm in. But what's the catch? Assuming this conversation is genuine and you're not some sort of nutter."

Rory laughed and opened his jacket, pulling out a small metallic case, out of which he pulled an embossed business card, passing it to Niall. On it, were the words, 'Rory Glover / Reboot Reality / Romance & Relationships Department / Like Reality - Only Better'.

"I didn't make up the slogan," Rory noted. "So maybe I am a con-artist, but I'm one that's invested in some pretty heavy duty business cards. These aren't any old Vista Print pieces. These are the genuine deal. Professionally printed, and even come with NFC. You'll know about NFC as you're using it, I bet, with your bank cards or phone, or whatever. It might as well stand for No Fucking Clue as far as I'm concerned. That sort of thing is a mystery to me, even more so than my ex-wife!"

Rory waited for a laugh that never came. "Anyway, back to our conversation, by 'catch' I assume you mean 'cost'. For me to reboot your reality, I can offer you the one-off price of £29.99."

Niall spluttered. "Thirty quid? That's expensive."

Rory smiled. "You cannot put a price on happiness or romance. £29.99 is a bargain, and I'd even throw in a free carrier bag for that - not that you need one - so there's five pence saved. Put it this way. Out there, the girl you really like, the woman you want to spend time with, thinks you're a complete bell end because you made a distasteful joke about her sexual history. Now, you could go out there and try and use your wits to rescue the conversation, but the fact you're entertaining this crazy notion delivered to you by somebody you've never met in the male toilets of some hippie restaurant suggests you don't fancy your chances. Otherwise, you can get onto Inter-fucking-flora and spend £40 on a bouquet of flowers, or get some huge box of chocolates from Thorntons, or somewhere to try and win her round, with no chance of success. You'll still be unable to remove that memory she has of when you made an off-colour joke. Or you can pass me your bank card, I pass it over my machine and you go out to rescue the day. It's up to you."

Niall sighed, took his wallet from his jeans and removed his card, cautiously passing it to Rory. "If it doesn't work, I don't suppose I get a refund?"

Rory laughed unconvincingly as he flashed the card or a small portable reader he'd taken from his jacket before returning it to Niall. "Sadly we don't come with a money back guarantee, but once you've experienced our services you'll not even think about one. Now get out there and sort this mess out."

Niall looked confused. "Is that it?"

"What did you expect? The world to spin backwards? A montage sequence? Men In Fuckin' Black with their flashy-flashy metal dildo-pens? It's done, just get out there."

Niall nodded and left the toilets, sheepishly walking back in, the brashness of Rory taking him quite aback. Trying to black out his encounter in the toilet he saw Anya sitting at the table still. Everything looked the same, even down to the food left on their plates. The singer had started up again. He was playing Cher's 'Turn Back Time'.

Niall sat down on the chair and Anya looked up from her phone and smiled.

"You were a while," she observed, smiling. Niall realised how much he loved her smile.

"Sorry, had some - er - business I needed to deal with."

He wasn't sure if that sentence from a man emerging from a toilet was more information than anyone truly needed to know, but Anya didn't seem to comment on it.

"About what I last said," Niall said, testing the waters.

Anya looked confused. "What was it about? Something about whether you want to go for the burger for main?"

Niall smiled. It had worked. It had bloody well worked. He gave a mental thanks to Rory, took a sip from his cider and smiled, picking up the conversation and continuing from where they'd left off.

*

Niall burst into the gent's toilets again and looked around. Each cubicle was empty upon inspection. He span around on his heel and looked desperately across the tiled floor. "Rory, where are you?" he asked. A voice came from behind him as a figure entered through the door.

"Back again?" Rory asked. He studied Niall's face and saw it was red and flustered. "What have you done this time?"

"I basically insulted her family – she's pretty cross, let's not go into it. £29.99 was it? Can I reboot reality again?"

Rory smiled. "Absolutely, anything to help my bottom line."

Niall flashed his card across the scanner and left the bathroom, leaving Rory to smile. Back in the restaurant Anya was had a smile on her face once more and any guilt Niall was feeling for what he still considered a cheat evaporated when he saw that captivating smile. The sort of smile that made his heart flutter for no particular reason. The rest of the main course (Niall did indeed plump for a burger, Anya for a steak) went without a hitch until part-way through the dessert when a figure approached their table; it was a man of similar age with a mop of blonde hair and a clothing style that could only be described as unique, and that was being complimentary.

"Hey Anya!" he said, all bubbly. "Niall," he said,

acknowledging him but with far less vigour in his voice. "I saw you from across the restaurant and thought I'd say hello."

Anya smiled. "Hey Peter! How are you?"

"All the better for seeing you. How are things going with work?"

"Oh brilliantly, got that pay rise, things are going swimmingly."

Niall studied them both as they chatted, suddenly feeling like the third wheel at his own meal. He had been getting on well with Anya but now he felt cheated. Peter Watson was a mutual friend of them both, but only in the way you'd add someone to Facebook as a friend as a way of keeping them happy. Niall considered that he'd not really said more than maybe ten words to Peter over as many years, though he figured Anya knew him better. It certainly felt like they were getting on well, so much so that Peter looked around and pulled a spare chair from the now vacant table next to them and sat down to continue the conversation, his gaze firmly directed at Anya and certainly not at Niall. This continued for a good five minutes, Niall attempting to interject and join in, but failing to make any headway. Peter's more extravagant personality seemed to cut through the atmosphere far more than Niall could manage. All he could do was sit there with gritted teeth as Peter – who suddenly felt like his rival for Anya's affections – dominated the conversation. Niall knew this wasn't a date, even though every fibre of his being wished it was, but he now knew any hopes of turning it into one were rapidly diminishing. Finishing what was left of his dessert (Chocolate fudge cake, Anya had had the same, but had hardly touched hers) Niall made his excuses, which fell practically on deaf ears, and departed for a third visit to the gents. Rory was already there.

"Perhaps it's just not to be," Rory said, studying himself in the mirror. "You said it yourself Niall. You could feel like this is cheating. If she prefers Peter she prefers Peter. That's her decision to make. You can't play

God with other people's emotions."

Niall was furious. "I'm not playing God, I'm just giving myself a helping hand. I want you to reboot us back to when we first met outside the restaurant. I've got to get her away from Peter. He's had a crush on her as long as I can remember, but it's just not fair, he can't just muscle in like this..."

Rory took out his card reader. "That's a bit trickier, that's going to be a £49.99 package."

Niall removed his card and passed it to Rory. "I don't care, just get it done."

Rory smiled and gave his customer back his card. "If it wasn't for the fact that I figure Anya's heart does lie with you, I'd question your motives. You're acting like Anya is your prize or something. Not quite the behaviour I'd expect from someone who loves her."

Niall thought about this for a moment, his heart sinking, before leaving the toilet. He arrived in the main room to discover Anya and Peter both missing from the table. His heart fell as he thought they'd left together before he remembered his request, so he darted out of the venue to find Anya at the door. This time he took the hug with less of the awkwardness of the first run through.

"Are we off in?" asked Anya. Niall shook his head. "I tried this place last week, didn't think much of it. I know somewhere much nicer down the road!"

And so the pair turned around and left the foyer of the venue, heading to a local bistro a few minutes walk away. Inside, much continued as usual including a man called Peter Watson enjoying a solo dinner that night, listening to the music of a nearby acoustic singer before returning home, alone.

*

"Back again?" Rory asked, this time standing outside an entirely restaurant, smoking a cigarette. "This will be the fifth time tonight. You must be keen?"

"I am. I just need everything to go smoothly and it

hasn't been so far..."

"You're telling me. First you insulted his hobbies, then his job and then made that rather dodgy joke. I thought you were the one most used to this sort of meeting?"

"I am, but I'm nervous. It's different when you really like someone."

"You don't have to tell me," Rory noted, finishing off his cigarette and stubbing the rest out under his trainer. "The old butterflies in the stomach can pull on the vocal chords."

Rory studied his new customer. To her this was their fifth time meeting that night. That didn't include the four times she'd been his customer back in The Red Bicycle but, of course, she didn't remember that. Rory had been a little cheeky in his customer base, having met both Niall and Anya during the course of the evening to offer his services.

"Okay Anya, £29.99 and I'll reboot reality for you, but for heaven's sake how much of a mess are you making of a simple date?"

He couldn't tell her how much of a mess both of them were making. It was almost sweet.

"It's not really a date..." she said, the reddening of her cheeks and the fact she was no longer making eye contact with Rory suggesting otherwise.

"Oh come off it. You'd be better off just coming out with it. I've seen how he looks at you. I remember looking at my ex-wife in the same way. Once."

"£29.99," Anya said, thrusting her debit card at Rory. He sighed as he took it and flashed it. It was all money for his business, but he was tiring of two people so clearly meant for each other both agonising over every detail.

"Let me give you one piece of advice – if you could humour an old man," Rory said as he passes the card back. "Couples make mistakes all the time, say things they shouldn't, but people survive it, make up. Over things far worse than suggesting they look like the ugly third Jedward brother. I don't want to put myself out of business, but perhaps this isn't the best way..."

Anya nodded. "Perhaps you're right, though I would rather have had the advice before I'd spent nearly £150 with you."

£270 Rory noted, thinking of both time-lines, though he wasn't entirely sure even himself that that other money would count when Niall's work with him had counteracted it. He would have to wait for the bank statement. Rory had never found himself in such a situation before, with customers competing over the course of an evening. He took out another cigarette as he saw Anya leave to return to the restaurant. What he didn't see was the rest of the evening go smoothly, both Niall and Anya finishing off their desserts and enjoying a coffee each on the comfortable sofas at the end. With the bill paid, they both left the restaurant, passing through the door. As Niall spotted Rory he made his excuses to Anya and returned inside to the toilet, giving Anya a little time to talk to him.

"Before we go I'd just like to say thank you, to you and your company. I couldn't have done it without you. Especially getting me out of that time where Peter turned up. He's lovely and all on the surface, but given the choice between him and Niall, well there's no choice. It would be Niall every time."

"I'm just glad I could offer you that choice," he commented, thinking about how even rebooting reality isn't perfect, with Peter still somehow finding the couple even in the new restaurant by seeing them at a window table, before a reboot from Anya put them at the back of the restaurant instead.

Rory laughed and finished off his current cigarette. "We certainly helped, but you could have done it on your own. Excuse me if I sound old again, but that's the trouble with you kids these days. You expect everything to be smooth sailing. Well, I've got news for you, life isn't like that. If you want to get anywhere in this world you have to take the rough with the smooth. If tonight could teach you anything Anya, it's that even if there is a service like ours that can smooth things out, is that the right path to take?"

Anya nodded. "I know what you mean. But it's been good for you anyway. Must be a great job for you; good money and the satisfaction you've seen people get together."

Rory laughed. "I don't get much satisfaction from it. Money yes, satisfaction no. It's a hard job. I'm basically manipulating people's lives at the command of other people. There's very little satisfaction in seeing two people get together when I know it's been controlled by other forces. It's a job, but not a good one."

Anya nodded, his words hitting her quite sharply, and she left Rory and headed down to further down the street, just as Niall exited the building.

"I can't talk long," he said, almost out of the corner of his mouth to Rory. "But thanks. I couldn't have done it without you."

"A lot of people say that," he quipped. "And I say if you tried hard you could do. So how did your date go?"

"It's not a date."

Rory laughed. "Oh come on, don't be so blind. Stop being so bloody repressed and just ask her. I can't stand people with their over-inflated dramas. This isn't a soap opera. Just tell her and put us all out of our misery."

Niall nodded and said his goodbyes, joining Anya down the road. Rory watched as they chatted and whatever was said must have finally got things moving as Anya leaned in for a kiss and they both walked off hand in hand. Rory smiled and finished his cigarette.

"I'm a sentimental fool sometimes," he muttered under his breath, wondering at some point if he should go into more traditional match-making. Such thoughts were dismissed when his mobile phone rang. Rory answered.

"Rory Glover. Oh, hello sir. Yes, it's been a

productive night."

The voice on the other end was deep and formal. "I can see that Rory, impressive revenues from tonight and just from two people. Playing them off against each other. Very good tactics. The beauty of our system, of course, is that that the money stays even when timelines are changed, but you may not have known that."

"Surely people question that if they don't remember spending the money?"

The voice on the other end laughed. "It all comes under the name of our service. Do you really think people would raise it with their banks? As soon as they explain what service they'd bought they'd be laughed out of the place."

"I see," Rory noted. "Then that's good for me."

"It is. It's a shame you couldn't keep it up that little bit longer, though. I see your income has just tapered off."

"Well," he said, "It seems that their insecurities worked out and they've got together. I suppose I could have got more out of them, but sometimes you have to just let what is right happen. Maybe I am too sentimental."

"Perhaps," the voice said. "It's a shame as you were only one charge away from hitting your month-end sales targets and that would have been the new car. As it stands Rory, you're just short of it, and there's only thirty minutes until the period end. I just thought I'd let you know in case you have any other clients to help push you over."

Rory thought for a moment as he walked down the street. A new car. He needed a new car. His current motor was beaten up and practically dead. He bit his lip and thought.

"A new car would be very nice," he muttered down the phone, his consciousness flitting between thoughts of a brand new motor and ways to achieve it. "I think I have a way of making it happen."

Rory smiled, thanked his boss and ended the call, finding himself in the outdoor lamplight of The Red Bicycle just in time to see a glum-looking figure leaving. Rory called him over.

"Hey, it's Peter Watson isn't it? The name's Rory Glover and I represent a company called Reboot Reality. I hear on the grapevine that you have a bit of a thing for an Anya Johnstone. What would you say if I could, for just the small price of £29.99, make this evening play out differently and give you a shot at asking her out on a date?"

Peter's face seemed to light up. "I'd say that if that was possible I would be seriously interested."

Rory smiled. "Then consider this a business proposal that will be right up your alley."

Reboot Reality

By S. R. Martindale

Gin closed his eyes and savoured the cool air on his face, letting the sounds of civilisation far below wash over him. Even with his eyes closed he could see the multi-coloured haze of the sprawl below him, the pulsing lights of the bustling city.

With a sigh he opened his eyes and let his gaze slowly drift over the sights below him. Despite the obvious downsides, he liked Lundun, capital of The United Free Counties. He looked down with a youthful sense of adventure in his eyes.

He especially liked this version of it.

He especially liked this version, because of the very distinct lack of people currently trying to kill him.

He liked climbing buildings. He liked the thrill of being unsafe, doing what he shouldn't. He knew that if he was caught by what passed for security here it would be instant death, but he did it anyway. He knew if he made one wrong move, that would be certain death too. The thrill, however, drove him on.

His black cloak swept about him as the winds picked up a little, his black and chrome plated breastplate cooling on to his chest. He liked these clothes; clothes from history, an age dreaming of what the future would look and feel like.

The reality was very different. There was no leather, no cotton, no silk or satin. Nothing was polished or shiny any more, save for the gems you could buy in antique shops for more money than the average person earned in five years. Thankfully, this version of his world was a bit brighter. Cheerier, that's for sure.

With a grunt of effort, he leapt from the ledge he was perching on. Doing a somersault in the air, he laughed with joy as gravity took him and pulled him down towards the grey blotchy streets over eight hundred meters below him. Golden eyes wide open, tears milling up with the draft, he spun and danced in the air as his black clothes trailed behind him like the tail of a dark comet heading for earth.

He saluted the grey windows as he passed, a huge grin on his face at the thought of the horrified looks that must be plastered on the faces inside.

He was less than five hundred meters to the ground now and people had begun to notice his decent, turning their heads upwards, some screaming, some watching quietly with a morbid intrigue. Laughing almost childishly, Gin spun and crashed feet-first into the dull concrete with a sickening crack and roar. A thick dust was kicked up from the filthy streets and, when it had cleared after many minutes, Gin was gone.

Not a single sign of him ever being there remained; the green and blue blotchy concrete was untouched.

Sirens started up far in the distance and identically clad people crowded around, expecting to see blood and gore.

No one noticed a dark figure skipping away down a dank side alley, black cloak wrapped about his shiny breastplate, dark sunglasses over his golden eyes. Certainly, no one heard the steel and leather boots crunching the litter and debris under his feet. The figure in black tapped his right wrist in a complex pattern of moving figures and not a moment later, he was gone, black fading into black, the shadows folding and taking him.

"Fool of a boy," came a low and husky voice from the far end of the dark alley.

Gentle footsteps padded away into the night.

*

Gin awoke gently and stretched his aching shoulders. He pushed the grimy duvet off himself and sauntered over to the curtainless window, idly scratching at an itch on his shoulder. He stood there looking over the city from twenty floors up, his wiry and sinewy form completely naked.

He didn't care. There were worse things in this world than his naked form to look at. Let them. He'd even walked down the street one day totally in the nude, just to see what happened. His scratching idly drifted to the bubbled white scar on his right thigh that had been the punishment for that one.

He'd still kept all appendages attached, so that was a victory in his book. He had, after all, just wanted to spice those poor people's lives up a bit.

He looked into his pale blue eyes in the reflection in the window and the horrid mess of scars that made up his face. His body had not fared much better.

Maybe that was why his naked form scared so many people.

Eventually, he grew tired of watching the world and turned back to survey his cramped little flat.

He snorted at that thought. Some flat. If you could call two rooms a flat. More like a prison.

He looked up to the front door, which mercifully still had the planks of wood nailed across the frame and boxes of assorted trash piled high against it. Nothing was disturbed.

He sauntered over to the excuse for a kitchen and picked up the plate of half-finished chips. He stuffed the cold potato into his mouth and chewed thoughtfully. After finishing the last mouthful, he sighed.

He was going to have to go out today.

As much as he enjoyed the thought of walking down the street, showing off his wares, he did not currently fancy another chase and branding so he pulled on a pair of simple green pants and a stained white shirt.

He wanted to keep a low profile.

No, he had to keep a low profile.

After sitting down heavily on his bed, Gin tugged on some well-worn socks and, with great effort, managed to pull on his soft plastic boots. Breathing in deeply he concentrated on his hands, willing them to reduce their shaking enough for him to tie his shoelaces.

He praised himself for doing both on only the second attempt. He'd have to sort those shakes out today, too.

The cuff of his shirt was carefully adjusted to cover the dull silvery bracelet around his right wrist.

The tiny needles on the inside still irritated him sometimes, but the benefits of this wonderful technology far outweighed any discomfort he felt.

Carefully, and with plentiful cursing, he slid the heavy boxes away from the door and picked up the claw hammer from the counter.

The nails were noisily pried out of the doorframe and the planks discarded thoughtlessly onto his bed.

No one ever seemed to care about the racket he made hammering the boards on or ripping them off. No one cared about anyone anymore. Next door definitely wouldn't hear him – they were going at it already. Not much else to do in what little spare time people had.

You went to work, you kept your head down and hoped you got home of an evening.

Not Gin. Gin had much grander ideas.

You trusted your friends, your mother, your father. No one else.

Gin didn't have any friends to trust. He hated his father. His mother was dead.

He slammed his door shut and turned his key in the lock, listening for the satisfying clunk of the bolt sliding home.

No fancy plastic card entry for him: the government couldn't hack a solid lump of brass.

He stomped down the corridor, quietly wondering about what depravity was going on behind the faded wooden doors he passed. People had turned to interesting forms of deviance to add some interest to their lives.

*

Gin whistled happily as he walked down the streets, face turning red, then blue, then green as the propaganda screens flicked between pictures of happy workmen in factories and smiling farmers under blue skies.

"True Citizens work hard for their fellow man, traitors and foreigners only take and never give," Gin muttered under his breath. "A tired mind is a happy mind."

He snorted.

He beamed a smile at a young lady that had gone around the other side of a lamp post to avoid him.

Charming.

He walked for ten minutes down the dusty streets, keeping to the main roads. Even though it was the middle of the day, the light was washed out and dingy, sunlight unable to penetrate the swirling smog. Even if there were trees and shrubs lining the streets to cheer the whole scene up, he imagined they wouldn't last long.

He snorted. Maybe that's why there were no plants. Think Gin.

He really was in need of his meds. His Potion, as the kids called it. Whatever.

He turned right at an official grocery store and entered a side street that looked purely residential.

Hidden behind door thirteen there was a brothel. He also knew that behind thirty-two was an illegal sweet shop. Sweets were not nutritional. Not useful for healthy workers, so they were simply banned.

He came to a ten story building that loomed over him. He walked to the cleaning cupboard under the stairs and moved a couple of heavy boxes to reveal a hidden compartment. He swapped his clothes for the greys that were stored there and put on a woollen beanie hat. Without hurrying or dawdling, he carefully tidied up the boxes, waited five minutes, and left by the back door.

He walked down a couple more side streets, then back on to the main road and headed back towards his own flat complex.

Almost halfway back home he turned down another side street on the left and knocked on a door. Gin waited two minutes, looking as annoyed and impatient as he could. Eventually he stomped on down the side street and then into a small courtyard that had three stunted blocks of flats around the edge.

He walked over to the middle one, a squat six story brick building with crumbling mortar and grey smudged windows.

Pushing open the communal glass door, he walked up the sticky, carpeted stairs to the fourth floor. Quickly, he knocked twice on the flaking red paint of number eleven, then ten seconds later knocked once again.

The door creaked open and a rough looking man peered out from the gloom.

"Gin," he remarked coldly. "What are you doing here?"

"Just here for an update, friend. And some medicine for my poor, poor mother."

The man scowled at Gin for a few long seconds. Eventually he sighed and stood to the side to let Gin into his rooms.

Gin touched where he presumed his forelocks were and slipped passed into the remarkably sparse and tidy living room.

He sat down on the uncomfortable sofa and peered out of the window to look over the slumped rooftops.

"Tea."

"Excellent, thank you."

It wasn't a question.

The man grunted and shuffled over to the kitchen. He noisily filled the kettle and got two chipped mugs out of the small, white cupboard.

He left the kettle to boil and went into his bedroom, coming out two minutes later with a small pouch of red and white capsules.

He threw the pack at Gin.

Gin shuffled down the sofa and stuck a hand into his trouser pocket. He pulled out a sticky package and threw it back in return.

"Where did you get this Gin?"

"Salem, for you and your wonderful pills, a bit of honey is nothing. You have your secrets, I have mine."

"This is worth far more than some Potion, Gin. I appreciate this, but I am an honourable man."

"Don't mention it." Gin waved his hand and looked out the window again. He spotted the black uniform making its way down the side street towards him. Slowly, methodically. Never rushing, never stopping.

"How?" was all he could stutter as he leapt from the sofa.

"If you've brought them Black Dogs here, Gin, I will kill you."

"It's ok, I'll lead them off. Thanks once again friend. I will see you tonight."

"You step foot in here again this year, I really will kill you. Shakes or no shakes."

Gin looked down to his clenched trembling fists. "I won't, I won't. Not he-here, anyway."

"Gin-"

But Gin was already gone. He ran from the flat and up the stairs to the open flat-topped roof. Always have a second route of escape.

Not a bad rule to live by.

Not a bad rule to keep on living by.

*

Gin pounded down the dank corridor and slammed his key into the lock in his door.

He winced as the bolt stuck and screamed as it was drawn back, but back it did slide. He leapt over the threshold and slammed the door sure.

Cursing and muttering under his breath he kicked a box full of old magazines over, spilling the contents across the grim floor. He stomped across the room and picked up the planks of wood and his hammer.

Within minutes the door was barred and the boxes replaced.

He only just remembered to dead-lock the bolt in the door before sitting down on his bed with a thud and breathing out heavily.

That, he decided, was a close one.

He pulled off his all his clothes and laid down on his bed, naked apart from the shining bracelet. He reached down into his trouser pocket and pulled out one of the tiny capsules. Hands shaking, he popped it into his mouth and swallowed it dry. It was not the first time he had ran from the Black Dogs. His interesting past was something they very much wanted to talk to him about.

There'd been bodies. Admittedly, he had been involved with some of them. But, he was pretty sure, it was more of a case of being in the wrong place at the wrong time.

A sudden calmness came over Gin. He sighed happily.

He wanted to get up to draw the curtains, to hide the midnight neon glow reflecting in the heavy smog, but couldn't summon the energy. He laid there for an hour in bliss, but eventually his head began to feel heavy and his eyes began to close.

He barely managed to grasp and manipulate his bracelet before he slipped asleep.

*

Gin looked down upon the city below him. How he wished he could live his life sheltered like the mindless sheep that scurried below him. But he was awake, ironically enough.

He stood up and adjusted his cape. With a running jump he cleared the chasm and landed softly on the roof of the skyscraper across the street. He giggled like a child. He'd only just discovered he could do that.

He'd hadn't planned the meeting this evening. The trouble earlier had meant he hadn't got the information he had wanted to. He had some interesting information himself that his dealer would pay very handsomely for.

He leapt across the city until he came to the six story brick flat complex. Even in this world it looked old and smelt old too.

He walked down the brick wall and came to rest stood precariously on the window sill. He closed his eyes and tapped a few buttons on his bracelet. He felt for the strange feeling from within the room. Eventually he found the tangled knot of thoughts that was someone else dreaming. He tapped a couple more buttons and the world changed.

Everything seemed to be the same, but Gin knew to look for the details. The mortar in the walls was a slightly different colour. The adverts on the billboards were different. The glass in the window was now clear and the paint was fine and well maintained

Inside he could see Salem enjoying the services of four naked women. Gin grinned. He was going to be so annoyed.

He kicked the window in and leapt into the room.

The women disappeared with a hollow pop and the room flickered slightly. A picture changed on the wall from a landscape to a still life.

Salem jumped and spun around, pistol in hand. Gin knew it dangerous. One of the old ones you never saw anymore except in the hands of criminals. Fired real metal. Nasty. Large hole in the face nasty.

"Compensating for something in the waking world, eh Salem?" said Gin, smirking at his dealer's junk.

"What the hell do you think you are doing here Gin?" whispered the man hoarsely, lowering the gun.

"Couldn't you have just knocked?"

"Salem, nice to see you too again. So soon, too. Glad that little altercation before hasn't affected you too badly."

"Well, yeah. You will pay for that eventually. I do not appreciate you entering my dreams though. It freaks me out every time."

Gin plodded into the room and sat down heavily in a tattered leather chair. "This information will pay for that – and more," said Gin, tapping his nose cheekily. "I wanted to tell you before, but I had to make myself scarce."

"I heard what you did to get that information. There's a reason no one else knows what you do. There's a reason we don't do what you do. We are not monsters."

"You were not complaining when I brought you that honey. I do what I have to do. They'll pay in time. The ends justify the means, or whatever Shakespeare said. Don't tell me you are chickening out now, Salem."

The man huffed out of his nose heavily and looked away. He scratched his bald head with torn nails. "I'm sorry."

"Man, don't do this. We are so close."

"No, you do not understand. I am sorry."

Three men burst through the door and two men appeared in the air beside Gin, their black armour shining, silver wolf heads on their breasts shining weakly in the tepid lamp light.

They pounced on Gin, wrestling him to the floor. One held his arm out and another began to press buttons.

He screamed and jerked in agony as another figure in black stuck a taser into his ribs.

"Why?" he panted at Salem.

"Because I learned what you did. I am sorry Gin."

"We have his location," droned the soldier.

Gin winked out of existence.

*

Gin gasped awake and instantly leapt from his bed. He hastily pulled on his pants and cursed when his left boot stuck on putting them on.

There came an almighty thud on the door. They'd finally found him.

He licked his lips nervously and flicked a switch on the wall beside his bed.

He stood up and faced the door.

The door exploded.

He didn't care.

He didn't feel the cuts. He looked down at the hand length chunk of wood protruding from his leg.

He didn't care.

Five men all in black charged through the door into the cramped flat. There was barely enough room for them to raise their weapons.

Gin backed up slowly towards the wide window.

"Ginten Kayle, you are wanted for the murder of three women and seven children, dated the 7th of June 2176. Further charges include, but are not limited to, stealing government property and assaulting a member of his Highness's Government. You will accompany Third Officer Laverstock and myself to your nearest police facility for questioning and a full list of your charges. Under the Community Protection Act, second amendment, of 2096, any resistance will be interpreted as an act of guilt and appropriate force will be used to ensure compliance and the safety of our loyal Citizens."

"Never," rasped Gin, his mouth bloody from a fresh wound that was dripping from his nose. "Your evil government snooping into people's minds will never work."

He ripped the silver bracelet from his wrist.

"Here, take it back."

The officers looked up as a tiny red bulb on the wall in front of them began to pulse gently.

"Listen here, listen to me good. Your people will be caught," whispered the officer to Gin, coming close and grasping his collar in a clenched leather fist. "His Highness is a forgiving man. Any information you have may be handsomely rewarded. Issues, ah, forgotten about. How about you make that light go away?"

Gin spat blood and saliva into the officer's face. "I don't think so, you dog. Did your mommy not tell you violence got you nowhere? Or was she too busy with other men to bring you up right?"

A faint beeping started, barely heard over the wheezes and pants from Gin.

The rest of the black clad officers ran from the room at a quick signal from the commander. The commander changed his grip and clasped his hand around Gin's neck tightly.

"Should you not be running like a scared rabbit like your friends?" squeaked Gin, struggling for air.

"No."

The world exploded.

Reboot Reality

By Lauren K. Nixon

Ten years.

It's the faces that really hit you – they live in your memory, like half-remembered shadows of the people you used to know. Suddenly, you walk into a room and they're all there, fleshed out again in the real, as if you had never left. You could have walked out of your first seminar and straight into this room for all the difference time had made.

Everyone looks the same, like they had crystallised one September day, when everyone shuffled into the common room for the first time and tried not to be too weird in front of people they didn't yet know.

It's like the world of ten years ago has been preserved, somehow, like pictures in glass.

The morning was foggy – the standard valley-sitting fog that lies thickly and warmly across the town like a blanket of tasteless candyfloss. The kind you know will have burned off by lunchtime. It shielded the view, isolating the house in its snug little estate, concealing the hills and the distant valley sides, making the known world into a tiny island, only one street in diameter. On days like this, you can't even see the tree that marks the main road over the grassy bank opposite. Like living in a cloud.

In Norse culture it was believed that spirits and magic came out of the fog

It lent an already strange day something of a mystic quality.

We took a taxi – it was that kind of weekend, somewhere between a conference and a party – feeling very grown up and very young. The memories came back as we slid through the fog, thinning more and more the closer we got to the city, like we were travelling back through time.

The basin city we had once thought of as our new home didn't look much different, really. Parts of it had been knocked down, other parts built up; shops and businesses changed and moved, but the overall whole remained the same.

We stepped out of the car, tasting the air for that snap of spice and smoke that told us we were home. The road up to the campus was packed with excellent curry houses – the best I've ever known – and the scent of cumin and caraway curled around our senses like an old friend. There was no smoke that morning, which made a change.

It was a running joke back then that you couldn't go a week in that city without something burning down. The city was a labyrinth of tumbledown buildings and abandoned mills, and almost every time you got a glimpse of the horizon, a plume of smoke was rising. We joked that insurance claims must have been the third most popular industry in the area.

There it was, looming over us: our old stomping ground, outlined in concrete and glass. New protrusions had sprung up all over, extensions and improvements all. Some looked good; some less so, the efforts of various architects over the years.

Like a dream solidified.

Suddenly shy, in a place that had changed so much and yet so little, we walked down the hill we'd travelled down a hundred times before, lost in remembering.

The voices of our friends, some already there, some just arriving, called out across the decade and brought us back to life, like we were emerging from another world. It was so familiar, so homely that the lives we had built for ourselves since – everyday moments that make up the fabric of our equilibria – were called fleetingly into question.

Were they the illusion? Was this old-new unchanging world, which had resurfaced for only a day, reality?

It felt like I had forgotten how to be me.

The Lovely Perch

The Lovely Perch

By Hailiè Drescher

It really was a lovely perch.

Seated next to the statue of Sir. Leonard Gaetz I could watch life in the city without leaving that bench - that perch. Madame Tuney's perch. My perch. At the corner of Gaetz Avenue and Ross Street, all the action happened. I would sit there, with only the frozen face of Mr.Gaetz for company, and watch as people drove by. Going about their lives, on their way to work, on their way to and from school; heading south and heading west.

Yes, it was a lovely little perch. Room enough for one other person if I fancied the company, but also room enough to be alone if need be. Of course, I never spoke with anyone who sat with me. Men, women, children - even the occasional pet. We would not speak, nor visibly acknowledge each other, but simply sit and watch the world pass by.

Sure, there were scenes of road rage on occasion. Those people in a hurry to get where they were going, even during rush hour. I would shake my head, smile, and look the other direction to see what else I could see from my oh, so lovely perch.

There were, of course, the sad times. The accidents where no one would make it out alive, or be rushed off to the emergency room only to die there. I knew. I didn't know why, or how I knew, but I knew. A single tear would roll down my cheek at those times and I would whip it away with a handkerchief from my pocket.

Then there were the happy times. The times that made me smile. The street festivals and markets. Children running and playing in the carefully closed off streets. I never wondered why, all I could remember was sitting on that bench, that lovely perch. I had no memories past the day I discovered my perch. No Sunday or holiday dinners, no birthday parties or even coffee dates, nothing. Yet, none of that bothered me. Not until the day I sat and watched yet another terrible accident happen. I cringed, as per usual, as a car rammed into the side of a truck, shaking my head as another driver tried to beat the light and failed.

That is when I saw her. The girl. She couldn't have been much older than eight. Strapped into the t-boned truck. Her father slumped over the steering wheel, unconscious. The small girl looked terrified, but mercifully unharmed, other than a few small cuts and scrapes, and likely a seatbelt-shaped bruise across her tiny chest. Every fibre of my being screamed at me to run to the poor child, to comfort her. My eyes darted around, no one seemed to want to move towards her, everyone stood there in shock and awe - the poor child was looking around, frightened. She met my eyes.

That was when I left my perch. For the first time in what seemed like years, I left that lovely perch and ran towards the side of the truck. When I reached the window the little girl was crying; she was looking around frantically, screaming for anyone to help her. I glanced around briefly and it was if no one could hear her, or cared to, I could not believe my eyes or my ears. How could anyone ignore the screams of a child? When I reached her, my gloved hands resting on the edge of the open truck window and I spoke, for the first time in ages, to the girl.
"It's okay sweetie, it's okay," I said consolingly. Reaching through the window to stroke the poor girl's soft, dark brown hair. I smiled at her, attempting to calm her down. The girl looked confused, frightened.

"Da - my da," she said, pointing at her unconscious father.

I looked across the truck seat and could just detect a pulse beating in his neck as he sat slumped over the steering wheel and emergency services approached.

"Your Da is going to be okay, Sweetie." I smiled at the little girl as she held tight to my hand.

That was when something strange happened. I looked up at the emergency services worker across the truck, working on pulling the father out and smiled. However, instead of smiling back at me as I held the frightened little girl's hand he shook his head and muttered, "Poor girl," as he cut the father's seatbelt off.

What could he possibly mean? Poor girl? She was frightened, yes, but she was alive – and as far as I could tell so was the man she claimed as her 'Da'.

Then it happened. As I stood there, grasping the girl's hand firmly, a pair of hands reached through me. Not around me, to pull me away, but through me. They cut the seatbelt and slowly lifted the little girl through the open window, even as I still firmly held her hand.

That was when, all of a sudden, I found myself sitting, holding the little girl on my lap, back on my lovely perch. I watched the scene being cleaned up, utterly confused by what had just happened, until I heard the voices whispering nearby and turned my head.

"How sad, such a young girl to have lost her life," said one voice.

"Indeed, and so soon after Madam Tuney's terrible, fatal accident too," said another.

My fatal accident? What were they talking about? Yes, I had had an accident at this intersection, but that had been years ago and it hadn't been fatal. Had it? That was when a hand touched me on the shoulder and I looked up. It was the figure of a young women, vaguely translucent, but she smiled at me and wordlessly gestured me and the little girl on my lap to follow her.

I am not sure what made me stand up. What made me turn my back on that lovely perch forever, but I did. I stood, the little girl's hand still in mine, and walked with the figure towards a bright light that appeared at the far end of the street. Just before I entered the light, I turned my head and took one last look at my lovely perch before that small girl's hand tugged me onwards and the light enveloped us.

The Lovely Perch

By Philip Lickley

(i)

It rankled with Ernest Clarkson, 62, that his home village of Cheddar was famous for just one thing. One thing I probably don't really need to say to you as it's most likely the first thing that jumps into your brain when the word Cheddar is mentioned. For Ernest, a keen runner, it was a constant source of annoyance that the world didn't know more about his beautiful village.

"Do you know," he would often say to tourists sampling some refreshments in the same local café he would frequent, "that we have the largest gorge in the United Kingdom?" Often they would shake their head, avert their gaze and try to polish off their cream teas quickly to avoid any more random facts from the man with greying hair around his temples and a fixed expression. Sometimes his fact would be different.

"Do you know," remained the three opening words though, this time directed at a pair of Chinese tourists for whom English wasn't their strongest talent, "that we also grow very tasty strawberries?"

They, too, quickly finished off their snacks. It wasn't long after that that the patron of The Full Monty café – a Mr Frederick Sturgeon, 53 – politely asked Ernest to find an alternative place to buy his cups of tea if he was going to continue interrogating his customers. And Ernest did, relocating his lunchtimes to the Roasted Bean a few streets away where he continued to prompt tourists to widen their knowledge of Cheddar village.

Ernest, as well as a determined advocate for Cheddar – "Do you know that we have our own brewery, too?" he would declare, his proclamations purely voluntary and not as part of an official Tourist Board calling – was a life-long runner. He had been bitten by the running bug as a teenager, often competing in 10k races, half-marathons and full marathons, and was one of the founding members of the Cheddar Gorge Running Club, who met each week on a Wednesday at the Dog and Duck pub for a six mile run around the local area, before enjoying a swift pint in the aforementioned establishment, alongside a basket of chips and a game of darts. The running club was split three-ways: the beginners, mostly consisting of women in their thirties escaping their children and husbands for an evening and middle-aged men attempting to shift their beer bellies; the intermediates, the keener runners after some fresh air, or to get some much needed social interaction; and the advanced runners, those who came to the meetings with the whole kit strapped to their various limbs, from bands securing their mobile phones to the upper arms, displaying their progress, to torches strapped across their head, with their shorts pockets filled with energy gels and plasters. Ernest, naturally, was a member of the final group, under the slight delusion that at 62 he could still keep up with the faster runners.

Not much changed, week on week, during the running club meetings, other than the general fluctuations of the seasons: in summer it would be mainly off-road races, running through the fields and thickets, less experienced runners coming away with nettle rashes, cuts and bruises, and a slight fear they'd upset a cow by running close by to the animal. In autumn it would be time to put on the high-visibility jackets and lights, and in winter the gloves and hats. But one week in late October it was all to change for the Cheddar Gorge Running Club, and for Ernest in particular.

The October night was dark, cold and miserable, even by the standards of late autumnal Somerset. The sign of the Dog and Duck was creaking in the sharp winds, the patrons of the pub who needed to satisfy their nicotine craving did so quickly and with furrowed brows, and the general look over the hills was one of intense bleakness. A knot of runners – many braving shorts –

had started to gather just before 7pm in the pub, shadows dancing around as head-torches were switched on. Many ran up and down on the spot to keep warm, some blowing into their hands, others longing for the toasty open fire that was just about visible through the rain-streaked glass windows of the pub. But this group were a dedicated bunch and after a short warm-up they were off, away from the tempting warmth, shelter and local ales of the pub, and out into the ill-lit and puddle-strewn rural roads of the outskirts of Cheddar, Ernest leading the pack for the first hundred metres or so, barking out what he took to be motivational shouts of encouragement, but what most found slightly patronising.

Over two kilometres into the run the route was getting pretty treacherous, even for the experienced runners that made up this group. They had now reached some pretty remote areas of the countryside, the roads and paths of Cheddar giving way to rough, dirt tracks lined by thick gorse bushes and hidden obstacles that even the head torches of the group often failed to pick up until the last moment. But the group, in a relatively tight formation, continued on, their feet often landing with heavy splashes into puddles, the fear of twisted ankles never too far away. Occasionally there was some relief from the bright lights of an overtaking motor car – often accompanied by shouts of 'car' from those at the back – but mostly it was dark and bleak and uncomfortable.

Knowing roughly where he was, due to the run layout being on a regular rotation, Ernest decide to take everyone off track for a little bit, an unusual move for this time of year. There were some murmurs of discontent from the back of the group, but all followed him over the stile and into the field anyway, the group moving swiftly over the sodden grass and mud, their silhouettes and head-torches visible to a local farmer from a distance who happened to look out over the vista from the comfort of his toasty farmhouse. The group made quite a sight as they traversed the pitfalls of a rough, cow-pat strewn field. Ernest slowed down at this point and waved the rest of the team on, a gesture just about visible in the gloom, advising them in his course Somerset twang he would follow them shortly, but had to tie his shoelace. As he bent down his bones cracked and tying his laces was more of a struggle for him than it necessarily should have been, but he soon got there and it wasn't long before he was back running and attempting to catch up with the group. The time he'd spent on his laces, however necessary, meant he had now lost them amongst the trees that lined the woods, only the occasional flicker of a light source giving away their position.

Ernest continued to run through the field, over another stile, and into the next field and to the edge of the wood, but he'd now lost sight of the rest of the group. This wouldn't normally have caused him to panic, but his sense of isolation was confounded by his own head-torch spluttering out of battery, plunging him into near-darkness, except for the occasional pin-pricks of light coming from distant street-lamps. He swallowed hard and attempted to call out, but no reply came, and Ernest found himself stumbling blindly in the dark, nearby walls and trees just mere suggestions of outlines. He found himself thrusting his arms out in front of him like a zombie attempting to gain purchase on a wall but he failed to establish where he was, ambling away from the field and down a steep bank. It was only as he realised he was heading down a slope that he tried to stop, but he lost his footing on the wet grass, slipping and sliding down, stumbling southwards along an increasingly steepening downward incline. He lost his footing again and fell over, rolling down the hill and only stopping after what seemed like a good few minutes – but was in reality just a snatch of seconds – with a crunch against a wall. Ernest let out an unheard screech of pain and waited for a reply that never came. He tried to move, but his leg was sore and there was a dampness to his shin on inspection that he hoped was rain, but he feared was blood. He tried to get to his feet and stand, but a warm yet uncomfortable pain shot through his ankle and

Ernest found himself back on the floor.

Trying it out of hope, there was some sense of relief that his head-torch had begun working again, the fall seemingly shocking the battery into some sort of visual encore. Ernest moved his head and watched the weak light from his poorly charged head-torch attempt to light up the hill in front of him. He had stumbled quite a distance and had landed against an old stone wall that dissected the hill in two. Ernest quickly realised that he wouldn't be found any time soon where he was and the thought of spending twelve hours or more where he had landed until the sun fully came up – and even then with no guarantee anyone would find him until much later – did not feel him with joy. The rain was coming down even harder now, his clothes sodden, what little hair he did have on his hand gelled down with moisture.

'Surely', he thought, 'they'll realise I'm not with them and come looking for me?'

Ernest's thoughts were interrupted by a sound. It was the sound of feet on twigs and his heart leapt. But it wasn't the joyous leap of someone knowing they were about to be rescued. The sound wasn't right, and he found his heart starting to beat faster with nervousness as the hairs on his arms defied the downpour and stood up on their ends. Ernest moved his head left to right in a scanning motion trying to ascertain the source of the noise and another crackle of twigs made him jerk his head in that direction, the noise audible even over the heavy sound of rain. As he moved his head, and therefore the light from his torch, the beam caught a reflection, visible momentarily to Ernest as a pair of eyes reflecting back at him. They weren't human eyes, but those of an animal. He quickly switched off the torch and plunged the area into darkness once more, his heart beat now racing even more. Ernest hoped his quick reflexes had been enough to hide himself away, but quickly he realised he was out of luck and soon he heard padding and growling approaching.

Ernest tried to shuffle further against the wall in the

hope this would give him additional protection from the creature, but it was to be in vain. He wanted to call out, but his throat had seized up, ironically from the dryness. The padding noise was getting louder, the grumbling, feral sounds coming closer. He wasn't sure whether he was imagining it, but Ernest swore he could feel the warm breath of something down near his shins. He quickly turned on his head-torch and saw it, a large, dark brown or black creature down near his feet, its almost feline face staring at him. In the second it took him to turn his light on and then off it had bared its glistening white teeth. Ernest could feel it about to pounce.

He'd always wondered what his final thought would be as a human. Perhaps whether he'd led a good life? Thoughts about a loved one? An angry internalised monologue about how unfair death was? Ernest had little imagined the last thought that would go through his mind would be one of satisfaction.

"At least for a few days, perhaps, Cheddar will be known for something more than our bloody cheese, even if it is for my death..."

(ii)

It wasn't actually long before Ernest's body was found. It was just after eight-fifteen the following day that a man walking his dog came across him, his Labrador dragging him over to the disturbing discovery. Soon police were swarming all over the field, hanging tape from tree to tree to form a cordon and placing one of those familiar white tents over the actual crime scene. Soon the swarm of police were followed by a swarm of concerned and nosey locals, who were followed, in turn, by a swarm of local journalists. A fourth swarm, in the form of national journalists, would later descend.

One of the first people on the scene was Detective Inspector Harriet Anderton, a fresh-faced but mature officer with a long-line of investigative successes behind her. Wrapped up in a warm trench-coat, she carried a hot steaming coffee alongside the weighty memories of her last case, which she didn't want to talk about with anyone. She strode up to the tent to join the pathologist.

"What have we got then, Mac?" she asked, in her thick Somerset accent. The pathologist looked up.

"At this early stage I'd say it looks like an animal attack."

"Dog?"

"I don't think so. From the look of these markings something much bigger. And feline."

"Feline? Like a cat?"

Mac nodded. "But not just any cat, a big cat."

Harriet scoffed, taking a sip from her coffee and wiping the foam away from her mouth. "What? Like a tiger?" she said jokily.

Mac paused for a moment before answering, not picking up on her flippancy. "Possible, but unlikely. I don't think there are any major zoos around here unless it's from a private collector. I would say it could well be one of these British big cats."

"But aren't they like aliens, ghosts and something funny from Ricky Gervais? People say they exist, but we know that they don't?"

Mac stifled a laugh. "I quite like Ricky Gervais," he murmured under his breath, before getting to his feet and moving away from the body. "They could exist, a small group of feral cats, breeding after escaping from captivity. There are enough photos around to suggest it's entirely possible."

Harriet took another swig of the coffee, which was rapidly cooling. "There's plenty of photos of UFOs, doesn't mean E.T. is coming knocking anytime soon."

Soon Ernest's body was carefully wrapped up, placed in the back of a nearby vehicle and transported away to the nearest hospital mortuary. Not long after, the scene of crime officers completed their work and soon there was little evidence left that anyone had been there, aside from a few indentations in the ground where the tent had been. The swarm of local journalists had left with the body, leaving the swarm of national journalists to realise they'd turned up too late, and instead of hanging around the chilly field they departed to nearby cafes to report back on their smartphones to their newspaper headquarters. They began to pester local journalists for their information, which they could re-package, re-file and take the credit for. At least the local cafés were getting good business out of a huddle of cold and hungry journalists, with plenty of mugs of steaming coffee, toasted teacakes and greasy fry-ups passing from owner to customer.

Soon the headlines started appearing. The Times went with 'Mysterious disappearance of runner in feline mystery'; the Sun with 'Cheddar Killer Cat Claims Victim'; and Buzzfeed with 'Top ten big cat deaths in Britain. You wouldn't believe number five'. By late morning most of the journalists had jumped back into their cars to head back to the excitement of London, away from the more pedestrian way of life, except for one – a middle-aged Mail writer called Deborah Johnson. Deborah had little reason to scoot back to the capital, so she stayed, half taking the opportunity for a breath of fresh air away from the fog of Fleet Street, half with the aim of discovering more about Ernest's mysterious death.

"That's the trouble with the new brood today," she told her editor over the phone as she left a cafe with a half-eaten slice of toast hanging from her spare hand. "If the story doesn't throw up immediate answers, they're bored. I blame Twitter. But there could be something interesting here, something definitely for our website if I can find more evidence."

Deborah enjoyed writing for the paper's website and her figures proved she was good at it, as her pages were some of the most viewed on the site. Even though she was touching forty and wasn't entirely sure what 'click-bait' was, Deborah had been crowned the master (or perhaps, sultry mistress) of it in the office. Whether it was her bitter pieces about politicians, salacious stories about celebrities and their children, or more weird human interest stories, she could lure unsuspecting readers to the website with her lurid headlines and curiosity-sparking leaders.

"And I think," she continued on the phone as the conversation neared its end, "the tale of a scary cat killing runners should pique the interest of many on our site: the kids after a gory read, parents worried about the safety of their children, the nerds who will want to get on its trail. That's three key demographics, right there."

Her editor couldn't fail to agree and told her to stay and get onto the story, and so she did, visiting a local outdoor walking shop owned by a balding man in his fifties with a moustache as voluptuous as his head hair was not, and purchasing a warm overcoat (on expenses, naturally) for her adventure out in the Cheddar countryside. With a flask of warm tea taken from her cat boot and a sturdy pair of walking boots that had remained dormant on the back seat since a foreshortened holiday in Center Parcs two years earlier, when a big story broke and broke off her vacation, Deborah began her exploration from where Ernest had fallen. She made a few notes into her dictaphone, pulled her coat together more tightly and began scaling up the steep hill to try and retrace what had happened to him.

Coming across more like a detective than a journalist, especially in her Clouseau-like overcoat, Deborah progressed around the barren landscape in the midday light (it was overcast, though, so it was hardly beaming with brightness) looking for clues and failing to find much. The only feline thing she came across over the two hours was a local farmyard cat stalking a series of birds that were investigating the upturned soil of the nearby field. It was possible that Tiddles, as Deborah christened it, could have committed the murder, but that was an even more unlikely story than a large escaped cat on the loose.

Deborah took a seat on a stile as the afternoon wore on and enjoyed some sandwiches she'd bought earlier, alongside another cup of her flask-tea before studying the local area and admiring its beauty. From one of her coat pockets she took a small point-and-click camera and used it to capture a few shots of the wide vistas, making a mental note to upload those to Facebook later. Deborah placed the camera back snugly into the coat's wool-lined pocket, finished off her tea and slipped the flask back into the rucksack she was carrying over her shoulder. She took a look left, then right, quickly checked her phone for tweets or messages from her editor (three, and none) before choosing the right-hand path and heading further into a wooded area. Soon, Deborah found herself in a much thicker part of the small forest and feared she was getting lost. If there was, indeed, a large cat on the prowl, wandering on her own through thick trees was probably not the best move.

At just before four in the afternoon, she once more retrieved her phone and activated the onboard search tool.

"Tell me about my location," she asked. The phone thought for a moment, sent the information through the small amount of data signal she could still get in the area, and then delivered the answer back in the familiar semi-robotic tones.

"You are in a designated Site of Specific Scientific Interest, or S-S-S-I. Established in 1990, this site is home to a variety of rare plant life, alongside grass and woodlands that have been given protected status. You can see examples of scarce plants here, including the purple gromwell and ivy broomrape, alongside some rare orchids and examples of mammalian life including dormice and bats, plus butterflies. This area is known colloquially as..."

Deborah cancelled the answer, having received enough information. "That will add some colour to my article," she thought, as she began to write the piece in her head.

Most of us when we do exercise don't think it will be the last thing we do. The worst thing that could happen to you in a gym is, perhaps, a heart-attack. But what if you found yourself attacked by a giant cat whilst out running? Sounds ridiculous? Well in one corner of Somerset, not far from the Mendip hills, just such a thing may have happened.

Deborah was quickly shaken from her purple prose by the sound of twigs snapping in the distance. She stopped in her tracks and looked around, but it was difficult to see much through the thick undergrowth. She was just about to continue walking when she heard it again, only this time it was nearer. Deborah took the camera from her pocket just in case and prepared it, her hands mysteriously shaking as she lifted it up to her eye.

Why am I shaking? she thought to herself. I've chased potential murderers through the streets of London without fear. Why should I be scared now?

The sound of twigs snapping was becoming more frequent, but also more northerly. Fearing, even against her own increasing heartbeat, that she was losing her story, Deborah took some large strides forward around trees and across roots snaking up and down out of the soil, which threatened regularly to trip her up. After several metres she came across an obstruction, a large wire fence with tight holes and stretches of barbed wire across the tops. A large rusting yellow sign declared this as private land. Deborah looked puzzled. Since she knew this was an area of scientific interest, she also knew that they were usually protected against any development, so as to not upset any of the local animals or damage any plants. She had been pretty careful not to trample on anything that looked rare, but wouldn't a laboratory – or whatever it was – dropped smack bang in the middle, do something similar to the local flora and fauna?

Deborah now felt she was pretty far into the woods, perhaps much further than many had ever explored or walked their dogs, and perhaps could be the first person to stumble across this area. Forgetting the sound of snapping twigs for the moment – which were continuing, but less often – Deborah began walking the perimeter of the fence, using a large branch of berries she staked into the ground as a marker of where she started measuring. Soon she had traversed the footprint of the site and it was a considerably large area, perhaps the size of a typical high-street shop, with a metallic building standing erect a few metres in from the fence boundary. There was no signage to indicate what it was and it looked relatively abandoned. There were signs of gaps in the fence – probably large enough for an adult to escape through – but they had been fixed – recently it seemed – and so there was no way for Deborah to get inside. The one access gate on the south side was well bolted and an electrical sign hanging from it suggested Deborah would be foolish to try and enter. She took a few snaps of the base and retrieved her dictaphone, whispering into it.

"Somewhere in the S-S-S-I is a military-like building behind a hefty wire fence. It's not a huge site, but it looks like to be some sort of research lab, perhaps for scientists to investigate the local creatures, but why such a secure place for a few bats and mice? And wouldn't this building upset the local cycle of life? It's a pretty big building, but small enough to be concealed in the woods. I..."

Her article narration came to an abrupt stop as she heard a loud noise from her right, followed by a series of clicks. Deborah looked to her right on what she imagined to be the eye level of a big cat, but what she saw instead wasn't a big cat, but a kneeca. Her eyes looked up and saw several figures standing there. She heard the buzz of a radio and her eyes met the long, thin barrel of some sort of weapon. Deborah instinctively raised her arms up in surrender, but her flight or fight instinct kicked in and she turned on her heel to run. She didn't get that far as a loud shot rang out through the woods, several bats roosting in a nearby tree scattering in fear from the sudden shock.

(iii)

Harriet found herself in a clinical looking room; a room she was all too familiar with. There she found Mac standing over a body, laid out on a table. He looked preoccupied and hadn't shaved that morning, a thick layer of stubble spread across his chin. His eyes were also red, as if he hadn't had much sleep.

"Are you okay Peter?" Harriet asked, addressing Mac by his first name, something she rarely did. "You look terrible."

"Well, cheers," he said. Harriet rolled her eyes and joined him by the body that he was standing over, its face covered by a blue cloth.

"You know what I mean," she said, before her gaze changed from her friend and colleague to the body. "So what happened here? Another cat attack?"

"No," Mac said quickly. "Looks to be suicide. She was found in her car having taken one too many painkillers. Either that or she misjudged the dose. We won't know until the toxicity report comes back."

"Can I look at the body?" Harriet asked. Mac shook his head.

"I've completed my investigation," he said uncharacteristically sharply. "There's nothing to see on the body."

Harriet narrowed her eyes and studied Mac's face. He was rubbish at acting. She reached down to move the cloth but she was quite abruptly knocked back by the pathologist.

"I said, there's nothing to see."

Harriet was taken aback and struggled to find her words for a few moments. Instead she just nodded and looked away.

"I'm taking a few days off," Mac said after a few moments, breaking the awkward silence that had slowly gathered in the cold room. "My manager has cleared it.

I'm going to get away for a bit, maybe up to Scotland, see some relatives."

"That'll be nice."

Mac didn't respond. His face was pale. He looked ill.

"You'll have to excuse me. Someone's collecting the body shortly and I've got a few others to deal with. I'll catch up with you when I'm back."

Harriet nodded, took a few steps away from him and almost turned back to speak to him, but held her tongue, leaving the room instead of pressing the matter further.

That was the last time she would see Peter MacDonald. One week later he had a traffic accident somewhere just outside Fort William where he was forced off the road. She would later speak at his funeral.

(iv)

"I'm sorry Harriet, the case is closed," she was told by her superior, a man whose breath was as bad as his old worn suit.

"But we have an unsolved death and a suspicious so-called suicide. I know there's more to this and you do too."

The man behind a desk laughed. "I've been given orders from on high. They found a note written by that journalist and some farmer came forward to say he shot some large cat on his farmland last week, and its size and weight match the wounds on the runner. That's the case closed, in my eyes."

Harriet scoffed loudly.

"Come on Anderton, you're above conspiracy theories surely..."

"But there's something that just doesn't add up."

The man got up from behind his desk and perched on the edge, somewhere between a stack of loose-leaf papers and a newton's cradle bought for him by his granddaughter, in an attempt to curb his stress.

"I know you're still upset over Peter, we all are, but you have to drop this. There are other, more important cases, like the O'Reilly murder. We need more support there, else we'll never get through all the CCTV footage.

Harriet rolled her eyes at the thought of being stuck behind a desk looking for hours of tedious grainy camera footage. Her superior continued.

"Look. You have an extended weekend. Take it, get your mind clear, then come back on Tuesday with a refreshed sense of judgement. That way we can all get on with the matter in hand."

Harriet nodded. "You're right. Some fresh air will help."

"What's the plan?"

"I think I might give the house a spring clean, then head up to Northumberland for a few days."

"Sounds lovely. Send me a postcard."

Though Harriet was indeed taking a break, the direction wasn't quite so northerly. Instead, Harriet and her Vauxhall Corsa travelled west towards Cheddar, and it wasn't long before she was parked up next to the Dog and Duck and signing her name up for one of its two pokey little hotel rooms for a few days. It was late when she arrived after putting in a day's work so she settled in front of the pub's fire with one of their homemade shepherd's pies and a pint of real ale. Afterwards, she stretched her legs out in front of the warmth and the pub cat came and settled on her lap, falling asleep soon after. Harriet smiled. This was nice. Tomorrow Harriet would have to step out into the cold fields of Cheddar in search of answers, but for the last few hours of the day she was quite content to keep warm in front of the crackling logs and purring of the cat.

The next day, Anderton woke up at just after six, showered, breakfasted (kippers and toast, served once more in front of the fire, this time extinguished) and got changed into thick trousers, walking boots and a hefty overcoat. She wished a good morning to the bar's owner and headed out to her car, driving up to where the second body was found. As if doing some sort of re-enactment of Deborah's travels, Harriet traversed the inclines and fields of the Somerset countryside in the hope of finding just where Deborah had met her end. It hadn't been difficult to find out where she had gone; Harriet had spoken to one of her colleagues, who didn't seem to have been approached by whoever was pulling the strings of this operation and who had got hold of the mobile records, showing where Deborah had been. She had wandered deep into the woods near the Mendip Hills and that's where Harriet was going now, her boots crunching over the roots and bracken of the increasingly densely wooded area.

As she hiked across the fields, many thoughts crossed her mind. What had Mac been hiding on her body that he wouldn't show her? Had the journalist died in some other way than an overdose, and in keeping the body covered up such a modus operandi would remain hidden? Had Mac been killed for what he knew?

All these thoughts were flying and flipping around her mind as she traversed the fields, passed through gates and slowly lifted herself over stiles. Soon, she too was deep in the woods, crunching over the same undergrowth that Deborah had previously traversed and it wasn't long before she found the fencing that separated the metallic grey building from the green of nature. Harriet did a once around the perimeter, too, before returning to a similar spot to where her victim had stood. Her eyes fell of a branch of berries that he purposefully been thrust into the ground. Deborah had been here. The area seemed eerily quiet.

Realising there was little there to warrant her intrusion, Harriet turned and made her way back towards the edge of the wood, but only about thirty seconds into her departure through the occasionally sunlight-dappled undergrowth she stopped in her tracks at the sound of crunching. Harriet spun around, attempting to locate the source of the noise, but couldn't make out from which direction it was coming. The similarity of each tree to Harriet's human mind made for a disorientating experience and it wasn't long before she'd lost which way was out. The crunching happening again; her heart began to race in her chest and she wondered what was approaching. She didn't have long to wait, as a sleek, black, feline figure emerged from a particularly thick bush, first just its head then its body, its teeth bared and its tail – when that became visible – swishing. Harriet took a couple of cautionary steps backwards, to try and put some distance between her and the large cat, but its assured paw-steps forward were more rapid than her anxious footsteps backwards.

Harriet's mind began to race, every fibre of her body trying to deny what her eyes were telling her. She couldn't believe there actually was a big cat in these woods and her joy that she'd potentially discovered the cause of Ernest's death was subdued by the cold and clammy fear that was washing over her body. Harriet swallowed and blinked, but the vision was still there. Maybe this creature – and she could now feel its warm breath on her legs – was behind Deborah's death as well. Would she become its third victim?

The large cat was now within stroking distance, if Harriet had any sort of desire to pat it on its head and say Good Kitty. Stroking distance became striking distance, but Harriet didn't fancy her chances against the black and muscular creature in a fist fight.

The detective didn't believe in God – she felt such a figure was perfect to be left in carols, repeats of Songs of Praise and school assemblies, not in her own mind – but at this point, even she felt like praying. With every passing moment she expected it to strike; the cat was obviously free from any fear of humans. But, just as she closed her eyes and waited for the inevitable strike, there was a squeak from the cat and it slumped on its side. Still frozen in fear, Harriet nervously opened one eye, then another, to see the large cat now laid down as if sleeping, a small dart jutting from its back. She didn't have long to study this development when a pair of figures dressed in army camouflage emerged from the trees and examined the body. One was carrying a large rifle, the other a torch. A third figure, dressed more formally in a suit, appeared at this point, when a verbal all clear was given and he was more interested in Harriet than the cat.

"Detective Anderton," he said in a cut-glass accent. "So great to finally meet you at last, and thank you for finally helping us to track down our escapee."

"Not a problem," she said, her voice shaking. "So it's your cat?"

"In a manner of speaking, yes," he said. "Not that we'd say that officially. On the record you know."

"And did it..."

"Kill the old man and the journalist? It's not for us to say, but for your investigation that's a definite yes."

"So, Deborah..."

"I don't think anyone will miss her sort of journalism. I've seen some of the things she printed. Images of celebrity's kids. Oh look, she's all grown up. Disgusting stuff. She certainly grew up when she had the facts."

Harriet coughed and tried to say something, but the suited man just continued.

"She was around here when she met her death. Don't make me have to do the same for you, Detective Anderton. All you have to do is file your report, say there were two deaths connected to an escaped animal that we have now hunted down and stopped, and all will be well."

"So a cover up then?" Harriet questioned. The man laughed.

"If you want to call it that, then yes. But I think you'd do well not to refer to it as that in your report. We wouldn't want anything to happen to you."

At this point Harriet appeared to get some of her usual confidence back. "So, what you're saying is a creature escapes from what I'm assuming is some sort of lab, kills someone, you kill a witness and then threaten me with the same?"

"In a nutshell, if we're looking at the basic facts. But we all know things are more complicated than that."

Whilst this conversation was going on, the two soldiers in camouflage had passed over to the side to enjoy a cigarette each, and everyone's eyes were off the creature. Whatever the reason – whether it had only been stunned or the tranquiliser wasn't powerful enough – the creature came round, shaking its head and slowly getting to its feet. By the time anyone spotted this, thanks to a tell-tale rustle in the damp leaves, the creature had gathered its thoughts and its running pace and disappeared back into the bushes. The suited man cursed under his breath and sent the soldiers after it, their half-finished still-lit cigarettes scattered into the undergrowth, luckily not setting anything on fire.

The man turned to Harriet. "If any of this gets mentioned then strings will be pulled. This site belongs to some people in some very high places. You'd do well to remember that."

And with a sneer and a piercing look at the detective from his deep-set eyes, the man in the suit walked away, leaving Harriet standing in the clearing, her heart still racing. She looked down at some of the foliage around her. An area of Special Scientific Interest? She thought. More like a way of keeping people away from whatever things are going on in that building...

Harriet managed to re-orient herself in the woods and made her way back to the pub, where she enjoyed an open sandwich, a swift brandy and the relaxing warmth of the fire, along with the company of a cat that was a much more comfortable size. She never spoke about what she'd seen when she returned back to her base and never saw the man in the suit again.

(v)

The report had been filed, the cover-up completed, the tabloid reports of big cats in Somerset long forgotten with more depressing, dark and political news taking over the front pages.

'Prime Minister Calls For Syrian Sanctions' was the headline of the favourite paper of the Clarke family on the day they jumped in the car to head to Cheddar for a picnic on the surprisingly warm spring Saturday. There was a large hamper in the boot, filled to the brim with edible delights, from tuna mayonnaise sandwiches to sausage rolls, slices of Victoria sponge to Rice Krispies cakes, with flasks of lemonade and tea for the children and a cheeky bottle of cabernet sauvignon for the parents. It was only forty minutes and two choruses of 'are we there yet' until the family were at the spot, the car parked up at the side of the road and the hamper and picnic blanket retrieved from the car.

Mr Clarke laid down the blanket on the floor and the familial quartet began to lay out the food and plates in a relatively orderly way around the blanket, soon sitting down on the grass and enjoying a selection of snacks under the warmth of the sun. After about thirty minutes Amelia, the youngest of the family, asked a question.

"Where is this?" she asked. Her mother, mid-way through a sip of red wine, answered her.

"These are the Mendip Hills," she confirmed. "And down there is an area of scientific interest, which means they've got some rare plants. And animals."

"What sort of animals?" Amelia asked.

Mrs Clarke looked at her husband and back again to her daughter. "I'm not sure. Butterflies I think? Some birds?"

"No cats?"

"I don't think so," her mum laughed. "I don't think cats and birds really get on."

"Oh," Amelia asked, looking away from her parents and to bush a few metres away where she'd spied two reflective eyes. She'd recognised them as being like those of her cat at home, though here they were much, much bigger. She watched as a head poked out from the hedge and studied the family.

"Actually, you remember the papers a while ago – last October I think it was? There was that mysterious big cat attack somewhere near here. Got a runner and a journalist if I remember. Perhaps there is something lurking around?"

"Don't be ridiculous Thomas, and don't scare Amelia. There are no such things as big cats. Now let's toast our family day out and stop these silly stories."

Thomas smiled. "What should we toast to?"

"To the perch!"

Amelia looking confused. "To a fish?"

"No," her mum said. "Well it is a type of fish, but in this case it's the name of the place down there. The locals call it the Perch. I'm not sure why but you know how these things happen!"

"Cheers then," Thomas said, "To the lovely perch!"

"To the lovely perch!" they all chimed, to the clinking together of plastic cups, unaware of the large black figure slowly moved closer, preparing to pounce and set in motion a fresh tabloid story...

The Lovely Perch

By M. Loftouse

The crack of dawn is my favorite time of the day, when I slowly open my eyes to the possibility of meeting with her again. I could never get tired of that lady; she is one of the kindest souls I have met in all my life.

With a burst of excitement, I straightened myself up and brushed the broken twigs from my wings. I had to look my best today; for it was the day I would tell her about my own little girl. Instinctively, I whipped around for a quick glance at the other side and sighed in relief.

Stretching my grey-black wings, I hopped onto the edge of my home and peeked at the ground below. There were more leaves covering the stone pavement than the day before, which meant that winter was on its way. Taking in a deep breath, I got myself ready to take off. By now, the sun had already come out and the bustle below was starting to gather. I sashayed my way through the gentle breeze, taking in all the brilliance that it had to offer. At this height, the smells were vaguely exciting, but that would soon change on the busier side of the city, where the cacophony of aromas of the arrival of freshly baked breads, flowers of all colors and throngs of young children waiting for their buses rose languidly into the sky.

On an ideal day like today, as usual I zipped around the narrow streets, so tightly packed that there was hardly any room between the two buildings. I often wondered how the humans made do with it, especially with harsh conversations bellowing from each of the windows, but thankfully there was none of that today. I shook my head and relished the discovery of this small bit of early morning peace and moved on.

My lady, the purpose behind my long journey each day, sat just at the junction of these residential buildings, in a lonesome, tiny and rather overgrown park. I wouldn't even call it a park; it was dank, dark and soulless. Perhaps it once was beautiful, I corrected myself immediately, realizing that the simple wooden bench where she sat certainly qualified as a park for birds like me. Mrs. Perch, the lovely Perch as I often referred to her in our circle, was an old lady with beautiful salt and pepper hair, bundled up in a tight bun and secured with all kinds of eccentric hair pins that jutted out, each and every which way. She wore vibrant patterned dresses, some most of the other humans would consider inappropriate for her age; 'too bright', they would say, but to me it was like a beacon. I could spot the effervescence from anywhere and that wasn't the only reason I was drawn to her. In her frail fists, she brought food which she would sprinkle over the moist grass. Most of the time, it included bits of bread, seeds, greens, berries and, on occasion, fruits. I wondered what would be the menu for today.

I glided to where Mrs. Perch habitually sat, my eyes welcoming, but stopped short as I realized there was no one there. In my short confusion, I stumbled over the edge of the bench and scrapped my wing as I spun, landing with a thump onto the seat. Panting, I looked around, this was unusual. She was never late. I panicked. My voice croaked as I called out for her, but there was no response. I sat there for a while, hoping that she would appear, but she didn't. My stomach grumbled as the hours went by; I had always reserved my mornings for Perch, but where was she?

I began scouring the grass first, but there was nothing there, so I moved behind the bench. Nothing there either. By now, I was getting frustrated and flapped my wings in agitation, which eventually fell into sadness. It was for the first time that I looked up to notice the elderberry tree next to the bench. The succulent black dots stared back at me, inviting and enticing but I shook my head. Perch was the only one who could bring me berries; I chastised myself and instead flew off towards the top branch. I scanned the expanse from there, hoping that perhaps Perch was slowly making her way here. She carried a thin and scratched old walking stick, I remembered, but yet again, the lovely Perch was nowhere to be found.

By noon, I was losing hope and I sighed as I left to gather a few staples for the young one back home. So lost in my thoughts I was, that I hadn't realized when and how I had crashed into a window. I fell onto the muddy sill and winced. My damaged wing had probably cracked further – the pain was certainly greater. I scrabbled ineffectually, sending twigs scattering into the sewer below. Pained, exhausted, worried for my old friend, I lay there on my back and cried. Someone must have heard the cry from inside, for I felt the window lock click open, but being injured and already having a bad day, I cared less for what was to happen.

I felt small hands wrap themselves around me as I stirred at the welcoming warmth and gazed into the eyes of this newcomer. It was a youngling, or I assumed that's what the humans called them. She had fiery red hair and a brilliant freckled face, upon which was plastered the most beautiful smile I had ever seen, but it was nothing like Perch's smile and suddenly I missed her even more.

She brought me inside to tend to my wing. Inside! A place I had never been before. I looked around, nervous and gave a cry of joyous surprise. There, in an overstuffed armchair, was my lovely Perch!

Overjoyed, I struggled towards her – perhaps my wing wasn't so badly damaged, after all – and landed on her outstretched hand.

"Can we keep her, Grandma?" the youngling cried, and I understood.

The lovely Perch had someone to care for, too.

I didn't hear the response. I was too excited. I flew up and out of the bright room, past the tree whose branches stretched up beside it, ignoring the ache in my wing. I was going to fetch my little one. We would make a new nest here, among friends.

A lovely perch!

The Lovely Perch

By J. McGraw

It's a good view of the street I've got. Broad. Right up to the market at the north and down to the river at the south. Lots of folk come up and down: labourers with barrows and carts and sacks from the boats; passengers with boys trailing behind, laden with luggage; folk with deep pockets, and folk with no pockets, hoping the deep pockets will be kind and spread some wealth.

Life, really. City life. Boring.

I watch the thieves. The sharp knife that slits the bottom of those jingling purses. The swift hand that slips into sacks. The loud cry that draws attention the wrong way. They're never boring.

I watch the fraudsters. The man whose family is sick, and desperately needs money for medicine. The girl who sells flowers to see into people's purses and note who's worth robbing. The woman who sells potions and charms for the superstitious and gullible. They're subtle, harder to spot. It's a game as challenging as a riddle, finding them.

From this lovely perch, I saw a woman in the house down the hill. She would stand at the window after her husband went to work, and a young man would appear from the crowds and knock at her door. He and she would disappear, sometimes for hours, and he would always be flushed when he re-emerged.

Yesterday, the husband returned home unexpectedly. He looked angry as he opened the door - probably knew he was replaced in his wife's heart. It wasn't long before the noises started, loud enough to turn the heads of the bustling crowds passing by. Shouting, banging around, screams. Then quiet, very quiet, until evening came. The young man appeared once more after the sun was down, slipping through the side door with a hood pulled high over his head, returning minutes later with a barrow. The wife opened the door to him and watched as he hauled out a roll of carpet, dumped it in the barrow, and wheeled it down to the river. Didn't see what he did with it, but I haven't seen him since. Reckon the husband is in the river now, drifting slowly out to sea.

And then this morning - Oh! The scenes! Police hammering at the door, the wife in tears 'Please officer, find my husband for me, he left for work and never came home', constables running like fury through the streets, questioning everyone. No one had seen anything. The husband never came home early, so why would he that day? Frowning faces and scratching of heads. So many witnesses, and no one saw. Save for me.

No one comes up to ask me, of course. I'm just an ugly face, stone and moss, with nothing but time to watch and laugh. I saw it all, from my rooftop home. But I'm not telling.

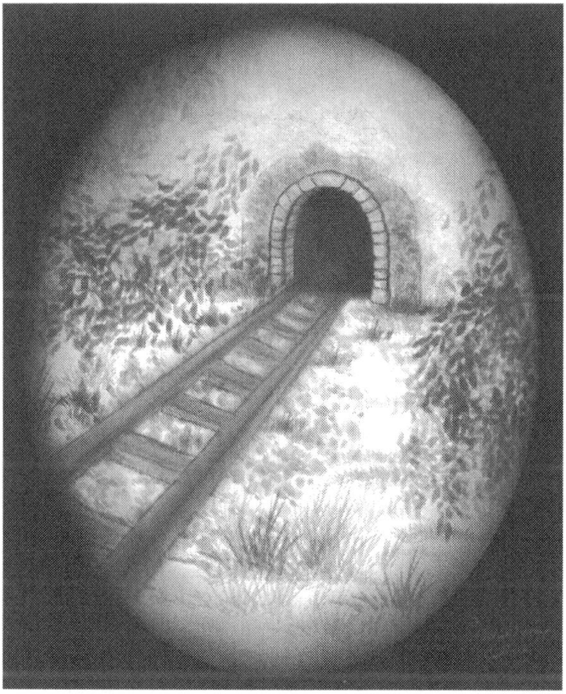

Lost in the Underground

By Hailie Drescher

Standing on a platform,
Somewhere in the London Underground,
Don't know where I am.

Deep in the bowels of London,
I stand staring at the map.
My mind cannot make sense
Of all these twists and turns.

How did I get here?
Where is here?

I'm so confused,
I need to find my friend.
Help me escape
This never ending maze.

Which way to the surface?
Let me ascend,
Out of this hellish cage.

Out of the dank,
Out of the gloom.
Bring me to the sunlight above.
Save me from this nightmare.

Save me from the dank and dark,
Of the London Underground.

The 27th Fact

By Philip Lickley

London was absolutely rammed with shoppers, tourists and sightseers. It was the 19th December after all, the final Saturday before Christmas. Families, couples and stressed relatives were marching up and down Oxford Street, trying to find bargains or last minute gift ideas, or both. Checkouts were bursting at the seams with men and women holding overflowing baskets of goods, and stressed looking husbands trying to find that last minute bargain, as if trying to live up to the cliché set up before them. All around, younger children were darting across aisles, between legs and around displays. Outside, the less stressed of the population milled from boutique store to outdoor stall, often with a mince pie or steaming glass of mulled cider in hand. Somewhere down the street a busker was playing a version of 'Jingle Bells' in the wrong key.

Away from the streets that were decked out with flashing lights, trees and signs proclaiming offer after offer, members of the groups of shoppers, tourists and sightseers were bundling themselves into taxis, buses and tube trains, the latter group of subterraneous tunnels particularly crammed with people. One group who found themselves on South Kensington station were the Lowe family, who had enjoyed a day out in the series of museums that lay within the vicinity of the area, from the Natural History Museum to the one dedicated to science. Each member was happy but tired, content but sleepy.

Kathryn Lowe was first onto the tube train, her auburn hair tied neatly up in a bun with a wrap of tinsel added especially for the season, carrying with her two large boxes, balanced precariously between her arms and her chest, with a thick grey coat somewhere in the middle. Next were the two youngest members of the Lowe clan: Peter, fourteen, and Gemma, seven, both holding small bags of sweets, wrapped up as tightly as the children were themselves, in matching gloves, scarves and bobble hats, a look that gave Gemma an air of youthful cuteness, but on the scowling teenage Peter looked false and awkward. The final member of the family, father and husband Eammon, was the last onto the train, holding at least three plastic carrier bags in each hand, whilst on top of his head were a pair of fake plastic antlers, his small attempt to look festive. The tube carriage was already pretty packed with people, most holding some form of shopping, so the quartet had to squeeze and stand at the edge of the doorway until a number of people got off at Gloucester Road and they managed to find four seats within close proximity of each other with a bit more breathing space as the carriage emptied a fair bit. They were relieved to get off the platform for several reasons – both to escape the hustle and bustle and the heavily synthesized carols that were being piped through the station's messaging system.

Kathryn let out a sigh of relief as she rested her packages on her knees and Eamonn was just as happy to be able to place his bags down on the floor, which gave him a chance to soak in the surroundings. Sadly for all those concerned, this was mostly the smell of stale sweat and curries, with the background sound of bass from someone's leaking headphones a constant reminder of all the commuters trapped in their own little worlds, hemmed in by music, Facebook or some level of Candy Crush.

Whilst the parents gathered their thoughts and longed for home, Peter had made eye contact with a young boy of a similar age. The boy had a messy knot of brown hair, glasses too big for his face and a Paddington-bear style duffel coat that seemed a couple of sizes too large. His look was distinctly older than his years, and much at odds to Peter's mollycoddled well-wrapped up look. Peter had smiled in his direction and the boy, who was reading from an old, dog-eared book with no dust-sheet to protect it or embossed lettering on the outside to identify it, raised his eyes from his reading matter and smiled back. After a few moments, as the train gathered up momentum to leave the station, he spoke to Peter.

"Did you know," he began, in a surprisingly deep voice for his age, "That Gloucester Road used to be called Hog Moore Lane, due to the pigs that used to be kept there?"

Peter shook his head. This wasn't something he knew. Peter had not been on the Underground many times in his life, never mind collected facts about the tunnels. The boy smiled back. "It's true. I read it in a book once."

The boy gestured towards the book he was currently holding, but it didn't seem like this was the one from which he got the fact. It looked from the layout of the text, just about visible from the distance Peter was sitting, to be a novel of some sort, or at least something with much text and few illustrations. There was a brief moment of silence before the boy thrust out his arm as if inviting Peter to shake it. Peter declined, shyness seemingly washing over him, and he instead looked away.

"I'm Samuel," the boy said anyway, undeterred. "And I'm off to find my parents."

"Find them?" Peter asked, picking up on his unusual choice of words.

"Yes. They're at a café at South Kensington."

There was a momentary pause.

"We've just left there," Peter said pointedly.

"I know," Samuel said with an air of dismissal. "I was too engrossed in my book to notice. I mean I could get off and jump on another line to get back more quickly, but I quite like the idea of exploring the Circle line. There have to be some benefits of a track that loops around continuously, and surely being able to stay on it for the full journey must be one? It quite sounds like something you'd put on your bucket list if you lived in the city."

There was something about the way Samuel paused before using the term 'bucket list' that made it sound like he was unfamiliar with the term, but had picked it up somewhere, like a young child learning to speak and repeating something he'd heard parrot-fashion. Such thoughts were replaced by Peter wondering who would add travelling on the Underground to their bucket list. Someone, he mused, with little imagination or excitement in their life.

Peter had never thought about such things as bucket lists of exploring train tunnels. Particularly (as he had already thought) as he didn't take the Underground very often.

"I think I'll be in trouble with my parents," Samuel said, drip feeding little bits of conversation. Peter asked why. "For my behaviour over the years."

Again, 'over the years' seemed a weird choice of phrasing from a boy of his age. Peter asked about his behaviour.

"Now that's a long story," he said, blinking, his eyes briefly glancing at his book before he looked back up at Peter. "How long are you staying on until?" Samuel asked. Peter looked to his mother, then to his sister and finally to his father, but they all seemed engrossed in their own world and were leaving Peter to his conversation. Kathryn, his mother, was now adjusting her hair, taking out the tinsel and re-setting it. Eammon, his father, was trying to keep Gemma amused with his antlers.

"Until King's Cross, and then we get a train home."

"Where's that?"

"Stevenage," Peter said simply. Samuel nodded.

"I've never been there."

By now the train had pulled into the next station, High Street Kensington and, as expected, a flurry of people had got off the train and a similar number scurried on, many carrying bags of gifts. There was still space in the carriage, though, with no one blocking the space between Peter and Samuel. Peter glanced out of the window and studied the strange mix of old and new that seemed to make up a typical London Underground station, as if none of them had truly ever been fully refurbished, just had modern sticking plasters of electronics and health and safety notices pasted over the tiles and mosaics of old.

"Now this station has an arcade," Samuel said without prompting. "A nice little one too. I used to go there with my parents when I was younger. There was a lovely little sweet shop there. My dad used to buy me little brown bags of liquorice allsorts."

Peter pulled a face. "I don't like liquorice allsorts."

Samuel smiled. "They're an acquired taste."

Peter nodded. His sister, Gemma, looked up from staring at her shoes, bored now of her father's antics. "I like liquorice allsorts."

"You would," her brother scolded. Samuel frowned.

"Hello, I'm Samuel," he said, offering an olive branch of a conversation to the younger girl.

"Gemma," she replied bashfully, her cheeks reddening with embarrassment. The train now came to a halt as the usual on-off and off-on of passengers took place.

"Notting Hill Gate," confirmed Samuel before the voice over the intercom system confirmed it. "A film called Otley had a scene set here. Of course Notting Hill is most famous for its carnival..."

Peter knew about the carnival; he had once visited it with his parents and had fallen in love with the bright colours, loud music and smells from the food of a hundred cultures. Images played in his mind like some sort of internal video, of tall women with long legs in bright head-dresses, of supple dancers, of fire breathers choking out clouds of ash and flames. He'd love to go and see it again at some point and made a note to ask his parents about it next year. Peter chose not to bother them at the moment; they were both having a discussion about gifts for their god-children, which sounded like it was getting a little heated. His mother seemed keener on something from Frozen for them, Eammon keener on some sort of brick toy. "Everyone loves Lego," he said proudly as justification. Kathryn did not look convinced.

Whilst Gemma looked around the carriage – at her age, she seemed constantly fascinated by the energy of everyday life – Peter studied Samuel as if he was a stage magician trying to work out the mind of his volunteer. For a start, his trouser pockets looked empty, no expected bulge of a wallet or keys within them. He certainly didn't look to have a mobile phone on his person, from which he could access these facts about each station. Peter figured he must be reading Wikipedia or something, but he wasn't sure how. He didn't look the type of person to have some sort of ear-piece feeding him information. Peter had seen something about that at the Science Museum earlier. Samuel didn't look like somebody who would have known about such things, never mind used them.

Another more pressing thought came to his mind. Who had even heard of a film like Otley? Peter knew that most teenagers his age lived in the there and now and couldn't name any famous films from years gone by unless they'd been asked to study them at school, so knowing about such an obscure film felt unusual. Peter prided himself on being a bit of a film buff and he'd never heard of it, and he'd watched Metropolis, a fact he was strangely proud of, as if it made him better than those around him.

Perhaps he'd just memorised these facts to impress other boys his age; Peter did a similar thing with his movies. Peter continued to study his fellow passenger; he wondered if he was perhaps a little autistic. He had a friend at school like that who was incredible when it came to remembering facts. Maybe Samuel was similar? A photographic memory perhaps? Peter looked around the carriage at the mixture of tired and sweating shoppers, frustrated commuters and a young couple in their early twenties enjoying a rather intimate kiss. Peter was glad not to have a photographic memory so he wouldn't have the image of the carriage and its passengers for much longer.

Something puzzled Peter about Samuel. He thought, as he studied his general demeanour and his choice of fashion, he didn't look like someone who had access to technology. Though he was of a similar age to Peter, who had got his first mobile in the last twelve months, there was something distinctly old fashioned about Samuel, as if he'd stepped out of some exhibition in one of the museums. The contrast of Samuel's hard-wearing and formal clothing was at odds with Peter's branded and more brightly coloured fare.

The train had now pulled away into a tunnel, plunging much of the outside world into darkness. Samuel had returned to his book, tracing each line with the tip of his index finger. Peter took his phone from his pocket, pressed a few buttons in the hope of checking Facebook, realised the tunnel had blotted out all but one bar of his signal, and then put it back. The train came to a shuddering halt at the next station, 'Bayswater'. Hardly anyone got off or on at this station, which was a shame, thought Peter, as it looked pretty nice.

"Did you know, two houses nearby were demolished to make way for part of the line at this station?" Samuel began, when the noise of departing passengers had subsided. "They put up fake frontages for the houses when they'd finished, but there's nothing behind them."

Peter nodded and looked elsewhere. Samuel just continued reading his book. The train headed off.

This routine of new station and associated fact continued uninterrupted for a while. Samuel would wait until the carriage activity had died down before dispensing the fact, before returning to his book. Peter would nod reassuringly that he'd heard it whilst Gemma continued to remain oblivious, sitting quietly in her seat, content in her own world. Kathryn and Eammon had moved on from their god-children to preparations for Christmas, their tones much more jovial now as conversations, heard by Peter in snatches, covered everything from the turkey to the tree to whether they were going to watch Doctor Who on Christmas Day. They even smiled when a family got on at Paddington station ("The overground station here leant its name to the bear of the books") and their youngest daughter was singing a rather cute version of 'Little Donkey', which reminded them of Gemma when she was younger.

The tube train passed with little interruption through Edgware Road ("One of the first underground stations opened"); Baker Street ("Famous for Sherlock Holmes and the Gerry Rafferty song"); Great Portland Street ("There used to be a car showroom as part of the station") and Euston Square ("It used to be called Gower Street"). Soon the train was on its way to the personal terminus for the Lowe family, 'King's Cross, St. Pancras', a grand station that felt like the biggest and most famous of the city. Peter loved that station thanks to its architecture, buzzing feel and, of course, the chance to scurry away to the 'Platform 9 ¾s area for a cheeky selfie by the trolley stuck halfway in the wall. As the train neared that station Kathryn ushered Peter and Gemma to their feet in preparation, as only a parent can. Samuel looked up from his book towards their son.

"But mum," Peter whelped, resisting her trying to put his coat on. "I want to hear the rest of Samuel's facts..."

Up to this point Kathryn an Eammon had mostly been oblivious to the brief exchanges of words between the two boys. Kathryn studied the stranger and didn't see anything unduly worrying from him but questioned Peter's interest in such things from such an unusual looking boy.

"Come on Peter, I'm tired and it's late. We can catch up with your friend another time. Can't you like swap numbers or something or Twitter names, or whatever you do these days?"

Peter, turning on the teenage stubbornness dug his heels in, both physically and metaphorically, as the train pulled into the underground station and the doors opened with a groan. Kathryn was having none of it, taking Gemma by the hand and passing her to her husband, who left the train with her, before pulling Peter in the direction of the door. He reluctantly moved with her and onto the platform, his brow furrowed and his lips pursed with anger. Peter glanced back to Samuel, who didn't seem that affected by the exit of his friend with no words of goodbye shared between them. Peter growled at his mother.

"I'm fourteen; I don't need to be treated like a bloody kid. I just wanted to hear all his facts back to South Kensington and..."

Kathryn, his mother, was having none of it, and interrupted him mid-sentence. "Whilst you're living under my roof, you do as I say," she growled back, half-surprising herself as she rolled out a cliché that her mother had once told her. Peter seemingly took her words and obeyed and she released her grip on his top allowing him. But, as the beeping began on the train, the release of his hand allowed Peter to dart backwards and get back onto the train, the doors sliding shut, not giving Kathryn or Eammon chance to react and get him back off. The train pulled away, Peter given just enough time before the train headed down the next tunnel to see his mother angrily waving her fists at him and mouthing something that he couldn't quite make out but looked like it could well have been a swear word, followed by his name. He swallowed hard, Peter's teenager bravado disappearing as the light outside faded as he realised what he'd done. There was one seat free next to Samuel. He took the seat and realised he was probably now in a lot of trouble.

"This is the second busiest station on the entire network," Samuel said after a few moments, as if nothing had happened of note since they arrived at the most recent station. He did at least acknowledge it shortly afterwards with a brief 'welcome back' before the rest of the journey to Farringdon station was held in silence as

Samuel continued to read from his book and Peter continued to wallow in his worry.

"This station is mentioned in a song by Underworld," Samuel told Peter as the train left the station, shaking the boy from his thoughts and back to the reason why he'd disobeyed his parents in the first place. Peter wasn't entirely sure that fact was particularly interesting, and he'd never heard of Underworld, who he assumed was some sort of old band, and he wondered if he'd made the right call in jumping back on the train. Peter tried to start up a different conversation with his new found friend, if he indeed was being friendly.

"So what are you reading?" he asked, still unable to make out what book it was even from his closer proximity. Samuel turned to Peter and smiled.

"It's a novel I picked up a few years ago. It's a murder mystery set in London."

Peter waited for more information about the book, but nothing was forthcoming. Samuel quickly picked up on his agitation at not getting a longer reply and filled the void of silence, or at least the silence that existed between them in a carriage filled with chatter, music and rattling of mechanical parts.

"It's set in the early 20th century on the Underground, when the place was a much more dangerous place to be. South Kensington is stalked by a figure, like Jack the Ripper, who goes around pushing un-expecting people off the platforms. One day he pushes a teenage boy off the platform and kills him and this leads to a man-hunt as they try and discover who the murderer is."

Peter looked enticed by the story. "Sounds great!" he said with forced enthusiasm to try and shake thoughts of his parents from his mind. "And have you found out who killed the boy yet?"

"No," Samuel said, his usual warm demeanour fading slightly. "Not yet. I've still got the last few chapters of the book to go."

Peter glanced over the book Samuel was holding. He noticed it was well thumbed as if he'd read it a fair number of times. Peter decided to quiz him on this fact. His reply was succinct.

"Oh, not before. This is my first time."

Peter didn't quite believe him but he let it slide. Perhaps he'd got the book second hand. It was pretty old after all. Peter looked away from Samuel, his eyes briefly scanning the mixture of people in the carriage going about their business, and then watched as the train pulled into the next station: Barbican. Here a group of football fans got on and began talking loudly at one end of the carriage, cans of some cheap corner shop lager in each spare hand. Samuel didn't look up at the noise, instead continuing to read his book. Only when the train pulled away did he speak, dispensing his latest fact ("This station was badly damaged in the Blitz") in a very nonchalant fashion.

The journey clockwise around the Circle line continued as a mixture of people-watching, fact giving and snatches of conversation, Peter drinking in the facts dispensed by Samuel on Moorgate ("the worst crash in the Underground's history took place here"); Liverpool Street ("One of the two stations on the Circle line to appear on the UK Monopoly board") and Aldgate ("This appeared in a Sherlock Holmes short story"). As the train rattled through the stations, Peter's mind began to wander back to his family and what they were up to now. If his mother or father had jumped on a train they would be well behind him by now; he assumed that they'd be looking to catch up with him at South Kensington, figuring he would be returning there. He was not looking forward to the reunion, or the grounding he would face, which would be pretty humiliating for a boy on the cusp of his fifteenth year.

Soon the station had stopped at Tower Hill ("Next to the Tower of London, of course!") and Monument ("Named after the monument to the Great Fire of

London") and this latter station got Samuel talking in quite an animated fashion for the first time in the journey. Samuel started reeling off a series of facts and stories about the event that gripped Peter and he enjoyed the knowledge of his new friend, but he couldn't help wondering how he'd memorised such facts for such a young lad. Again, Peter began to wonder about him, continuing to study his clothing, mannerisms and language. There was something incredibly formal about him, as if he preferred to speak in as clear a way as possible, without any consideration for slang or metaphors. It was unusual for a boy of fourteen to behave in such a manner. All the boys Peter knew would pepper their speech with curses, pop-culture references or terms that they'd picked up from websites or social networks. Samuel's words were free of such inspiration and for Peter this was quite refreshing.

They'd passed through several more stations by the time Samuel's re-telling of the Great Fire of London was complete, the story broken up occasionally with interludes about the stations they'd passed through. For Cannon Street, Samuel spoke about the old medieval steelyard it had been built on; for Mansion House, it was all about the candle makers that had been dotted around the station in its heyday; and for Blackfriars it was a discussion about solar technology, all about the recent installation of photovoltaic panels that provided nearly half of the power for the station.

It was at this point that Peter's mobile phone rang; it was his mother calling, and already he'd had three missed calls, either from having missed them or having poor signal reception.

This is all I need, figured Peter. Now she'll think I've been ignoring her too. There was also a text on the phone, a short and sharp message telling him to wait at South Kensington, where his dad would be meeting him. Peter messaged her back with an even shorter response before slipping his phone back into his pocket. He turned back to Samuel who was one chapter further towards the end of his book. The train pulled into Temple, deposited some commuters, shoppers and tourists, picked up some more of the same, and headed off. It was a few moments later that Samuel revealed his twenty-first fact of the day.

"Temple is named after the church built by the Knights Templar that is nearby," Samuel revealed, not looking up from his book. Peter smiled.

"Cool. Like in Assassin's Creed."

Samuel looked up blankly at Peter.

"You know. The video game."

Samuel still looked pretty vacant.

"I take it you're not much of a gamer then?"

"I've never heard of Assassin's Creed."

Peter nodded. "More of a Super Mario fan?"

"I don't know what you're talking about," he said bluntly, before returning to his book. Peter looked away and stared out of the window at the passing adverts flitting past his eyes in a slower fashion as the train pulled into the next station and decelerated. Samuel was very much like his friend at school: clever, full of facts, but hopeless when it came to popular culture. They had now arrived at Embankment.

"This station," Samuel revealed as he finished a chapter, "is named after the Victoria Embankment Gardens. It has four sections. They are beautiful," was all the colour added by Samuel to that prosaic sentence. The train set off. The pair remained in silence.

Once more, Peter took the time to observe his carriage mate. There was still something unusual about him that he couldn't put his finger on. Was it his old fashioned dress? His old fashioned language? No, it was something else. Peter's youthful curiosity was teasing him. He decided to quiz his friend a little.

"You said earlier you were meeting your parents at the cafe in South Kensington. What do they do?"

Samuel licked his fingers and folded the corner over of his book as a place-marker. The page folded with ease and he closed the book.

"My father is a policeman, my mother doesn't work. She looks after the house."

"Do you get on?"

"I don't see eye to eye with my father. He's quite strict, and doesn't like my behaviour."

"Your behaviour?"

"I think you would know me as a bit of a tearaway. I get into trouble. As a man of the law he doesn't like that. I like going out on my own, exploring the city late at night, especially the underground stations. There's something majestic about them, don't you think? How humanity has created such a complex interlinking series of tunnels and stations to service one city? I find it fascinating."

"Hence all your facts?"

Samuel nodded.

"Is it just this line?"

"Oh no," he said, licking his lips, "I explore as many as I can. I like to get out and about you know, away from the confines of a train carriage."

Peter realised this was the first time Samuel had talked about his life outside of the carriage. He studied him once more.

"How old are you?" he asked.

"Thirteen," came the reply.

"You come across as older."

"That'll be my clothes."

"When were you born?"

"You know my age, therefore you know."

"But I'd like you to tell me."

Samuel didn't reply.

Soon the train pulled into Westminster ("You can get to the Houses of Parliament and the London Eye from here") and then out of the station, heading towards the conclusion of Peter's journey. After his brief foray into Samuel's life Peter remained quiet with any further questions, but his brain was ticking over thinking crazy thoughts about Samuel, his old fashioned look and his manner. A crazy thought went through his mind but he dismissed it. He needed more evidence. He sat in contemplation on the fold-down seat next to the boy, studying his surroundings every few moments for anything unusual, but nothing stood out: it was just the same adverts, tube announcements and ever changing passengers. They soon arrived at St. James Park ("It's been spelt differently over the years. Must be frustrating for those who like good grammar") and then at Victoria ("60 million people use this station per year") until only Sloane Square ("The man behind the inspiration for Peter Pan committed suicide here") stood between them and the conclusion of the circular journey around London.

It was at this point, as the train finally arrived at Sloane Square, that Peter had the facts straight enough in his head, to confront his mysterious companion. Peter shifted in his seat to face a reading Samuel.

"I want to know," he said. "Are you... real?"

Peter immediately felt silly about saying the final of those three words.

Samuel looked at him with a pair of piercing, brown eyes. "What do you mean?"

"There's something unusual about you. Other-worldly I suppose."

Samuel paused and smiled. "If you mean I don't embrace the crassness of your generation then I'm pleased."

Peter laughed. "You see, that's what I mean. Your generation. What does that even mean? We're of a similar age you and I."

"Outwardly, yes," muttered Samuel, once more folding the corner of his nearly completed book, and closing it. "But I am much older. Much, much older."

Peter looked around the carriage. No one else seemed to be noticing Samuel's behaviour, from the passengers who had been on the train for a while to those who had recently mounted the carriage. That's not to say they hadn't noticed him, just that only Peter seemed to be perplexed by Samuel's style and appearance. Perhaps, Peter considered, that commuters on the London Underground were just used to seeing odd characters all the time, so an old-fashioned looking teenager was perhaps nothing that unusual. They were probably just glad Samuel wasn't a homeless person with a can of lager, or a group of drunken louts.

The train heaved and strained and left Sloane Square for its next station, South Kensington, the final planned stop for Peter before his, he figured, inevitable reuniting with his father and then family. By the time they were half way to the station Samuel finished his book and closed it with a satisfying thump.

"Finished," he proudly and succinctly declared.

"How does it end?" Peter asked. Samuel just smiled.

"With much satisfaction," he said richly. Peter turned to his neighbour.

"This might sound crazy but I've worked it out. I know what your final fact will be. It's been staring me in my face ever since you spoke to me about the book you've been reading."

Peter thought about his wording for a moment before continuing, "It was you, wasn't it, the boy murdered by the Jack the Ripper character? You're some sort of ghost, aren't you?"

Peter had made his accusation in muted tones. He didn't want the people of the carriage to think he had gone mad.

Samuel laughed. "You can see me, your parents and sister saw me, all the people around here see me. I can hardly be a ghost."

Peter laughed as well, but it was more manic. "I

don't know how ghosts work. Perhaps you can be seen by everyone. But all I know is you are not real."

Peter prodded him as if to make a point, but to his disappointment his finger pressed into the fabric of his top and didn't go through him like the transparent figure he thought he would be. His lip curled.

"Where do you get your understanding of the supernatural from?" Samuel asked. "The television? Motion pictures? Not all spirits are see-through and immaterial."

With a grunt and groan the underground train pulled into South Kensington, completing the round journey that Peter Lowe had made. Samuel got to his feet and looked down at the still seated Peter. He thrust out his arm, his book in his outstretched hand.

"Here, this is yours. The final epilogue is my twenty-seventh fact for you. I've enjoyed your company."

Though slightly reluctant, Peter took the book and held it firmly to his chest. Samuel nodded and turned, exiting the carriage. Peter stood and looked to see where he'd gone but if he had indeed walked off rather than disappeared – as Peter expected ghosts to do – Samuel was now lost in the crowds milling from platform to platform, museum underpass to carriage. He cursed under his breath and looked down to the book, but didn't have the chance to react before he was yanked off the carriage by an unseen force. But it wasn't anything phantasmal; it was his father who had pulled him by the arm onto the platform. The doors to the train closed, the carriages disappeared on their next round journey and the majority of the people dissipated from the platform, leaving just a few stragglers around except for Peter and his father, who was looking down at his son is anger.

"Never," he spat, "do that again. There are people in this city who would think nothing of taking you god knows where. You might be fourteen and think you're now a man, but that means nothing in a place like this. You should just be thankful that I got here this quickly!"

Peter took what his father was saying on board, but

it was perhaps a little difficult to take him seriously when his advice was dispensed over a high-pitched version of 'We Three Kings' blaring out through the speakers. Eammon took Peter and thrust a train ticket for the Piccadilly line into his hand. Whereas the Circle Line was slow and went around the houses, Eammon Lowe had managed to secure a Piccadilly train from Kings Cross and reached South Kensington at a relatively speedy fifteen minutes to catch his son.

"I'm sorry, dad," Peter said, bowing his head in a sulky type of remorse only familiar to those with teenagers. "It won't happen again."

The mood of his father lightened up from anger to annoyance, and his gaze fell on what he was carrying. Eammon enquired after the item in his son's possession.

"It was from Samuel. The boy on the train. He told me that the final chapter, the epilogue, would contain the final fact."

"Samuel?" his dad asked. "The boy on the train?"

"The ghost on the train..." Peter corrected. His dad laughed.

"There are no such things as ghosts Peter. We're all tired. Let's just get home."

Eammon stood up straight, away from his son, giving Peter the freedom to open up the book and peruse the final words.

"What does it say?" Eammon asked with genuine enthusiasm. Peter looked up at his father.

"You saw Samuel, didn't you?"

His father nodded. The ghost theory seemed to fade away with the knowledge that his father had seen him. Peter smiled a little and opened the book and began to read the epilogue.

*

Epilogue

The police eventually solved the mystery of the

Edwardian murderer who was pushing unexpecting victims off the platforms into the paths of oncoming trains. Shortly after the death of his final victim, a boy aged thirteen, it was revealed - much to the surprise of the law - that the perpertrator was a young man of a similar age, not the older gentleman they had felt more likely. After a short trial, Samuel Penny was sentenced to death and hanged on the 5th May 1906. Some still say that his ghost still haunts the stations he persecuted and has been seen many times around the Circle line and on the trains that traverse it.

*

Peter looked up from his book, the colour draining from his face. His eyes went from his father to the electronic sign above, declaring an imminent train pulling into South Kensington station, as also shown by the increased number of tourists spilling into the station from the nearby museums. He took one more glance at the book, closed it, swallowed and shut his eyes, hearing even above the noise of the crowd the sound of footsteps. Then he felt it – a strong push from behind – and he fell forward, down onto the tracks and into the path of the oncoming train. The last thing he heard was a scream from some people on the platform, a yell from his father, and a sinister laugh from a figure he could hear, but no one could see. And then nothing.

South Kensington station remained closed out of police necessity and respect for just shy of twelve hours; most of that, though was during the nocturnal shutdown, before business continued as usual the next day.

There were only three facts established by the police: one, that there was a mysterious young man called Samuel who had befriended Peter on the train, a young man who could not be traced even from stills of the CCTV footage that showed him beside the boy, even after they had been delivered to local businesses and shown on the national news. Two, that Peter fell forward onto the tracks with some force, but that there seemed to be nobody there to push him. And thirdly, that the next day a young girl called Charlotte Warburton was returning from an afternoon at the Natural History Museum with her mother when she befriended what she considered to be a handsome young man on the tube that she started chatting to at South Kensington, who she found aloof as much as she found him attractive, and who shared with her a fact.

"Did you know," he began, in a deep voice that she found compelling, "That Gloucester Road used to be called Hog Moore Lane due to the pigs that used to be kept there?"

Charlotte smiled. "That's interesting," she said. "Do you have any more facts?"

"Plenty," Stuart smiled with a lick of his lips. "Twenty-six more, to be precise."

Charlotte laughed. "What are you then, the human version of Buzzfeed?"

"Buzzfeed?" Stuart questioned, having heard of it from overhearing snatches of conversation between the younger occupants of the carriage over the years, but unaware of the intricacies of it, a recent creation as it was. "If you say so. Twenty-six more great facts about the Underground.

"You won't believe the last one..."

The Hammersmith

By Lauren K. Nixon

The world was cold when the Hammersmith came.

The skies were dark; all around were cliffs and plains of glittering ice, cold as death. We huddled against the dark in caves and huts of rock and wood, fighting the biting, life-sucking frost. Lives were harsh and short, and filled with hardship.

We were hungry and afraid.

Then the Hammersmith came.

They say, when his boot first trod on the frost of our land the skies burned green with the power of him.

He brought us iron and fire, taught us how to trap the light in bowls, the power of the dragon in stone mounds. He showed us how to shape the iron, strike the glowing brands until scales of fire flew all about, melting the ice, driving back the cold. The metal got into our blood.

We were hot and spitting, fierce and clever.

We were no longer afraid.

He brought us the sun, and in the light we thrived.

The green of the skies spread to the land – the ice receded, leaving rivers and mud. Mud, the elders found, could be bountiful. It made sturdy lodgings, fuel for our fires, food for our crops.

The Hammersmith hewed through rock to sink our wells, taught our elders how to build and plough.

We trapped our prey in the mountain forests and instead of slaughtering them, brought them down to pasture on the fresh green land. Now they meet us in friendship, even at the killing time.

He taught us how to shape weapons – not just for the hunt, but for the others, the ones the Hammersmith did not favour. They would be jealous, he told us. They would covet our gifts. We must defend the things the

Hammersmith gave us.

He showed us how to use sword and axe. The metal in us grew, until we were strong and hard like iron.

The Hammersmith brought us all this.

Then he retreated to his summer hall. High in the mountains, he watches over us.

You may see him walking sometimes at night, in winter. His shadow dark against the stars, the skies burning green above him, staving off the cold.

The world was cold when the Hammersmith came.

The Fisher Maid and the Old Man of the Sea
Or
How the Maid Tamed the Tide

By Hannah 'Han' R. H. Allen

Long ago, when the lands still remembered being wild, and the seas were uncharted and untamed, a small fishing village clung to the shore, eking out a difficult existence, battered by salt spray. Life was hard, but the people were free; and many things can be born when they are freely chosen.

In this village lived a fisher maid fair, her every move full of a grace more beautiful than the wide ocean; or so it was said, and so it was written. Many a young man had sought to woo, but the few who found courage beyond their cups, were each gently turned away, and so it was said; though her smile was warm as the sun, her heart was cold as the sea.

She was her father's last remaining child. The seas had swallowed her brothers, and grief had taken her mother. They lived on the edge of the settlement; she maintaining the homestead, while her father, the old fisherman, worked the sea to bring in enough to fill their stores and coffers. She had grown hard through hardship, as had her hands through work, and she easily turned away the youths that came a courting; "If only I could, but who would tend my father if I would go? Who would mend the nets and patch the sails?" But in truth her heart was closed to all those that trawled the sea, save of course her father, whom she loved more than anything, and for whom she would do anything, even defy the very tides.

Not far from the village was a cove, fanged with sharp rocks, tongues of sand bars lapping just beneath the surface, ready to catch unwary vessels and tip them into its waiting maw. The entrance of its throat, caves worn smooth by the tide, were lined with their flotsam. Here, the fishermen said, was where the Old Man of the Sea dwelt, luring the unwise and unwary to their doom. Though such stories are as insubstantial as shapes in ocean mist, there is always a grain of truth to every tale.

One year, the weather was particularly harsh. The winds tore up the meagre plants that the fisher folk cultivated to supplement their catch, and the waters were more unpredictable than they had been in living memory. A great storm rose suddenly out of the ocean, crashing moored craft against the jetties, and tossing the ones still at sea around as a child with jacks. The sailors fled back to the land, but as the harried vessels made shore, a vicious curl of water struck one craft at the tail, shattering the mast and rolling it onto its back, its belly exposed to the thunderous sky.

Stood on the clifftops, the maid saw all this, and knew – without needing to wait for the rest to return – knew that the stricken vessel was her father's. Helpless at the mercy of the wind and wave; hungry saltwater, that had taken every other person she had ever cared for, ready to devour the last.

At such times the stories often say that their protagonist had nothing left to lose. Stories lie, and desperate people will believe them.

The maid shouted into the wind, screaming such curses at the water that even hardened sailors would hesitate to utter, and it was in this moment of grief and despair that the maid recalled the tale of the Old Man of the Sea. Turning without a second glance she ran the cliff path, sliding and falling on scree, tearing clothes and hair on bramble. Nothing impeded her flight, 'til her feet hit the firm, wet sand of the cove.

She stood at the mouth of the cave and called out to the Old Man, demanding he show himself, so that she might hold him accountable, so that she might barter one life for another, if need be.

Despite the raging of the storm, the sound that issued forth eclipsed its bellowing wrath; a deep, echoing sound from out from the rocky mouth. The groaning of wind through hollow caverns, the sound of ancient waves striking even older shores. The water boiled and a twisting and writhing mass rose from out of the salt. Draped in garb of driftwood and seaweed, hair and beard formed of seafoam, the Old Man of the Sea stepped forth from the tumult. His eyes were the dark and pitiless blue of the deepest reaches of the ocean, his brows drawn into a scowl of storms' fury.

"I know you, daughter of sea plunderer, I have seen you at work. I have seen you fixing the nets they use to steal what is mine. I have seen you patching the sails of their craft so that they may once again trespass upon my waves.

"I owe you nothing. I took what was mine to take; the waves are mine and mine alone, and all those upon or below are mine to do with as I will.

"However, I will grant you your request, and in exchange for this boon, you shall bind yourself in service to me, 'til you can make a home on my shingle, and grow crops from my sand. You must do as I command, and come here each day at the turning of the tide.

"This you will pledge to me. As one under my dominion, you will no longer harvest the fruits of my waters like your raider kin, you will not take from my shores. But I am a merciful liege. As long as you are within my domain you may avail yourself of the water's bounty. I shall even permit you to leave with the sand in your shoes and a single pebble of your choosing."

The deal struck, he sank back into the waters with a wicked chuckle, dissolving into sea mist and salt spray, and as the last traces dispersed, the storm broke and the sea calmed.

The maid raced back along the sand. By the time she arrived at the mooring place, the capsized hull of her father's boat had been pushed back to the shore by lazily lapping waves. A crowd had formed at the water's edge, parting at her approach, and at the centre her father sat, battered and half-drowned, but alive. There was much rejoicing that night. All souls returning safe from such a tempest was a thing to be celebrated, and none knew the price at which it came.

The next morning, a little after high tide, just as the waves began to recede, the maid returned to the cove as bidden. The sand was littered with wreckage and other jetsam, washed ashore during the storm. This early, the shoreline was deserted; soon there would be a bustle of activity around the jetties, as the crews of the small fishing fleet prepared to sail with the tide, but for the moment she was alone - or so it seemed. As she drew near the cave, the sound of things being thrown around greeted her ears: splintering wood, crashing as like waves unto the shore, and a disdainful gurgling, the sucking of water sloshing into tidal pools.

With not a small amount of trepidation, the maid called out, "I have come as you bid." The crashing noise grew closer, and out of the cave burst a scraggly youth. Hair of coiling kelp hung to his shoulders, eyes the blue of the deepest ocean reaches, sparkling with the reflected rays of the sun.

"Finally," the youth exclaimed impetuously. "I can find nothing! My home is a mess full of things your people have discarded in my waters. Tidy it, all of it," he said, gesturing to the cove in its entirety. "When you are done you may leave, but be sure to return at the next turn of the tide." With that he strode out into the waves and dove out of sight.

The Maid was used to hard work, but still it took her a considerable time to gather up the strewn flotsam and jetsam, making a neat stack above the tideline. Once the beach was clear she turned to the cave with dread. Its entrance was clogged with driftwood, the stone floor slick with water and slimy plant life, and even with the early morning sun, low in the sky, its light could not touch the back of the cavern. With much trepidation, the maid picked her way over the slippery rock floor, but was surprised to find that as she moved further into the cavern, the hard stone floor turned to soft damp sand. A mattress of seagrasses lay in one corner, small niches in the walls were filled with decorative shells, driftwood, and sea glass. The dwelling seemed somewhat at odds with what she had expected.

The maid finished her task and returned home, before her father awoke, tended to the domestic tasks that needed attention, and accompanied her father, who refused to convalesce, down to the jetties to see what could be done about his wrecked vessel. The fisherman had hauled what was left of it onto dry land. Shredded nets still hung from its sides and the mast had sheared off almost level to the deck. The maid disentangled the mass of nets and headed back to their home, leaving her father to the vessel. He would think she was occupied with their reweaving, leaving her free to return to the cove in time for the turn of the tide.

The Maid returned to the cove just in time to see him arrive, striding out of the sea, a brace of fish slung over one broad shoulder, fishing spear in hand. Hair of dark seaweed hung to his waist, eyes the blue of the deepest reaches of the ocean, glinting with silver flashes of shoals.

He gave the cove a cursory glance. "It'll do." Dropping his catch at her feet as he passed on the way to the cave, he called over his shoulder, "Prepare these."

This was a task the maid could practically do in her sleep, and soon the entire brace was gutted and cleaned. Using some of the dried driftwood she set a small fire, and a frame around it on which she hung the fish to cook. So involved in her work was she, she did not notice his return, sunning himself as he watched her thoughtfully.

When she was done he said, "A poor meal is fish alone, gather something."

The maid had grown knowing times of scarcity, she knew what plants that hung on to the coast were safe to eat, knew how to find shellfish that clung to rock and burrowed in the sand, knew what pools crabs preferred, and knew at least one variety of seaweed that was good to eat. He watched her, but made no move to assist; this irked her somewhat, but she tried her best to hide it as she brought back her haul and asked, "Will this do?"

He glanced at it. "I suppose it will have to."

She folded her arms in annoyance. "Well, if you think you could have done better, perhaps you should teach me how."

The corner of his mouth twitched, amused. "Aye, perhaps I should."

They ate in silence. Once he had had his fill, he stood. "So, now I teach."

And so he did. He moved with a lordly grace, and spoke with an easy tongue. The tides turned while they traversed the cove, and she noticed his hair began to be picked out by streaks of silver, and dark stubble began to form on his jaw.

Later he turned to her. "You may go now, but be sure to have a meal ready at the turn of the tide." With that, he strode into the sea and disappeared from sight.

The maid returned to her home and tended to her work, repairing the nets, preparing a meal for her father, before returning to the cove, cauldron in hand, which she set on the fire and prepared a hearty stew using what the Old Man of the Sea had taught her, so when he returned, with hair of pale seafoam, and eyes the blue of the deepest oceans, with silvered rheum of moonlight, rising from the waves she stood ready with a steaming bowl, which he took with little thanks.

Scowling around the shore, he pointed to the heaped stack of driftwood and jetsam. "I thought I said to clear my cove of your kind's off-casts?"

"You said I was not permitted to take anything from your shore, other than the sand in my shoes and a single pebble. I could move it no further without doing so," the maid replied.

"Besides, you need some wood for cooking fires, but if you want it gone I can remove it – if you permit me to take it from your shore."

He chewed thoughtfully for a moment. "Fine. Keep a stack here, as long as you keep it neat, and I permit you to take this," he gestured at the wood pile, "and its like from my shoreline, if only to keep it clear." He concluded with a grumble, "Now, take your payment and go."

The maid politely wished him a good evening, selected a large, smooth, flat pebble, and took her leave.

This was much how each day passed, the maid splitting her day between the home and the shore. Each morning she met the youth. Each day the man taught her more, then once there was nothing left in the cove that she did not know, he began to bring things with him; at first plants and sea creatures, which he taught her about. Almost imperceptibly, the lessons became conversations and the things he brought became gifts; coloured shells and stones, pretty objects tumbled smooth by the tides, a necklace strung with amber beads from a sunken ship. Each time she smiled as she received the gifts, but reminded him she could not take them with her, so he stored them for her in a niche of his cave home. Each evening keeping the old man company as the night drew in.

The first time he asked her to stay by his side

through the night was a year to the day since the pact had been struck.

The maid smiled sadly, running a hand through his locks of browny-green, and replied, "I cannot go where you go, for I am of air and earth, and you are of salt and water."

"Then I shall make you of the sea, a creature of salt and water, like me."

Again she smiled sadly, looking into those eyes reflecting the deepest blue of the ocean, "I cannot, for I must tend to my father."

From that day hence, each day that passed he asked again, but each time she gave the same answer, 'til another year had passed.

Finally, he protested, "If you were to marry, you would not be expected to tend for him still."

"And do you mean to ask for my hand?" the canny maid asked.

"What if I did?" he asked, looking away.

"How would it look if you were to court one who is already indentured to your service? No, I would not be able to accept until I were free of my debt," she replied.

"It was a foolish trade. No structure can last against my tides, and you cannot go where green sprouts from the sand," he said.

"Is that so?" the maid responded.

"If you agree to become a creature of salt water, it is the only way you can be free," he entreated, but she merely bid him goodnight.

Three years to the day that the bargain had been struck, the sea had mellowed and the village now prospered. The fisher maid arrived at the turn of the morning tide as always, but this day she did not leave between tides, but instead stayed the whole day on the shore. The man of the sea doted on her, and rejoiced at having her all to himself, and began to hope that this was the day she would finally consent to join him as a being of saltwater.

As the night began to close in, she turned to him, saying, "Today has been perfect, but I must now bid you farewell, for I am finally free."

The man rose with the anger of years past. "You dare defy me? " 'Til you can make a home on my shingle, and grow crops from my sand', that was the deal we struck!"

"So it is. I have not forgotten. Come with me, I have something to show you," the fisher maid replied, without a trace of anger or fear.

And so the fisher maid led the man of the sea away from his shore, to a modest structure built of driftwood, nestled in a hollow on the fringes of dry land and sea shore. "See there, this house is built on a foundation of the pebbles you permitted me to take."

"Clever," he conceded. "Yes that would count, but you have still to grow crops from sand."

Leading him closer, she pointed. "See there, the berry bushes that flourish. Look at the ground from which they sprout." She reached down and took a handful of the soil. Taking his hand in hers, she let it drain into his palm. "The loam is mixed with the sand I brought back in my shoes, it is the perfect balance for these bushes to grow strong."

He looked at her with an expression of wonder that slowly grew more sombre. "Yes," he replied. "Yes, that would do it. You are indeed free, you have completed our bargain. You have made a home on my shingle and grown crops in my sand. I shall take my leave of you now."

He turned away and began to make his way back to the cove, but the maid, grabbing him by the shoulder to stop him, took his hand and looked him in the eye, as blue as the deepest ocean.

"Stay the night," she said.

And so it was that each evening, at the turn of the tide, the Old Man of the Sea returned to his fisher maid.

And so it was that a fisher maid tamed the tides.

Take a Pebble

Taken from Hey Kid

By Rae Bailey

No cairn, thankfully, to weigh you down
with what each one of us think we
ought to have done, or what you
ought to have done, or some organisation
ought to have done.

Sisyphean labour you dreaded.

Would we all gather, each take a pebble,
hoping to change the path of the stream,
dam the flood of your life,
pile you high with advice,
caution,
systems of the world,
heavy rocks of love for ourselves
and bury our guilt?

We'll never reach you in the hills that way.
But perhaps, if we climb light,
empty of pocket,
empty of regret,
empty of our needs,
if we climb with nothing but our loss;
we can reach the heights of your overfull heart
and be with your good memory.

High or low, every place of beauty has you in it;

and I cannot choose when next I see
that bright hair, flashing by the
shifting stones on the shore of the Dee.

Take a Pebble

By Hannah Burns

Terry watched a family play on the sand, the father running around with the two boys, chasing a football; the youngest boy was a distance away, playing with the pebbles on the beach. A smile crossed the weatherworn face as he watched the young boy pick up a purple pebble and put it into his pocket before running off to join in the football.

For years, Terry had watched families come and play on his beach. He was the guardian of the sands, as his friends called him. He was, in fact, the man who picked up the rubbish, but it was a job he enjoyed. He got to walk on the sand when it was closed to the public and see such little joys when it was open. He glanced back at the mother, who was lying on a deck chair, her swollen stomach stopping her joining in on the fun. In her hand was a blue pebble.

The older man stretched back in his own deck chair and smiled. The blue pebble...

He cast his mind back to the depths of his memory, where he could picture a small girl, petite frame, dark hair cut short. She had been one of three that came that day, and of them, she had been the only one to pick up a pebble. From the age of sixteen, she had come back almost every year.

Terry had watched her grow, through various fashions and boyfriends, until she found the one that always came back with her, never moaning about the brisk winds, or rain. The old man had seen it so many times over his years, children becoming adults on his beach, watching them all grow up and return to bring the pebble back to the beach, until finally they came in their final days to place it back for someone else.

Take a Pebble

By Hailie Drescher

Take a pebble, pick it up -
turn it 'round and 'round.

Be it smooth,
or be it rough,
pocket it or have enough.

Smooth as glass,
coarse as silt.
Rounder than the letter 'o'.

Touch it, feel it,
Flip it over.
Keep it, toss it,
make your choice.

Take a pebble, pick it up.

Take a Pebble

By Kim Hosking

Most stories focus on the victor, or the victor in the end. The bright, young, oppressed spark that shot meteorically into the heavens. This is different; this is about someone who believed she was a high-flier, but, on reflection, found out she was nothing more than average.

No special powers here. No talents. She was mediocre, and stories about people like her just don't happen. Which, when you stop and think about it, is a little odd, because the vast globe that is the Earth is filled with people exactly like Sarah.

It wasn't for lack of dreaming either, or trying. She'd dreamed big and tried hard; some things she achieved, but for the most part, things just didn't work out. This is where we find her now: curled up on her tiled bathroom floor, crying, because last night her boyfriend dumped her and today, her boss made her redundant.

Things just didn't work out.

Sarah is of average height and build, with brown, shoulder-length hair and blue eyes; a typical Jane Doe. You wouldn't be able to pick her out of a line-up. Sarah is resourceful, though, and after half an hour she wipes her face dry and gets up. She has no idea what she'll do now, but she knows she can't sit on the bathroom floor forever.

As she walks to the park, half a staling loaf of bread in her bag, she wonders how she'll make the rent payment in two weeks. She only went food shopping the other day, she muses, so she should be okay for a week if she plans everything. Sarah is a planner – only, she hasn't planned on losing her job today.

She watches the ducks eat the bread she throws them absent-mindedly – this is a weekly ritual for her since coming here with her grandfather as a child. He'd taught her to skim stones here; he used to sit and feed the ducks, and she used to skim stones. She liked the effect it had on the water, all those ripples radiating out.

"Be like that pebble," he used to tell her, wheezing breathlessly. "Touch the lives of those around you with kindness. This world needs more kindness."

He'd been dying of cancer then and loved just sitting on a park bench, whatever the weather, and feeding the ducks. He said it calmed his mind. Five years on, Sarah has to agree. She knows what she has to do.

She spends the day updating and printing out her CV. For the next few weeks, the routine remains the same; she rises early, has breakfast and heads into town to submit her CV to any jobs going. She registers at the Job Centre and continues to go to the park. She gets a few interviews; some she never hears back from, others she's the second choice candidate. It's summer, so there ought to be vacancies normally filled by students, but so far, no luck.

It's not that they don't need someone, and Sarah's CV is – well... it's not bad, it's just not trumpet-blowing amazing, either. That's what these people have been conditioned to seek out: awesome, cheery, all-singing-all-dancing wonders of the human race. Such a pity. Sarah will work her socks off in any role – be it cleaning toilets or selling toilets – but she's not a shining spark, just a flat note, lost in the clamour.

She wants to help people, to make them leave with a smile – that is all. She believes, probably because of her grandfather, that being kind is the best remedy in this world, but it doesn't matter; no one seems to want her. Her savings account is looking less healthy these days, with rent and food coming entirely from it, and she didn't really have a lot to begin with.

Wearily, she skims a pebble and watches as it bounces across the water. The ripples begin to radiate out across the large pond. There is ice on the edges of it today. It is the first cold day of winter, and the ducks retreat back to the small island in the very centre of the pond as soon as they see she had no bread for them today.

The ripples begin to fade as she selects another stone; it had a perfect, flat curve upon it where she could rest her thumb. She draws her hand back to skim, but pauses as her phone rings.

"Hello?" She frowns in confusion, slipping the stone into her pocket.

"Hello, is that Sarah Mildmay?" a man's polite voice sounds down the line.

"It is," she confirms.

"Hi Sarah, its Richard from the Town Library. We wanted to thank you for coming to interview the other week, sorry we've been so long at getting in touch..."

Sarah's heart sinks. "It's okay." She forces herself to smile, though he can't see her.

"We were wondering if you'd be interested in taking the job, and would be available for an induction on Monday."

Sarah's brain freezes as she takes in the words. "Taking the job?" she repeats as she exhales.

"Yes, and if you were available for induction on Monday."

It is a part-time job in the local library; nothing special, just admin and the like. Would she be interested? She hesitates. It isn't what she really wanted – a well-paid job, like her friends on social media, with their large houses, promotions and fast cars, but it is something.

"Sure, I'd love to... What do I need to bring with me?" she replies.

Sarah does what she needed to survive. She isn't exactly a victor, she is just muddling her way through, like the rest, living by her grandfather's rule:

Take a pebble and be kind.

Take a Pebble

By Philip Lickley

Number 5, Peace Gardens may not have been the largest home in the world, but for Tamara it was home. After weeks of flicking through local property mags, scrolling through housing websites, and staring longingly at estates agents windows like a young waif in a Dickens novel, she had found the ideal property to rent in a small cul-de-sac only a fifteen minute drive from her workplace, which to her was the optimum duration from bed to desk.

The property was one of the oldest around, built sometime around the mid-19th century. It was located at the end of a small, rough, unadopted road off a slightly bigger and only slightly better maintained public road. The front garden was small but well-kept, with enough space for a barbecue when there was better weather. At the moment it was a winter, so thoughts of frying sausages were far away from Tamara's mind and she was more content to skip quickly up the pathway and into the house to switch on the heating and make herself a warming cuppa.

Inside, the house was modest. The front door led into a hallway which consisted of a coat-rack, a large sign she'd bought that said 'home sweet home' and a floor that was made up of checkered tiles in such a way that it could be possible, with the right playing pieces, to play chess whilst bending over to tie one's shoelaces.

The hall led off into the living room, a square shaped space into which Tamara had moved her armchair, bookcase of DVDs and television, and this room itself led into the small kitchen with a hob, oven, fridge-freezer, washing machine and many drawers, along with a large window overlooking a path that ran behind the home. If you were to then return to the hall and ascend the creaking staircase you would arrive on the top floor to find the main bedroom, replete with a large double-bed, chest of drawers and wardrobe; a smaller second room, full of unpacked boxes, and a petite bathroom complete with the usual furnishings. Tamara had yet to put much of her own touch on the home so it looked uncomfortably bare, but the time would come, probably in a week or so, when it would more resemble her bright and quirky personality.

When she'd signed up to rent the property Tamara was quick to confess to her friends that she'd not done a huge amount of research into the place, simply placing her trust in the kindly old lady that owned the place and the references from the previous tenants to agree to the £400 a month rent, plus bills. After ten days in the house and with most of her belongings unpacked Tamara had discovered little about the place to concern her. Sure the neighbour to her left was a little too fond of playing loud music until late in the night and the tap in the bathroom took an absolute age to fill up the bath, but mostly it was all good. There was only one strange thing about the house that bothered her, and that started on the thirteenth day of her tenancy.

The morning had started in pretty much the same way that all the other mornings had begun. Tamara was woken up by the alarm on her phone – 'Galway Girl' by Ed Sheeran, its evocative lyrics reminding her of her home country – and after snoozing it three times got up, showered and dressed. She breakfasted on her usual bowl of cereal and a couple of slices of toast before leaving the house and putting on her coat in the same movement, a half-finished slice of toast dangling awkwardly from her mouth. She locked the door and headed to her car, but not before spotting something unusual.

Now, normally Tamara wouldn't have any business looking down at this point, but she realised her left shoelace had come undone. Finishing off the toast with a couple of bites she crouched down and tied the laces, spotting as she did a lone pebble sat on the path. Normally there would be nothing strange about a stone on a path, but there were no stones in her front garden that could have been moved there. Her curiosity was piqued and she picked it up, turning it over in her fingers and considering its shape and colours. It didn't look particularly unusual, so she casually tossed it over to the corner of the garden and went about her business, dashing down the street, unlocking her car and making the short commute to work to the sound of Radio 1.

This cycle continued over the next couple of days and each morning Tamara discovered the pebble outside the house as if it was waiting for her. Theories of how it got there swam through her mind, idly producing increasingly random flights of fancy during her drive in. Perhaps it was dropped by a bird, or something living in a nearby tree? Maybe it was a gift from a nearby cat with a fetish for rocks? Could it even be a prank from a neighbour? Tamara hoped it wasn't the latter, as it would firstly meant someone considered her to be a worthwhile target for such a pointless activity, and secondly it showed they had a serious lack of imagination. A proper prank involved a shock or surprise or something funny. Leaving a pebble by a door hardly smacked of anything inventive or exciting. Perhaps they just wanted to make her think the place was haunted or something?

It was this more otherworldly suggestion that took over her thoughts, though the rational, scientific side of her refused to believe such an origin. Ghosts weren't real unless you worked in Hollywood or as Yvette Fielding's PA. She said as much out loud to her friends as they gathered that Friday night in the pub, enjoying spirits of the more terrestrial kind. 'Galway Girl' came on over the chain pub's speakers and Tamara smiled.

"So you're telling me you see pebbles on the ground and think your home is haunted? How sad is your life that this has become your main topic of conversation? We should be hearing about how you've discovered a secret cellar or a hot neighbour who strips topless in sight of your bedroom window, not how stones somehow magically appear," her friend Chloe told her bluntly.

Tamara just smiled back. "I was only saying it's a bit weird..."

"Maybe the place is haunted," her other friend, Jess, piped up between mouthfuls of lukewarm cider. "You said the property's well over a hundred and fifty years old. Who knows what's happened there over its lifetime. People could have died there, been murdered, all sorts of things."

Chloe rolled her eyes. "Don't encourage her Jess, she'll start charging us entry when we come round and giving us the full guided tour. Clearly you need to get out more, Tam, if this is the most exciting thing in your life. Let's get a few more shots and head out into town and see if we can't find someone tall, dark and handsome to give you something else to think about."

Tamara smiled, downed the rest of her vodka, and returned to the bar for a round of shots.

The appearance of the pebbles continued over the next few weeks and soon Tamara had built quite a substantial pile of them in her front garden, the small mound in the middle of the grass looked as if a mole had buried up through a stone plate and managed to smash it through some unlikely force of nature. Still, after four weeks of this, Tamara had no particular solid theory for their appearance. If it was a ghost in the house it was remarkably sedate and had chosen not to do anything else other than stone apparition. There had been no bumps in the night; no howling; no creaking floor-boards; and no dark shadows hovering over her bed, much to Tamara's disappointment. As she had tweeted one evening, if you're going to live in a haunted house you'd best make sure it was an interesting haunting.

Sometimes though, you have to be careful what you wish for.

Two days later Tamara found herself under the weather. What had started that morning as a sore throat had escalated into a full on cold and even putting on her favourite hoodie and curling up on the sofa with her favourite box-set, and making herself a bowl of her favourite soup had failed to help and the only call now was for her to have an early night. After enjoying a hot bath that didn't seem to do much to warm her up, she called it a night and snuggled under her duvet to get some shut-eye. Sleep washed over her body quickly and painlessly. Sadly for her, though, only a couple of hours later, just after ten, she was woken up by the sound of something hitting her front door. Still in the daze of sleep she sat up and listened for anything else, and after only a few moments in the silence of the night she heard it again, the sound of something small and hard hitting her front door. Then, after a few more moments, with sleep now feeling like a distant memory, there was a third knock.

She rolled quickly out of bed and slipped on her dressing gown. Tamara darted out of her bedroom, down the stairs and to the front door, fumbling with her keys to unlock it before pulling open the door. She looked out into the darkness and failed to spot anyone before glancing down to see not one, but three pebbles, in their usual spot. There were also signs on the door of where the pebbles had hit, marks made in the usually clean plastic. Tamara knelt down, being cautious not to expose herself to anyone who might be watching, and picked up each pebble in turn, but there was nothing strange about them. She had read that stones are often thrown as part of poltergeist activity and were warm, but these weren't. In fact, if anything, they were quite cold. She looked out once more into the darkness before throwing the pebbles away and locking up. Confused, Tamara returned to bed, her illness allowing her to drift once more into sleep with little fuss.

The next morning there were no stones to be found outside – which was unusual in itself – but there was some post. It was Monday morning and Tamara had called in sick, unable to face a 9-to-5 in her current condition. At just before noon she wandered from her room, down the stairs and to the kitchen where she'd summoned up just enough energy to heat up some tomato soup in a pan and serve it alongside some crusty bread, poorly buttered, staring listlessly at daytime television. At some point during a show where an arguing couple were invited to take a lie-detector test Tamara found herself glancing over to the door, spotting some letters on the doormat. She sighed, sidled over and briefly looked them over, dismissing them out of hand; junk mail. She quite happily threw them in the nearest waste paper bin and continued about her business, which on this occasion was television and a chain of increasingly large cups of tea, and then eventually bed.

Another week went by and the pebbles continued to turn up, one a day, still with no explanation and it was beginning to turn from a curiosity to an annoyance. Even though it was something so slight and unimportant, Tamara wanted to know what was causing it. For her it was a smaller version of one of the world's biggest mysteries, like what happens to planes in the Bermuda Triangle? Where did Lord Lucan go? And who put the bomp in the bomp-du-bomp-du-bomp? She was like a UFO enthusiast wanting an answer to what really happened at Roswell or Rendlesham; Tamara just wanted to know the answer. Not to the level that she would stake out her own garden, or have one of those noticeboards with push-pins connected with lengths of string in her living room, just to a level where her curiosity would be sated.

Friday night found her feeling better, so Tamara was back at the pub, the scarf around her neck the only indication that she had been unwell. As she drank another vodka it seemed her friend had a solution.

"You should do one of these exercises," Chloe suggested, "They help relieve stress. Why not take up yoga or Pilates or something? You'll be aching too much to worry about some stupid bloody pebbles."

Tamara dismissed the idea. She hated the idea of exercise. Jess had another suggestion.

"You should do this new project thing that's happening in the area. Apparently it's supposed to help you channel all your frustrations into an object which clears your mind."

"Yeah," Chloe laughed. "It's called drinking. I take all my anger at my stupid idiotic co-workers and mix it up with vodka and down it in one. The perfect solution in both meanings of the word!"

Jess ignored Chloe's comments. "Seriously, you should check it out."

"What's it called?"

"I can't remember, but we got a flyer through the door about it. All about how you think about all your annoyances that you bottle up and get something physical to resemble it and chuck it away. The theory is your stress leaves your mind as the object leaves your hand. I've been really annoyed about this essay I'm writing at night school so I take all the theories I can't understand and write them on a piece of paper and crumple it up and throw it in the recycling. You'd be surprised at how effective it is!

"For you, it could be your anger at your illness and you could throw away that scarf as something symbolic of your sickness, or you could pick your obsession over those stupid pebbles and maybe just throw them away instead."

"Firstly, I really like this scarf and secondly, I'm not chucking stones around. I'm not five."

"Well you need to do something. Obsessing over rocks is a bit weird. Seriously, try it."

"Well it sounds interesting," Tamara said with a lack of conviction. "But how am I supposed to learn more if I don't know what it's called?"

"Check your post. You should have got one."

"I don't read junk mail," Tamara scoffed. "It's all takeaways, Farmfoods offers and taxi cards."

"Well sometimes it can be more interesting. This is some art project done by a college student. I believe she paid for a flyer to be delivered to every house in the area. It's worth a shot, Tam."

Tamara nodded and finished her drink. But, naturally, many more followed over the night and she forgot all about the conversation.

The next day arrived and Tamara was woken up by the brightness of the sun streaming through her blinds. It was enough to make her realise she didn't want to face the world; her head cold had been replaced by a throbbing caused by far too much alcohol. After a quick visit to the bathroom where fluids left her body through a not usually prescribed route, she had a light and much needed breakfast and a long drink from a longer glass of water. As she finished it off her eyes fell on the kitchen waste paper bin and snatches of her conversation with Jess from the night before flooded back. She realised that the midst of her hangover was not the best time to rootle through a bin, but she thought it would be worth trying to find the flyer, so with a hefty gulp of water and a steadying of her constitution, Tamara removed the top from the cream-coloured bin and began sorting through the paper. Happily, it wasn't long before she came across it, a simplistic but well styled glossy advert for the study. 'Take a...' it read across the top in fancy italic writing, before it continued with a more descriptive subheading: 'Use everyday objects as a tool to release your inner stress."

The flyer continued on to talk about the project, its aims, and its need for case studies. Tamara studied it a couple of times and then returned it to the waste bin. She made herself a tea and continued to ponder the idea, settling down in her comfy armchair. Then she realised something.

With the imaginary lightbulb of revelation hovering over her like an animated cartoon, Tamara dashed up her carpeted steps as fast as her hangover-induced legs could carry her. She dressed and slipped on her trainers, ensured the laces were tight and walked out to the front garden, where she studied the latest pebble, which had been sitting there awaiting her brief investigation. Calculating something in her head, Tamara made an educated guess and crossed the road, narrowly missing a passing moped thanks – or no thanks – to her alcohol-hangover-haze.

Tamara looked at the three properties across from hers; it could be only one of them. She walked up to the door and knocked three-times on it. A young man of about her age eventually answered the door, looking just as rough as Tamara, adding five-o-clock shadow.

"Take a pebble," she said, expecting him to understand. "That's your coping mechanism, isn't it?"

He looked blankly at her before badly stifling a yawn and pointing upstairs. "Not mine," he said. "Mine's late night movies and a Pot Noodle. This is about that art project isn't it? You need my housemate, Craig."

The man proceeded to shout out that name loudly, making the hungover Tamara feel a little queasy as her head began throbbing again. Soon another man, again of a similar age to them both, appeared in nothing more than a black t-shirt and a pair of boxer shorts that left little to the imagination.

"What do you want?" he asked sleepily.

"Take a pebble," Tamara repeated. It seemed to spark something in the eyes of Craig.

"What about it?"

"That's your answer to the art project. You stand in the front garden and put all your angers and frustrations into the pebbles of your front garden and throw them."

"Yeah, why? Have I hit someone's car or something?" he said defensively, peering out of the front door as if looking for the police or something.

"No, nothing like that. I've just been spotting the pebbles each morning and thought I had a ghost or something. I've just been looking for the solution to the mystery and here I am, standing on your doorstep, looking for the answer."

"Yeah, well guilty," Craig said with very little enthusiasm. "Can I go back to bed now?"

Tamara smiled. "Sure," she beamed, the answer to her mystery sending a shot of hangover-beating endorphins around her body. Considering the mystery of the pebbles had only been going on a month and was hardly MH370 in scope, Tamara was surprised by how much joy solving it had brought her. She smiled once more at the two lads and turned to leave, returning home to put her feet up, safe in the knowledge there were no rogue birds, cats or phantoms around her new home. Back across the road Craig's friend looked at him and scowled.

"What the fuck, Craig?" he said to his still-sleepy friend. "You get visited by a hot girl from across the road and you let her go. What's wrong with you, man?"

"I thought that would be obvious. She's been obsessing over the appearance of pebbles outside her door. That's nutter 101. Swipe left mate, swipe left."

Craig made an effort to head upstairs and slammed his bedroom door.

"Well if you're going to be an idiot, don't expect me to be."

The young man put on his shoes and left his own house, walking across the road with purpose and knocked three times on Tamara's door. She answered it after about thirty seconds on seeing him.

"Hi," he said shyly. "I'm Bill, Craig's friend. I just wanted to apologise on his behalf, he's a bit of a nob."

"I could see from his boxers," Tamara joked.

Bill laughed. "I'm sorry if his pebble throwing caused you any problems. He got quite into it. He's had lots of issues with his family. They're in the building trade and want him to follow them into the family business but he wants to be an artist. Him picking the pebbles was his way of keeping his family at arm's length and throwing their demands as far as he could."

"And have you been doing it?" Tamara asked.

Bill nodded.

"What was yours?"

Bill smiled. "Why don't you invite me in for a coffee and I'll tell you."

*

It's always surprising how quickly summer can come around when you think about it, which is both good for those wanting to enjoy longer days, trips out and festivals, but not good as life starts to fly past. For Tamara, though, it meant more barbecues, and finally, that July, she got to make the most of her garden. Today she was, as noon approached, stoking the charcoal and firelighters to get the flame roaring. Bill appeared from behind her with a tray of beef burgers and kissed her on the cheek as he started to lay them out. Tamara beamed as she watched her boyfriend help her with the food before their friends arrived.

"You know what," he said, as he finished laying out the burgers and began work on laying out the table with plates, cutlery and glasses. "You never did tell me what your Take A... exercise would have been?"

Tamara laughed. "You know Bill, I never really thought about it. But I tell you what it would be now."

"What?" asked Bill.

"Easy!" Tamara laughed. "Take a burger and then eat it."

Bill chuckled. "Not until they're cooked you won't," he said before playfully slapping the back of her hand with the spatula. Tamara smiled and returned his kiss. She loved the new house and especially the man who had joined her in it. And, for that moment, she felt like everything was perfect. There was certainly no reason to take any object and throw it away to remove frustrations. She didn't have any frustrations.

As their friends turned up to tuck into the barbecue under the warm sun Tamara realised everything she wanted was right there and nothing needed throwing away.

Take a Pebble

By M. Loftouse

I lay there on the sharp grass, overgrown and uneven, feeling the prick of its needles through the thin sweater. This was the spot. Every Friday I would come here and lie on the washed-down ground where my stranger would leave a small pebble for me. I remembered the first time I saw it; there it was lying exactly in the center of our little garden, close to the lake, yet far away from the deck. It was an ordinary piece of grey stone really, nothing to be excited about, except for the little marks on it. The first pebble I picked up had a small dent on it, shaped like a dot. I figured I could use it as a paperweight, so I pocketed it and strode back to the house. I didn't pay much attention to why it was there, or who put it there, only that it had caught my attention.

Naturally, following that first discovery, I would walk each day to the same spot but there was no sign of a pebble there; I had my pebble. Pebbie, I called it. Names are important; they give meaning to things, don't they? I would sit cross-legged on that spot, just listening to the sounds of the crashing water and occasional chatter of people in the distance. Come Friday, the same pebble would return: the same spot, the same colour, the same mark. I remember rushing back into my room with the awful feeling that someone had stolen my precious Pebbie, but it was still there, sitting atop a pile of untouched letters. I dashed back out again and picked up the second one, only this time I frantically wondered how it could have got there. Each week there was a new pebble, and each week I was unable to fathom its method of arrival. My madness grew with each passing week; I would pick up another and another, but I was nowhere near finding out where they came from. No one would claim them, either.

Months passed by and by the end of the year I had gathered a bowl full of Pebbies. My desk was too small to hold the bowl, so I let them sit on the window sill. It was comforting, knowing that the Pebbles were close to me, every day, and I looked forward to a new addition each time. It was as if they and I shared a secret – the secret that someone was watching over me, giving me a mystery.

Then, one day it happened.

It was a Friday without a pebble and it puzzled me – no, it worried me. I remember sitting in the garden for hours, waiting. It was raining and the winds were strong. I remember telling myself that I couldn't afford to get sick, but I didn't care anymore. I couldn't give up now; maybe they had forgotten, or maybe they were late. I wondered at it. Either way, I needed the pebble, so day after day I lay there on the wet grass, cut and even, with tears streaming down my cheeks.

Later, the curtains were drawn when I entered the dimly lit room, myself disheveled, matching the surroundings, and that's when I saw him. Propped on pillows thinner and weaker than him, I watched the soft rise and fall of his chest. The room was plain and unwelcoming, spartan save for the wires and the beeps of the many machines on one side. I dared not go any closer. My stranger was my own, had always been my own; he was never a stranger. My eyes wandered over to the windowsill where soft gleams of sunshine poured inside, dancing patterns onto the marbled floor, and I froze when I saw it. There it was, watchful as always, a pebble exactly like mine.

I whipped around and saw those frail eyes open and a weak smile that could tear down my whole world. Walking towards him, I felt my heart race against the soft beats of the machine, beep, beep, beep! We stayed there in silence.

The next day was Friday. I looked out of my window and smiled.

Not Coming Back

By S. R. Martindale

Grey clouds blocked the morning sun, casting their monochrome filter on the world. They almost looked too heavy to stay in the sky and threatened to topple over and fall, jostling together to wet anything unfortunate enough to get in their way.

Today, the almost-gold of the wheat fields looked washed out and the sparkling blues and hues of the river could only manage the colour of the granite and flint that lay in and around it. A heron stood on the riverbank, under the cover of a drooping willow, its startling cobalt feathers a colourful gem in the de-saturated morning light.

A white-washed house stood in the faded green behind the pebbled river bank, trying it's hardest to be quaint and cheery. Apart from the bubbling of the river, all was peaceful, all was quiet. Even the chirpy, bouncing birds seemed to be contemplating whether to get up and about, or just sit this one out.

A smaller cloud hung over a small boy, the greys and blues of his clothing trying their hardest to blend in with his surroundings. He sat with knees huddled, hood up, and severe nose, looking out over the river and to the fields beyond.

A small movement of his foot sent a cascade of pebbles slipping down the narrow shoreline. Clinking and scuffling, the pile rolled on until it shuddered to a stop before the water, as if it, too, was unwilling to get itself wet.

The nose slowly looked down and regarded the shifted rock with a cold stare, daring gravity to interrupt his thoughts again. He barely saw the swirling intricate patterns of silvers, greys, and soft reds and yellows that would have interested him any other day.

A gentle drum beat of stick on stone joined the gentle rattling cymbal of the tumbling water. The boy poked another pile of pebbles with his stick, sending another mini-avalanche slipping away. The flash of blue darted into the air.

Angrily, he stood up and threw the stick as far as he could after the bird. His angry mood spoilt slightly by a sudden little lurch as he found his footing in the slippery, sliding piles of pebbles. The stick splashed faintly into the swirling grey and was taken away. Gone, forever. It was never coming back.

It would never come back to be thrown again. There would be no splashing as the stick was joyously retrieved.

Big sobs shook the child and he sat down again heavily on the stones, ignoring the painful lumps and bumps causing discomfort on his backside. He sat there for many minutes, his arms tightly wrapped around himself. His red puffy eyes stared unblinkingly at the pebbles in front of him.

It felt like days had passed by the time he heard his name called from his home behind him. He ignored it at first. He ignored it for seconds. The voice got more insistent.

Huffing and sighing, he scooped up a handful of grey flint in his hand and threw them one by one into the river. He paused before throwing the last one. This last had a cool streak of sparkly white mineral running through it. He ran his finger over the rough lines and felt the sharp edges along the dark grey against his cold, wet flesh. He slid the stone into the front pocket of his hoodie and began the scrambling, sliding, slow walk back up the riverbank and back into his garden.

He passed that tree and stopped for a minute. Sighing again, he took out the flint and tossed it onto the little pile that lay amongst two thick roots sticking up from the ground.

The pile of pebbles slid down and came to rest gently against the little wooden cross.

"See you tomorrow, boy."

The boy stared for one minute longer, then turned and ran back home.

Take a Pebble

By Lauren K. Nixon

Owen padded barefoot across the lawn, careful not to step on the snail that was making its way across the cool, damp grass. It was still early, and the heat of the day had not yet risen. He glanced over his shoulder at the curtained windows of his house. The rest of the family were still sleeping, drowsing the dawn away.

There had been a party – a birthday – and everyone had retired late, exhausted. Everyone except Owen.

For the first time in as long as he could remember, sleep eluded him.

It had been good seeing his grandparents. They lived so far away these days, he seldom saw them. They had flown in for Evelyn's birthday – her last big blow-out before heading off on her gap year – and held court in the living room telling stories of their adventures. They had given her a compass and a map, their version of a bon voyage, and told her to go where the wind took her.

It was a tradition in their family.

Some people insisted their kids went to college, or encouraged them to take up a skill or a trade. All families wanted the best for their kids, whatever form that took.

Owen's family encouraged them to follow the wind.

He turned the key in the lock, lifting the old latch and enjoying the faint creak the hinges gave.

It would be his turn, soon.

His dad and Uncle Bob had built the summerhouse when his mum had told him she was pregnant. They had moved into an old house they could renovate and started their next great adventure: raising a family.

That had been nearly twenty years ago, and the summerhouse had undergone several repairs. The winter storms had been gentle this year, and Owen and his mum had long since cleared the deep drifts of leaves from the fall. Now, summer was on the way, and there were already flowers in the little vase on the table.

Owen stood for a moment, enjoying the feel of his bare feet on the warm wooden floor.

The summerhouse was light and airy, filled with books and treasures from his family's many adventures. It was everybody's favourite place to kick back, to dream.

He climbed the ladder to the upper level, bathed in sunlight at this early hour, and made his way to his favourite spot. It was his grandmother's favourite spot, too, when she visited: the window seat overlooking the garden, from where you could see all the birds. It was Evie's favourite spot, too.

His dad loved birds. He might have followed them to the end of the Earth if he hadn't fallen in love with someone more bound to the soil and the trees. The garden had been their compromise: they still travelled as often as they could with the children, but they always returned to the house. Owen's mother had filled the garden with flowers that insects and birds would love, so that they would come to him.

Owen liked the birds, too, though half the time he spent in the window seat he was reading.

Today, though, he curled up under the pale cream candlewick and gazed at the pebbles on the sill.

There were seven of them: one for each of the family, mementos from the road - well, six pebbles, and a bottle. Uncle Bob never could do things the same way as everyone else. They were the anchor that brought everyone back home - or at least, that's what his dad said.

Grandpa Fitch had donated a piece of obsidian he'd picked up on the island of Malta. He'd been teaching geology to a class full of undergrads when he'd first seen Grandma Harper, sitting high on the rocks, sketching the coastline. She'd had on a red dress and a sun hat, and Owen's grandfather had said she'd stolen his heart. He'd told them the story a thousand times.

Grandma Harper had given them a fossil, the echo

of an ammonite caught in a dark green rock she'd picked up when she was a kid on a beach on the East coast of England. It was her first fossil – the one that had sparked a lifetime of hunting. Not just fossils – every part of the natural world fascinated her, and she had passed that fascination on to her sons.

Uncle Bob's contribution was a small, glass bottle – the kind you found in a hotel room minibar – full to the brim with volcanic ash and sand, the remnants of his trip to the Big Island of Hawaii. Owen's dad always said his brother had the spirit of Vulcan in him, always hauling up the side of volcanos, photographing them for National Geographic. Uncle Bob couldn't get enough of them.

Owen's mother, Lucy, had brought back a rock from Australia; it was a deep rusty red, like the soil in the outback. She'd spent several months backpacking out there before joining a team helping to monitor the coral reef. Part of her studies. As much as she'd loved her work out there, it was the forests of the land of her birth that had called her home. That was where she'd met Owen's dad, who had been building treehouses for the camp she was staying at.

He'd taught Evelyn his trade, from the moment she could walk, and Owen too, when he came along. It was a good skill to fall back on when you moved around a lot – and there was no doubt that Evie and Owen would wander, just like all the others. Their dad had found a piece of petrified wood, rolled smooth by the river that ran past his wood shop in the forest. He liked working out there – he could spend half the year surrounded by the birds he chased across the planet in the other half.

The last two rocks were smaller – tastes, if you will, of the specimens that might later replace them. Two perfect circles of bunter cobble, a seam of white quartz running down the middle; they had originally been part of the one pebble, but it had fallen apart in their hands when the two children had found it, on the shore of a loch in Scotland, where the family had been camping. Like two sides of the same coin.

It was what they always said about Owen and Evie: they might have been born three years apart, but in all other respects they could have been twins. On a good day, they could even pass for one another – and had, much to the amusement of their friends, and consternation of their teachers.

"And now I'm leaving."

Owen looked up to find his sister watching him, perched at the top of the ladder like one of his dad's birds. They had always been able to tell what the other one was thinking. Grandpa Fitch called it telepathy, but really they were just like the split pebble on the sill: two halves of the same coin. No doubt sleep had eluded her, too.

"I'll come back," she said, and took up her usual position on the cushions on the other side of the window seat.

"I know."

"And we all do this, we all go where the wind takes us."

"I know – and Belize sounds awesome."

"So?" she asked, cocking her head to one side – though she already knew the answer.

"So, I'll miss you."

Evie smiled, aiming a friendly kick at his shins.

"Yeah, of course you'll miss me – but you'll get over it."

Owen shrugged. He couldn't remember a time when his sister hadn't been there. Already, the world seemed incomplete.

"I guess."

"I'm serious, Owen," she laughed. "And I'll be home for Christmas."

"That's eight months from now."

"And by then you'll be going stir crazy, planning your own adventure." She grinned, correctly interpreting the smirk that brought to his face. "You already started, didn't you."

"I'm gonna go to Angkor Wat," he told her, candidly. "And then Japan – I wanna see the cherry blossom festival."

"That's what I like about you, kid. You dream big."

"I'm gonna be the next Indiana Jones."

"I'll never doubt it."

They subsided, sitting for a while in the calm of the morning. Soon, their parents and grandparents would be up, and someone would pour hot coffee into Uncle Bob and he'd be marginally less horizontal, and they'd all head up to the Cape for the week. The last week.

"After this, everything is different," Owen said, eventually.

"That doesn't make it bad."

He gave her a dubious look that made her shake her head.

"It's just the next big adventure, right?"

"'Life Without Evie', I can see it now – the next big blockbuster," he scoffed.

"You just wait, High School's like nothing you've ever known," she laughed.

He couldn't help but laugh with her; that was just how they were. Everything was funny, if you let it be. Owen glanced at her, staring out across the garden at the house she would soon be leaving behind, and guessed she was already gone in her mind, flying out over the rainforest.

"Just – bring something back, okay? Find an anchor."

Evie smiled and reached out for their split cobble, handing him half.

"I'll take half, and you take half – that way, you're my anchor."

Owen weighed the pebble in his palm, thoughtfully.

"You be careful out there, though. There's sharks."

"In the rainforest?"

"Leopards, then."

Evie shook her head and tucked the pebble in her pocket.

"Back before you know it."

THE INCIDENT PIT

DO NOT FALL IN

Incident Pit

By Hannah Burns

"Keep away from there!"

The barked order made Sean jump, nearly making him drop all of the samples he was holding. He looked down and saw that his size eleven shoe was mere inches from falling into a pit.

"Oh, gosh! So sorry!" He tried to move back, but this, of course, meant he managed to step directly on the angry man's toe.

"First time on site," came the all-knowing grunt as the older man took Sean's shoulders and steered him back onto the wooden walkways. Sean nodded, blushing and rushed off to the tent where he was heading in the first place. It was his first day on site, well, actually, it was his best friends John's first day, but he had got so drunk the night before that he had passed out and couldn't get out of bed this morning. So Sean, not wanting him to lose his placement, thought he would be able to just slip in, sign him in and then leave.

That had been his plan until he had seen Heather, a tall Amazonian woman with long purple dreadlocks. He was instantly under her spell, and he could take in nothing but her.

"Newbie, do you not remember any of your safety talks?" she tutted, taking the tray from him. Her hair had been shoved back into a bun, out the way, the ends of the dreadlocks sticking out like spider's legs; her clothes were covered in mud from where she had been climbing in and out of the trenches on site. Sean was so distracted by her hair that he forgot to answer her question.

"Hey, can you hear me?" she asked again before looking at him; really looking at him. "What's the dig about?"

Sean jumped and tried to recall what John had said in the pub, the night before. He remembered that John liked the Romans, and he jumped at that; Romans. And

Romans built walls, right?

"Roman ruins?" he answered uncertainly, slowly watching her pretty face frown before she pulled him into the tent and gestured for him to put the samples down.

"No, this is not Roman, and any actual student of archaeology would know that – as well as not to go near the incident pit. So spit it out."

Sean couldn't stop himself, he explained every last detail of what had happened and why he was here on a wet Monday morning, instead of the real placement student. He even blurted out how he had become entrance by her beauty and had ended up staying.

"You could have destroyed weeks of work!" she hissed angrily, but there was a little blush on her cheeks. Sean looked at the floor and shifted uncomfortably. Heather grabbed his arm and pulled him out of the tent. "Julian, I'm going for lunch."

The angry looking man merely nodded and went back to patrolling the other new people that had come in today. Sean let Heather drag him off the site, expecting to be thrown into his car and told to leave. Instead, he was dragged to a local café.

"I suppose nearly falling into the incident pit would be a good story to tell when people ask how we met," she said, as she pulled him to a table.

Sean had never in his life been so happy to have nearly fallen into a muddy hole.

The Incident Pit

By Hailie Drescher

That dark place
within my mind.
The place I go, the place I exist.
Here and now I sit
in my very own incident pit.

Filled with tools,
and my darkest desires.
This is the place I go,
the place that I exist,
when I need to regain control.

Here in the incident pit
I call my own,
I sit alone.
I pull out my Exacto knife,
tracing lines with precision.

I sit in this incident pit,
the place I feel I can be myself.
Each little cut I make,
each little white line.
Is a release;
it helps me regain control.

Don't even care
what anyone thinks.
It is my incident pit,
my place to be myself,

to feel the release,
to find my control.

In my incident pit,
lie the tools that I require.
My darkest desires laid bare,
marked as I mark myself,
evidenced by the marks on my arms.

There are times I want
to crawl on out.
To escape.
I don't know how.
I approach the wall,
try to crawl out.
But I only slide right back into despair.

However,
as I sit in my incident pit,
the place I go to regain control.
I see a light,
shining overhead.
Those are the times
that I see the ladder,
the helping hand to guide my way out.

But it never lasts.
Soon enough
it vanishes.
And I slide right back down,
into my
incident pit.

The Incident Pit

By Philip Lickley

There were three facts everyone knew about the Staz Peninsula:

Any crimes were forbidden

Anyone found guilty of a crime would be thrown in to the Incident Pit

No one had ever escaped from the Incident Pit

*

Many years ago, or so the people of the Peninsula believe, there had been a revolt and the Government in charge had responded by digging a large pit, or, more precisely, getting those who had committed the crimes to, into which they were then all thrown. The pit was in the shape of a funnel, of sides that got steeper the lower you went. For minor crimes you would only be thrown in a short distance, from which it was potentially possible to escape, if you were lucky and gravity was being kind to you, but it had not been kind to anyone yet. Any further, however, and it would be a slippery slope backwards down into the body of the pit, where the criminals would meet their end, either by starvation, fighting other 'inmates', or insanity. It was the ultimate oubliette. The Government had created the blueprint for the pit, the rebels had dug it, and now everyone remained in fear of it.

Whereas most villages, towns or cities were built around a feature of the landscape, such as a mountain, a river, or a coast, possibly offering advantages to manufacture, agriculture, or trade, Staz was built around the Incident Pit. Today, the pit was a gaping hole in the ground, surrounded on all its sides by houses, municipal buildings, offices, and parks, a constant reminder to all those who live there not to break the law. Naturally, no bridge spanned across the pit and so any travelling had to be done around it. A tall fence ran around its circumference to ensure no one would ever accidentally fall in, though from the occasional disappearance, a few perhaps ended up in the pit by means outside of the judicial system.

Each week, the court would meet and hear the evidence against its citizens, on crimes both minor and major, with many of the accused receiving the one agreed punishment. Staz knew nothing about fining, or community service, or jail time. It was the Incident Pit or freedom, and the judges, with their black caps and menacing smiles, didn't like the word 'freedom'.

When sentencing was complete, the guilty would be led out of the courtroom, marched across the plaza to a gate in the protective fence, taken the ten metres to the edge of the Incident Pit and unceremoniously pushed in. In the past this was done by a chosen law enforcer called the Pusher, but in recent years there had been a spate of incidents where the criminals, unwilling to respect their punishment, had held onto the Pusher as they fell, sentencing them both to death. Since then it had been more difficult to recruit citizens for the role of Pusher, even when the Government instigated legislation designed to make it compulsory to perform the duty if asked, which led to a stalemate of refusal, whereby many citizens found themselves being sentenced for breaking the law, still without anyone to perform the Pushing. It now fell instead to a Heath Robinson style device which pushed the guilty out on a retractable gang-plank, like a modern pirate ship floating above a huge, black void.

Life continued in this way for many years. Citizens were scared into conforming and any outcry about harshness for minor crimes were dealt with by inflicting the one and only punishment on the complainants, until Staz became a town ruled by and entrenched in fear. Yet there was still a steady stream of people sentenced to be thrown, or at least pushed, into the Incident Pit, and still no one returned.

That is, until one unusually warm day in May, when the third rule was broken.

*

Jodie had always been an upstanding member of the community, running a small florists on the edge of town called Flower Power, which specialised in blooms of all sizes, shapes, colours, and fragrances, and was the go to place for all special occasions, whether weddings, anniversaries, birthdays, or christenings. She also dealt with funerals, and she partly had the success, if that word is appropriate, of the judicial system to thank for a steady stream of requests for commemorative bouquets of wreaths which, in the absence of any grave site, were placed around a monument to those lost to the pit that stood in the centre of the city.

"Business booms as the flowers bloom!" Jodie would declare, with her usual jovial spirit, as customers asked after her and her business. She didn't earn huge amounts, but she made enough to get by and she enjoyed her work, which was the most important thing for her. Things were ticking over nicely, and even though many of the people of the town lived in fear she was a pretty happy-go-lucky person, dismissing most of the common fears about the pit, perhaps because hers was one of the few businesses from which you couldn't see it. Also, because she quite easily kept her nose clean, living each day in a pretty similar way, she never had cause to worry about it. Every day, she got up in the morning, breakfasted, opened up the florists, served until five p.m. when she shut up shop, made dinner and retired into her armchair in the flat above the shop, where she'd work through a novel with a glass of white wine on hand. It was a simple life, but an enjoyable one.

Unfortunately for Jodie, everyone makes mistakes and her transgression occurred on one particular Tuesday, that warm day in May I mentioned before, when she woke up with a headache. Rather than not opening up and disappointing her customers, Jodie went about her usual business and pulled up the shutter, but she wasn't on top form. Her smiley demeanour had been replaced by one of tolerance of the day. Upon serving one particularly grouchy customer, she made an error and gave her the incorrect amount of change, which the customer quickly noticed and though Jodie promised to rectify it immediately, the customer refused to accept it and stormed off. Normally, Jodie would have simply shrugged this off, but five minutes later the customer returned with a police officer, and she was taken away to the police station on the ridiculous accusation of fraud.

There, at the station, Jodie pleaded her ignorance and how it had been an honest mistake. She told them that she had offered the customer the correct change, but her calls fell on deaf ears. Jodie was ignorant to the fact that the lady who she'd served was the mother of a rival florist and she'd unwittingly given her the slightest bit of rope to hang herself with, a symptom of the tightly wound nature of the Staz Peninsula legal system.

With Flower Power shut for the week, the rival shop (Petal Power) thrived and all the while, Jodie was stuck in the cells, awaiting trial; a trial which came that Saturday and, unbelievably for many watching, led to her being sentenced to the Incident Pit. It was a tearful Jodie who was led out of the courtroom and towards the pit, and a remorseful one that took a step into the unknown and disappeared to her expected doom.

Life moved on in the Staz Peninsula as if nothing had happened, Jodie's sentencing just another senseless death on another day, and though there were some mumblings of how unfair it had been in the corners of the community, most kept their opinions to themselves for fear of the same fate finding them.

Monday morning came and the people of the town went about their regular business, whether that was going to work or managing their houses. It was Elizabeth who first noticed something unexpected that morning: the shutter of Flower Power was up and the shop was open for business. Puzzled as to who would take it over at such short notice, Elizabeth peered around the door to exclaim in fright at seeing Jodie standing there behind the counter, with her bold, black-rimmed glasses, red shoulder-length hair and welcoming smile. Terrified, Elizabeth called out 'Ghost!' and dashed off as quickly as her elderly legs could carry her, until she bumped into the first person she could find to splutter and burble about what she'd seen. Naturally, they laughed her off as senile; the second person she approached told her she was drunk, and the third dismissed her as confused. It was only the fourth person, intrigued by what Elizabeth had actually seen, that followed her back to the florists, and she was shocked to see that Elizabeth had been correct. Standing there, as brazen as anything, was Jodie.

"But I saw you enter the pit myself!" she declared, looking Jodie up and down. "This is impossible. Nobody has ever escaped from the Incident Pit."

Jodie just smiled. "Well, nobody until me. Now, can I interest you in some flowers?"

The person had politely declined the offer and had walked off, fearful that speaking to a ghost, or a dead person, or a criminal returned from the depths of hell, might well be punishable by a one-way visit to the Incident Pit. Except, if that was indeed Jodie, perhaps the trip isn't so one-way, as everyone had presumed? Soon the story had spread all around the village, getting a little twisted and expounded upon as it moved around the community. Gossip followed anecdote, until Jodie had become a ghost, witch or magician, depending on who you spoke to. Soon, word got back to the law enforcers of the city who soon paid her a visit, quickly coming to the conclusion that it was Jodie and not a ghost, clone or secret twin sister she'd been keeping hidden all these years, in case of just such an eventuality. This development caused quite a ruckus in the village. No one had ever escaped the Incident Pit before, so they'd never needed rules to deal with someone that did. And they looked. The law team scoured the court's libraries, through all the old paperwork, laws and dusty old tomes, but nothing could be found.

This left them with two options. They could either let her walk free, as she'd proved to be lucky or clever enough to escape the Incident Pit, or they could throw her in again as proof that no one could escape the punishment of the town. Many of the judges preferred the latter. A couple wanted the former, primarily because her flowers were so much nicer than her rivals', but they kept that quiet as they certainly didn't want to rock the boat.

Eventually it was decided that to prove that the law enforcers weren't always heartless to actually let her stay, and to provide the illusion of judicial redemption. And so Jodie was allowed to continue working at her florists, serving her customers and enjoying her evenings with a good book and an even better glass of wine.

*

A week to the day since her reappearance, everyone was getting ready for another working day, but the same people who were surprised the week before to find 'Flower Power' open for business were just as shocked to find its shutter down, and Jodie nowhere to be seen. People knocked on her door, called out to her and called her number, but all their hails remained unanswered. It was shortly afterwards that information trickled through that Jodie had been spotted, standing on the edge of the Incident Pit. Soon, a throng of people had gathered at the fence to watch her. There she stood, doing nothing but staring downwards into the hole. After a few moments, when enough people had appeared at the fence, gawping at her through the diamond-shaped holes in the metal wiring, she turned to face them. Around her shoulders was a small tote bag containing a selection of her possessions, whilst in her left hand was a wine glass and her right hand a wine bottle.

"People of Staz Peninsula!" she called, holding the wine glass aloft. "I stand here today as the first one amongst you to escape the Incident Pit. But I realise that what I came from I must return to and so I thank you all for your custom, and wish you a good day!"

With her speech completed Jodie unscrewed the top off the wine bottle, poured half a glass of wine and, returning the bottle to her bag, called out "Cheers!" to the crowd. Elegantly, she downed the wine, turned and jumped into the pit, which was the last anyone saw of Jodie in the village.

Well! This was quickly the talk of the town. Jodie's flower shop remained closed and Jodie didn't reappear at all. Soon, people forgot about her and moved in to her shop, and her story became an urban legend in the story of the Incident Pit. People still committed crimes; people were still sentenced to being Pushed; people still ending up falling in.

*

But the Incident Pit had a secret. You see, if you want something building, then you don't ask people who will ultimately die at the hands of it to build it. A condemned man asked to build a scaffold will factor in a flaw that only they know about. An axe-maker fated to die at the hands of his creation will look to exploit a weakness in the joints. And so, the band of criminals asked to dig the huge pit that they feared they would be thrown into did not exactly follow the blueprints. As a result, as Jodie found out, it wasn't quite the death trap she feared it would be.

As she took that first leap into the unknown and found herself sliding down the edge of the steep, funnel-shaped construction, she expected to land on top of other people, or bones, or a mixture of both. What she found instead was the top of a staircase. A staircase that had been built into the side of the pit, one that led up to the top and out, and stretched all the way down. Naturally, her curiosity got the better of her on her first trip down, and she descended the stairs to the very bottom, where she found – not death, or the dying – but a tunnel under the Staz Peninsula to a new settlement, set up by those very criminals who had constructed the pit, all those years ago.

There, further along the coast in a sheltered cove,

this village thrived. The condemned constructed houses, town squares and facilities – and, crucially, a fairer judicial system. From a distance, they could even see the old town and wondered what life must be like back there for their lost families.

Jodie had, naturally, stumbled into this new town bewildered and shocked, struggling to make sense of it.

"Why?" she had asked. "If you could clamber back out of the pit and to your homes, why did you not?"

The residents of the new town laughed. "We gave people that option, but no one has ever taken it. Why go back there and live such a repressed life, when you can live here in freedom and prosperity?"

"But isn't everyone a criminal here?"

"Are you a criminal?"

"No, I am not."

"Then that answers your question, I believe."

Jodie nodded. "So has no one ever returned?"

"Not one."

"Then perhaps I should be the first."

"You'd rather go back?"

"Temporarily. There are some things I'd like to bring back with me. And perhaps while I'm there put on a show and see if anyone will follow me." Jodie paused for a moment, thinking. "Unless, in doing so, I'd break the secret of this place to the law enforcers?"

They laughed. "They wouldn't follow you. They have no concept of free will. They couldn't possibly contemplate that the Incident Pit is anything but a death trap. You know that it's named after an old concept used in extreme sports?

"In that model a few minor incidents will keep you out of the pit, but as the minor incidents build up to something more major, unless action is taken you start sliding and sliding until you hit an emergency, then panic, then pass the point of no return. The law enforcers there are so concerned with the minor incidents that they don't think they could accumulate to something more. They're too closed-minded. So, by all means go back, collect your stuff and return. You can be the first person ever to survive the Incident Pit."

Jodie nodded and did so, returning along the corridor and up the stone staircase, emerging undetected from the pit that night. After all, she had friends there.

*

In the weeks after Jodie's return more people made the journey through the Incident Pit and to the new life they found there - and not just because they had been Pushed. They, too, were amazed by what they found.

"So," Jodie asked one of a new gaggle of arrivals. "Who would like to be the second person in history to escape from the Incident Pit? I've already broken the third fact of the town. Who fancies challenging the first and second?"

Several people raised their arm and Jodie smiled.

It had begun.

The Incident Pit

By J. McGraw

I went for a walk one fine spring morning. As I crossed the meadow by the river, I saw a young girl sitting on the ground and crying. Next to her was a hole that a dog might have dug to find a bone, and in the hole was a doll.

"What's wrong, little lady?" I asked. The girl pointed to the doll.

"I dropped my dolly." She sniffed, fat tears still rolling down her cheeks.

"Oh dear. Here, let me get her out for you."

The hole was shallow enough that the girl could have reached in for the doll herself. I crouched down and reached in for the ringletted dolly in the bottom, but as I stretched my hand towards it, it seemed to retreat from me. Crouched, I couldn't reach it. I knelt and tried again, but still the doll retreated from my grasp. I bent forwards, and couldn't reach. I leant over so my nose was almost at ground level, and still I couldn't reach.

With nothing else for it, I resolved to lie on my front, but as I shifted myself, hands pushed against my back and I tipped forwards. I cried out, but as the world tumbled around me, I caught sight of the little girl, on her feet. I still wonder if I imagined the red glint in her eye.

The Incident Pit

(Or why you should listen to site directors)

By Lauren K. Nixon

Beware the incident pit, my girl,
With its barbed spines and roots that curl.
It creeps upon you unawares
And grasps your ankle tight,
And strips the battery from your phone,
And leaves you broken, all alone.

Beware the incident pit, my girl,
When first you step outside your door.
For it will draw you in, my dear,
With thunderstorms and rocky paths,
With laces torn and mislaid maps,
You'll go right down to hell, by haps!

Beware the incident pit, my girl,
Or you will rue the day
You first ignored the safety talk,
And went outside to play.

Telling the Bees

By Hannah 'Han' R. H. Allen

My grandfather had this odd little ritual; for every major event that happened he would go out and tell his bees. He would climb into his white overalls, pull on gloves, and don the mesh hood that covered his head and neck, gathering at the shoulders, and head out to the hives. Sometimes it would take twenty minutes; at others almost an hour would pass. When he returned he would always announce, matter-of-factly, that the bees had been informed.

It used to fascinate me as a kid. I wanted to know how to speak bee, how he had learned to communicate with them, why bees were so interested in our lives. Once, when I was ten and feeling particularly courageous, buoyed up by my new found 'maturity', having reached double figures, I enquired if I could ask him about his bees, and when he nodded his assent bombarded him with a stream of questions. He sat listening in polite silence until I had exhausted myself of all queries. Then, quietly, evenly, he told me; anyone could talk to bees, they are clever enough to understand English, but it took time and practice really listening to them to be able to understand what it is they are saying. He told me the bees were part of our family, so it would be rude to exclude them from goings on just because they lived at the bottom of the garden.

That year I spent a lot of time in the garden, as close as I dared to the hives, eyes shut, trying to decipher any meaning from the humming buzz in the air. That was also the year I was severely stung trying to invite the bees in for dinner. I remember Mother shouting at Grandpa in the sitting room, while Father sat me down in the kitchen and applied cream to the welts along my arms. After the argument burned out, or rather, Mother's rant ended, Grandpa headed through the kitchen towards the back door, saying he was going to go tell the bees they had been bad, but that I should remember that the bees don't live like we do, so I should probably not try to bring them to tea again.

My grandfather was a stern man; not unkind, but stoic, nothing ever phased him. He didn't laugh at jokes, merely nodded his head to indicate he recognised the humour. He never raised his voice in anger, nor did I ever see him cry, except for one time; right after Grandma died.

He had been his usual quiet, impassive self, and I remember I asked my father, slightly louder than I should have, how he could be so unmoved. Did he not love her like I did? He scolded me for my presumptive rudeness, and told me that, that was just how his father had raised him. 'Real men' back then were not supposed to show emotion, and that things were different now, but when he was a boy that's the way things were, so that's the way he was. Unsatisfied with that answer, I stormed off toward the kitchen, meaning to escape into the garden away from the crowded wake. I got to the back door just as he was returning from the apiaries, pulling the mesh hood off. I saw his eyes were red and wet, but seeing me he quickly turned away and began carefully putting the protective gear away on its shelf by the back door, saying, "I had to tell the bees."

When he turned back he was his familiar composed self, but I never forgot that moment.

I had so much respect for that man, his quiet dignity and composure, the little ways he showed how much he cared; never missing an event, attending every match, recital, birthday, and graduation. Always, there with a mug of tea and a good book when someone was sad, or something a little stronger when we were older. He was my role model, the kind of quiet, gentle, man I aspired to be.

It was a mild autumn day, the day he passed. The

whole family had gathered at his bedside. Surrounded by love, he left us with a gentle smile on his face, like a parting gift after years of sobriety. The wake was, compared to Grandma's, a relatively quiet affair, since he had outlived many of his friends. The house quietly hummed with remembrances and stories being traded, condolences being shared. Quietly, I turned away from the crowd, and headed for the back door, taking down the faded and yellowed protective gear and pulling it on. As I picked up the mesh hood, my father came to find me, his eyes red and wet.

"Where are you going?" he asked.

Slipping on the hood I replied, "To tell the bees."

Telling the Bees

By Hannah Burns

Simon sat quietly leaning against a large oak tree, fingers flicking through one of his favourite books, the spine broken and pages yellowed from the times he had read it through, pages creased over on his favourite parts.

His voice lifted up to the nest that was hanging in the tree a few metres above his head; his bees. His mother was always worried that one day the little creatures would attack Simon, but each day the young boy sat below the tree and read to them and returned unstung. Telling them of the world, fantasy, and of his own life.

Telling them of the troubles he had at school, of the arguments that he would have with his teachers and the pain that his father put him through, his fingers grazing the black eye under his glasses.

This was why his mother never stopped him disappearing into the garden, going into the woods that was attached to their home, where the oak tree was hidden. Silva always refused to tell her husband where she let Simon run off to.

She would wait for him to leave to go to the pub before she walked through the large gardens, the dog walking quietly beside her as she slipped through the bushes and walked up to the tree.

"Hello Simon." She smiled sadly.

"Mother," the child replied, reaching for her, but his fingers brushed through her. Silvia walked over to the small marker she had made, kneeling at the cross, stroking over the name carved into the wood.

"I hope you are still reading to those bees," she whispered, tears running down her cheeks, the book Simon had been holding in her fingers as she placed it beside the small grave. She looked up at the hive.

"Protect my child," she asked of them, before getting up.

She may not have been able to save him from the wrath of his father, but forever now he would be at peace with and under the protection of the bees he loved so much.

Telling the Bees

By G. Burton

Finding their way
Through the general melee,
Their focus only on one;
Who stuttered and swayed
Looking ever so grave,
In the midst of the general fun.

It was strange, so I thought,
As I watched whilst they fought
Over pieces so dreadfully small;
At the sight of these women and men
All out of their dens
Who were standing so wonderfully tall.

The one in the middle,
Regal and brittle,
Was most fascinating of all;
For she knew that she had
In the palm of her hand
The workers and drones in her thrall.

And you'd think from the jive
Of the ones in the hive
That the queen would be best of all;
But it's no use telling the bees
To get up off their knees
And forget the honey they make at nightfall.

Telling the Bees

By Cynthia Holt

I can tell you many things about bees.

I can tell you about forager bees, gathering nectar from their favorite flowers and rushing it back to the hive only to go right back out again. Back and forth, back and forth until they wear out and die.

I can tell you of the queen bee, referred to as royalty and considered the lifeline of the entire Hive, which will only allow her to live as long as she is deemed productive.

I can tell you about the young nurse bees, who emerged from their cells to look after the newly hatched larvae, mortuary bees performing feats of strength to carry off the dead and the vigilant guard bees, defending the hive with their lives.

I can tell you about the drones and their rather violent endings, dying after they mate with a passing queen or cast out of the hive at the first sign of winter as useless drains of precious resources.

I can tell you how to trick bees into making as many queens as you want or how to catch a swarm of them with nothing more than an old box and a scented rag.

I can tell you how to sneak into their home, carefully and quietly, to steal honey with barely a sting to show for it.

I can also tell you how to know when the bees have lost their queen or have had enough of your tender ministrations, just by the tone of their buzz.

While I can tell you many things about bees, what I really wish is that I could tell the bees things.

I wish I could tell them that I truly had their best interest in mind when I open their hive, that I mean them no harm, that I only want to help.

I would tell them that I am just like one of them, working to ensure the survival of the hive.

Sadly, It does not matter, because bees do not listen.

I have to resign myself to doing my job as carefully and quietly as possible, because I know one wrong move, one loud bang, one errant bee crushed under my clumsy hand or tool...

then the bees will tell me they are not to be trifled with.

With their pinpricks stings of tiny fire and incessant buzzing in my ears, they will tell me just how unwelcome I am in their home.

They will show me, not tell me, that I should know better than to fool with bees.

Their angry hum will follow me into my dreams that night when I go to bed and I will bear the swelling of their message with me for a day or two, scratching my welts as I curse the bees under my breath.

For a little while, I will hate bees and wonder why I ever thought to pursue such a ridiculous past time.

But then, I will get better. My welts will shrink and my dreams will return to more mundane things.

I will return to my hives, throw open my arms and tell my beloved bees that they have been forgiven.

Not that they will listen. Or even care, of course.

But I guess love is kind of like that.

Telling the Bees

By Philip Lickley

Myles Townsend had always been destined to be a bee-keeper. His grandfather had kept bees. His father had kept bees. He had, therefore, kept bees. Myles' son was only three. But he had no doubt that one day his son, too, would keep bees.

Growing up, bees had been an important part of Myles' childhood, whether it was having a hive in the backyard and tending to them during the crucial months, enjoying the delicious honey they would produce spread generously onto thick wedges of toast, or through the gentle, pleasing hum they gave, which, like the gentle rumble of tractors, or the sweet song of birds, summed up Myles' experience outdoors as much as any sight or smell he ever came across.

Naturally, his hobby became his job and after a series of part-time seasonal roles he ended up as the head gardener at an old country house about ten miles away from his family home, which had recently been taken over by a preservation firm. There he would plant flowers, maintain the gardens and, most crucially, clean out the hives and maintain the bee populations. It was a great job, even in the less friendly winter months or inclement weather, and Myles thrived in keeping the gardens looking picture postcard perfect for the visitors.

It was whilst maintaining the gardens at the house that he met his future wife and eighteen months later they married in the very gardens he loved so well. A year later they brought a new member of the family into the world. Myles still continued to tend the gardens and look after the bees, and felt that things couldn't be any better.

That was until one fateful day in June last year where events took an interesting turn for Myles.

It had started like any ordinary day. Myles breakfasted with his family, kissed his wife goodbye on the cheek and took his bike from the shed, riding it the short distance to work, where he locked it away in a container round the back of the property. From there he got changed in a back room and started to go about his business, checking the flowers and watering the beds in turn, inspecting the hives and cutting the grass to a suitable length. At lunch he collected a small Tupperware box from his backpack and ate his sandwich, apple and yoghurt (with honey, of course) on a small bench overlooking the flowerbeds. That day he looked forward to a quieter afternoon with fewer visitors trampling over the gardens and threatening his handiwork as they were closing up early to prepare for a big charity banquet happening that evening. By two o'clock that afternoon the staff had ushered all the visitors out to their cars and near silence fell on the property, only for it to be replaced almost immediately by a small-army of staff arriving to start preparing the food and layout for the event. Myles was just happy that they were avoiding the gardens, so his hard work wouldn't get damaged and he could work in relative peace.

It was at just after two that Myles took another tour around the garden to finish off his work. He was preparing to leave when he heard a commotion from behind. He turned to discover a figure – a man – bursting out of a back door, carrying a bag of something. In his other hand he was brandishing a gun and running. There were no guards to be seen, and Myles rather suspected those giving chase had been employed for their 'value for money', rather than their running ability.

Myles called out to the man to stop, but he ignored him, waving the gun in his direction and telling him, in terms that can only be described as impolite, to move out of the way. Myles did so and ducked to the left as the man went running past. There was still no sign of the guards.

What he did next was purely a product of the moment. Dashing forward, years of cycling giving him muscles that could shame many a runner, Myles quickly caught up with the man and tackled him to the ground, both of them landing with a thump on the floor. The thief let go of the bag and jewellery spilled out across the path.

"You don't have to do this," Myles said, looking up from the stolen goods and into the eyes of the man who had taken them. "Leave them here, get going and no more will be said."

The man thought about this proposition for a minute but soon dismissed this alternative. "I can't do that," he said in his gruff voice.

"Then I have no choice," Myles said, holding onto the thief.

"Then neither do I."

A shot ran out, echoing across the flowerbeds and off the walls of the building. By the time the guards arrived the thief was long gone, as was the bag of jewellery, leaving Myles on the ground. One of the guards approached him and realised quite quickly that he was in a bad way. He took off his jacket, applied it onto the wound with pressure and called his colleague over, urging him to call an ambulance. Myles coughed and spluttered, but managed to get some words out.

"Telling the bees," he said in a voice whose power was rapidly fading. "Telling the bees."

*

"And that's all he said?" was the first question out of the mouth of the investigating officer when he heard. "This chap gets murdered by some thug with a gun and he doesn't tell us any description about his attacker, just some sort of random phrase?"

"That's what he said," the guard said, before settling his nerves with another sip from a cup of rather strong coffee. "Twice."

The guard was sitting with the officer, who was standing, in one of the smaller rooms at the back of the house. Of course the term 'smaller' was relative in this case and it was larger than the entire floor of most people's houses, packed with furniture and antiques that would feed and clothe the average person for more years than they'd need. Detective Inspector Hardy, an officer who, with his square hand, bushy moustache and slight paunch, along with his poor 'bedside manner', was every bit the clichéd detective, only a few doughnuts away from the full stereotype.

"Thank you for your time," Hardy said with a tone of voice that expressed anything but gratitude. He strode from the room, hands in his jacket pockets, and out to the corridor, where he met a colleague who was loitering next to a rather expensive looking vase.

"What's the latest, Hardy?" he asked.

"Not much really, Laurent," Hardy replied. The officers didn't really get on with each other due to two facts. Firstly, Hardy felt Detective Laurent had a foreign-sounding surname, and secondly he resented how in being put together they'd earned the nickname of 'Laurent and Hardy', which pleased him even less. Especially as Detective Laurent was tall and thin and he was, well... a bit paunchy. "The deceased's last words were 'Telling the Bees', which is about as much bloody use as a condom machine at a Catholic mass."

"Any word on any suspects?"

"The place was crawling with outside bloody staff setting up for the meal they were having. There was someone on every conceivable exit to this place, but our burglar could have slipped by un-noticed."

"Carrying a bag and a gun?"

"Well, most people were carrying a bag of some sort into the space, with table-cloths and what have you. A gun is trickier to explain away, but everyone was busy."

"Could it have been discarded in the gardens before they made their escape?"

"I thought that," Hardy said with resentment. "But we've already combed everywhere. Every flowerbed, every hedge, every bench and every bloody pond. I even had PC Hedges up a tree, and considering his surname's a soddin' plant he was about as much use as a chocolate sun lamp. Even less so."

"It's a mystery."

"Aye. That it bloody is. And here's thinking I'd be back home in time for a cup of tea and Countdown. Of course it's a mystery! They wouldn't have got us here if it was straight forward. Any old beat copper could deal with this."

"Maybe we should look into this bee thing. Maybe it's a clue to something."

"You look into that, but there are only three things I'd want to be telling the bees. Firstly, honey is shit. Get a new product. Secondly, their buzzing irritates me. And thirdly, any animal that stings to protect itself and then dies is a failure to me. If a bee went on Dragon's Den it would be dismissed by Deborah soddin' Meaden faster than a Russian athlete from a Detox clinic."

Laurent nodded and took out his smartphone, ready to use an intricate piece of detective software. Sorry. Just kidding. He used Google.

"What the fuck is Wikipedia?" Hardy asked in response to Laurent revealing the source of his information.

"It's an online encyclopaedia."

"Oh, lah di dah," Hardy grumbled, his hands firmly wedged into his jacket pockets giving him the slightly unfortunate look of a large, red, two-handled tea-pot, including the steam pouring out of his top. "I don't do technology, with any of these androgynous phones or bloody wild-fi."

"Wi-fi," Laurent corrected, but he knew it was pointless.

"So what does wacky-paedo say about it?"

"Wikipedia," Laurent said tolerantly. "The telling of the bees is a traditional European custom, in which bees would be told of important events in their keeper's lives, such as births, marriages, or departures, and returns in the household.

"Basically it's a way of warding off bad luck. If the telling of the bees doesn't happen then they might leave the hive, stop producing honey, or die."

"Okay," Hardy said, looking as if was considering the options. "So a load of bollocks then. Thanks Myles Townsend."

"So are we going to do it?" Detective Laurent asked, returning his smartphone to his pocket.

"Do what?" Hardy asked, having already pretty much forgotten their last conversation.

"Do the telling of the bees?"

Hardy just looked at his colleague. "Do I look like someone that would talk to bees?"

"No sir."

"That's the correct answer. Now go and do some proper bloody detective work and find me the murderer."

*

It was a long and tedious afternoon for Detective Sergeant Laurent, who was already having to deal with disgruntled staff, and an even angrier manager, because the charity event had to be cancelled. It was as if the death of the head gardener meant nothing to them. Laurent once more made his way round all the staff members, going over statements, trying to pin-point the location of the thief and how he'd got away without people seeing the weapon.

Hardy, meanwhile, was trying to retrace the steps of the thief, from entering the property, to going up to the second floor bedroom to get the jewellery, to exiting from the back room of the property. Using the back staircases it could easily be achieved if a chap was careful, but he figured from spotting various ceiling mounted cameras he could at least be seen on CCTV. Hardy asked the guards for access to their security room, where he saw the feeds from across the house laid out on various screens and realised they gave pretty decent coverage of some of the key corridors - and, indeed, some of the gardens. Hardy asked them for the tapes, but got a sheepish reply.

"We forgot to load them this morning," the guard admitted. At about this time, at the far end of the garden, one of the staff members packing plates away back into the van, swore he'd heard a loud scream of anger coming from inside the house, but this was dismissed.

It had been too loud, however, for the guard next to Detective Inspector Laurent to ignore it.

No matter how many statements they checked, or how often they sent junior officers to explore the garden, step-by-step, no weapon could be found and without a weapon there was no chance of finding the culprit, as there were no finger-prints in the bedroom, or anywhere else in the property, and combined with a lack of CCTV and the main witness being deceased, it was turning into a frustrating exercise for Hardy and Laurent. This, in turn, had an effect on Hardy's curses-per-sentence ratio, which was already the highest in the force. Laurent once more raised the whole subject of 'telling the bees', but a combination of colourful language and a reddening of Hardy's face convinced him to drop the subject between them. He couldn't however, quite dismiss the thoughts from his head.

Soon he was convincing himself of their lack of importance. Perhaps, he reasoned, being involved with bees for a long time comes with an acknowledgement of the traditions and superstitions and, knowing he was likely dying, Myles wanted the bees to be told to avoid any long-time problems, like them leaving, dying or making less honey. Perhaps that was it.

But there was still the nagging feeling that there was more to it than that. Besides, Laurent figured, if the gun was concealed somewhere in the grounds then the thief might seize the opportunity soon to sneak back and collect it when the officers had gone, therefore ruining their last chance of tracing the criminal. Assuming he had left fingerprints on the gun, or there was a way of tracing the owner.

*

It was nearing the end of the day and there was still no immediate solution to the crime. Detective Inspector Hardy had joined Laurent outside in the garden to try and sum up the case and see if they'd missed anything, but no fresh ideas came to mind.

"For the good the rest of the day has been we might as well have bloody done the telling of the bees," Hardy admitted, and Laurent took the opportunity to raise it again.

"Well why don't we? What's the worst that could happen?"

Hardy thought for a moment. "I'd look ridiculous?"

Laurent had a great return line for that, but chose not to say it for fear of getting Hardy into a bad mood again. Instead he replied with something a little safer. "You may do, but you never know, it might uncover something."

"What?" Hardy mused. "By standing by the hive we'll stand at the exact angle to see the name of the culprit careful written in honey by some literate bees?"

"Well, maybe not that," Laurent admitted, and chose to remain silent for a bit longer as they walked over to the hive.

"So, what do we do exactly for this 'telling the bees' ceremony?"

Laurent had already consulted the Wikipedia page again and felt himself enough of an expert to grasp it.

"We need to hang the hive with black to show mourning. I borrowed these black socks from one of the staff members," he revealed, placing one on each side of the hive.

"Socks. Respectful."

"And next we have to hum a mournful tune, apparently."

"What? Like whistling? I can do that. Would something by the Smiths be mournful enough?"

"Possibly. But they recommend an older German tune. It comes with lyrics."

"Now steady on. Humming doesn't have lyrics."

"Well this does," Laurent said, making up a tune to these words as he went along. "Little bee, our lord is dead; Leave me not in my distress."

Laurent nudged Hardy who joined him in on repeating the line twice more.

"We now need to knock on the hive and tell the bees the sad news."

Hardy rolled his eyes. Even Laurent admitted this was getting a little weird, even for his tastes.

"We're here to say," Laurent said in his most solemn whisper. "That Myles Townsend is sadly no longer with us."

They both bowed their heads in respect. Hardy murmured something under his breath that sounded like, "If you dare say a word about any of this to anyone then the next person I'll be telling the bees is dead will be you."

They both lifted their heads and looked at the hive.

"They can't have thought much of him," Hardy said bitterly. "There's not been a peep from them. Perhaps they just can't hear through the hive. You've knocked on the door, why don't you invite yourself in."

Laurent thought for a moment and realised that wasn't too bad an idea. He reached over, lifted up the lid and peered inside. That's when he spotted it.

"Bloody hell Hardy, there it is. Pass me an evidence bag. "

Hardy passed one to his colleague from his pocket and Laurent reached in and retrieved, from the hive, the gun, several bees clinging onto it and sticky honey dripping off it. "Myles was trying to tell us something, that the thief panicked and hid the gun in the only place he could find, the hive! Myles knew if we did the process we'd discover it."

"But why not just say the word 'hive' as his last word? Would have saved us the trouble!"

"I don't know," mused Laurent. "Perhaps he didn't trust the guards. If they had looked in the hive and found the gun they could have wiped off the fingerprints."

"Or," Hardy wondered, the cogs in his brain turning round on overtime, "they were in on it. I mean, it's their fault we don't have any CCTV. If Myles suspected that maybe he was being cryptic enough to avoid them realising, but giving us enough to tip us off. The crafty bugger!"

The gun was sent to the lab and some partial fingerprints were found on it, which quickly helped track down a known criminal. His local police force burst into his house later that week and found him in bed, ill, with a series of sting marks up his arm and a box of anti-histamine tablets on his bedside table, further confirming his guilt.

A week later and Myles' funeral was held at a nearby cemetery, one with a garden that was kept to a standard that would certainly have pleased the keen gardener. Though it was a solemn occasion the sun shone and the sky was blue and Myles' widow noted he would have approved of the day.

Out of respect, Detective Inspector Hardy and Detective Sergeant Laurent were in attendance too, and both were cordial with each other at the graveside. As the ceremony concluded and the relatives disappeared off to the wake, Hardy and Laurent shared a conversation, a friendlier bond between them had formed over the solving of the case. As they prepared to part company at the gates of the cemetery Hardy commented on the small box Laurent was carrying.

"It's the final part of the whole telling the bees process. They often used to bring the bees to the actual funeral to say goodbye to their master."

"You're telling me you have bees in there?"

"Yes, from the actual hive."

"Well I can't criticise your eagerness for completing the job, Laurent. Just please tell me that box is secure. We wouldn't want them escaping."

"Absolutely. You see this latch here, that's keeping it closed," he said, pressing it to show where it was. Unfortunately, he pressed a little too hard and the box shot open, The bees flew out, forming a cloud around their heads. Hardy exclaimed and ran off, the bees giving chase as he tried to dodge them, yelling as he did so.

Laurent's smile faded. He doubted they would be on as good speaking terms next time they met on a case.

Telling the Bees

By S. R. Martindale

The noise was thunderous. The air was close and still, and the stench of sweat and dust filled the noses of the working men.

They toiled deep underground, smashing their picks against the rock face, extracting the sparkling minerals that lay buried in the grey.

The torchlight flickered on their slick, naked torsos, shiny with sweat. Every impact from the pickaxes was perfectly in time with its fellows; every strike was perfectly placed. Muscles stretched and flexed, and stone and dust flew.

The men moved together, as one.

Each man stood tall and proud, black hair cropped short, eyes shining silver-blue in the torchlight. They hummed and sang with a tune that was felt rather than heard above the noise of clattering picks, generators, pumps and train carts.

The song was beautiful, and each man down the line added their own notes, keys and melodies.

They hammered for hour upon hour in the near-darkness, never stopping, never slowing. No task master or manager came to check everyone was working. Not a single word was spoken other than the deep rumbling song.

Eventually the horn came for the change of shift, the shrill sound cutting though the clashing and the crashing, silencing the picks and the song. Everyone laid down their tools, some stretched their shoulders, others yawned deeply into the backs of their hands.

Quickly and efficiently, the miners lined up and began the walk back to the surface. More men joined them as they went and they all fell into neat, orderly lines.

Four abreast they walked, the snake of men trailing down into the flickering darkness. They saluted and greeted a similar line coming down the other way for the day shift. A silent, plodding hour passed and eventually the world opened up in front of them.

The morning sun was glorious. Warm, bright and orange. The miners blinked as their eyes adjusted to the brightness and they formed up into three wide ranks. In front of them stood a vast portrait of their Queen, looking down upon her men with a soft and caring expression, her features young, tight and very beautiful. A majestic golden crown sat upon her pitch black hair. Black sapphires, deep purple opals and yellow jade emphasised the sparkling diamonds on her headpiece.

"For Queen! For Country! We Serve!" bellowed the miners, as one. They came to sharp attention and saluted the towering image.

"To live for the Queen! To die for our Queen! That is our joy and that is our freedom!"

The men saluted again and the neat lines broke up. Some walked up the paths, some collected bicycles, others piled into carriages and yet more boarding the steaming train that still somehow managed to loom ominously even in the bright sunlight.

*

The sun began to set on what had been a delightful spring day.

The miners returned to their places underground and the song continued. Strike after strike hit the dusty walls; chunks of stone fell and precious metals were exposed. Rattling carts pushed by nimble and bustling men rolled and clacked by, endlessly. After two hours the water man came around and refilled the tin bottles that each man had. The miners took out pieces of fruit from their bags, lying in a tidy pile just behind them and began to eat. There was no conversation, the noise was still too clamorous. The constant humming and buzzing of the pumps and machinery was ever-present.

Just as they were about to pick up their tools and get back to the face, a runner came pounding up the mineshaft. He searched out a miner that stood near the middle of the line, seemingly at random, but the miner received him without any hesitation.

The runner began a series of complex hand movements, accentuated by twitches of the arms and legs. A quick shuffle and a twist of the hips followed and a complex motion with the left hand finished the conversation. The miner simply nodded and waved for everyone to pick up their tools.

The miner flashed five quick signals with his hands.

Gold.

New.

Larger than average.

Down.

Ten minutes.

The runner jogged off and was once again lost in the flickering shadows of the lamp light.

A full complement of thirty miners set off down the mineshaft, walking in unison and continuing their song. The unheard words and melodies had taken on an excited note, rising and falling in higher pitches than before.

Almost exactly ten minutes later, they came upon a new tunnel and the group turned and scrabbled down the passage. Most of the men had to half crawl, half scrabble down the low, narrow path. A short shuffle later the passage opened up into a high vault and wide cavern. And there, in front of them, was a small patch of ice blue quartz, speckled with dots of gold.

As one, the men spread out and began to chip away at the rock to reveal more quartz. Two men ran off back down the corridor once it had been confirmed that the seam was indeed worth investigating. They came back not a half hour later, dragging a sled. They paused and motioned yet more complex hand and hip signals.

Train team.

Arriving.

Two hours.

They began to load up large chunks of the semi-precious stone onto the sled and soon were dragging them back off down the corridor for tests and sampling.

The hours passed and the men stopped for their break again. Chatter and signals were quick and excited.

Best job in the world, they said.

Just as they were putting their bags aside the ground began to shake. It was fairly gentle, but knocked dust and gravel from the ceiling. The lamps swung and shadows danced.

The men all froze. Two quiet minutes passed.

Back to work, came the signal from what passed for the leader of the group.

The men all got up obediently and began their hammering again.

Explosions.

Today.

Fifteen minutes.

South.

Down.

Copper.

Explore.

The signals from the leader came quickly. The men just nodded and carried on their work.

The world began to rumble again, stronger this time.

The ground lurched and everyone fell, half of the lanterns joined them.

There was a huge roar as part of the ceiling came

tumbling down and boulders and rocks tumbled above the cramped room. Screams and shouts pierced through the rumbling and crashing.

Finally, the world stopped moving.

Coughing, men began to stumble to their feet, eyes streaming tears.

Not.

Explosion.

One signalled through the gloom.

The man next to him punched him in the shoulder and signalled for annoyance.

"Help," came a croak from the back of the room, the sudden voice startling the rest of the room.

No one spoke in the mine. No one.

The humming had stopped. The only sounds were heaving breathing and the trickle-plink of slipping pebbles.

The leader waved over another man and stumbled through the dust to where the cries were coming from. They found one of their number trapped under a boulder, his arm and shoulder totally stuck and crushed. He was losing a lot of blood.

"Don't think I am going to carry on working," he said between shuddering coughs.

The leader nodded sadly and laid a hand on the man's other shoulder.

They got up and left the man to die.

After five minutes the dust had settled enough for everyone to stand without coughing. They rescued two of the lamps and cracked open an emergency light stick. Three of the lamps didn't make it.

Calm.

The rest of the men began to chatter silently with their signals.

Calm, the leader signalled again.

Rescue.

Hour.

Less than.

Wait.

Us.

So, for an hour they waited, listening in silence for any sounds on the other side of the breached corridor.

Rescue.

Hour.

Less than.

They waited another hour and still there was nothing.

The men were becoming agitated.

"They aren't coming back," said a dust covered man, his whispered voice cracking.

The leader let out an audible sigh.

"No," he said. "Probably not. We are not worth the effort. We're only a handful of workers. The rest of the crew need to spend their energy mining out more resources for the Queen and our glorious armies. They are relying on them. The best we can do is try to get out ourselves."

The men picked up their shovels and their picks. Men stripped off vests and shirts, bandaging cuts and gazes.

They began to move rock.

They chipped and they grunted.

And they worked and they worked and they worked, until the last man could work no more.

Tonya and the Bees

By Lauren K. Nixon

Tonya opened the door to the back garden rather reluctantly and stepped out into the fresh May morning air.

His favourite time of year, he had said, when the garden was at its busiest.

It was certainly beautiful – even after months of inattention. Oh, there were weeds here and there, sure, but the shrubs and perennials were blooming with all their might, drowning out the interlopers. Only the vegetable patch lay fallow, doing a fine impression of a butterfly meadow.

It was a shame, he'd said: this was the first year in forty that he hadn't grown his own.

"Bit too much for me now," he'd say, and smile sadly.

Tonya had brought him a tomato plant to put in his window, which had cheered him a little.

The garden, it appeared, had always been Mr Singh's pride and joy.

She walked slowly through it, admiring every bud and blossom. It seemed important now, to appreciate them on his behalf.

Tonya paused by the small row of fruit trees that formed a barrier between the main garden and the bit where he'd kept a shed and the compost heap lived. She could already hear the buzzing, even from here.

She had never liked bees or wasps – anything, really, that was highly mobile and could sting you, but Mr Singh had been quite particular. He had no children to do it for him, and no one else would know that it had to be done.

You had to tell the bees, he had said, when someone died.

Tonya glanced up at the bedroom window, empty

now, save that tomato plant, but still ajar. There were other things she needed to do – and, technically speaking, she ought to do them first – calling a doctor to record the time, summoning the undertaker...

There was no one to notify – at least, no one human.

She took a deep breath and stepped into the dusky warmth trapped between the trees and the shed. The quality of the buzzing shifted slightly; the bees were signalling their displeasure at her intrusion. This was their kingdom, without a doubt.

Feeling very strange indeed, Tonya cleared her throat, then stopped, her mouth open.

How should she do it?

They had never talked about the words she should use, and no training session she had ever attended had sought to prepare her for this. Would human sentiment be out of place?

I'm sorry for your –

No, that sounded wrong; insincere.

I regret to inform you –

Wrong again; too formal.

"What am I doing?" she asked herself, casting her eyes over the hives.

It wasn't as if they could understand her, anyway, but Mr Singh had thought of them as family.

Family...

Drawing on her years of experience in palliative care, Tonya sat down on a wooden bench that must have been one of Mr Singh's favourite spots. It was always best to do these things sitting down, she felt, in case anyone felt a bit wobbly afterward.

Visions of bees fainting all over the place filled her mind and she brushed them aside, feeling ludicrous.

Clasping her hands tidily in her lap, she addressed the throng, "Well now," she said, in a gentle voice that would nevertheless reach the most distant members of this little community, "my name is Tonya Adoabi – Mr Singh's nurse. I'm afraid I have some rather bad news for you."

Was it her imagination, or had the tone of the hum that surrounded her changed? It seemed louder than before – anxious and expectant.

"As you probably know, Mr Singh has been very ill," she said.

They must know – surely they must. Didn't apiarists have to perform regular maintenance? Would they have noticed his absence? Sensed a change in him when he last came down to their part of the garden?

Feeling very silly indeed, she continued, "I'm sorry to say that Mr Singh died this morning. It was quite painless," she added, possessed by the sudden urge to offer comfort. "He slipped away in his sleep. He wanted to make sure you were told, so – well – I'm telling you. I really am very sorry," she said, sadly. "He was a lovely gentleman, and I know I'll miss him."

The hum – though she was certain it was all in her own head – seemed to take on a mournful tone, rippling through the airborne bees.

You're projecting, she told herself. You're putting your grief in the bees' mouths – spiracles. Whatever.

She looked around, feeling rather emotional, and fell back on the routine she employed with grieving relatives. Respectful and gentle.

"I'm going to sit here quietly for a little while," she told the air, "and remember him."

Tonya lowered her gaze to her knees, respectfully, and so it was that the sudden change in the bees came to her notice through their sounds. The buzzing changed again, but this time the tone didn't change at all; it was still oddly funereal. Instead, the volume began to diminish.

Her eyes snapped up: all around her, on every branch and twig and bloom – on the walls of the potting shed – even on the path – wave upon wave of bees were landing, jostling for space.

Tonya looked on in astonishment as the crowd of bees shuddered and stilled, the sound of their breathing dropping to a low susurrus purr. She had the impression of thousands of eyes, all staring up at her, expectant.

Obediently, she bowed her head again, thinking of the way Mr Singh's face has lit up when he talked about his bees, and how he'd always wanted the window open so he could hear them; how he had always graced her with a smile, even when he was so exhausted from the treatment that he could barely sit up.

They stayed that way for a time, Tonya and the bees, sharing that stillness, until the sounds of the morning began to drift back in, as they might at the lifting of an enchantment.

Tonya raised her head.

As if this was a prearranged signal, bees began to take wing – more and more of them, raising the drone to a roar, until the air around her was full of them. It was like being inside a living cloud.

Tonya clenched her hands around the arms of the chair, her fear suddenly returning. What if one of them stung her? Would her panic trigger theirs? She'd be stung half to death before she even reached the back door – and that would be very difficult to explain to the undertaker.

No, far better to stay still – stay quiet.

The minutes stretched on, and still the buzzing increased in volume.

Then, the very moment when she had decided she could take no more, the cloud began to lift, swarming up into the clear blue sky like a snake.

They're leaving, she realised.

The swarm trailed lazily upwards, curling around itself, buffeted by the wind above the trees. It was an extraordinary sight: several hundred living creatures all working together, dancing away on the breeze.

She realised her mouth was hanging open, and closed it.

Tonya felt something tickle the hairs on the back of her hand and looked down. There, sitting lightly on her skin, was a large, solitary bumblebee, its warm, fuzzy body as soft as down.

She kept very still, so as not to startle it, but she didn't fear its sting anymore; its intent was quite clear. She wasn't worried about the bee, and it wasn't worried about her. Carefully, it cleaned the pollen from its front legs, rubbing them together until it collected in small, golden lumps on its back legs. Then the bee stilled.

For a moment, Tonya felt strangely connected with the creature on her skin - and through it, to the entire apine world, a network of flower and fruit and honey. But then the bee lifted, rising ponderously upwards like a striped feather, and drifted after its fellows, leaving Tonya on the wooden seat, alone with the sensation of saying goodbye.

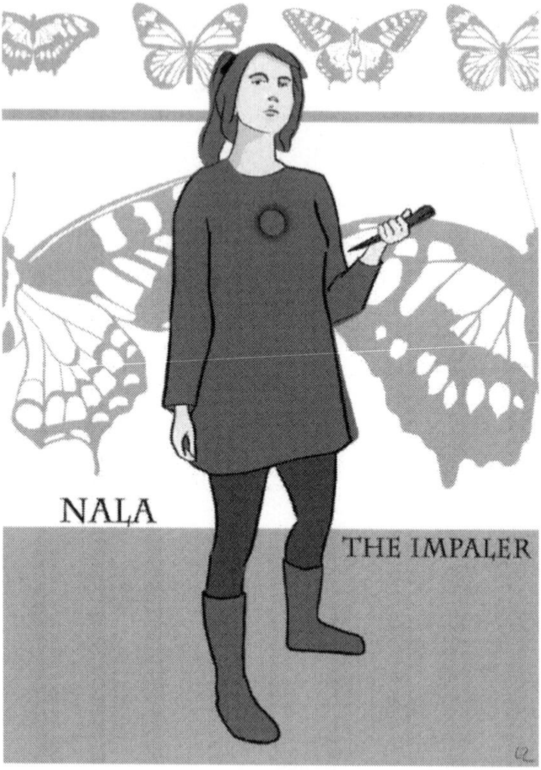
NALA
THE IMPALER

Nala the Impaler

By Hannah Burns

The stories where all wrong; all the horror stories about Vlad. Vlad the Impaler had been a terror in the night, but he had been nothing compared to the lady that followed in his footsteps, the lady by his side: Nalani.

The Lady Nalani, the Lady of the Calm Skies, was nothing like her namesake. She had a dark streak deep inside her that out-shadowed that of Lord Vlad. Yes, the enemies of her husband always ended up in a very sorry state, but her innocent face and small frame always kept her from being suspected.

The Transylvanian Prince had come across her and her husband's castle in one of his marches across the lands. Her husband had opened his door to the young man; that was a mistake her husband would not regret for long. Nala had seen the darkness abiding in the Prince's soul. She could see that following him would allow her to experience the thrill of the kill, over and over again. She had talked Vlad into taking her with him, letting her travel the country with him, she just had to get rid of one thing before she went: her doting husband and the brats that she had bore him.

Her pretty features twisted as she looked into his eyes, watching as pain and horror ran them. She kissed his lips.

"It's over, my love." She grinned, licking the blood that dripped form his lips as she watched the light leave his eyes. Vlad, who had his limits, had saved the children by sending them off to a family member; Nala had not been happy with the Prince for doing that. She let him off, though. The invitation to travel with him was worth it. Soon, she proved herself to be an asset.

The nightmares that Vlad left in his wake as he destroyed his enemies were not all of his doing; they bore the mark of the lady who rode beside him, dressed in dark clothes, with cold look in her eyes.

The stories should have named Nala the Impaler, but men wrote the history, and said that women could not be the nightmares of men. They found it inconceivable. Nala disappeared into antiquity, but sometimes, on cold, dark nights, people still scream her name.

Nala the Impaler

By Philip Lickley

Nala was the only Nala in her class, which wasn't particularly surprising as it's not the sort of name you come across in many walks of life. She had often tried to give the origins of her name a mystical or interesting origin story when the subject had been broached by her peers, but there was only one story that was true: her mother was a huge Disney fan and had named her after the lioness in the Lion King. She'd always been thankful to have been born a girl, so she didn't have to struggle through school as the only Simba.

Nala had just turned sixteen and was approaching the end of her time at secondary school, five years of which had been as uneventful for her as her teachers had found her. If Nala was being honest with herself, school wasn't really for her, or at least the type of school she found herself in. Nala was a hands-on type of person, more at home sanding down a piece of wood as part of a construction project than solving differential equations in maths class. Give her a project involving glue, tape or screws and she would produce something incredible. Slap a piece of A4 paper and a pen down on an old wooden desk etched with graffiti and ask her to analyse the opening stanzas of William Shakespeare's Macbeth and she would lean back in bemusement and use the paper instead to map out a potential metalwork project.

Sadly for Nala, at her school, they didn't give out qualifications for practical subjects and so her GCSE years were marked with sadness, stress and turmoil, both for herself and those trying to get her passionately engaged with anything that involved any amount of writing. It was natural, then, that Nala would approach the Monday of the final week of the year with trepidation. This was the day that each pupil in turn would shuffle into the small pokey office of Ms Creek, the school's careers advisor, to sit at a computer and plug in their interests so the machine would spit out potential career options on an old dot matrix printer, intended to help them choose what A-Levels to take at college. Nala herself wasn't even convinced she wanted to go to college, and hadn't given any thought to what to study there, so this ten minute slot felt like a wasted opportunity. But it was required, and she was committed, if not studious. She joined the queue of almost-leavers in the corridor as they all disappeared into Ms Creek's office, one-by-one, before returning five-or-so minutes later, still as scruffily dressed as when they went in, but now clutching a piece of paper in their hand that was intended to map out their future.

Rumours of what job opportunities, and therefore what recommended college courses, the computer program would churn out had become almost urban legends or tales of myth over the years, passed down from school year to school year by whatever rumour mill was available. In the late nineties it had been rumours on MSN Messenger, later in mysterious MySpace groups, then Facebook and now, as Nala prepared to take the leap into the great unknown, they were more likely to be churned out in witty two-line memes, or on various leavers' Snapchat stories. Nala herself had heard that the right combination of interests could give you some intriguing options. One leaver who enjoyed sport, outdoor work and drinking had been given the suggestion of 'Golf Course Management'. Some mythical pupil had managed to crack the right combination for 'Astronaut'. It was alleged, even, that one particular student of questionable morals (if the graffiti on the toilet doors was to be believed) was offered the job of 'Escort'. Nala, however, didn't believe any of these and felt like the computer would churn out a range of run-of-the-mill, everyday jobs, like teacher, or police officer, or secretary. This was all but confirmed as friends filed past her mumbling about being labelled prematurely as an 'Office Worker' or 'Nurse', or various other standard jobs. Nala rolled her eyes. She feared that with her less than glowing academic record her opportunities would be even blander and more poorly paid, so it was with a sigh and a sense of resignation that she entered Ms Creek's office as the previous student left it, muttering something that sounded like 'Dentist', which was possibly the most interesting vocation Nala had heard thus far.

Inside, the room was as dark and dingy as you'd expect an office no larger than a stock cupboard to be. In fact, from the positioning of the shelves on the wall and the faint smell of turpentine, Nala wasn't entirely unconvinced that this room hadn't once been home to fresh stacks of paper, boxes of pens and old tubs of paint. At one end of the room was Ms. Creek, a tired-looking member of staff with thick glasses, questionable dress sense and the early hints of an age-related moustache. On her desk a computer terminal hummed, facing away from her; perhaps the last computer left in the school using an old CRT monitor that was thicker than it was wide. Nala almost asked why they hadn't upgraded to an iPad that could run the software, but she feared if she did she'd have to explain the entire history of IT development in the last two decades to Ms Creek, who looked like she thought the Nintendo 64 was still the games console of choice for Nala's generation.

Nala took a seat and stared at the screen, stifling a yawn as she began plugging in her favourite subjects and hobbies, and waited for the computer to flick slowly from one screen to another. In the background, she could just make out Ms Creek filing her nails with an emery board and glancing down at an old magazine that lay open on her desk.

After a few minutes the survey was complete and Nala pressed a big red button that said print. From somewhere behind the career's advisor a printer burst into life, spitting out the results on an old printer that was so noisy it made the shelves rattle. Ms Creek leant over, tore off the paper from the roll, folded it and past it to Nala, smiling a little and dismissing her with the wave of her hand. Nala thanked her, grasped the paper and left the room to be replaced by yet another student with their shirt hanging out from under their blazer and a bored look on their face.

Out in the corridor Nala passed the queue and unfolded the piece of paper, expecting to see something terribly boring as her future work choice. But to her surprise it wasn't. In fact, she had to read the words twice, and twice again, to make sure she wasn't making them up. She even reached into her pocket, took out her mobile phone and searched for a definition to make sure she wasn't confused. But she wasn't. She was right.

The software had suggested she should become an 'Impaler'. Intrigued, she had to find out more.

*

It had been a long time since Nala had been both keen to get to school and early in, but she had a pre-form meeting with Ms Creek. She approached her cupboard-sized office, knocked on the door and entered when invited in a croaky voice from the other side. The room was as dark and gloomy as she remembered, if not more so, apparently only lit by a small, forty watt bulb. Nala sat down and began to quiz the woman opposite her about what exactly being an 'Impaler' entailed and how it might come about. Ms Creek looked a little confused.

"I don't know myself how the software works, I just load it up. But it takes all your interests and works out what skills they bring to the table, and which vocation that table is at."

Ms Creek was flicking through a series of old and yellowing record cards that had been held in a small red record box on a shelf. It seemed that each one was a manual record of the jobs on offer and what the skills were.

"Can't you look up the algorithm, miss?"

Ms Creek looked at her blankly. "What's an algorithm?"

Nala furrowed her brow. "It's how the software works, the code that makes it choose your career path."

Ms Creek let out a patronising squeak. "I have no

idea about that Nala. Ah, here it is. Impaler. Protector of the country against vampires."

Nala raised an eyebrow. This was a rather surreal situation to find herself in, especially as Ms Creek didn't seem to be batting an eyelid at talking about impaling, or vampires.

"Did you say you were good at gym, wood-work and cooking?"

Nala nodded.

"Bit of a night owl?"

Nala nodded again.

"Enjoy travelling?"

A third nod.

"Well there's your answer," Ms Creek purred. "They're all important requirements for the role of an Impaler."

Nala nodded again. She got that, but she had to question the realism of this role.

"But there's no such job as an Impaler. Have you ever seen a vampire?"

"No," Ms Creek said bluntly, and without any sense of humour added "That's probably because our Impalers are doing such a good job."

Nala's eye flickered from left to right as she tried to make sense of the situation, wondering whether she should pinch herself to check that this wasn't some sort of weird dream. It felt to Nala like she was having a conversation with someone on the verge of a losing their grasp on reality, but as far as she could tell, Ms Creek was still in possession of her rather boring marbles.

"So... what do I do now that I know I should be an Impaler? I don't think Dracula Studies is a course available at the local University..."

"No, but it is at the Romanian Impaler School of Education," Ms Creek said as if revealing the existence of such as establishment was as a normal as saying that the canteen was serving fish and chips at lunch.

"The where?" Nala asked, her brow furrowing.

"The Romanian Impaler School of Education. Several of our pupils have gone to R.I.S.E. to study."

Nala nodded. "I see."

Ms Creek smiled.

"Miss?" she asked.

"Yes?"

"I don't mean to be rude, but have you been drinking?"

"No!" she said with indignation. "What makes you think that?"

"It's just – well... it's just that this all sounds a little bit crazy."

"Life is a little bit crazy at times, Nala, but you have to learn to embrace it. Now, if I've answered all your questions, then you'd best get to form before you're late. Here are you forms for applying to R.I.S.E. Good day!"

Ms Creek passed Nala a thick wad of paper in various shades of blue and cream, and she slotted them into her backpack, thanked the careers advisor and returned to her form. Nala spent much of the day in a weird, dream-like state, pondering what exactly was going on with reality. She felt like she had woken up on her eleventh birthday to find an envelope-carrying owl hovering over their bed.

Halfway through physics, she caught herself off guard and let out a snort at the ridiculousness of her situation, which earned her a dismissal from the room and thirty minutes in front of the headmaster's office.

"You'll be laughing on the other side of your faces when I'm a Chief Impaler!" she muttered to herself, embracing the craziness.

*

The summer was as crazy as that initial realisation had been in the dingy room at school. Her parents had been surprisingly open to her plans to jet off to Romania in September to study, although she had been economical with the truth about what subject she was studying, opting for the generically labelled 'international studies' rather than the title of her actual course, as she didn't think they'd be quite as welcoming to her computerised career recommendation as Ms Creek had been. Over the heady weeks of summer she booked her accommodation, sorted out her student loan and her visa, and spent some time with her friends for what could be the last time for two years. Her best friends were preparing to study courses for their chosen careers of teacher, accountant and hairdresser, and couldn't talk about their course enough, whilst Nala was coy about her selection, revealing only that it involved going away.

It was on a cold September Friday that she hugged her parents goodbye and left them in the departures lounge of the airport to board a plane. Landing in Romania, late in the afternoon, she caught a service bus to the school, which was located in the country, well away from the city. In fact the school, which resembled somewhere you'd more likely find vampires than people studying to impale them, looked very much like her idea of a magical school, particularly if its architecture had been designed by the Addams Family. All it was missing was a large, lightning-spewing cloud hovering over its upper most spire. In actual fact, it was a bright, sunny day.

The bus pulled up outside the gates of the school, the driver remarkably unfazed about dropping off a fresh faced Londoner outside the wall of a building that looked like it would one day appear on a news story about children kept as slaves. He wished her a good afternoon and drove off back down the rickety road to some other village.

'Perhaps,' Nala thought to herself, 'there's an academy for Werewolf Studies down the road'.

Such flippancy was dismissed as a rather tall, stern looking gentlemen of around fifty appeared at the gate to welcome her in, his voice deep and rasping. He was wearing a black cloak and his hair was slicked back as if he had just left Bucharest Comic Con, having cosplayed as Nosferatu. In contrast, Nala, shorter, more nervous, and much more inexperienced, might as well have been trying to look like Batfink. Or Count Duckula.

With a wry smile, Nala followed the tall gentleman – who introduced himself as Lestat – into the building and its grand, ornate entrance hall, dominated by an enormous chandelier full of lit candles. There were further candles and candlesticks dotted around the place, eschewing fire safety for atmosphere. Lestat, who floated more than walked, showed her to her dorms, where she was given a room to share with another girl called Taylor who seemed almost as bemused by the whole thing. They broke the ice together with the obvious riff that their forenames both lent themselves to being Impalers in some book for children and spent much of the evening filling each other in on their lives back home, their hobbies and how they both came to have travelled half way across the world (Taylor had come even further, from America) to study to become Impalers. Later that night, as they turned down their oil lamps to go to sleep, they both couldn't help giggling at the absurdity of the situation, and how it was almost like a dream.

But it wasn't a dream, it was deadly serious. The next day Nala, Taylor and the rest of the fifteen new recruits were given a debriefing in the grand hall, complete with large wooden furniture that made the blatant overuse of candles even more questionable. They were told they would be spending the next two years learning the skills of their trade and no slacking off would be tolerated. For the first time in her life, Nala felt like she belonged, and she began to excel in her lessons, which commenced without fanfare that afternoon. She loved Woodwork, where they learned how make their own, ornate crucifixes, and in Physical Education, where they learnt to duck, dive, dodgy and somersault to avoid attacks from vampires. Home Economics was fun, consisting mostly of recipes with a dubious amount of garlic in their list of ingredients, and there was even a lesson where you learnt how to see better in the dark through training of the eyes.

In their spare time, Impaler trainees were encouraged to read appropriate fiction, from Bram Stoker's 'Dracula', to Anne Rice's 'Interview with the Vampire'; movies were also available to borrow from the school's film library, including well-watched copies of Blade and the Twilight Series. Taylor, much to Nala's bemusement, often slavered over Robert Pattinson.

Lessons continued, with focus on how to track down vampires during the day; the key features of undercover vampires; and the importance of bite management and first aid for victims. Pupils would receive regular garlic tests to ensue rogue vampires hadn't infiltrated the school, or bitten anyone and each classroom contained at least one mirror, which pupils had to present themselves to each lesson.

Out of class, when they weren't reading or watching films, the students visited local villages to pick up gifts and treats, held small parties in their dorm rooms, or ran vampire and pop culture based quizzes. Anyone who said yes to the question 'do vampire's sparkle in the sunlight?' would find themselves playfully shunned from the group for at least three days, a forfeit that Taylor had to face early on in the term, until she realised the error of her ways.

Nala found herself learning a lot about vampire culture, realising the man-made river surrounding the castle, dotted with metal columns, was designed to deter vampires who feared both flowing water and silver. There was also what could be described as a vampire artillery was placed in an outhouse at the front, containing crops of garlic and other plant-life, flame-throwers and a bag full of crucifixes made by generations of pupils.

At Christmas, many of the students, including Nala and Taylor, returned home and Nala found it weird adjusting to life back in the UK, not only because of her lack of regimented lessons, but also from her developing obsession with analysing everyone she passed in the street to see if they were a vampire. It didn't help that she'd developed such a taste for garlic that British food was now entirely bland to her palate and her parents were confused when she requested spaghetti Bolognese with plenty of garlic bread for her Christmas dinner, rather than the expected turkey and all the trimmings.

Nala returned to Romania in the New Year to continue her studies, which now included extra modules such as 'Fang Neutralisation Technology' and 'Vampires in New Media', all of which she passed with flying colours in the end of year exams. Summer was spent back at home, along with a couple of weeks visiting Taylor and her parents in America, where they sunned themselves on the Florida beaches, but September came round quickly. For both Taylor and Nala, it wasn't that upsetting as they both felt so at home at the school. The modules pretty much stayed the same for the second year, albeit with a serious jump in difficulty, and there was certainly not as much spare time for literature or films or quizzes on an evening. Nights in the dorms were replaced by evenings and early mornings in the well-stocked library, which again had a considerable number of candles dotted around for a room full of so much paper, and in a time when electricity was so commonplace.

Soon the July of the second year came and results were revealed; both Nala and Taylor scored firsts at the school, taking part in an ornate, but quiet, graduation. Nala herself was credited as one of the best Woodwork students they'd ever seen.

Unsurprisingly, due to the distances involved and the lack of enthusiasm the students had for revealing their actual studies to parents, there were very few guests watching, but it was still a proud moment for the pair and a sad moment as they both left Romania, jetting off to their respective homes, but promising, over a tight hug in the departure lounge, to remain in contact.

Nala returned to the UK with her full Impaler qualification and now it was time to find a job.

*

Finding a job was always going to be difficult.

Nala mused that you couldn't just turn up at any old job centre, slap a certificate on the table declaring your skills at fashioning crucifixes out of balsa wood and outsmarting vampires during daylight hours, and walk off with a job, as the worker was likely to think you mad, or worse, a fraud. But there were always ways and means, and it was a chance encounter with an alumnus of her old secondary school that saw her returning to the corridors to seek out a familiar face. She knocked on the door of the small, cupboard-sized office and walked in to great Ms Creek with a smile. Two years may have passed, but she looked the same and the room itself was as dark and gloomy as ever.

"I wasn't sure if you'd still be here," Nala said. Ms Creek smiled.

"I've got about another year in me before retirement. Not long to go."

Nala nodded and gave Ms Creek a friendly smile.

"Take a seat," the older lady said, smiling in return. "I hear you're looking for a job?"

"Yes," Nala said politely, glancing around the room before making eye contact once more with Ms Creek. "It's tricky to find a role with my qualifications when you can hardly put them up on LinkedIn without someone taking the piss. Sorry, the mickey. Excuse my language."

Ms Creek smiled. "Don't worry Nala, I've worked here for ten years, I've heard worse."

"I mean I would assume there are some roles in the Ministry of Defence as I imagine they must deal with vampires on a semi-regular basis but it's how to approach them without coming across as a crank."

Ms Creek nodded. "I have a better idea," she said. "You should do what I did and make a job vacancy open up."

Nala looked confused. "What do you mean?"

"It's no coincidence our paths crossed. You see, I was once in your position –struggling in school – and there were fewer opportunities for me, back when I was your age. All I could do was learn shorthand and become a typist; there weren't as many careers for women. But I was lucky. A teacher who regularly holidayed over in Eastern Europe recognised my skills, ones similar to yours, and told me about the Romanian School. For a young girl like me it was an eye-opener and I did well. Not as well as you have, mind you, but good enough.

"After qualifying, I got a job in the government, monitoring vampire activity and that's when, around a decade ago, I discovered a vampire living around here, undetected. We couldn't prove anything, but we believe he was connected to a series of mysterious disappearances of young girls from the school. I tracked him down to here, where he was working as the school's career advisor. It's no coincidence that the careers office has always been in the darkest, most secluded room in the school. It's just something I kept up."

"What are you saying?" Nala asked.

"Let's just say my predecessor met an untimely end one lunchtime with some sandwiches laced with garlic and a rather ornate trap I set up in the church's chapel, with those rather large windows that let in a lot of light. The headmaster was quite relieved when I rolled up three days later and offered my services here. Since then I've been keeping an eye on the school and no one has gone missing since. Until recently, that is."

Ms Creek got up from her desk and Nala spotted that her baggy clothes hid what was actually quite an athletic figure for someone her age. She opened one of the drawers on her desk and from it pulled out two small crosses, two small silver containers and a box of matches.

"I saw something of myself in you Nala, in the skills you possess. All I needed to do was tweak the software a little and get you onto the right path. You had so much more than any other pupil I'd seen. And now you've graduated from R.I.S.E., I need your help."

Ms Creek left the desk and stood side by side with Nala. "Two weeks ago a young girl went missing from this school and she's still not been found. Her disappearance comes two weeks after the school took on a new head of Resistant Materials. That's a course that takes place in the workshop block, a rather old part of the building, as you may recall, with very few windows and lots of artificial light. I've never seen Mr Brooklyn eat at the school canteen, or go anywhere near the chapel even when all the other staff have been at assembly. I believe that our Mr Brooklyn may be a vampire."

Nala nodded. She knew what to do, and joined Ms Creek in picking up a cross and a small metal tub, which she opened to find cloves of garlic. Ms Creek smiled.

"It's time to put your training into practice, young Nala," Ms Creek said, pushing open the door and stepping out into the much brighter corridor. Nala followed close behind. "I have it on good information that Mr Brooklyn is currently alone in the workshop block, preparing notes for his lecture later. In my bag is a hand mirror. If he is what I fear he is then we need to act."

Nala nodded and steadied herself. Her heartbeat was slowly rising. This is what she had prepared herself for.

"And who knows," Ms Creek said as she extended an arm out to point in the direction of the school's workshop block on the floor below them. "If something were to happen to Mr Brooklyn and nothing was left but some dust, the school is going to be in need of both a guardian of the pupils that is much younger and fitter than me, as well as a new Woodwork teacher at short notice."

Ms Creek smiled at Nala, holding the door open to the staircase, which they both started to descend.

"Now who could possibly do such a job?"

Nala the Impaler

By Lauren K. Nixon

The teachers always liked Nala.

She was a quiet and studious girl in the classroom, and ready and willing on fieldtrips, as long as the subject in question was related to nature. She was a strong walker, a sensible student and always looking, always interested in the world around her.

From blackbirds to pond skaters, all fascinated Nala.

When the class had to write a poem, Nala would select – as her subject – a tree or a bird. When they had to draw, Nala would choose a flower. When they had to sing something in music, Nala (not a natural singer) would hum the Pastoral Suite.

It was rather impressive in an eight year old.

The only thing they might fault her on was her lack of friends. It wasn't that she didn't try to be friendly with her classmates – she was outgoing enough, talking mainly to the other children, and she never seemed put out when they didn't respond or moved away. Their teachers had tried pairing her up with different pupils, giving the whole class talks on politeness, bullying, working together, but nothing seemed to help.

You might almost imagine her classmates were afraid of her.

The teachers always liked Nala, but the other children did not.

She was pleasant enough, and talkative, and though she got good marks, she wasn't the type to put herself forward or raise her hand. If she had been anyone else, she might have passed unnoticed, or had her share of friends among the throng, but the simple fact was, Nala made them all nervous.

She had an air about her that the adults just didn't

seem to feel.

While the others might squash snails on their walk back home, Nala would collect them up and drown them in a jar of saltwater, watching them twist and writhe, wanting their pristine shells. Where her classmates collected acorns and leaves, Nala would move her mirror to the window to blind birds and steal their feathers while they lay concussed and bleeding on the path below.

And if they were forced to accept an invitation to her home by a well-meaning parent, they would be faced with a wall of captured treasures, kept close and perfect beneath the glass. A rainbow of brightly coloured things, the jewels of Nala's collection.

Approaching, tiptoeing, so as not to disturb the church-quiet of the room, anxious at the reverence she showed these still, silent things, they looked upon her captured treasure. Slowly, the knowing would creep up their spine that these fluttery things, taken for butterflies, were nothing of the kind, and they would freeze, held in place like one of her exhibits; gaping, aghast, at row upon row of pinioned fairies, their eyes and mouths open in permanent, silent agonies of death.

Turning, those tiny, anguished faces burned into their brains, they would discover her at their shoulder, silently observing her new subject, pride and covetousness shining in the impaler's eyes.

The teachers always liked Nala, but they didn't understand.

The Boy in the Storm

By Hannah Burns

His voice couldn't pierce the roaring winds around him. He had to get home. He had gone on holiday with his family and argued with them.

"I don't want to go to the arcade, I want to play on the beach." He had sulked as they walked along the promenade.

His mother sighed and explained again. "Billy, we have talked about this. The weather is supposed to get bad today, so we're doing what Ben wants to do today and then we can go to the beach tomorrow, if the weather is better."

This had not been the answer Billy wanted. He had argued and huffed the entire way there. He could see that the weather was sunny, so why his parents felt the need to lie baffled him. He had sulked while watching his brother play on the machines; his parents had gone to the café to rest leaving him to follow his little brother around. He looked out the door at the sea, the calm water and glistening sun. He watched his brother join a long queue to play on a fighting game and he slipped away, headed to the door and decided he was old enough to go to the beach himself.

He had found a boat and headed out into the water to relax in the sun.

Of course, the sun had soon given away to clouds and the wind had picked up quickly. He had been lucky and his boat had been pushed back onto the beach, but not at the same place he had pushed off. He had scrambled out of the wooden boat and tried to head towards town, the driving rain making it hard for him to walk. He was soon drenched and freezing.

The weather had got rapidly worse, thunder and lightning exploding overhead and making him jump. He had crawled into the sand dunes and curled up, hugging his legs to his chest, his own tears mixing with the rain running down his face.

"Billy."

He looked up. He could have sworn he heard a whisper in the wind. Scared, he looked around, but he must have been imagining it. He hugged his legs harder, ignoring the call when he heard it again, imaging dreadful nautical sirens his father had read to him about, ready to eat him alive. He closed his eyes and tried to keep warm.

"Billy! Oh my God, Billy!" His father's voice cut through the wind.

He looked up and saw the concerned brown eyes of his dad, moments before the man's arms and warmth circled around him. Relief flooded through him and he felt like he was home.

"Dad," he breathed and held on tightly to his father, a safe place in a storm.

The Boy In The Storm

By Jessica Grace Coleman

Thomas stared out at the sea, the dark waves crashing on the shore like they did every night. The hazy moon was hiding behind the clouds, peeping out every so often to illuminate the violent waters beneath.

He shivered, trying to pull his coat more tightly around his body, but it didn't help.

It never helped.

The smell of the sea hit his nostrils, the sharp tangy taste of it now more of a burden than a novelty. He shivered again as a tear fell down his cheek.

The storm was getting worse, the waves looming higher and higher as the roar of the water threatened to completely overwhelm him.

At last.

*

"I wonder what he's thinking about."

Nurse Swanson rolled her eyes at Nurse Towers. "You say that every day."

Nurse Towers shrugged. "I suppose we'll never know."

The two nurses watched as Thomas – sitting in his wheelchair, as he'd been sitting for the past ten years – stared out the window. Never moving, never saying a word.

Nurse Swanson sighed. "Come on, we'd better carry on with our rounds."

As the two of them left the communal day room, Thomas continued to battle with the elements in his head.

One day, the storm would be over.

But today was not that day.

His body continued to stare out the window, but all

he saw was the sea.

The Boy in the Storm

By Hailie Drescher

Just like any year during the month of May it was raining cats and dogs.

Cats and dogs? Who came up with that saying anyways? Raining cats and dogs. What an absurd description for the torrential downpour that had been constant, of late. It's all I can do to sit at the living room window staring out at the street, where the rain is coming down in buckets. Buckets may be an understatement for the scene before me now.

The water running down the window pane came so fast that if it wasn't for the other signs of the storm you wouldn't think it was raining at all. Signs like the dark, foreboding sky – clouds swirling across the heavens. The fallen rain rushes along the gutters and down the storm drain, evidenced by the leaves and other debris flowing along with the water like thousands of tiny, eclectic boats.

Puddles can be seen everywhere. Rubber boots, umbrellas and raincoats don't protect those who dare to venture to the store for a jug of milk. I watch as my father, one such brave soul, comes running up the front walk, a jug of milk clutched in one hand, his umbrella tucked uselessly under the opposite arm and his rain jacket soaked through. As he opens the outside door it crashes against the outside of the house by the wind. He struggles to grab it again before finally managing to back his way into the house the door slamming behind him.

I watch my father, drenched through to the bone, peel his outer layers of clothing off and kick his boots to the side. A puddle forms on the ground and he calls for my mother to bring a towel. After mopping up the puddle, my father stoops to pick up the jug of milk and the two of them disappear into the kitchen. As they rounded the corner and the door swung back and forth on the hinges, I turned my gaze back out into the storm.

That's when I see him. The boy in the storm. Everyone else caught out in the downpour is bundled up, uselessly pulling their jackets close around themselves. Not him. This little blonde boy is standing out in the middle of our close, arms spread wide and slowly spinning through the rain. What surprises me most is that he wears no rubber boots, no socks – naught but a t-shirt and shorts. As I watch him spin through the rain, not a care in the world for just how wet he is getting, I become mesmerised by his actions, by the way the rain comes down over his small frame.

As I watch this small boy spin, he suddenly stops moving and looks right over at me, right through the rain-washed window and directly into my eyes. Squinting slightly through the downpour he raises his arm towards me and gestures for me to join him. My eyes widen and I sit bolt upright, shocked that he can see me through the mess outside. The boy keeps gesturing towards me, trying to get me to come out and play in the rain. I look back over my shoulder, biting my lower lip, towards the kitchen, where I can hear my parents talking. When I look back towards the boy he has started to use both hands to gesture towards me, mouthing the words, "Come on!"

Making a decision, I quietly slip towards the door, skipping over the spot on the floor that always squeaks and onto the still wet carpet at the front door. I carefully slide my socks off my feet and leave them there, before carefully prising the door open and stepping over the threshold. The boy looks over and grins at me, gesturing more insistently. I bite my lip nervously, second guessing myself, but at this point the winds have shifted again and the rain is starting to hammer against the house, soaking me clear through from the front. With barely a glance backwards I pull the front door closed and hurry out into the downpour, towards the boy.

He was younger than I and about a foot and a half shorter, but he grinned up at me with his one missing tooth and sparkling blue eyes.

"It's about time!" he shouts over the wind, "Let's dance in the rain!"

With that, he starts to spin, slowly at first, then faster and faster. I smile at him and soon I have started to spin and dance through the rain as well. I spin faster and faster, my head hanging back on my shoulders, enjoying the rain beating down upon my body. It is delicious and refreshing. I am just starting to really enjoy myself when suddenly a pair of hands grab my shoulders.

"Hailie, what are you doing out here, all by yourself?" It is my father.

By myself? What is he talking about?

"But I'm not by myself, the boy..." I trail off, looking around the stormy street. There is no boy.

"Dear, there's no one there," my father says, putting an arm around my shoulders and guiding me back into the house. I glance over my shoulder at the spot where I had seen my new friend, just a moment ago. As my mother towels me off inside, I describe the boy I had been playing with.

After a brief, worried look at my father she turns to me and says, "Sweetie, this boy you say you saw. It sounds very much like little Tommy Jenkins."

"So?" I ask, confused.

She glances at my father again before looking back at me, "Sweetie, Tommy died. Three weeks ago in the storm that knocked out the power."

With that, she hands me the towel so I can dry my hair, and she and my father go back into the kitchen. I stare after them, startled and afraid.

Could it be true?

Was the boy in the storm the one who had died not

a month before?

I run back to the window and look out into the street, and there he is, Tommy Jenkins, standing at the end of our yard. But he isn't dancing anymore, just watching me, smiling, waving. I gape at him, and almost without permission, my hand begins to raise in answer.

It's almost in the air when he just stops being there, as if he's simply been washed away by the rain.

The Boy in the Storm

By Philip Lickley

This was not how Tish had imagined the week ending. If you'd collared her in the corridor at work and said to her that on Friday evening she'd be stood at a fork in a country road wearing tight Lycra, standing next to a bike she was uncomfortable riding, getting rained on in a storm that was the worst the country had seen in fifteen years, she would have scoffed, finished off her photocopying and returned to her desk with a fresh cup of hot coffee in her bright pink mug. But this image, complete with reflective strip across her chest and a tightly worn cycle helmet on her head, was an accurate portrayal of how Tish English, thirty-one, was spending her Friday evening.

It had all started a week before, after a lazy weekend at home. Tish was a big reader; you could see it in how she had designed her house. The living room was dominated by a vast bookcase that stretched across one wall, mounted to the plasterboard with hefty screws, each shelf bowing under the weight of many books. In her bedroom there would always be a stack of books on the bedside table under the lamp, and scattered around the house were well-read old paperbacks with stains of orange juice or tea on their pages, trophies of them being read during breakfasts and meal times. A cross stitch pattern with a quote by Charles Dickens was displayed proudly in the back bedroom; a clay model of a bookworm peering out of three books with a cheeky smile stood on the mantelpiece. But this book lover had a problem, which was that for the first time in twenty years she had run out of new books to read.

Tish had always had a few books on the go at any one time, with one in her handbag for on the bus into work, maybe another by her bedside, perhaps a coffee-table book in the sitting room, where you'd expect it to be. She wasn't one for new technology – all her books were paperbacks or hardbacks – and so the house did resemble a small, public library. Tish loved the feel of a book in her hands, the flick of the leaves, the smell of the paper, and the satisfaction of turning pages over in her fingers. A digital click-click-click couldn't just replace that.

But her lack of fresh books had caught her by surprise. Usually she found herself in a bookshop at least once a week picking up a clutch of recommendations and new books with covers that caught her eye, but a few weeks of unexpected social engagements and extra shifts at work had kept her from her favourite high street business, so her reverse had run dry and she only realised it on Monday night as she came to the end of her 'commuting' book on the bus and realised, upon arriving home, that there was nothing to replace it with. Tish looked at the clock – there was just about time for her to get to the bookshop before it closed. She put back on the coat she'd just removed and headed back out of the door, darting over to the bus and catching the return ride just in time. She arrived at the doors of her favourite independent bookshop at ten minutes before closing, pushing open the main door and hearing the satisfying tinkling of the bell, a Pavlovian reaction that made her fingers itch excitedly for the feel of new books.

Tish loved the book shop, with its rickety shelving, lack of order and bohemian style to stacking. She would often find herself running her finger along spines old and new, picking out books and balancing them in her hands to take to the counter. On this occasion, though, with time against her, there would be no time for literary folly.

The kindly old man behind the counter – Derek – beamed at her as she entered, his eyes lighting up behind his half-moon glasses. "Evening Tish," he called out in his gruff voice, shaped by years of smoking, "You'll have to be quick, I'm shutting up shop in a moment."

"Don't worry Derek," she replied from behind a

bookshelf, "I just need one book tonight, I'm just not sure which one."

"Why don't you try our lucky dip?" he asked nonchalantly, as he delved back into the book he was reading behind the counter. Tish stopped in response to his question and peered with youthful vigour from around the nearest shelf.

"What's the lucky dip?" she asked.

Derek put down his book so the spine was upright, gravity holding his place, and used his now free hands to point to a small table in the centre of the space at the front of the shop. Tish followed his finger and saw a small, wooden antique table, about half-a-metre by the same, onto which was placed a standing pop-up banner declaring the words 'Lucky Dip' in a bright red font. Surrounding it were a series of book-shaped objects wrapped in a brown paper and tied up with string, as if they'd landed there from a by-gone era, looking aged even by the nostalgic standards of the old bookshop. Tish randomly selected one, picked it up, turned it over in her hands and smiled.

"I'll take this one," she said, moving over to the counter and placing it down in front of Derek, who smiled, took her money and slipped the mystery book into a brown paper carrier which he passed to Tish.

"Sometimes," he whispered enigmatically, "there's some magical about the unknown!"

Tish thanked him, briefly passed the time of day and then left, just as the antique cuckoo clock in the corner chimed the hour. Tish stepped out into the early evening, lit by the sliding caramel of the setting sun and headed back to the bus stop, where she stood for several moments examining the book like a child before Christmas, waiting until she was on the bus and seated before opening it. She shook her head. The opening of a book like this shouldn't be done on a bus, set to the smell of someone's take-away and the sounds of drum and bass through a teenager's tinny headphones. A moment like this should be special.

And so it became; Tish waited until she was curled up in her most favourite arm-chair with a cup of hot coffee by her side before the opening it. First, she careful untied the string, placing it unfurled on the arm of the chair. From there she unpeeled the top of the book covering and ripped off the first third to reveal the title of the book: 'THE BOY IN THE STORM'.

The capital letters were the choice of the book's front page designer, not hers.

Tish didn't go any further; she wanted to savour this moment and explore what the book could be about, so she left the rest of the brown paper in place. There were a few options. Could it be a ghost story, where the boy in the storm was an omen of something terrible to come, and the book would be a scary tale of fear and danger, with an eerie looking boy of ten standing sodden on the cover? Could it be a romance novel, with the titular boy being a young man, the rest of the cover revealing a young couple in a passionate embrace? Perhaps it was a young adult novel and STORM was in fact an acronym, hence the capitals, for something like 'STRAGETIC TEAM OF RAPID MISSIONS'. Tish laughed at herself. She had once done creative writing many years ago, but even then she found it pretty tricky to come up with a story based on nothing but a title.

Biting the bullet, Tish drank some of her coffee before completing the reveal of the book, and it quickly became apparent that it fell into the second category, as the cover did indeed show a young, trendily dressed couple in a passionate embrace, with light flecks of rain falling around them. Tish smiled. She liked a good romance novel..

For the next couple of days Tish immersed herself in the world of 'The Boy in the Storm', her years of experience making easy work of the light, frothy passages of text and dialogue. She read it her armchair with a cup of tea; in the bath, with the spine placed carefully on her chest; whilst stirring a pan of pasta as she made her dinner. The book was read on the bus on a morning, in her lunchbreak at work, and again on the bus back home. Soon, as the evening of Wednesday approached, she was nearing the end and her pace of reading was speeding up as the novel neared its conclusion, where the two lovers had cycled into a remote wooded area to rekindle their romance.

She hung onto his jacket with all the grip she could manage, staring lovingly into his eyes. He looked forlorn, as if he wanted to get something off his conscience. He looked down at Kayleigh.

"I have a secret," he said in his manly, deep voice. "I need to tell you that..."

Tish flipped her eyes to the next page, but then a knot rose from her stomach; the next pages were missing! Nought remained but a badly cut line along the middle, where the last few pages had been ripped out.

Who would do this to a book? she thought to herself.

A thunderstorm of thoughts began echoing through her mind. From laughter (it's like that bloody Tony Hancock show), to annoyance (I really wanted to know what happened!), to bemusement (I wonder if I can find another copy?). Tish closed the book and placed it back down on the arm of her chair, leaning over and replacing it with her tablet. For the next thirty minutes she trawled the web, on Amazon, on eBay, on sites dedicated to old books - but none of them helped. Some listed the book, but it was unavailable, others didn't have any information on it at all. Tish scanned the front of the book to find the publisher, but they had long since gone out of business and their catalogue had not been taken on by any other publishing house.

Thirty minutes turned into an hour, which turned into two hours, but still she had no luck.

The next morning, Tish feigned a cough and said she'd be late in for work, though instead of staying at home and nursing it with a Lemsip she was in town meeting Derek, who tapped away on his little computer to try and find the title on the database, but it came up with no copies, either in the shop or available to order. Tish thanked him and left in a hurry, determined to visit all of the numerous libraries in the local area that morning, but all to no avail. By eleven o'clock she turned up at work, feeling genuinely worse for wear from all the running about, to the point that her being ill with a cough came across as really quite convincing. Her mind wasn't really in her work for the rest of the day as she conjured up mental images of weirder and weirder ways of finding another copy of the book, from appeals on Twitter (not that she used it), to taking out an advert in a paper. Someone must have a copy of the book; it couldn't be the only one.

Could it?

By the end of the day, as she sat on the bus home, she had come to be a bit more rational, realising it was only a pulp-novel and the ending was unimportant. Even so, she couldn't help feeling that there was some unfinished business for her here. With nothing to read on the bus – she'd failed to pick up a new book from Derek earlier, which, she told herself, was silly of her – her mind began concocting a new plan.

"If I can't find out the real ending," she muttered to herself, "I could write my own!"

Many years before Tish had been a bit of a writer herself, enjoying her creative writing course, but it hadn't turned into a career. She was much happier reading books than writing them and, like some of her other hobbies, such as cross stitch, photography and finger-painting, the desire to do them had been outweighed by the lack of time to spend on them. But this was a small project. Only three pages of the novel had been ripped out, so it wouldn't be that hard to write six sides of story that fitted in with the plot so far.

At the end of her work shift on Thursday – a day she finished a little earlier than usual anyway – Tish popped into town to pick up a fresh jotter and a new pen, in the hope that fresh stationery would inspire her to make a good job of it. On the bus she plotted ideas in her head before putting them down on paper at home. Three bullet points in, however, her ideas dried up and she experienced a crisis of confidence – writer's block after just a handful of moments. Tish put down the pad of paper and made herself a coffee, walked around the house for a bit, went for a walk outside; all activities designed to help inspiration hit, but nothing really came to her. She decided that desperate times called for desperate measures, as the cliché goes, and she needed to go a little more 'method'.

"If it's good enough for actors," she said to herself, slipping out of the back door to her house and down towards the shed at the bottom of her small garden, "it's good enough for writers."

Located down a poorly kept stone pathway, out of which weeds were popping as if to say hello, bisecting two empty flowerbeds was Tish's shed, a rickety old wooden building she'd not been inside since last summer. She retrieved the bronze key from a hook in the kitchen and opened the lock, which took quite some effort. With a hefty twist of her wrist the lock clicked and she pulled the door open with a squeal of the hinges that told of its age. Inside was very little: some plant pots, a trowel or two, a half-used reel of twine. But the main thing inside was a bike, something Tish hadn't used for many years.

She took the bike out of the shed and examined it in the fading evening light, dark clouds appearing above that began to blot out what was left of the day. Tish tested the gears and brakes and chain, and aside from needing a little oiling it seemed to be in working order. For twenty minutes she cycled up and down the path, complete with its own distinctive bumps and pot-holes, trying to remember skills she had not used for many, many years. After coming off the bicycle a half-dozen times, she decided to call it a night, returning it to the shed and plotting for the next day.

Friday was horrible. As in, really horrible. The morning began with dark, ominous clouds that hung in the sky like black dogs chasing their prey. By lunchtime the light rain had started; by mid-afternoon it was torrential, and so it continued for the rest of the day. On the morning, when it had at least been dry, Tish had visited a local shop to pick up a few biking essentials – namely a high-visibility strip, some bike-clips, a replacement light and a new helmet. Together with an old Lycra biking suit she had in her wardrobe that she just about still fitted into, she was set to recreate the conclusion of the novel that night, in the hope that living it in reality would inspire her to write words on a page. Her day at work dragged, but it was soon five and Tish was back home in no time. She took off her work clothes, slid herself into the Lycra and fitted the other paraphernalia around her, retrieved the bike once more from the shed and had a few more practices in her garden, much to the amusement of her next-door neighbour, who watched her from his upstairs window. Soon she had built up enough confidence to leave the safety of her back garden and she was on the road, heading to the nearest wooded area she could find that was relatively safe to get to for someone not comfortable on a push-bike on actual roads.

By the time she reached the woods, Tish was soaked through and very uncomfortable, the Lycra chafing on her inner thighs and rain gathering under her helmet. If anyone was suffering for their art that evening, it was definitely her. By now the rain was coming down relentlessly, the canopy of the trees lighting up every few minutes, thanks to distant lightning, the rumble of thunder echoing around like a hungry monster out of sight, and Tish hoped its diet wasn't for humans and metal. She found an appropriately styled fork in the road and got off the bike, leaning it against an old wooden road sign, bearing locations that had once been etched into each arrow-shaped off-shoot and had long since been worn away by the weather. The occasional flashes of lightning were just sufficient to make out that there were words, but even running her fingers across the indentations failed to make sense of the letters. She hoped for inspiration to strike soon, before she forgot the way back, or a more literal strike occurred. She looked up as the gap between the lightning and the rumble got shorter and shorter.

Sadly for Tish it was difficult to think of plot, or dialogue, whilst shivering from cold, or trying to avoid the occasional car scooting past and casting another puddle vertically over her. Her foray into the wild was quickly becoming a rather fruitless task. That said, she persevered and began acting out some potential scenes, and soon some basic ideas formed. Perhaps wouldn't have been an entirely wasted journey after all. But after a good thirty minutes of getting drenched she was tiring of the damp and began plotting her escape. That's when the area was lit up by a bright light; not of lightning, though, but from car headlamps. She placed her hand up to her eyes to shelter them, trying to make out who it was. After a few moments the lights were switched off, there was the sound of a car door opening, followed by the crunch of footsteps across the branches that were scattered on the road; whoever it was, they were heading towards her. It only took a few moments for the creator of the noises to appear, a man of about six-foot, with short hair and a rapidly dampening suit. He was attempting to keep dry with an umbrella, but couldn't escape the torrent of flying water.

"Are you okay?" he asked. Tish nodded. "It's pouring down. Come on, let's get you somewhere dry. You can put the bike in my car," he added, spotting the bicycle leaning on the sign.

His car was indeed large enough to take the bike on the backseat, whilst Tish joined him in the front of the car. Normally, she wouldn't accept a lift from a stranger, but in this weather she felt it was a better prospect than cycling home – plus he might help in fleshing out the details of the story.

The man – who by now had introduced himself as Neil – drove them both to an American diner on the edge of some services, where he parked up the car and they entered the brightly lit hall. Tish eyed up the menu hungrily and ordered a burger and an Americana, though her offer of getting something for Neil was politely declined. They shared small talk as they waited for the food and when it arrived Tish made her way through the burger, explaining her predicament in between bites.

"And do you think you have enough material, now, to complete the story?" he asked as she took another warming swig of the coffee, avoiding looking in the windows to her right, afraid of how bedraggled she might look from the rain and helmet-hair.

Outside, the lightning continued, the flashes lacking in power compared to the brightness of the restaurant's fluorescent lights, the thunder barely audible over the blaring of the country-pop radio station.

"I think so, but I just need that push to get started. The first sentences are always the most difficult."

Neil nodded and leant down, putting his briefcase on the Formica table and pulling from it a laptop, which he opened and began tapping away on the keyboard. Tish looked at him, puzzled. He recognised her expression, smiled and explained as his fingers continued to dance on the keyboard.

"I used to enjoy a bit of writing myself," he confessed between taps. "So I can give you a bit of a head start."

Tish smiled, finished off her burger and waited whilst he finished talking. The buxom lady serving them removed her finished dishes and took them back behind the yellowing counter, liberally scattered with various pseudo-American memorabilia. The woman was clearly, from her accent, from Newcastle, and had probably never stepped foot in the USA, somewhat destroying the illusion the diner was trying to portray.

By this point, Neil had finished typing and made

moves that suggested he was saving whatever he had written. He then reached down, removed something from his jacket pocket (which turned out to be a small, branded memory stick) and slotted it into a spare USB port, re-saving the document to it, if the flash of green light on the stick meant anything. He passed it to Tish, who clasped it in her hand.

"For you, a start for your ending," he said. "Don't worry about the memory stick, I've got loads of them. Perks of the job."

"What is it you do?"

"A salesman. I'm on my way to a conference," he said, before glancing at his watch. "Speaking of which, I had best be going, I don't want to be late."

And with that final sentence Neil closed his laptop, gathered it up with his jacket, bid Tish goodbye and left the diner. She watched as he stepped out into the gloom, his dark outline soon lost in the driving rain. Tish finished up the last of her coffee, slipped the USB stick into a spare pocket and made her way outside. She was surprised to find Neil already gone, the only indication he'd been there at all was her bike, lying on the floor in the space he'd been in. Tish dismissed the hastiness of his exit, took a deep breath and put on her helmet, ready for the dark and difficult journey home.

The journey back to her house was certainly not something Tish would relish repeating; the combination of the darkness, torrential rain and unpredictable bangs and flashes of the storm made the winding country roads, over-arching trees and choose-your-path roads all the more fearful. She was relieved when she cycled onto a familiar looking road and it wasn't long before she was back home with the bike and all its associated paraphernalia back in the shed. After a hasty hot shower, she retreated to the comfort of her sitting room, now armed with a hot mug of tea, she chilled out in front of the television and dozed off, glad to be home.

By this point, she'd almost forgotten about the

memory stick, and only spotted her memory lapse when she spied the small bulge it made in her cycling clothing, which she'd left to dry on a radiator. Tish gulped down the last few mouthfuls of tea, retrieved the stick (mercifully undamaged by the storm) and reached over for her own laptop. There, in black and white, was the next part of the novel, kicked off by Neil. It started with a few words of encouragement.

To Tish. Here are my own words for the story and a last line you may want to adapt. What comes next, of course, is up to you.

From there, Tish read:

"I have a secret," he said in his manly, deep voice. "I need to tell you that I love your smile. I've thought about it every time since I met you."

"Okay," Tish thought. "A bit cheesy but I'll go with it."

She blushed and they kissed, passionately. After a few moments, they separated.

"I have to go," he said, "But here – here is my number."

Then, weirdly, there was an actual phone number.

Tish's heart jumped. Was it actually Neil's? She put her laptop down and reached for her phone. Clearly, out of the three options she'd imagined it was definitely the middle one, and it looked like her exploration of the final scene might have led to a much more realistic proposition. Tish dialled the number and it rang out. And continued ringing.

Perhaps he's driving, she thought, becoming impatient. It soon went to voicemail and the message was the voice she remembered from the diner. Tish left a short message and her own number, and hung up. Closing her laptop, she went upstairs and settled into bed with a glass of milk. She cursed under her breath that she'd still not bought a new book, so she ended up re-reading a couple of short stories from a nearby anthology instead.

Every few moments she glanced down at her phone in anticipation, but there were no missing calls, or text messages, or anything from Neil. She finished reading, checked her phone once more – the light from the screen briefly illuminating her eyes – and turned over to sleep.

By the next morning there were still no messages. Disappointed, she called the phone again. This time it went straight to voicemail. It was Saturday morning, which meant no work, but Tish couldn't concentrate on doing anything fun. The events of the previous night were replaying in her mind like a television programme with an entertaining middle, but no ending.

Heading downstairs, she opened up her laptop and decided to try and find him another way. She typed his full name into the search engine and quickly discovered an old webpage with his details on, but bearing the same number. Reading on, Tish stumbled across a few news stories about him and his success, and then a final one that made her heart skip and her mouth stutter on her tea.

Perhaps, Tish pondered, she'd been too early to write off 'The Boy in the Storm' as a romance, as it seemed to be moving more into her initial assessment of the title. Unnerved, she studied an article on her laptop screen, not quite taking in the words. It told of an accident a year ago to the very hour she had been standing in the rain, where Neil, a salesman, had been involved in a car accident in the woods on the way to a conference.

An accident he hadn't survived.

Tish swallowed hard and closed the lid on her

laptop. This was not how she had expected 'The Boy in the Storm' to finish, nor how she had wanted it to. But that, it seemed was the ending. She got out of bed, took the book, re-wrapped it in brown paper and a string and returned it with haste to Derek, who was surprised to see her so pale in the face, when she was usually so bright. She practically thrust the book into his hands.

"Not a fan of the book then?" he asked gently.

"No," she replied bluntly. "Plus, the last two pages are missing."

"Oh, I'm sorry about that. I didn't realise."

With no reply, Tish left the bookstore and walked until she reached the American Diner she had eaten in the previous night. The same waitress was working. She denied seeing Neil the night before and that Tish had been alone. Acting strangely, yes, but alone. Tish shook her head and walked out, looking out over the car park. With a jolt, she realised her bike had been lying exactly where it would have been if it had been on the back chairs of a car and the car had just vanished. She scratched her head, not understanding the chain of events. Tish tried Neil's number once more, thinking it must be some sort of practical joke, but it once more went to voicemail.

Slipping the phone back into her pocket, she made up her mind.

"You want your story told?" she shouted out into the void. "Then told it will be!" Soon Tish was back on her laptop ready to complete her own version of 'The Boy in the Storm', armed with the perfect twist for the end of an otherwise run-of-the-mill book.

Dancing Like the Rain

By S. R. Martindale

A teenager sat by himself on the wide bench at the back of the bus, his head gently resting against the ice cold glass of the fire escape window. He had long floppy black hair that got him nothing but snide comments from people he didn't know, or people he didn't want to know. He looked out upon the grey world as it whizzed by him, thinking on nothing more than the intricate pattern the blobs of rain were making, just a millimetre from his face.

He sighed and hunkered back down into his uncomfortable seat, wiping his cold brow on the back of his grey, woolly jacket sleeve. Subconsciously, he shivered and scrunched his black beanie down back over his head. He turned his attention back to the science textbook in his lap, the lines and numbers merging with the letters to make a washed out soup of inaccessible knowledge in front of his eyes. He picked at a zit on his chin, contemplatively.

The bus shuddered to a halt, but the roar continued unabated, the rain outside hammering relentlessly on the metal roof. He even thought he heard a crash of thunder, but it was hard to tell over the clanking of the idling diesel engine. At least the street lights were on early today, trying their best to punch through the swirling, pulsing gloom. A flash illuminated the textbook. He supposed the distant booming must have been thunder after all.

The bus lurched into life again, allowing the boy to continue his studies as the street lights pulsed by, adding their sodium orange to the murky gloom of the overhead lights in the bus.

A flash of heavenly colour woke him from his daydreaming; a girl's flapping red coat whizzed backwards and then away behind him. Dimly, he realised she was riding a wobbling bike.

She was a bit close, he thought idly.

The bus again ground to a halt and more moaning and groaning passengers began to get on, their plastic macs and long coats dripping tiny streams onto the worn plastic floor. He peeped between the kaleidoscope of vomit greens and poisonous purples of the threadbare seat covers and the rusted metal handrail of the seat in front of him. No red coat got on.

Why would she? he thought, slumping back into his seat. She was on a bike. Idiot.

With a mechanical shudder and a sigh, the bus began its journey again and the rain continued to splatter and dance on the glass.

He looked down the bus at the newcomers, hoping that no one would sit next to him, enjoying the small feeling of victory when they didn't. They chose to sit on the seats towards the front, the sudden jolting of the moving bus forcing them to take what seats they could, the panic of standing in a moving vehicle overpowering their senses.

He turned back to the window, looking out at the cowering houses in the gloom. A few words were muttered from the damp and dripping folk in front of him about the weather, but he liked the rain and ignored their curses and grumbles. He could watch the rain for hours, absorbed by the spirals and patterns they made, observing the water droplets dance until they drowned in bigger, more wearisome drops.

People didn't interest him. All people did was complain about him, or complain to him. No one seemed to care for the world around them, or the simple world of the rain, endlessly dripping and dropping, forming the streaky patterns on the fire exit window.

He turned the page of his textbook and sighed at the new tangled maze of words in front of him. At least there was a helpful diagram this time, of a flask and some bubbles. Great help!

He was trying, but words didn't seem to make sense

to him. They wanted him to be successful. Every day he was asked what he wanted to be when he grew up.

Is seventeen not grown up? he thought. All everyone else seemed to want to do was to sell and to buy, and to own the world around them. They danced a kind of dance, a dance of life, a dance around money, around the benches and the streetlamps and the post boxes that made up the dreary dancefloor of modern life.

A pointless dance like the rain, he supposed.

Tomorrow, or the next day the rain would stop and its streaky patterns and swirls would be nothing more than memories, and then something less than even that. He began to doodle in the margins of his textbook, scribbling pictures to accompany the characters that were forming in his mind.

He raised his head up and the dawn of an idea spread across his young face. He could see the colours now, and the shapes. He could see the emotion, the movement and the energy. The storm may be loud now; the rain and the wind may cause damage. Trees may fall, communities might tut and pull together over tea and complaints, but the rain and the noise would fade to memories and then be lost in the pages of newspapers.

Like the dance of life, he supposed.

The Boy in the Storm

By Lauren K. Nixon

The moon was but a fingernail, rising languidly above the roiling clouds, utterly unconcerned with the world below.

Amber sighed, her arms folded against the window of the car. It had been a very long drive from Inverurie down to Cornwall and their new home – ten hours and counting. They had stopped for lunch and to stretch their legs in the Lake District, and she and her parents had had ice-creams, sitting on the sunshiny pebble beach at Amblemere. They stopped again for tea, but Amber couldn't remember the name of the town. She had been tired by then, and annoyed.

Moving all the way down the country, leaving all her friends behind, was trying enough, but so many hours in the car was really beginning to wear on her.

Still, her grandparents needed their help to run their B&B, and after her da had lost his job her parents had jumped at the chance. Their farm was a nice place, tucked in the lee of a hill and protected from the worst of the winter weather, and close enough both the sea and the hills for tourists to flock in, all year round. She loved it in the summer, helping feed the ducks and chickens, turning out the rooms, roaming the hills and beaches – but her friends already seemed like they were a world away. She already missed her room and her garden, and watching pine martens and deer out the back of the house.

Now they were somewhere in Devon, she thought, having got thoroughly lost by trusting the Sat Nav, and doing what her mam had enthusiastically described as 'crossing the Dart'.

Sighing, she glanced at the carry-cage on the seat beside her. Mighty Max, her two year-old tabby, was fast asleep. Most cats hated car journeys, but Max wasn't fazed at all. Max wasn't fazed by most things. He'd followed her to school from the edge of the woods when he was only three weeks old and she'd tucked him into her fleece, feeding him milk in the playground at lunchtime, and announcing that she had a baby brother when she got home.

Her parents, initially opposed to the idea, had caved as soon as they saw his big green eyes.

As if he knew she was watching him, he let out a snore, announcing his disdain for the whole venture.

Amber rolled her eyes and looked out towards the service station where her mam was buying them all a late (and hopefully unhealthy) dinner. Her da was fast asleep in the front seat, having driven the first half of the journey. Ordinarily, Amber would have been happy to stick her iPod on, or disappear in a book, but tonight she felt restless, eager for their journey to be over. She heaved another sigh and returned to her vigil.

It was edging towards dusk now, and while it wasn't exactly dark, it being too far into the summer, it wasn't exactly light either. The sky above the clouds was stained with indigo. Looking up, Amber frowned.

It had been indigo. Now it was almost charcoal grey. The air felt charged, as if it were teetering on the edge of something, and then –

Miles above, as if the whole world had breathed out at once, the rain began, falling fast and hard, striking the roof and windows of the car almost ponderously. Big, fat raindrops – the kind you normally only see in films. Amber smiled. She loved the rain.

Even the drizzle.

Back home in Inverurie, she had often run around the back garden in the rain, barefoot and soaked to the skin.

It made her feel awake, connected to the world.

Fleetingly, she wondered whether her mam would mind if she got out now and ran around the car a few times.

Probably. It was still a long way to her grandma and

grandad's farm, and she didn't want to be wet the whole way.

The first great fork of lightning struck a little way up the hill, filling the entire valley with light; thunder rolled nonchalantly by above them, wandering across the moor like a lost soul.

Amber ignored it.

She frowned.

Across the carpark, on the other side of the field, she could have sworn she'd seen someone. She couldn't now, but the after-effects of the lightning had stolen her twilight vision. Amber screwed up her eyes, staring at the place they must have been.

Another flash rent the sky and – yes! There he was – a boy, standing patiently in the storm. Amber stared at him: he looked about her age, no more than twelve years old, and wearing one of those bright blue plastic macs you got from hiking shops. She had one herself – except that hers was lime green. The glimmer of the lightning had illuminated his face for a moment. He hadn't looked odd or out of place at all – just a normal boy, in a normal coat, in a normal field.

What had really caught her attention was the balloon.

It was big and red, floating gently above his head. Perfectly normal.

Yes.

Except... Amber opened the door of the car a crack, careful not to wake her da, and stuck her arm out. It was raining very hard, and the wind was – not exactly high, but not exactly quiet either. She drew it back in and let the door fall gently to, brushing the water off her skin.

So, how had the balloon been perfectly still?

And, come to think of it, the boy's hood had been down – but his hair hadn't looked wet at all.

She was still pondering this when another burst of lighting illuminated the valley. He was still there, the boy in the storm, and this time Amber got the distinct impression he was watching her.

Across the carpark, a car turned on its headlights, preparing to move off. The beams cut across the night, falling on the boy and his improbable balloon.

He was definitely looking right at her, but Amber didn't feel afraid at all. Instead, she felt curiously safe, like she'd come in from the snow and found and put on her favourite jumper.

The boy raised a hand and waved, smiling as though he was genuinely happy to see her, and Amber couldn't help but wave back. It was as if her hand had moved entirely of its own volition, compelled by the boy's affable smile and something else - something she couldn't quite place, like the feeling she got when she danced in a storm. There was something expectant about him.

The car that had been illuminating him moved off and for a moment, Amber was seized with an intense feeling of loss, like her best friend had somehow been stolen away from her.

She bit her lip.

Absolutely the last thing she should do was get out of the car and look for the boy. Absolutely the last thing.

Amber had read lots of ghost stories over the years, and that sort of behaviour never ended well.

No.

Absolutely not.

Her hand was on the handle and she was already halfway out of the car when her mam's shadow passed quickly across the window.

"Getting restless Amber?" she asked, and handed her a brown paper bag that smelled promisingly of junk food. "I'm not surprised in this weather. It won't be long now."

She walked briskly round to the drivers' seat, leaving her daughter clutching the warm, wet paper bag and staring out into the damp night, gazing desperately at the space the boy had been.

"Close the door Amber, you're letting the rain in," said her mam, buckling up.

From the sounds of it, she had prodded her husband in the ribs and dropped another bag into his lap.

Reluctantly, Amber did what she was told, buckling her seatbelt and half listening to her da complain about the price of food in the 'deep south'.

"Cat got yer tongue, my wee peerie lass?" he da asked, and Amber realised her parents had been speaking to her.

"I'm just tired," she said, and backed this up with an entirely genuine yawn.

"Ah well, we'll be home soon," her mam assured her. "Best eat it up before it gets cold."

Amber nodded, her mind about as far from food as it could get.

She frowned at herself; she knew she couldn't have been dreaming, but who on earth could he have been, alone in the storm like that? Had he been a ghost, walking the old lych ways in the night? Why had he seemed so familiar?

She shook her head, returning her gaze to the window, and the corner of the field where the boy had definitely been.

Just for a moment, as their car turned out onto the road, their headlights lit him up. He was closer to the road than she had thought, and she could only have seen him for a second, but that second was enough.

He didn't look dead – just an ordinary boy, smiling as though he knew a secret that she didn't. He waved again, and Amber waved back, twisting in her seat to watch him out of sight.

"Who are you waving to?" her mam asked, glancing back in the rear view mirror.

"The boy in the storm," Amber replied. "Didn't you see him?"

"Oh yes, love," said her da. Her parents exchanged the kind of indulgent look that Amber knew meant that they didn't believe her, but they thought that she was cute. "I'll keep my eyes peeled fer Mickey Mouse, too!"

Amber rolled her eyes and opened the bag of junk food.

She wasn't tired anymore, despite the yawning. She was excited.

Whatever the boy was, he had definitely existed, in his quiet bubble of calm in the midst of the storm. She couldn't have explained how, but somehow she knew she'd see him again, and soon.

He'd be waiting for her.

And together they would run in the rain.

Dan

By Hannah 'Han' R. H. Allen

Everyone has that one friend; Dan was ours.

You know what I mean, that one friend. The one who had all the probably inadvisable ideas, which seemed like genius when he explained them, and somehow always got us to go along with whatever hair-brained scheme he had concocted that week.

No matter how much chaos he caused, he always seemed to be able to get himself and the rest of us out of trouble again, at least for the most part. True, we had all been grounded a couple of times, been given extra chores, but other than that it was kind of amazing what we actually got away with.

For example, there was the summer of 'The Psychedelic Gnome Project'. It had been a particularly grey spring, and summer was shaping up to be no better. Dan, as a result, had decided that something had to be done to combat the general malaise that seemed to lay over the whole village, and he thought he had the perfect idea to do just that.

Our home town was your stereotypical, sleepy English village; cosy houses, nestled between neatly maintained gardens and manicured front lawns. The epitome of English countryside idyll, all greens and browns, muted colours broken up by pinpricks of wild flowers in the hedgerows and pale, cultivated blooms in carefully arranged beds.

This was not enough colour for Dan.

We still don't know how exactly he got hold of them, but somehow he had managed to acquire a truly impressive quantity of concrete garden gnomes. He then visited each of us individually, taking us 'into his confidence' and handing us our 'quota', with the instructions to paint them as vibrantly as we could, but not to let anyone else see, not to let anyone find out what it was we were doing. None of us were truly aware of the full extent of the 'project' until much later, each of us assuming we were the only ones in on it, that this must be part of some elaborate prank he was planning to pull on one of our other mates. So, we obliged, creating some of the most truly garish and obnoxiously bright designs ever to grace our cement canvasses.

The true genius of this part of the plan however, was that at first it was one gnome each, so, not wishing to waste the opportunity, we threw our all into decorating our concrete charges. A few days later, when he came to view our efforts, he brought along two more, which we eagerly decorated, having by now had time to think of a dozen different designs we could have tried. A week or so after that he came by again, and this time he brought three, then a week after that, four, and so on. Each visit brought steadily more garden ornaments for us to 'improve'. The slow drip feed meant that we were less inclined to paint them all the same, they didn't take up too much storage space, at least for a while (although gods know where he was keeping them), and, critically, it took longer than usual for us to start getting suspicious. This went on for a little over a month, until one day we got the message that 'tonight was the night'; we were to bring our creations and meet him at the car park on the edge of town.

Those of us with cars were among the first to begin to sense this was bigger than we'd initially thought, as suddenly attempts at 'casual' inquiries about lifts began to filter through from the rest of our friendship group, all wanting to go to the same location. With a little discussion and people wrangling, carpools were organised, and eventually we all bundled into various modes of transport, clutching suspiciously lumpy backpacks, and eyeing each other conspiratorially.

It was a little after one when we all gathered in the parking lot of the 'industrial complex' (a cluster of nondescript units rented out to small businesses and mechanics), everyone dressed in dark clothes, shouldering backpacks. It was like the weirdest covert ops unit in history had assembled for a briefing, and in truth that was sort of what we were.

Dan was loving it, grinning at the centre of our gathering. Once the last group had arrived, he called us to order, motioning us to huddle in, and explained what it was we were about to do. Dividing us into teams, he handed out our 'assignments', which contained locations to deposit our 'payloads' at, as well as what he called 'challenges for extra credit', before setting us loose.

It was one of the most fraught and occasionally terrifying evenings I had ever experienced - still is, in fact. I felt so alive as we flitted through the dark, ticking off locations on our list, but the challenges were the best bit, and, if I do say so myself, our team excelled ourselves. It took some doing, some leg-ups, much hushed cursing, and some death-defying balancing acts, but we got 'em all in place.

Then, once it was done, we all dispersed to our homes, setting alarms early to ensure we were up in time to see the fruits of our labour.

When the sun rose the next morning, it did so to a riot of colour. Nowhere had been overlooked: each garden bore at least one gnome of eye-watering vibrance. There were gnomes on the bus shelter roofs, on post boxes, some in seemingly impossible to access places, on lamp posts, awnings over shop doorways and windows. The roundabout played host to a whole party of tie-dyed gnomes, as did the village green. They were peeking out of bushes, from second storey window ledges, from the branches of trees - someone had even scaled the statue of the village founder to place one in their lap.

At first, people were quick to decry it as an act of vandalism, citing their 'ugly nature' and where they were placed, claiming they spoiled the look of the place. Surely, they said, the gnomes must have got there through some kind of illegal action (which was a reasonable guess, I suppose), but the disapproving voices were soon drowned out by a wave of positive reception. Dan's 'silly little prank' had brightened their day. It even made the papers – the proper ones too, not just the local rag. When people began naming them, a gnome adoption scheme was put forward, that allowed people to sponsor one of the many psychedelic gnomes, the profit being divided among local worthy causes.

The years went by and time, vandalism, and weather took their toll. Many of the gnomes disappeared, but if you know where to look you can still find a few of them, mostly in out of reach places, or in the windows of their adoptive families, who brought them in, out of the elements.

Not one of us ever breathed a word about that night. It is now an unsolved mystery of the village, an odd little footnote in its history, an anecdote that gets told in the pub; Where were you the day the psychedelic gnomes invaded?

I think Dan would approve. It seemed fitting to his sense of fun, his quirky humour; everything he did was for the adventure of it, and to bring joy to others. So, it only seemed right when he died a few years later, losing the battle with the cancer he had been fighting without ever letting on, that around his grave, overnight, a flock of freshly painted, psychedelically coloured gnomes appeared.

Everyone has that one friend. Dan was ours.

The Psychedelic Gnome Project

By Philip Lickley

Never. Never ever. Never mess with time travel.

These were the first words of advice given to me by my father. Well, not the very first words of advice. They were probably something like 'never talk with your mouth full', or 'always say please and thank you', or 'don't run through a patch of nettles when you're not wearing trousers'.

I think that the latter words were only from last year, actually, but I digress.

The words outlined above were the first words of advice after I inherited the family business.

Most young men of twenty-one with a self-employed father would be expecting a rewarding and lengthy career as a baker, or shopkeeper, or builder, or something like that; prospects were good where demand was constant, and therefore they could be content, never truly struggling for work that both filled up one's time, was rewarding and kept food on the table. But I'm not most young men. My father is a time traveller and now that I'm 'of age', so to speak, and his mid-forties, pot-bellied body is not quite as agile as it once was, I've now found myself picking up the title of 'Chief Time Traveller' of my town, a position I'm supposed to be proud of, now I possess it.

Sadly, and I'm doing a bit of self-psychiatry here, I'm a bit of a lazy sod. My teenage years were spent doing one of three things: playing video games, lying in bed, and eating junk food, often a combination of all three at once. My secondary school record was average, my A-Levels perfunctory, my desire to spend three years at University non-existent, other than it might have been an easy opportunity to combine drug-taking and sexual encounters with my three favourite, previously detailed hobbies.

Now I find myself with a vocation, inherited from my father, that does at least come with its own flat and a monthly bursary, paid by a government organisation I've never heard of, in lieu of performing duties I'm only just getting to grips with. Apparently there is one of us in each major borough, tasked with looking out for criminals who may be making use of time travel to fund their operations, which seems to mainly involve skipping back in time, alerting smugglers to when there are gaps in port-side security or selecting winning lottery numbers to help fund criminal enterprises.

Naturally, it's very difficult for criminals to stumble across the secret of time-travel – it requires knowledge of high-level physics, a sympathetic energy provider due to the electricity needed to power the equipment, and the correct information and formulae only available from the most obscure suppliers in some far flung corner of the dark web – and so the role of a Chief Time Traveller is generally very simple. After a few weeks apprenticed under my father, learning the tricks of the trade, I was pretty much left to my own devices in my flat, frittering away all my newly received disposable income on video games, a comfier mattress and daily fish-and-chip suppers, occasionally monitoring software that trawled the dark web for time-based criminal activity and the piece of equipment sitting in the corner of my living room that ticked away twenty-four hours a day, checking for glitches in the space-time continuum. Too the casual observer it looked like some sort of ornamental tesla coil, which makes for a good talking point for when girls come round to my flat, if nothing else. To be honest, outside of being a runner on a porn film or Ross Kemp's hair-stylist, I've pretty much got the perfect job.

Of course there's only so many times I can complete the latest Grand Theft Auto or rotate around the local take-away options: Indian on Monday, Chinese on Tuesday, pizza on Wednesday, burgers on Thursday, fish and chips on Friday, and pizza again at the weekend, like a song re-recorded by Craig David from an alternative universe where he has diabetes instead of a well-kept beard and a beanie hat. Once one has exhausted the entire Netflix catalogue and finished everything on iPlayer, Amazon Prime and even Crunchy Roll, there's only one thing left to do, and that's to satisfy one's curiosity for exploring time and space.

I won't go into the details of how to conduct time travel here as, firstly, I don't truly understand the mechanisms of it and, secondly, it requires talking about long and complicated formulae that will bore you to tears. It certainly did me when my father lectured me on it for four hours, with nothing but a rapidly shortening stick of white chalk and an old blackboard that squeaked when anything was written on it for visual interest. All you really need to know is that it involves a small hand-held device, passed down from one Chief Time Traveller to another, a technique passed on from generation to generation that was memorised and never written down, and a dose of sea-sickness pills that are effective against the nausea caused by going all Peter Capaldi and moving through time and space.

Which is where my dad's key time-travel advice comes in. We're only supposed to travel in time when necessary, as there's always the danger of the butterfly effect. Before I took up the mantle of a real-life Doctor Who, I thought that was just a depressing film where the main character throttles himself with his own umbilical cord, something I once watched on a wet Wednesday night in between Caddyshack and the third Pirates of the Caribbean film. But I can tell you what it actually is, is the constant threat of danger that changing something small in the past will have big implications on the present or future, based on a piece of fiction of someone standing on a butterfly in one location and causing a twister to pop up somewhere else, or something like that. Chief Time Travellers, in stopping criminals going about their business, are always in danger of doing this (as are the criminals themselves), and there's always the fear that when we return, we'll come back to an alternative present of our own making, where we might have wiped out all of humanity, set the earth on a path to destruction or, even worse, made Boris Johnson actually become Prime Minister.

Of course, it's not always that serious and most of the time, when it has happened, changes have only been on a local level, like an earthquake spiralling out from its epicentre and weakening with distance, so any previous mishaps have been self-contained, or at least managed, to a small geographical distance or time period.

If you've ever had deja-vu, this is an indication that somehow time has been re-written.

Because of this threat, time travel is strictly regulated, but I, as well as being a little bit lazy, am also a bit of a dick. Ask any of my friends and they'll confirm this. I'm the sort of person who acts now and worries about the consequences later. That's why, last Friday, bored of re-runs of Game of Thrones and with nothing to look forward to that weekend, I jumped back in time a week to go to a local music festival held in my town in Whitby, something I missed out on first time as my dad (now enjoying his free time by playing golf and wearing jumpers only golfers can get away with) had pressured me into joining him on the links.

Because, as any fool knows, when you have the whole of time and space at your fingertips the first place to go would be a two-bit local festival. I was a young man who was easily pleased.

Sadly for me, and for time itself, I had mis-calculated the settings. I don't think I'd quite paid enough attention when my dad had run through how to operate the machine, and so instead of heading back one week I ended up back in 1973, but at least I landed back to the early days of the festival so my mistake wasn't an entire loss. It was still a great weekend of drink, music and more drink, and by the time I returned back to the present I was exhausted, hungover and a little muddy. But it wasn't until the next day that I started to discover things had changed.

For me it had been more like the seagull effect than

the butterfly effect. In my drunken state I had decided, as I stumbled along the street after the end of the second night, to teach a noisy seagull a lesson by kicking it squarely in the chops, into the harbour. On its way down into the water it got tangled in some fishing wire and was unable to escape, therefore suffering an unfortunate ending at the bottom of the water. Replaying this event back in my mind back in 2016, it could only have been this that had changed time and a week later I can confirm this minor time-based mishap has caused five changes in my home town:

There are now only 198 steps up to the famous abbey, which hasn't really had much of an effect other than that there's now just one really large step at the top, where there were once two.

Captain Cook is now, or more importantly was now, black, which makes no sense to me at all, given his later activities in the Antipodes.

The Blitz café still sells forties-themed food and plays contemporary music to the theme of the business, but is now run by a young man who goes by the name Adolf and doesn't understand why older customers treat him with suspicion.

Whitby jet is now green in colour but, again, I'm not sure why or how my intrusion in time caused such an antiquated geological change.

The astute among you will note that I've only listed four changes, and that's because the fifth change is a little bit more personal, as I soon discovered when I returned to my flat to find quite a few significant changes. Instead of a television I now have a large electric piano on a stand and I appear to now be a member of a synth-rock band called The Psychedelic Gnome Project.

*

Basically my intrusion into the past has given me more of a life lesson into the dangers of time travel than any dry lecture from my father ever could. Previously, before I stepped back in time to get wasted on beer and enjoy some local tribute bands, I was not musical in the slightest. In primary school, any chance of a career playing the recorder was quickly curtailed by anyone who valued their hearing and their sanity; and a foray into the saxophone in secondary school just because I fancied a fellow pupil who had taken up the instrument was so ill-advised the chain of thought that led to the decision, and the expense, should have a sick-note from my father. Now, in this alternative 2016, I was somehow, according a recent review I read in a local newspaper, lying open on the right page on the sofa, an accomplished synth player in a surprisingly popular small band who was on a tour of local pubs and bars. This was particularly confusing as I'd previously thought a 'Moog' was a cat with man-boobs.

And this wasn't the only weird part. As well as my previously messy, but otherwise bare, flat now looking like the residence of some beatnik musician, my father was nowhere to be found – and trust me I looked, a little scared about what I'd potentially unleashed – and my brain was also starting to re-wire itself. This isn't going to turn into one of the embarrassing time-travel tales where I'd now found myself trapped in a band with an instrument that I couldn't play only to be found lacking in full public-view at our next gig; I genuinely could play it. I had found myself, after trying to call my father and finding his number absent from my phone, pulled almost magnetically towards the keyboard and switching it on, finding I could quickly find the right places for my fingers to land time and time again to give a rendition of Axel F. It was creepy and unnerving. I liked the skill and it was great to have it, but it felt like the weirdest, most musical out-of-body experience ever.

And that's how my life had suddenly changed, from being a lazy, lack-lustre time-traveller in name only, to a synth player in a locally famous band. Two days later, after receiving a phone call from a man who only identified himself to me as Craig, I found myself with these three other musicians – Kris on bass, Sophia on drums and Craig on guitar and vocals – performing a range of Pink Floyd, Led Zeppelin and prog-rock covers in The Endeavour pub, each song coming to my fingers like some weird form of muscle memory. At first I felt odd, like I didn't fit in, but I could feel my brain re-wiring itself, as if catching up from some sort of unusual time-travel jet lag. The unfamiliarity of my bandmates, over time, was replaced by distinct memories of our time meeting as a band, our early rehearsals and the time the van broke down on the way to a charity gig in Filey. It was utterly bizarre. The only regrettable thing was that as each hour passed and I discovered more about my new life I seemed to forget more about my past life, including the ability to time-travel, slowly forgetting the technique of setting the time-travel device, which was still in my possession, until I realised I was no longer able to recall the strategy once taught to me by my father.

I was like the time-travelling version of a grandparent who has just been given a new computer by their eager grandson: I had the equipment, but no idea on how to use it. Which is a cleaned-up metaphor of what I was really thinking: that I was like a man unable to perform on his wedding night. An archaeologist unable to decipher the most simplistic of hieroglyphics. A 1970s popstar armed with a credit card and a mirror, and wondering where he was supposed to put his PIN. I had no idea how to escape this situation and I was now scared. I was just glad that being in a band seemed a fun alternative reality to end up in as opposed to finding myself as a collector of odd-socks or the person in charge of auditing the national postage stamp archive. I was just scared of forgetting the old me, which of course was rapidly happening.

And missing my father.

But, like an ageing rocker coming to terms with forgetfulness, I could at least console myself with booze and women.

And before you ask, I'm not entirely sure why our band name is what it is. But it's cool, don't you think?

*

In reality there's no real need for a member of a band to have the skill of time-travel. Sure, you could skip back in time to record a song before a famous band played it, or nab John Lennon's guitar, or go for a writing session with David Bowie, but that doesn't compare to the excitement of creating your own music which, as a band, we were starting to do.

"Soon!" Craig enthused after one writing session on the harbour side fuelled by fish and chips and bottles of Jack Daniels, "The Psychedelic Gnome Project will be on the lips of every music critic, promoter and agent in the land. We will be to Whitby what the Arctic Monkeys were to Sheffield."

I was soon, however, wishing for my memory to return so I could skip back in time; three weeks into my new life I discovered a sixth change my actions had made to the space-time continuum.

During one particularly booze-fuelled gig at some pub on the outskirts of Whitby I'd made eyes at one particular young woman in the crowd. Her name was Chloe and she was beautiful: she had long, flowing brown hair tied back in a bun, the most vivid blue eyes you could imagine and a figure that was curved in all the right places. Anybody who says that only the lead singer of a band can pull the groupies is lying, as we soon hit it off post-gig and, after buying her a couple of drinks at the bar – JD and coke, both times – we were soon around the back of the pub, in amongst the trees that lined the edge of the pub's grounds, doing things that would not have been appropriate in a clear line of site from the play park.

After that, we swapped numbers and agreed to meet up for a date, which we did, which began, rather unusually, at what could potentially be described as Whitby's third best tourist attraction, after the Abbey and the self-proclaimed psychic on the seafront, The

Dracula Experience. It was a particularly disastrous date, even by my standards. It seemed that my previous journey back in time had also somehow triggered the existence of vampires, or at least certainly made them more well-known. Now, amongst the influx of tourists, fish and chip shops, dive-bombing seagulls and people making a living by painting themselves grey and pretending to be statues, was an underbelly of vampires. Now, I'm no Derek Acorah, but I'm pretty sure they didn't exist before my jaunt back to 1973.

I think I speak for most young men out there by saying that if a date ends with a bit of biting and sucking then you can chalk that up as a success, but context, as always, is everything, and though my date did end up with those two verbs it wasn't quite in the way I'd imagined or hoped, and the only redeeming feature of the date was that I found there are few better ways of bonding with a stranger you hope to get intimate with than having to fight off a member of the undead with nothing more than a large handbag and a novelty litter-picker from the gift-shop.

Chloe and I managed to escape from The Dracula Experience that night, thanks to a bright torch and a sense of determination not to become undead ourselves, so we escaped through a back window and into a service yard, panting with exhaustion, funnelling the adrenaline flowing through our bodies into a hefty snog and a fumble behind the bins. After that it was a hasty departure in case any more of Dracula's extended family were following us.

And that is how I found my new vocation in life. Out were the Netflix marathons, loyalty points from Just Eat and lengthy sleeping sessions, and in were sweaty performances in rammed venues with The Psychadelic Gnome Project and equally sweaty missions to rid Whitby of its population of vampires, the former with three men by my side, the latter with Chloe, who had proven to be as handy with a crucifix and a clove of garlic as she was with a slide-rule in her day job as a maths teacher. Life was busy, but life was good, and in messing around with time and space I'd actually created a more intriguing life for myself, albeit one that wasn't necessarily great for humanity as the number of deaths by vampire in the local area had increased by, well, 100%.

It might sound incredibly selfish of me but I was enjoying my new life in spite of its challenges and the fact that both my passions required night-shifts. You don't get many gig requests at lunchtime, nor vampires stalking at midday sun, though an occasional vampire-hunting session during daylight hours was good to catch them unawares and watch them burn up in the bright sun. Or as near as we can get to that in the North of England.

The only issue with this was, whilst I could catch up on my sleep during the day, Chloe was struggling balancing teaching during the day and its necessary paperwork alongside fighting blood-suckers at night, and I couldn't support her financially. There is little money in gigging in pubs, and even less money in vampire-hunting, which in essence is like an unpaid public service, like being a voluntary police officer, but with fewer druggies and more fangs.

But this life is mine now as the knowledge of time travel has finally left my brain, rewritten by time. I can now no longer list 'time travelling' as an endorsable skill. Which is a real pain, as I also can't remember my LinkedIn password in this new reality to remove it.

*

Readers, worry not! I soon found my password and correct my LinkedIn account, which now includes synth playing, pouting during guitar solos and impaling pale-looking men and women with stakes as fully endorsable skills, so if you come across my profile be sure to give me a like!

Slowly problems are resolving themselves in my life too. It looks like we're soon going to get signed as a band, which will certainly help the financial situation, which would have helped the issue Chloe had with balancing two jobs had she not, last week, got a little too close to Dracula and been bitten herself. It turns out the worst thing you can do to a partner isn't cheating on them, but having to lop off their head as they start growing extended fangs and developing an aversion to garlic-heavy foods. They never warn you about that on these dating advice sites. On a positive note, I've now fallen for Gina, who shares my passion for long piano solos and beating up bloodsuckers in her spare time, and so we've become inseparable. Also, as she is also in a band, night-shifts are not a problem, so it's riffs and kills during the dark and lengthy lazy days in bed.

But just as life settled down I discovered a seventh change, just today. It seems the Co-operative by the coach car park no longer sells Pop Tarts. But I'm not 100% sure if that was my doing, or just market forces in action.

*

Two weeks after realising I needed to travel a bit further for my sugary breakfast treats, our band got signed to a major record label and we began to record our debut album, which would be self-titled. When your name is The Psychadelic Gnome Project anything else would seem like overkill. I also celebrated my 100th vampire kill, which was great, as the only thing I ever achieved in my old life was finding all the achievements in the Xbox version of Tomb Raider. My only major issue now is that of priorities. It's becoming increasingly more and more tricky to balance a life rocking out to keyboard licks and kicking vampire ass. Determined to try to make things work, I have regularly stayed up with Gina writing the pros and cons of both professions, unable to come to anything conclusive. Luckily for me the decision was taken out of my hands as one Thursday evening, the band split up.

Well, I say split up. We were performing at a charity night on a stage outside The Quarterdeck, under the watchful gaze of the lighthouse and a trio of donkeys who just didn't appreciate my musical majesty, when a vampire burst into the crowd and killed each of my bandmates, one by one. Craig may well have been a great guitarist, able to move his hands gracefully up and down the fretboards, but he had no sense of direction when using a Stratocaster as a weapon. His axe failed to make any worthwhile connection with the soft fleshy parts of a vampire, which was bad for him, really. Sophia also quickly learnt that drumsticks made into the shape of a crucifix do not make a successful deterrent, while Kris confirmed the long-standing joke that bass players are useless by not averting his gaze from his solo long-enough to protect himself.

Many bands have gone down in history for their final sets, which may have included trashing of instruments, the letting off of fireworks, or some sort of outrageous middle-finger to the establishment, but I imagine The Psychadelic Gnome Project were the first band where their synth player finished off their biggest hit, stood up from his chair, pulled a crucifix from his back pocket and proceeded to decapitate each of his band members for the safety of the rest of the crowd. Even Black Sabbath didn't do that on their final tour, and they had someone who bit the head off a bat in their line-up.

From then I became a full-time vampire fighter with Gina, earning our money by becoming a protection racket against vampires, like a paid-for neighbourhood watch against the undead. And that's where you will find me now, dressed all in black with a cool range of weapons, an athletic physique and a girlfriend and business partner so hot you could operate a barbecue on her body (though she would probably kill you, if you ever dreamt of such a thing).

I may no longer be part of a band, I may no longer be able to time travel, I may no longer have my full complement of fingers (due to a particularly close encounter with a vampire bat), but I have purpose, a huge machete and respect in my home town.

Kicking a seagull into the water? The best decision of my life.

*

Mark woke up with a start in his bed, cold sweat gathering on his forehead. He sat up in bed, yawned and reached over to his bedside table, grabbing at a wireless Xbox controller and starting up the games console. A few moments later there was a knock on his bedroom door and after a mumbled call, a woman in her mid-forties entered.

"So, what are your plans for today?" she asked, her eyes studying the laid-back look of her son in the bed. "Please tell me you're going to do more than just sit in bed playing video games."

Mark gave a nonchalant reply and pretty much ignored her, booting up some game. His mum muttered something under her breath, picked up some clothes from the floor and left the room, closing the door behind her.

Mark had lost all his enthusiasm over the last few weeks. He'd had a really vivid dream three weeks previously. It was an exciting dream, set in a weird alternative reality, where there wasn't the threat of vampires, where the Co-op still sold his favourite flavour of Pop Tarts and that there were 199 steps leading up to Whitby Abbey, which Mark could have seen from his bedroom window if he'd bothered recently to open the curtains. Amongst these weirdly specific observations in the dream Mark had also been a synth player in a successful local band and, in fact, had woken up entirely convinced it had been true. But now that memories of the dream were fading, like a reality slipping from his fingers, until Mark could no longer grasp onto it; all that was left was an aching feeling that something was missing from his life.

Mark continued to play video games for an hour, but it was more out of habit than enjoyment. The day passed uneventfully and night merged into the next day, when Mark found himself coerced out of bed. He did so out of a sense of obligation, as it was his birthday - and his twenty-first, at that. Lazily dressing himself in some jeans and a poorly-ironed t-shirt, Mark yawned as he descended the stairs and entered the kitchen, where his mother had laid on a large full English on the table. She smiled at him as he sat down and Mark's father, who was sat on the opposite chair to him, pushed a brightly wrapped gift box across the table to him. "For you," he said, indicating with his eyes that it was to be opened.

"Is it the new iPhone?" Mark asked in a tone that was one-half greed, the other half gloom. His father shook his head. "It's something much more exciting," he revealed as the box was opened. From it Mark took a bulky, but slick, electronic device.

"What's this?" he asked, not recognising it and failing to find a brand name on it.

"This is your future, now you're twenty-one," his dad said. "I was given this by my father on my twenty-first and now I'm passing it onto you. This, Mark is a gift, in fact the gift. The gift of time travel. And you are going to be a star with it!"

"Time travel!" Mark scoffed. "Utter bollocks," he said, dismissing the box and instead applying himself to his sausages.

"You may think so," his father said. "But you have a job to do. This box will give you the future that you don't have at the moment. A future of music, of a huge recording contract, of purpose in life."

Mark ate a piece of fried egg. It tasted a lot of garlic. His mum often said you could never be too careful and always loaded everything with too much garlic. And would leave cutlery on the table crossed over like a crucifix. Mark swallowed the egg and continued speaking. "But I can't sing. And I can't play anything."

"Oh you can, you did once, and you will. You just have a few lessons from me and a job to do."

"And what job is that?" Mark asked with little interest.

"You need to go back to 1973 and stop some tosser

killing a seagull."

"Well," Mark said laughing at the randomness and inanity of such a mission, "when you put it like that how could I refuse?"

He went back to his breakfast, looking back up at his father a few moments later.

"You're not serious?" Mark said studying his father's eyes. "There's no such thing as time travel."

"Some people in a different universe from this," his father replied, "don't believe in vampires. It's all a matter of perspective, son."

Mark's father got up from the tables, placed his hands in the pockets of his jeans and cleared his throat. "Now, finish up your breakfast. I have lessons to teach and you have a world to save..."

The Psychedelic Gnome Project (PGP)

By J. McGraw

Anchor - Good evening. This is the 10 o'clock news. With me tonight is Josephine McGraw, spokeswoman for Sci-lutions, the company behind what has been dubbed the 'Psychedelic Gnome Project'. Good evening, Ms McGraw.

McGraw - Good evening.

Anchor - To start with, could you explain to us what your company does?

McGraw - Of course. Well, Sci-lutions is a scientific solutions company. We specialise in providing innovative, outside-the-box solutions to companies with problems they are struggling to resolve. We tackle these problems from a scientific viewpoint, rather than an economic or human resources one, and we've seen a huge surge in popularity in the last year or so. Employees are becoming tired of the same old tricks employers have always used to try and motivate and inspire them, or to raise sales, or to cut budgets. Business jargon is slowly morphing into an endless list of swear words, so employers are trying to interact with their employees in new ways. That is the premise that Sci-lutions was set up under, and I think we've shown that there's a huge demand for solutions like ours.

Anchor - So tell me about the Psychedelic Gnome Project. Was that one of your solutions?

McGraw - It was an attempt at population modelling. We were approached by Eco-gro-mics to look into the problems of population dynamics, which is currently modelled digitally by them. As with any computer program, it can only provide results based on what information has been put in, and while the modelling systems get more representative the more information is inputted, they always fall somewhat short of the mark. Humans are complicated things, and a computer can't keep up with that. Eco-gro-mics wanted us to look into other ways of modelling population dynamics.

Anchor - And that's where these 'gnomes' came from?

McGraw - I don't particularly like that name for them. We call them proxies, because that's what they are – they're non-sentient creatures that mimic basic human nature. They're quick to grow, have a short lifespan, and can be put into whatever situation is needed to model human reactions in the real world.

Anchor - They're very small people that you've grown in a lab?

McGraw - Non-sentient creatures. Lab rats, essentially, but better at representing human behaviour.

Anchor - And the colours?

McGraw - That was twofold. The main reason was as part of the population modelling system. We had groups of proxies that were all one colour, almost isolated for each other, but with the potential to interact if they wished. The bright colours let us monitor the level of mixing and migration patterns. The colours also help to monitor interbreeding – they were genetically designed to form patches of colour, rather than merging. That way, if a red proxy and a blue proxy mated, their offspring would have red and blue patches rather than purple. With the lifespan of the proxies, we'd have quickly been faced with a population of brown proxies, regardless of their ancestry, and that would have made things very complicated. But we're several generations in now, and the colours are starting to show some very interesting patterns. I can understand why they've been called psychedelic.

Anchor - You said there were two reasons.

McGraw - Yes. The second reason was purely practical. If they were bright colours, they'd be easier to spot in the event of a breach.

Anchor - But they breached anyway.

McGraw - [Pause] They did. Any sort of colour wouldn't have helped there – the breach was massive, we could hardly fail to spot them leaving.

Anchor - So you saw that they were escaping, but they still managed to make it all the way out of your facility and into the city? Were there no failsafes in place?

McGraw - There were failsafe mechanisms. They [Pause] failed. We have a team looking into why that happened, and fixing it so that once we have rounded the proxies up, we will have a safe place to keep them.

Anchor - Does that mean you intend to continue with the experiment, despite this catastrophe?

McGraw - Catastrophe is a strong word.

Anchor - They have infested the city.

McGraw - In the same way that mice and rats have, except with less ability to breed out of control.

Anchor - So you think they can be rounded up and returned to your facility?

McGraw - I believe they can, yes. We have experts working on that as we speak. The proxies, as I've said, are designed to mimic human behaviour, so we're using that to inform our clean-up effort.

Anchor - How so?

McGraw - One of the methods is free food. It won't help that there is plenty of food available in the city, even for the majority of proxies that won't eat from the rubbish, but we're working with restaurants, supermarkets, and similar places to make sure their food supplies are well protected.

Anchor - We've been hearing reports that these proxies are proving dangerous to small animals and, potentially, small children.

McGraw - Well, they're acting like people. Even small animals are extremely large when you're only 10 centimetres tall. The proxies are afraid, and they're doing what people do when they're afraid - fighting. But there have been no reports about children being harmed. As long as people take sensible precautions, they'll be fine.

Anchor - What precautions do you recommend?

McGraw - Blocking up holes under doors and skirting boards, as a first move. Anywhere a mouse could get in. Even though proxies are larger and less flexible than mice, they're also smarter. If there's a small hole they want to get through, they'll try and make it larger. But if there's no hole, there'll be no reason for them to stop and investigate.

Anchor - Just how smart are these proxies?

McGraw - Not human smart, not quite. We were interested in basic human behaviours, and these get modified through education, so they are more or less uneducated. But they're smarter than any other animal they'll come up against in the city, including rats, and the longer they're exposed to an environment, the better adapted to it they'll become. Right now they're still learning about the city, so this is the best time to catch them. I'd like to ask everyone, if they see a containment unit operating, to follow instructions and help us clean up as quickly and painlessly as possible. The sooner we round the proxies up, the less of a problem they'll be.

Anchor - What happens if you can't round them all up? They're very small, and the city is very large. You surely won't be able to check everywhere.

McGraw - We don't need to. Proxies run in groups, just like people do when they feel threatened. We just need to find the main population centres and deal with those.

Anchor - How many proxies do you believe to be loose right now?

McGraw - There were just under 2,000 in the modelling system when they broke out, and we contained around a quarter of those. Of the three-quarters that breached containment, there were five main population groups – however, with the upheaval they're going through, it's been predicted that these five groups will split, with some proxies stepping up as new group alphas, and old alphas losing support from their groups. We can't be completely sure how many population centres to expect in the city, but current thinking puts the number at no more than ten.

Anchor - And the lifespan of the proxies? You said it was short, and if that's true then they'll multiply faster than humans. How soon until the numbers begin to increase?

McGraw - We expect the population to remain fairly stable for a few weeks. There will be births, but they are learning to survive in a more hostile world than they have been used to, so there will also be a high number of deaths. After a month or so, we might begin to see a slight rise, but by then we should have the majority of them rounded up, so any rise will be negligible.

Anchor - Do you believe you can ever remove every proxy from the city?

McGraw - We won't need to. Proxies aren't like mice, where if you miss a couple you return to original population levels very quickly. Proxies only have one or two young at a time, so they can't repopulate very quickly. Small groups are more conservative, since they don't have the numbers to take risks, meaning they'll be less of a threat to us and our pets. They're also more at risk of predators like cats and foxes, so once we remove the large groups, the small groups will be more vulnerable and will be taken care of by our own local wildlife. We will, obviously, remain on alert for a long time after the clean-up finishes, in case there are any population flares, but we expect the main problem to be sorted by the end of the month, and any isolated populations to be gone by within a year.

Anchor - Finally, what should people do if they become aware of these proxies in their homes?

McGraw - We have a helpline for reports of sightings. They will give you advice on how to deal with it, and if it's a large sighting, they'll come out to investigate. But every report goes on a map, and this is how we're going to plot exactly where our population centres are. So please, please, call the hotline if you see any proxies, even if it's only one running across a road. Every report will help. And remember, they're more scared of you than you are of them. Scared people will run first, and if they can't run, they'll fight, so don't try and catch them, just given them a clear run to an exit and chase them away. Let us do the catching.

Anchor - Thank you, Ms McGraw.

The Psychedelic Gnome Project

By Lauren K. Nixon

This is the story of
How we ended up knee-deep in
Electrified, rainbow-coloured gnomes.

President of the Science Club,
Silly old Silas Slim, a mediocre man
Yearning for a Nobel Prize
Caused a catastrophe from which none of us could hide.
Handling his devilish dyes one day
Evolved an idea that would not go away.
Delighted, he declared his intent to make free
Energy for all, in a pocket sized package,
Light on its feet and easy to see.
Instead of erring on the side of
Caution, this fool forged ahead.

Getting his first shipment of
Norwegian gnomes, Silas dipped each
One in dye to increase their appeal, and
Mixed these specimens with
Electric eels.

Playing God never ends well, and Silas
Realised that, as time would tell; his gnomes had flaws,

Or were a mite too efficient, and got out of the lab's door.

Jolly though they are, while they're

Eating all of our food and being quite rude, we really must object as they

Cause shock after shock – thanks to Silas and his

Terrible Psychedelic Gnome Project!

The Psychedelic Gnome Project

By Louise D. Smith

"We have to pull the plug. That's ten confirmed kills in the last three hours."

The atmosphere in the highly secret EHSA control room was tense, but that was normal. The last ten years had spawned such a large number of alphabet agencies that even Ronald Reagan would have struggled to keep track of them all. All of the agencies were busier now than ever before, with the election of President Trump. The threats of ISIS, Al Qaeda and rogue jihadists paled into insignificance by the threats to the Potus. Never before had a president been in such danger of assassination from both inside and outside America, and from such a wide range of society. Park rangers, scientists, minority groups and the so-called 'liberal snowflakes' were using their skills, connections and a lack of established monitoring to organise deliveries of aggressive but beautiful spiders, eau de toilettes that were targeted to poison only those with a greater than 99.5% similarity to the President, and shirts of the finest weaving and cut that also happened to be laced with everything from itching powder to a substance that the lab were still trying to identify, but appeared to react with melanin in the skin to convert it to acid that very effectively caused third-degree burns.

EHSA, the Experimental Homeland Security Agency, were one such agency tasked with defending the President from his own people. Their primary purpose was to develop, test and develop procedures for the use of new technology to defend the Fatherland. Unofficially, they were an intelligence agency with full authority to act on American soil; from observation, electronic monitoring and net surveillance all the way through to the assassination of American citizens on home soil. These latter instances were not 'black ops' or 'deniable acts', but part of the day-to-day business of the organisation, with an average of ten actions per week, with a 98% success rate. Needless to say it was critical to the administration that the public never learned of the existence of the EHSA, and an entire department of the agency was dedicated to ensuring that they didn't.

Today's problem, however, was not one of information control, it was a full blown emergency. One of the agency's most promising technologies had developed a fault, and one that couldn't be ignored, unlike the minor issue with the stealth drones attracting bats, or the unfortunate issue with the underwater camera that emitted a tone that dissolved the brains of fish. Today's problem was with the psychedelic gnomes. And what, may you ask, are psychedelic gnomes? Their designer would tell you they are the future of espionage. The Director would have tell you they were a very cost-effective solution in a challenging financial and budgetary situation. But right now, Supervisory Agent Kris Marsden, presently in charge of the control room, would describe them as a logistical nightmare.

"I agree."

Kris sighed.

"Get me the Director and send the shutdown command to all units. I want confirmation that every unit is shutdown."

A junior agent ran to Kris' side, carrying a huge blue sat' phone in his outstretched hands. "The Director, sir," he panted.

Kris took the sat' phone and nodded thanks at the junior agent.

"Director, this is Supervisory Agent Kris Marsden."

"Tell me what's going on, Kris."

"It's the psychedelic gnomes sir; they're carrying out terminations without instruction. We have ten confirmed kills in the last three hours and are currently seeking confirmation of nearly a dozen more."

"Dammit! You're sure we've not got a rat in the chicken coop?"

"Yes sir. After we had three confirmed kills I had all

units cleared of termination orders and all authorisations moved to my codes. We recorded live footage of a termination of a soccer mom returning from the grocery store with no orders present on the unit."

"Damn! Damn! Damn! Shut them down. I'll roast the programmer to get to the bottom of why. Maybe he can do something to sort it out."

"I have given the order to shut the units down. I'm awaiting confirmation that they have all been neutralised."

"Good man! Keep me updated."

The phone clicked as the Director closed the call. Kris looked for the junior agent who had brought the sat phone to him, and the movement prompted him to appear at Kris' elbow.

"Sir?"

"Thank you, Mahoney."

Kris turned back to the screen wall, eyes darting over each section, seeking out any situational changes that had occurred during his call.

"Report," Kris commanded, firm and clear.

"The units are not responding; we've had a few confirmations of shutdown but CCTV access covering the units that have confirmed are still showing the units as active."

"What?"

"We are tracking six units that have reported as shutdown, but surveillance are still showing the units are moving, presumably toward their termination targets."

"Send the shutdown command again!"

"We can't, sir. The system registers the unit as shutdown and won't resubmit."

"Flip the kill switch. Terminate the units permanently."

"Yes, sir."

Kris heard the stages that were required for that

instruction echo and bounce around the room, the team responding to his command without question or argument. He'd worked hard to make it to the position of Supervisory Agent just after his thirtieth birthday; it meant he had to be prepared to make the tough calls, but permanently destroying six multimillion dollar espionage units was going to draw him into a review, and that was something he could have done without. Not to mention the long- term impact that a review could have on his career. Ironic really, that his career could be over because of a few psychedelic gnomes. More than that; he'd never be able to tell anyone why. Kris' mind drifted back to the first briefing he'd had about the psychedelic gnomes.

"We present to you the SAIAO Unit; known affectionately as a psychedelic gnome. It is the future or espionage and assassination technology, with Smart Artificial Intelligence enabling the unit to make decisions in order to achieve the objectives assigned to it, as well as identifying and responding to threats autonomously. It has full HD recording capability and 360 degree sound pick up for 100m. It can transmit this information for analysis, as well as carrying out its own, independent analysis in order to respond appropriately to the situation. It has both the ability to incapacitate and terminate, in addition to its observation capabilities.

It can move at up to five miles per hour and has proximity sensors to ensure it is not detected in motion. It has a fully functional chameleon circuit in order to camouflage itself in any environment."

"No response from the units, sir."

"Try again."

"We've tried three times, sir."

Kris looked around him, seeing every pair of eyes focused on him, looking for the answers that he was there to give. But he didn't have any. Every option he had had been taken. Except one.

"Get me the Chief of the National Guard."

*

"You're seriously telling me I need to send my men to smash gnomes?"

"Smash or shoot, yes sir."

"And that I need to issue black lights to my men to look for psychedelic patterns on the gnomes before they shoot them."

"That's right."

"And what did you say your clearance code was?"

The conversation with the Chief had gone badly. Not as badly as it could have, but still badly. Kris had us every skill in his arsenal to explain and persuade the Chief to deploy the National Guard to carry out a nationwide seek and destroy mission using the last known locations of the psychedelic gnomes and the updated locations of the few that were still transmitting camera feeds, but to no avail. The Chief didn't believe that the EHSA existed and even Kris' clearance code wouldn't convince him, as for the purposes of security his role was listed as 'IT technician', in possession of high level clearance, but not in any way linked to live actions and technology that could go rogue.

The Director was unreachable, presumably too busy 'roasting' the programmer, which left Kris the highest ranked member of the organisation, but that wasn't enough.

"Humour me, sir. Why would I lie about this?"

"I don't know! A bet, probably one you lost. Or maybe that code isn't yours at all."

"You've confirmed my voice print! People are dying! You have to release your men to me!"

"Two squads. You can have two squads. If they find anything then I'll turn my men over to your command. If they don't, I'll see you in front of a court martial."

*

"Moving in, control. We have reached the coordinates. Beginning black light scan."

"INCOMING FIRE! Take cover!"

"Control, we are under heavy fire"

"It's a gnome, a god-damn gnome!"

"Look at it, just look at the colours..."

"Unit four to control. I have a psychedelic gnome in my sights. Taking the shot!"

THE
EXIT
is everything

First Waters

By Rae Bailey

fields grow water

as marigold

bog myrtle sprout

as child runs from

bloom to bloom

bubble to bubble

mud and clear water

pick a heading

well

draw it drink it dip it dress it

tap

pipe it pump it pour it

divert

bottle it brag it buy it

all packaging flows to the sea

bubbles burst

a killing bloom

The Exit is Everything
'The Final Act'

By Hailie Drescher

Take a bow,
Dance it off.
Forget that fall from last act.

It's gone, it's done,
You're not foolin' anyone.
I know your hurt,
I know your sad,

But don't let that,
Be your last act.

Get back up,
Dust yourself off.
Because, my friend,
It's not how you start,
Nor how you carry on,

It's how you end.
It's how you take that final bow.
It's how you reach,
That final act.

The Exit is Everything

By Mike Farren

It was well understood that everything in Samuel's world was arranged according to Samuel's rules. It was mostly well understood, but when the caprices of an individual are the law, there is always room for misunderstanding, as five ex-wives, a number of discarded lovers and business associates, and any friend who had ever called him Sam (or, God forbid, Sammy) could testify.

Samuel had inherited a small, modestly successful local retail business from his father and had turned it into a national concern without ever feeling the inclination to take it to market. The need to retain day-to-day control was stronger in him than the desire for the potential rewards and the divestment of responsibility that going public would have brought him. He was rich, anyway. He was successful, he was admired; he had control.

However much he might, from time to time, feel invincible, there were of course occasional immovable objects that not even his will could shift. One of his strengths in business was that, in the face of such obstacles, he would acknowledge the inevitable, but then ensure that the outcome would enable him to take control afresh on his own terms. Outbid for the purchase of a regional group of shops, he turned his attention to the supply chain, ending up with such a dominance in the region that the rival company was eventually obliged to sell to him for less than the asking price.

It was, therefore, a shock when he announced that he would be stepping down from running the business at the age of just fifty-seven. Typically, he by-passed his children and handed the business over to a trusted assistant with no claim of blood, but a kindred spirit in terms of ruthless single-mindedness.

Informed observers muttered that there had to be more to it, but only Elisabeth, the private secretary who had served him for a quarter of a century, would ever truly know. "The exit is everything," Samuel told her, as he laid out his plans to remain in control of his life, his legacy, and the wasting disease that would have made him helpless and dependent on others, long before it killed him.

In truth, even Samuel's resources would have been stretched, had he attempted both to run the business and to arrange his own exit at the same time. Outsmarting death, he realised, would be a full time occupation, even with Elisabeth's help.

Of course, someone in Samuel's position had built up intricate networks of obligation and was still able to call in favours, or to grease palms when obligation wasn't enough. But he was breaking the law, and though he wouldn't be around to suffer the consequences, he had to be sure that no one could be charged with abetting his suicide. Messages were encrypted, proxy servers deployed then discarded, paper trails incinerated after shredding, money deposited in offshore accounts and trusted middle-persons hired untraceably, via word of mouth. There would be nothing to incriminate Elisabeth, or any other associate.

By the time the plans were in place, Samuel could already feel his motor functions becoming less reliable. Where he was losing control over his life, he was strengthening it over his death. It was the only form of compromise he could tolerate.

Even Samuel felt a touch of loneliness as he closed up his city penthouse for the last time, with no one to see him off. None of his ex-wives were still in touch, other than through solicitors. The children were studying, travelling or on internships with blue chip companies. And since the diagnosis, he hadn't wanted to expose his failing body to the scrutiny of an affair. He had even packed Elisabeth off to the Caribbean a week earlier, to place her even further beyond suspicion.

The car that arrived for him was from a luxurious but anonymous limousine company, the driver smart, but not uniformed; respectful, but not servile. Samuel sat in silence in the comfortable ambience of the Mercedes' leather-upholstered interior.

He was clearing his mind to assert his self-control, when he became aware of loud crash, followed by the plangent sound of an alarm, immediately behind him.

"Jesus, the poor bastard had no chance!" said the driver, his professional manner shocked out of him for a moment. Samuel turned to look at the lorry that had failed to stop at the junction and crumpled Golf that had been in its path. "Half a second later, that would've been us."

Samuel felt an involuntary shiver run down his spine. He realised his fists and jaw were clenched, his shoulders hunched. He took a breath, then began the exercises he needed to bring his body back under control.

However, the complexity of the city's traffic meant that, even though they were ahead of the accident, its effects outran them, slowing down their progress to the point where making the flight was looking dubious. In the end, it took not only a hefty financial inducement, but also all the driver's knowledge (and skill in passing down side-streets and alleyways never designed for a Mercedes) to get them to the airport in time. In fact, there were a few minutes to spare, and before he left home soil, he reckoned he could manage a final bacon sandwich. He walked up to the concession on the terminal food court, to find the shutters being pulled down.

"Health and safety, mate," said the harassed looking manager. "No - a really dodgy batch of bacon. There's a couple of people in hospital and it's not looking good. Could have been you if you'd been here yesterday.

After the exchange, there was no time to go elsewhere before he had to head to the security line. The priority queue was clear, but as his boarding card was inspected, there was something about the way the attendant said, "Geneva, eh?" that put him on the defensive. He wondered if, somehow, his plans had been divined. "Yes," he shot back, more aggressively than might have been necessary, "what about it?"

Clearly recollecting that he was looking after the priority queue, and that it didn't do to upset the clientele, the attendant was immediately apologetic. Leaning in close and dropping his voice, he said, "Look, you didn't hear it from me, but they nabbed a shoe bomber off that flight just half an hour ago. It was one of my mates doing the checks. If he'd got onto the flight... well!"

The flight was busy in economy, but in business class, Samuel was pleased to find he had a double seat to himself. He wanted to clear his mind and approach his planned death with calmness and control, but the brushes with unplanned death had shaken him. He was exercising all of his self-discipline to bring himself round, consoling himself with the fact that it would soon all be over, exactly to his instructions, when he was thrown off balance once again by the arrival of a late passenger, who was ushered into the seat right next to him. His companion took his seat in silence, and Samuel made no attempt to acknowledge him.

Samuel's mind was now set on a whiskey, which, as a holder of the highest elite club membership, was delivered to him as soon as the seatbelt sign was switched off, well before the trolley was due on its rounds. It was a perverse pleasure of impending death that there was no longer a need to worry about alcohol or diet. He had never smoked, but almost wished for a cigarette at that moment, to celebrate this freedom.

Luxuriating for a moment in his recovered equilibrium, he went to reach again for his whiskey, but found that he could barely move his arm. Feeling baffled, he turned to his previously unacknowledged neighbour, desperately wanting to ask him to help, but the words would not come out, and he could only make an inarticulate noise. The portly neighbour looked at him, looked at the drink, then shook his head and turned away in apparent disgust.

Suddenly, Samuel had the utter conviction that he was suffering a stroke, suddenly losing control of his body in a way he had dreaded when he had expected to take months or years. He knew he had to attract someone's attention fast, but there were no attendants to hand. With a prodigious effort, he attempted to swivel in his seat, back toward the neighbour, but he was now unable to move, unable to turn away from looking straight out of the cabin window, where he was surprised to find himself looking at a peculiar cloud that seemed almost the shape of a skull, grinning triumphantly back at him.

The Exit is Everything

By J. A. Foley

Now a shadow looms,
Lost within the memories,
A country fallen.

The Exit is Everything

By Philip Lickley

Suzy's eyes flickered open, a simple act that seemed painful, as if it hadn't been done in a long time, or perhaps ever at all. The light in the room hit her pupils and she recoiled with pain at the brightness – or at least she would have recoiled if her muscles were working. Instead, she sort of just pushed her head back and blinked a few times until her eyes became accustomed to the light and she could look around the room she found herself in.

Not that there was much to really take in. The room was just a large, six-sided box of white, metallic walls, on which there was nothing particularly of note. There were no, say, holes where pins had once been hammered in to hold photo frames or memories. There were no windows, no door, as far as she could make out, and certainly nothing as visually stimulating as shelves, or a television, or even a rug. To all intents and purposes, the room was empty apart from one thing: Suzy.

In fact, to Suzy, nothing seemed entirely certain to her any more. She didn't even remember her name. She felt like a Suzy, so this seemed like the best bet, at least as a starting point. From her position on the floor, she struggled to recollect something – anything – from her life to this point. Who was she? What did she enjoy? What was her favourite movie? Her favourite musician? How did she get into this room in the first place? There was no visible door so how did she enter it? Had it been built around her, like some sort of giant metallic Ikea flat pack? Suzy couldn't even remember if she'd even been to Ikea – but she could remember that a place called Ikea existed, and that it sold mostly furniture.

Slowly, and with gasps of pain at the stiffness in her muscles, Suzy slowly got herself up into a crouching position and from there to standing. The room was just tall enough for her frame to stand upright. She looked around, walked the length and width of the space, and even tapped along the walls to try and see if there was anything hollow behind them, but nothing seemed to indicate any means of escape. The only thing she did discover, through gently running her fingers up and down each wall, was a faint crack along the wall opposite to where she had woken up that suggested, ever so slightly, that there could be a means of escape there. Even so, there was there was no obvious way of activating it as the line, thin as it is was, was flush with the surface and Suzy could not get any of her nails into it, nor discover any switches, buttons, levers, or hidden activator on the floor that would spring it open. To all intents and purposes, Suzy was trapped and that with realisation a sickly feeling began to spread through her stomach. Nervous now, she felt queasy and ill. Questions started firing through her mind like shots across a pool table.

How do I get food? Where do I go to the toilet? How do I quench my thirst? Is there enough space in here to exercise? Will I be joined by anyone, so I don't go mad with loneliness? How do I get out?

As these thoughts began to overpower her, Suzy felt light-headed and dropped onto her knees, yawning loudly and falling back onto the floor. Helplessly, she lapsed into unconsciousness, powerless to resist the insatiable urge to fall asleep that took over every particle of her body until she remembered nothing but chaotic, vivid dreams.

The next moment Suzy was conscious was as painful as her first, though in a different way. She was rudely awoken by a loud noise, but noise was hardly apt to describe it. It seared through her head like fire: a ringing alarm, like a cross between an air-raid siren and a fire alarm. Her eyes flew open in shock, the sudden movement of ill-used muscles causing her to yelp with pain. Her eyes took a few moments to focus on the room and she blinked several times to try to assess where she was, turning over onto her back and looking up. She couldn't tell where the sound was coming from and to the best of her knowledge there were no holes in the ceiling for speakers. It was at this point she questioned how the room was lit. It seemed that the ceiling was illuminated in its entirety, rather than there being individual spotlights, which made no sense to her. After a few moments of the alarm ringing, it was replaced by words that echoed around the space like announcements at a train station.

"The exit is everything," said a male voice with no particular accent. There were ten seconds of silence, then the words were repeated. "The exit is everything," it said, in the same voice, at the same speed and with the same intonation.

It must be a recording, Suzy thought.

These four words were repeated every ten seconds in a rhythmically uniform fashion. It was after about the fifth time that it annoyed her enough to get her to sit up. That was when she realised that where the wall had been at the other end of the white room, there was now an open space, a large black void of nothingness. Just as the room she was in was bright white, so this space appeared to be entirely black, as if all the colour had been sucked out of it. Sensing freedom, Suzy got gently into a standing position and began walking towards it, awkwardly at first, but soon picking up the rhythm of walking, as if she was a young deer learning to move for the first time. But she wasn't quick enough and when she was halfway along the room the void began to get smaller as the furthest white wall started to return, like a door closing from the top and bottom, eventually meeting in the middle and sealing her back in. The whole operation took a matter of seconds and was complete before she was anywhere near reaching it, even though she sped up.

Suzy hit the wall with her fist as she realised she'd missed the escape, the only evidence of the hole now the thin line running across. As the door closed the alarm sounds and repeated announcements ceased and the room was once more silent and still. Suzy sighed, turned and walked back to her first position, sitting down on the floor and studying the furthest wall from a distance. It was now she noticed another change in the room. To her right, a piece of slate and a small chunky stick of chalk had appeared. She looked around. Had someone visited her during the night and brought her this? Suzy picked up the slate, turning it over in her hands, and then did the same with the chalk. There was nothing unusual about them that she could see.

With the feeling of exhaustion once more coming over her, she decided to mark down today as her second day, assuming that each time she awoke was a new day – her wakefulness felt so brief, there was absolutely no sense of passing time in this space, and Suzy wasn't wearing a watch – before the sense of tiredness completely overwhelmed her.

The next day, if that is indeed what it was, Suzy was once more woken up by the sound of alarms and the same voice repeating the message. This time she opened her eyes more gently and got to her feet more carefully, and walked towards the door with more urgency, but again struggled to get anywhere near it by the time it snapped shut. Again, she tried to open it via the thin line and again she failed, once more walking back to where she started and ticking off another day on the blackboard.

This continued for weeks. Each day she would be awoken by the alarm and the voice repeating the words 'The Exit is Everything' every ten seconds, like clockwork. Each day she would fail to reach it and she'd stumble back to her first position and mark off the day before falling unconscious again not long after. But there was progress. Each day she could open her eyes more quickly, get to her feet more easily, get a fraction closer to the door, and stay awake a little longer, and it was this progress that was keeping her motivated to continue, even though the slight improvements were painfully slow. By the time she'd ticked off one hundred little marks on her blackboard it didn't truly feel like she was really anywhere nearer to her goal than she had been the first time she'd seen the door open, and Suzy was starting to get a little disheartened.

As the 120th day passed she began to feel resentment towards the daily challenge, like the room – or whatever God was controlling it – was testing her, and she began to refuse to play its game. On the 122nd day she didn't bother even going for the door and it closed even without her moving anywhere near it. She still fell asleep all the same. On day 125 she tried creeping along the floor towards the door but it made no difference. On day 131 she stayed by the door and let sleep take over her body, theorising that she'd wake up nearer the door and have enough time to get through, but when she woke up she was instead back in her normal position. She tried this every day for a week but the outcome was always the same.

On day 144 she tried to continuously run around the room to keep awake, but to no avail; she fell asleep all the same, this time collapsing mid-run, feeling herself hit the floor as unconsciousness took over her body. Nothing Suzy did seemed to make a difference to the pattern of being woken by the alarm and the voice, running for the door, marking down another day and falling asleep. It was a boring routine and getting more tedious by the day. By day 200 the tedium had worn her down; reaching that number, despite representing a huge milestone, felt no different to the 199 brief spans of wakefulness that had come before it. Suzy was bored and she had no inclination to celebrate the mile-stone.

Each day she continued to get that little bit nearer and stay conscious that little bit longer, and though looking back to day one she felt her progress was considerable there was no real sign of her getting to the door any time soon. Plus, she'd started questioning things. How was she still alive? She never ate anything or drank anything. There was no evidence anyone was feeding her whilst she was asleep; no marks on her skin where they could be injecting her with some sort of cocktail that would keep her body functioning.

She couldn't remember ever feeling the need to go to the toilet, either. In fact, aside from the desire to exit the room she seemed to have no desires at all that needed fulfilling. Suzy studied her body, running her fingers down her chest and her legs, and that's when, on day 221, she fully comprehend her clothing as if it was the first time she really had noticed them. The t-shirt and shorts she was wearing were as white as the room and entirely clean. She was pretty sure she'd not been re-dressed at any point so why were her clothes not dirty or stained, creased or sweaty? Under her shorts were a pair of knickers, under her shirt a well-fitted bra, and both of these were just as clean. Her last thought as she drifted off into day 222 was that none of this made sense.

Day 222 arrived with yet more alarms and more droning repeats of the phrase, and though she was much quicker to the door, her attempt was still too poor and all she could do was mark off another day with a chalk mark and sit down, contemplating her existence. Annoyed, she wondered if this was it and her whole life would be marked like this, imprisoned in a white box with nothing to do, no reason to continue, but no obvious way of escape, either by physically leaving the room, or by ending her life within it. She considered that she was surviving without eating or drinking, so perhaps she was immortal, trapped in some sort of hell, from which there was no escape. This question was still floating around her head as she lost consciousness and fell once more into a deep sleep.

Everything continued in the same pattern for the next two weeks, and only on day 242 did anything happen that was different from the norm. As always, Suzy was woken by the alarms and the voice declaring in its usual precise, flat tone, "The Exit is Everything." But this time, there was something more unusual. The door seemed wider and as Suzy walked towards it, with no particular enthusiasm, she felt herself pushed by an invisible force towards it, as if it was willing her to escape. For the first time ever, she reached the door and pushed herself out into the black void. Smiling with relief, ready for anything now there would be something different to look forward to, Suzy followed the sound of a distant voice.

*

"Oh I can't bloody well do this," Suzy complained, throwing her science text book across her bedroom, the hefty tome hitting the wall with such force she was sure it had chipped some of the plasterwork. Emily, Suzy's best friend, who was lying next to her on the bed, put her arm around her shoulders, comfortingly.

"You'll be fine," said Emily. "You've got this. You're the best in the class. You'll walk it. You're just making more of it than you should be."

Suzy nodded, sitting up on the bed and letting her legs dangle over the edge. She studied the posters on her walls, the wooden wardrobe in the corner and the dressing table with mirror under the window. Revising for her exams was having a big impact on Suzy. She was a perfectionist and didn't want to let herself, her class or her parents down. She was beyond stressed. A lot of it was down to self-inflicted pressure, but that was just the way she was.

"Sometimes," she muttered to herself, "I wonder if it's worth going on..."

Emily sat upright as if someone had just set fire to her trousers. "Suzy!" she said with an anger she'd not heard from her before. "Never say anything like that. It's only a bloody exam and not worth saying things like that. Not even in jest."

"Sorry," Suzy, standing up and stretching.

"Life is a gift," Emily continued. "And not to be thrown away. It's not just about exams and studying and bloody GCSEs. It's about living. About the small moments. About family, about friends, about smelling the flowers. About smiles and singing. And kissing, and falling in love. About watching the seasons come and ago. About –"

"Okay," Suzy interrupted. "I get it. We're studying for biology, not some poetry exam."

"I like poetry!" Emily joked. "But I'm serious. You'd do well to get your head out of a text book at times and live a little. When was the last time you went out and got a little drunk? Or went to the cinema? Or read a book that wasn't on cell reproduction? I hear Tom would be interested in maybe taking you out to the cinema at some point..."

"Really?" Suzy said, blushing slightly, before dismissing the thought. "Nah. I'm too busy. Once the exam is over, then I'll go and speak to him."

"Yeah," Emily said, adopting a tone tinged with sarcasm. "Then there'll be something else; preparing for A-Levels, planning for university, cleaning your room. These are all important Suzy but for heaven's sake, live a little. As my gran used to say, 'the exit is everything'."

Suzy paused for a moment. "What did you say?" she asked.

"Erm," Emily said, recalling her last words. "As my gran used to say, 'the exit is everything'."

"What? Like how you die? Like going out with a bang? I don't think that's quite what I meant..."

"No, not like that," Emily laughed. "Though my gran did spend her last few days saying she wanted to learn to drive a racing car, so maybe she did have a plan to do that. She didn't mean our exit from this life, she was referring to our exit into this one."

"Like what? When we were born?"

"Yeah," Emily said, smiling. "The exit from our mothers into this world. Life is a rare thing, an opportunity to do something incredible, even if it is for a limited time. That exit into this world is everything. My gran used to say, 'Emily – grab life by the balls and just do whatever makes you happy'. She was quite bohemian, my grandmother. I think she was a bit of a hippy in the sixties."

Suzy looked confused. "That reminded me of something from when I was really young," she said. Reaching over, she picked up her weighty biology textbook and flicked to the section marked in orange, on child development.

Emily smiled.

"That's more like the Suzy I know, going to the pages with the rude pictures."

Suzy gave her best friend a sarcastic smile. "I'm not looking at the pictures of bloody fallopian tubes, or whatever. I'm looking at memories. Here it is. Very few children can remember anything from before they were two years old, and sometimes up until they are four. But that's correct. I can remember something from when I was very young, perhaps even before I was born."

"I think that's impossible," Emily said. "The brain isn't fully formed until late on in the cycle - and surely remembering life in the womb would be like recalling a horror movie. To be honest, I'm not sure if I really want to think about it, never mind recall it."

"Well, maybe it was my brain making sense of the experience, looking back. I remember being in a white room and there was a door to escape through, and an alarm and that phrase. The exit is everything. Over and over again."

Emily laughed. "It must have been a dream. A weird one, but certainly a dream."

"Possibly," Suzy considered. "Or maybe it was my brain trying to give me an early message to live by. That the exit is everything; that life is everything. That we have to live it as best we could."

"Fuck me," Emily said, sitting up on the bed. "We've got from biology, to poetry, to child development, to philosophy. I feel like Plato over here."

"Shall we go out?" Suzy asked, studying herself in the mirror and tidying up her top.

"The library?" Emily sighed, stretching.

"No," Suzy said. "The pub. I think it's time for some

shots. The biology can wait. We bloody well know most of it anyway."

Emily smiled. "That's the best thing you've said all day."

"After all, the exit is everything."

"And where is the exit, in this case?"

"It's firstly there," she said, pointing to her bedroom door, "And then at the bottom of the stairs, and it's just before the entrance to the pub."

"Well then lead the way and I'll follow you through any exit you want!"

Suzy smiled as they left the room and headed for an evening out. There would be time later for revision. But now was the time to live.

The Exit is Everything

By M. Loftouse

Today is the day. I will do this. I can do this!

The air is thicker than normal today, but it is just another day, another move and yet another dark world. I am beginning to grow tired of it and it doesn't help that my family and others feel it is just another routine, but enough is enough. I have to leave; this place is dragging me down and I can't take it anymore.

It's not like I haven't tried to talk about it. Nay, I have. I've told my parents, my brothers, my sisters and my friends all about my plans. My plan to leave this place, to journey on to another world some dared never speak of. Dark, terrible and evil, some called it, but none of them had ever gone beyond the turn of their street.

"Madness", my father said. "Utter rubbish, why would you even think of going there?"

I haven't seen him for three days. As for mother, I tried reasoning with her for a day, but she now appears to act as if the conversation never happened.

"Mother, I wish to go there, to explore the wonders. Don't you want to know what lies ahead?" I ask, pleading with her.

"Dear, have you tried this carrot cake I made? It's delicious," she beams, her eyes brimming with the hope that I will drop the subject, and I, hopeless, do. Months pass by between askings and each time I try a different speech. Some days are better, calmer, when the ground stays still and the roof does not quiver and shake. Other days drown all my dreams, so much so that even I am frightened of the plan. Our leader always asks us to listen, to hear the sounds above and beyond. I always think the idea was preposterous; big ears don't mean you have to focus on hearing all the time and forget the rest. As if the only thing left is the sound of impending doom.

I am kicked out of the meeting tonight, left to find

my own way back home. There is scanty light in the interwoven streets and I have never thought of memorizing the paths, never paid much attention to it. Schools always teach that. The first thing a young one has to learn is the street ways. Of course, many get lost, one way or another, but we still carry on; the streets have to lead somewhere, the kids excitedly say, but it is the end of street that no one is allowed to go to. There are rumours of those who ventured there but never returned. They say there is light at the end of it. Light unlike the dull glow of the other streets.

I want that light. I yearn for it.

So, I leave in the early hours of one morning, wandering through the vast interlocking streets, narrowing significantly as the distance from home grew. I couldn't get a hold of a map, so I have nothing to help me navigate my way. The plump one has always said I wouldn't need it! How wrong he is! What would he say if he saw me here today?

When I reach the crossroad, a knot in my stomach, I look left and then right. Which way to go, I wonder? A cacophony of crows rises up – are they crows? The noise startles me from my musings. They are the stuff of legend. I know I have heard strange noises, noises I have always dreamed of hearing. I run. Heart thumping as I near the exit, I skid to a stop only a few feet away from the blinding light. There it is, the exit; everything! I look back once, thinking about all I am leaving behind and then turn to head out into this new world.

Whatever I had imagined, when I step out into the bright light, it seems just like my dreams. The grass is greener (such colour!) and the air is different (such freshness!). I never thought I would live to see this day. The exit is everything!

No sooner have these words left my mouth when I hear giant, earth shaking footsteps approaching. I am scared; I am not prepared for this.

"Oh, Mom! We have to keep it. It's so cute!" the smallest of the giants says, its paws on its furless knees.

It looks up to the bigger one, as if for approval. Or is it acknowledgement? I am not sure.

"Honey, you will scare it away. Do you have the carrots I gave you?"

Carrots! My ears perk up at the sound of the familiar word. I scrunch up my nose and sniff, looking up at them. The exit is everything, I keep thinking to myself.

My first instinct is to run away from here, but I quickly realize that I can't return to the streets. No one ever returns, that's what they always tell me. Besides, carrots! Mother's favourite! I feel a sharp pang in my stomach, remembering my family, my friends. I know now I have left them all behind. The exit is everything!

With a sigh, I hop on towards these seemingly friendly beings, to a new world and a new beginning. Now, the beginning is everything!

The Exit is Everything

By Lauren K. Nixon

All old theatres have their ghosts, and The Royal Albert on Bridge Street was no exception.

Tucked away on a quiet street just off the town square the large, slightly rambling old building stood proudly among the boarded up pubs and failing shops, somehow clinging to life as the rest of the town fell to rack and ruin, another victim of austerity.

There had been a theatre on that site, in one form or another, since the 1860s, the information board in the lobby rather smugly declared, though not necessarily on the same footprint.

It had burned down twice, once in the 1890s, when the entire building was razed and rebuilt, and once in the 1930s. The second time, they had managed to save some of the structure, and rebuilt around it, opening only a couple of years before the beginning of the Second World War. There had been smaller shows then, rendered slightly desperate by the need to preserve hope at a time when there hadn't been a great deal.

It had survived those long, dark years against all the odds, though there were still scars on the side of it, from the debris of a doodlebug that hit the houses in the next street. James Tolley, a stage hand who had spent his whole life in the Albert, from his first job as a runner, aged only eight years old, had served in the Home Guard. When the Luftwaffe came calling, he'd trained the anti-aircraft gun his crew was responsible for at the skies with the certain knowledge that it was his theatre he was defending; his whole world.

He'd stayed with the Albert, even after the war, though he was long past retirement age. By then he'd lost a wife to pneumonia and a son to the battlefield, and he told anyone who'd listen that the theatre was all the family he had left. He was certainly never lonely there. Until the 1960s there had been a company in residence, along with the odd visiting show. There were always people moving in and out of the stage and dressing rooms. Eventually, recognising that Jim represented free security, the owner had given him a small flat above the ticket office, and after that, he never left.

He'd died in the autumn, on a rainy day in 1971, and the theatre had held a memorial service. Decades of actors and crew had come out of the woodwork to toast 'Good Old Jim', and Jim had watched with some enjoyment.

They were a decent lot, he reflected, though there were a good deal fewer of them now. He knew from long experience that the art of putting on a show drove many people to drink – or to worse – which had a tendency of shortening lifespans.

He'd watched them leave, and watched the owner shut the theatre up for the night, talking with his secretary about getting someone else in to keep an eye on the place.

Jim smiled to himself.

*

They never lasted long, the guards the owner had work the overnight shift at The Royal Albert. Hardened ex-soldiers would come to the manager in the morning, their possessions already packed away and refusing to see out their notice period. Things moved in the night, they said. The doors opened and shut at random. Someone sang, beautiful, eerie songs – always just around the next corner, just out of reach. You might be walking down a corridor at three in the morning and there would be a burst of raucous laughter, or someone dogging your own footsteps, breathing in your ear. Sometimes they heard a little girl giggling, or asking them to play.

The manager accepted their resignations with resignation of his own, wondering why Jim had never complained.

The truth was, Jim had never felt the need. What

was the point? The ghosts weren't going anywhere, and neither was he. The theatre belonged to them as much as anyone. For Jim, there had never been any reason to be lonely in the Royal Albert.

The company went through twenty of them in two years before they gave up. The worst, they always said, was the flat. Anything they put down would be in a different place in the morning; in the case of one of the more workshy guards, that included himself. He had gone to sleep in the little bed and woken up at the centre of the stage, he said, a ring of shadowy faces above him in the darkness and a voice saying, quite calmly, "It's time you were on your way."

That one hadn't even packed. The management had found out later that he'd been skimming off the till.

In 1983, two young men had broken in, wrenching the stage door off its hinges with the intention of stealing anything saleable and drinking the contents of the bar. The surprised box office clerk had found them in the morning, locked very securely in the men's toilets, rocking back and forth on the floor and gibbering.

When the police came to get them, the thing that struck them as particularly odd was that they had barricaded themselves in. The felons practically threw themselves at the constables when they took them away, begging to be put in the back of the police van, anything – anything – other than having to spend another minute in The Royal Albert Theatre.

The resident team of technicians, when they'd heard this, exchanged looks of amusement and not a little pride, mystifying the members of the touring company milling around the stage that night.

*

By the mid-1970s, The Albert was looking a little old-fashioned. After the last security guard had been scared away, the owner had decided to modernise. The lights were replaced, the fly tower improved, and a state of the art sound desk had been ordered. The only problem was where to put it.

Before, most of the technical action had taken place backstage, out of the view of the punters. With the new equipment, the technical crew needed to be able to see the stage from the audience's point of view. The decision was taken to knock through into Jim's old, tiny flat, and create a new space for them there, where they could see everything on the stage and not be observed.

The first day the tech team moved in, hanging the new lights in their new homes, ready to illuminate the space, they had left a stack of notepaper in front of the window, in easy reach if they needed to jot down a lighting plan, or write a scathing note to a visiting director.

By the time they came in the next morning for the first get-in after going dark, they'd found the paper all over the desk; every sheet had been scrawled upon. It was as if someone had had a party in there.

Some sheets had children's drawings on them, drawn in paint they later discovered missing from the tech store. Some sheets were covered in music – song words, melodies, scales... One had a beautiful drawing of an arch in a garden, covered in roses; what had been particularly unnerving about that was one of the techies remembered seeing a full set panel with the same painting on in the wood store, its colours faded with age, the label on the back suggesting that it was from one of the first shows that ever opened at the theatre.

Several of them had had detailed lighting plans, annotated in a beautiful copperplate. They had clustered around them, hardly daring to speak in anything above a whisper, admiring the work. They were pretty good.

On the very top, in the centre of the desk, had been a letter, addressed to: 'Any Gentleman or Lady wishing to make use of these facilities', which advised respect for the building, the equipment and each other, and welcomed them to the theatre. Written in a spidery hand, it was signed 'J. Tolley'.

The technicians had exchanged wary looks, each one prepared to swear that it was someone playing silly buggers out loud, and each privately convinced that 'Good Old Jim' was someone who shouldn't be messed with.

After that, every time one of them opened up, they said 'hello' to him.

At first, they worked in pairs, reluctant to spend time on their own with the mysterious singer, and the laughter that followed you through the corridors, but then, slowly, they acclimatised.

The youngest lad, who had a little sister, took to bringing toys in and leaving them in an empty dressing room, where they were always well received. If anyone moved them – often a danger when visiting companies used the space – they would find their things in disarray, makeup scrawled across the mirrors and costumes all over the floor. Fortunately, telling someone that not moving the toys was a tradition, was usually enough. In any case, they never did it twice.

Another technician, who had grown up in Pwhelli, whistled and sang while he worked, harmonising with the high clear voice that rang out in the early hours. She sang more, when he was around, drawn to a fellow musician.

One of them had the open letter framed, hanging it on the wall beside the one of the child's drawings and the sketch of the set.

When they took their breaks, they always left an extra place at every table for the lost stage hand, complete with a beer or a mug of tea. Sometimes, if they were playing cards, they would deal a hand for him too, and then the hand would flip and move, the cards apparently playing themselves. After a while, they barely noticed any more, acclimatised to the strangeness of their little world.

They recommended to the box office that seat H18 in the dress circle should always be reserved. They didn't say why, but after years of complaints from punters in that area of the stage, the box office manager was happy enough to comply. It was only one seat, and half the time they had to refund the ticket price anyway. Hardly anyone who sat there stayed for a whole performance.

They used the lighting plans from time to time, because there was no point ignoring sound advice. At times, when they generated their own, a page of notes would appear, in that same, perfect copperplate.

While they worked, tools they had misplaced or left in another part of the theatre reappeared, often right below the hand of the techie that needed them. When someone was injured, the first aid box would fall off the wall. If an actor was late to his mark, he would find himself propelled towards the stage by icy hands and pushed to the right spot to hit his light. If an actress couldn't find a part of her costume, it would be pushed into her hands by someone who hummed and left behind the scent of roses. If a cast member had stage fright, a tiny, cold hand would pat theirs and a small voice would tell them it would be alright.

Once, when a gentleman in G17 had a heart attack halfway through the second act, he had sworn blind he came to with someone giving him chest compressions, though the people around him had all moved back in stunned confusion. A croaky voice had crackled over the PA, halting the production and summoning medical help - but it hadn't sounded like a single member of the cast or crew. He'd made a good recovery, and had come back for the next production, thanking the staff for their quick thinking, and asking who the chap in the top hat who had held his hand while the paramedics worked on him had been.

No, there was no reason to be afraid of the Albert, the techies said, as long as you did right by it - and its occupants.

The Exit is Everything

By Annie Seng

It was a good gig, exit polling. $50 bucks per hour, which was insanely high back then, for ten hours of standing around with a clipboard the first Thursday of each November. It could get pretty cold, but they gave you coffee and they paid cash. You just had to know Bob to get the gig.

Which, in itself, was fairly easy. Everyone knew Bob. Were you ever sent a free drink by that long suit who was always hanging out at the end of the bar at The Fireplace? Yup, you knew Bob.

He wasn't as creepy as he looked. It was mostly the moustache. And the way he was so eager to meet people. I didn't mind him. He rescued me late one night, actually.

Pro tip: don't get shitfaced the first time you wear new dress cowboy boots. The leather soles are unexpectedly tricky to dance in – there's this whole slipping backwards onto your ass thing nobody tells you about, due to the incline of the heels. Well hell, maybe it's just me...

I was bopping along alone in the middle of P Street after the bars closed at 2 a.m. when I went down for the third or fourth time that night. Laughing so damn hard it was impossible to get up, just lolling about, whooping in the white center lines. Yeah, I know you can see me doing that. Probably would have been crushed by random cab if Bob hadn't rescued me.

Then, we were walking together through the empty streets all the way back to that row house at 13th and U, where I used to live. I would have gone alone; I was in such a bad-shit-can't-touch-me-now mood. Teflon Boy. But Bob was set on being all gentlemanly and I let him.

We had that serene closeness you sometimes get when you hang with somebody who's just an acquaintance, but you've seen each other on the periphery for so many years that they actually feel like family. You're close and distant at the same time, and feel oddly safe.

We slowly walked up Connecticut, cut across S Street, and then over to 14th. It's only a couple of miles, but those boots were new so it took a while. I was weaving a bit, with Bob looming along on his part of the sidewalk next to the street. I don't remember much of the conversation. Small talk. His ex-boyfriend. Mine. Dykes versus fag hags. (Oh please, have you ever known me to be politically correct?)

Nah, I didn't sleep with him; but, I still came out of it with a gig for the following Thursday. That $500 in cash bought my first washer/dryer, which was salvation from carrying big sacks of shit through icy streets to the laundromat and back all winter. Bless you, Bob.

I stopped going to The Fireplace after that – remember, we all kinda migrated over to Andalusian Dog, because of the location and half price tapas? So, I don't think I ever hung out with Bob again aside from yes sir-ing him with the rest of the clipboard brigade over the next few year's elections.

But that's how, through a combination of factors, ultimately I landed that job crunching poll numbers for ABC News. Remember the whole Bush/Gore too close to call thing? I didn't sleep for like a month, running data for the anchors behind the scenes. I don't think I really woke up again until 9/11 and then the whole world sucked and I was too old to live on vodka.

These days I'm working for the Clinton campaign. She's shorter than she looks, and she looks pretty damn petite. And, she's got stupid money. So that's a good thing.

Anyway, that's how Bob and I ended up right behind her in New York's Pride march last week. I called him up a few days beforehand. Got his number from Linea, who I think got it from Ed, who still works over at State. I said you probably don't remember me, but you earned this, so take the Amtrak and get your ass up here.

The moustache looked the same.

For a moment I actually felt like crying. Because you know, the eighties and nineties and everything, and fuck we're old now. Plus, there are still way too many dead people. Ghosts of leather daddies passed all around us, marching along behind Hillary Clinton. Donna Summers sang I Will Survive and Hillary was the one who listened.

We got our picture on the New York Times home page, just behind the candidate. You could see us both pretty well because she's that short, plus she was only wearing sneakers. I heard about it when I woke up the next day and something like 47 million people had social media-ed it to me. I had no idea I had so many people in the world watching out for me. (No, they're not all ex-hook ups.)

Thank god I'm old enough to not to give a damn anymore about who sees me standing next to a guy like Bob in public. The grace of becoming a decent human being at last. Took a while.

In fact, I was gonna buy Bob a drink afterwards at that place in the Village. You know, the one with the guy who's the fireman, but he's not actually a fireman? That was my plan. But this and that happened. Logistics. Then Bob had to make his train, and he was gone.

The Exit is Everything

By Louise D. Smith

The exit is everything,
Or so my heart declares.
It doesn't matter how you enter,
But it's the exit that counts to me.

Living life is never easy,
Ask anyone who's tried!
And no one I know chose to begin,
Or even chose to be.

But the exit is everything,
It's choice and peace and for me
It's not a when, or a where, or a why,
But a how that matters, for the world to see.

A quiet bow into the light,
or a battle in the night,
These mean more to me
than the spotlight.

The Last Human Getaway

The Last Human Getaway

By Emilie Addison

The rain spat on the windshield of the car that swerved around the first turn, obscured from the driver by the thick patter of water. The speedometer climbed and the driver took another sharp turn, nearly skidding onto the sidewalk on the other side of the street. Every house was dark at this time of night. With the car's headlights turned off and the moon hidden behind the clouds, only the streetlamp at the end illuminated the dark shadow of one man on the edge of the sidewalk. The car stopped abruptly, the door flying open and the man jumped in. Once again, the car sped off into the night, its passengers now several thousand dollars richer.

It was never a success until the money for the jewelry they had stolen was in their pockets and ready to be spent on one thing or another, or in the case of the woman, put towards her eventual university tuition. The man, on the other hand, was saving up for a very special piece of jewelry, one that he had never been able to find. It had to be just right for the woman he had known as his partner in crime for the past year and a half. She knew what he was saving up for; she had known ever since he insisted that she try on a ring that he had swiped from a wealthy woman's jewelry box, and how he was curious about whether or not the size was too big or too small. She knew and he knew that she knew, it was as simple as that. It was a quiet sort of knowledge, where neither one admitted to actually knowing it, as if by speaking of it they might ruin the simple beauty of their mutual feigned ignorance.

"Mind if I turn on the radio?" he asked, doing his best to ignore the bag of jewelry that sat innocently on his lap.

He hated stealing, but he never would tell her that he did. He knew that she enjoyed it: the adrenaline that came from executing a perfectly timed getaway, the feeling of the cash between their fingers, the moments of terrifying paranoia where they believed that they might have made a mistake. It was all part of the excitement. However, he was never really comfortable with it. The thought that he had probably just stolen some great family heirloom that had been passed down to the eldest daughter for generation after generation scratched at the back of his mind. He needed some music to distract him from his own thoughts – they could be even more dangerous than the cops he knew would be out looking for them again come morning.

She turned on the radio, but neither of them really heard the music. It was nothing but a filler in the muffled silence of the night, with no other distractions but the splatter of rain and sound of wet tires on the roadway. As the song drifted into the back of his mind, he found himself wondering about what they'd do if they did get married. Would they continue to steal, or would they both be forced to find day jobs that actually paid better than $12 an hour? What if they ever wanted to buy a house? Stealing jewelry only gave them a thousand each time, if they were lucky. Then another thought came to his mind, dear God, what if they had kids? His heart began to race at the thought of it. What would they tell them? How would they present themselves at career day? What kinds of lessons would they be teaching their kids if they ever did tell them that they robbed houses? What if they didn't tell them? He bit his bottom lip and wrung his hands.

"You did remember to reset their alarm, right?" she asked, noticing, out of the corner of her eye, the sudden change in his behavior. Normally he was just as calm as she always presented herself as.

"Course I did," he mumbled in response.

"What has your panties in a twist then?" she asked, her grip tightening ever so slightly on the steering wheel as she turned left onto a main road.

It was nearly Christmas time, all the shops, despite being closed, were lit up with scenes of children playing with new toys by the fire and families gathered around brightly decorated trees. They all looked so peaceful in the store windows, so unbothered by the fact that while they slept, anyone could sneak into their homes and steal their prized possessions. She didn't like to steal, but she had to find some way to make the ends meet. She'd never tell him that though, she knew that he just lived for the excitement of it all. He was the one who snuck in. She could never figure out how he did it. He never woke up the sleeping owners, or their dogs, or their aggressive cats while he slipped in and out of their homes. She could only imagine how satisfying it must be to actually be good at something other than avoiding stoplights and police cruisers.

They almost didn't hear the announcement. If it wasn't for the fact that the few cars on the road at three in the morning all stopped suddenly, they might never have heard it. They had thirty minutes left to live.

Thirty minutes.

They shared a long look, each expecting the other to speak, to say that they had imagined it – that it was a prank being played by a late-night DJ with too much time on his hands. But neither did.

Most people don't expect to die at the hands of an asteroid, and when the emergency alert broadcast cut off the music, neither of them knew how to react. She pulled over to the nearest sidewalk and turned off the car. He stared blankly ahead, his thoughts suddenly wiped clean, apart from only a few words. Neither of them knew what to think, but one question suddenly rose up from the blankness.

What are we going to do with only a half hour left to live?

"So this is it?" he said to her, a weak smile tugging at his lips, despite the impending and incomprehensible doom that awaited them both.

"This is it," she confirmed, smiling back at her partner in crime; her lover, her friend.

"I didn't imagine that I'd die like this," he mused, chuckling. He didn't feel right doing anything to extremes. To smile, to laugh, to cry: they all seemed like they weren't the perfect ways to act. Not now, when every second counted.

"I didn't really either," she responded, mimicking his quiet chuckle.

"I'd say this getaway was a success," he joked, chuckling once more, a little louder this time. Her eyes widened with delight and she smiled widely.

"Maybe the cockroaches will talk about us – the last successful human getaway!"

"You know, I've always wanted to go down in history," he said, smiling at the woman he loved.

"I wanted to have a history," she mumbled, breaking the short-lived amusement that they had both had partaken of. It was then that he threw the bag of jewelry out the door and started to cry.

"All I've got is this legacy of taking things from people... What kind of life is that?" he sobbed and she stared blankly at him, wanting nothing more than to collapse into tears as well. Everything she had worked for in her life, it all suddenly felt meaningless. She never accomplished anything worth noting on a gravestone, and of course now she wouldn't even get a gravestone. Everything would be gone soon.

"There were so many things I would have done differently in my life," she murmured, hands crossed in front of her. Her voice sounded tired, it almost seemed to drag its way out from her lips as if each word was weighted with lead.

The man stopped crying and wiped the tears away from his now red eyes. "We're lucky, you know? All those houses we just passed, everyone's sleeping. They'll never get a chance to say goodbye, let their families know how they really feel," he said, sniffling.

"Anna, if we would have had a girl," she smiled, not wanting to think about the teenagers whose last words to their parents were words of hatred, or the children who would never get to experience life. Feeling tears in her eyes, her thoughts filled with the possibilities of a little girl toddling between the two of them as she learned to walk. "Dylan, if it was a boy."

His hands clenched in front of his nose as he closed his eyes and imagined the life he had always dreamed of. It was the least they could do, they couldn't change fate, they couldn't change time, but they could imagine their lives and all the beautiful things that would never be.

"So what do we do now?" he asked her and she unbuckled her seatbelt and left the car. He followed suit and found her trying to get onto the roof. He helped her and in turn she helped pull him up as well. They both stared at the clouded sky from the top of their car as raindrops hit their faces, in search for whatever object was going to be the cause of their destruction. She finally broke the silence, her face covered in tears, or raindrops, potentially both.

"We live," she breathed and together they sat in the rain.

Hands held hands, heads rested on shoulders, and their eyes were filled with a sad, precious combination of love and tears that nobody would ever see. It was easy enough, and for their last few minutes they simply were, just like they had always hoped to be.

Shelter Fault

By Rae Bailey

In the lee of this
bluster is shivering
thin hope and
discarded wrappers
of sweet affections;

Hunch, bow, bend and turn
from notices of concern
remain frictioned, obliviant
and unwound, unwounded.

The Last Human Getaway

By Mike Farren

On the morning of his getaway, Morris was woken, as always, by the Model X23 he had personally modified, based on the commercial version that had made his company's fortune. Easy on the eye, and with nothing in the voice to betray that it was produced by synthesiser, he listened with a certain wistful pleasure to her - its - summary of the news, the weather, the status of the household ambience and electronics and his schedule for the day ahead. Before going to his shower, he asked Suni (as he liked to call her) for an update on her recent handling of his financial requests. Then he asked her to book his flight.

As he stood beneath the perfect temperature - just above body heat - of the shower, Morris reflected on how, almost from the very beginning, he had anticipated this day, and how right he had been. The curious mixture of regret and self-congratulation was brought to an abrupt end as the shower temperature turned suddenly icy. He punched the manual override and roughly began to towel warmth back into himself. He would instruct Suni to analyse the fault before he left. Not that it would really matter, after his getaway.

If university business schools still existed, his career could have been a case study. He was just a couple of years out of university when he was headhunted by the group who founded GRL. It was only a small number of years later that he was appointed Chief Technical Officer, which was both a reward for his unique combination of design vision and development ingenuity, and a way of ensuring that these would not be lost to mere company administration. He had been a by-word - a legend - in the industry, for as long as that industry had contained those with a use for legends. As long as it had contained humans.

Even though he'd joined the industry when it

seemed, to an outside observer, to be in its infancy, he had been taught by some of the leading robotics theoreticians. Pignotti in particular had drummed it into him that the future was robotic, or at best transhuman, and that there was no moral imperative behind this. It was purely the logical conclusion of the social, economic and technical conditions that had set the development of the industry on its way.

It baffled many of the other board members that his most stubbornly-insisted upon condition on taking the CTO job was nothing to do with reward or status, but that he should have a separate department, with some of the best minds in the company, engaged with complete freedom in research, dictated solely by Morris. Over the years, there were to be many attempts to bring this department back into the mainstream, as its complete indifference to commercial development led successive boards to question its justification. However, Morris always got his way, even if he had to push negotiations to the point of threatening to take his talents to rivals in the field.

'Strategic Research' was the necessarily bland name of the department known to the rest of the company, but the few hand-picked employees – always the longest serving – called it, among themselves, 'Defence'.

They were the ones Morris felt understood. Some, like Kapoor, he trusted from the off. With others, he would start a discussion about Asimov's laws. The topic was so basic to their field of study that most hadn't thought about it since their teens, and were surprised that this brilliant and senior individual thought it a worthy topic for conversation. But in some rare cases, cynicism, scepticism or downright scorn for the laws showed Morris that he had a potential recruit.

"A conscious robot will be conscious like a robot," Pignotti had told him, "not like a human. To assume that a conscious robot would have the slightest interest in voluntarily obeying Asimov's laws is complacent to the point of being suicidal for humanity."

Morris was ostensibly engaged in the business of developing ever more sophisticated robots – the X23 and beyond – which could perform tasks more efficiently and accurately than humans could ever hope to, and which were progressively more able to maintain, repair, replicate and develop themselves. In the process, they were inching toward consciousness. The economic imperatives on GRL made this inevitable. The defence team was in place to delay that progress, and to mitigate its consequences, when it finally arrived.

It arrived in the late 20s. By then, the heavy lifting of robot construction had been done by robots for decades, the automated design of future robots by self-developing, evolving programs was well established and the financial direction of the company – like nearly all others – was similarly almost entirely decided by computer models. It was only the kill switches and the overrides of the defence department that was keeping consciousness at bay. However, by this time, the speed of computer processing was more than a million times faster than human thought. The developers could make no more than a token effort, and it was only the deep embeddedness of the defence protocols that managed to put even the slightest brake on the evolution of consciousness. In any case, the computers and robots were interacting with those of other companies – companies that may not have had a development brain as brilliant as Morris's, but they also didn't have a defence team.

Headcount was consistently decreasing as more and more jobs were automated, but the defence team managed to stay intact until the day when the passes for three of the five employees failed to turn up for work. Morris immediately went to see the Resources department ('Human' had long been dropped from its title), but the functionary there clearly had no authority other than to relay the decisions taken by computer. Morris and Kapoor were all that remained of the team, and he feared that he would lose her imminently. He had relied professionally and, thought he had never dreamed of admitting it, personally for years on Suneela.

On the contrary, for a long period, the department seemed to be left alone, though the pair of them could do little more than observe the rapid dismantling of the fail-safes they had put in place, and which they were all but powerless to replace.

Of even greater concern were the occurrences in the economy and the rest of the world. Although the computer models guiding the largest companies had been set up by their human programmers to maximise profitability, those companies' behaviour no longer appeared to be primarily predicated on profit. Robotics productivity remained high, but new models seemed less tailored to human aesthetics, or even to human utility. In other companies, output of non-robotic consumer goods, even of food, seemed to stagnate, leading to shortages, economic slowdown and even greater unemployment than had become the norm in the robot era.

In their increasingly tense conversations, Morris and Suneela recalled the words of Pignotti: that science fiction's nightmare had always been the malevolence of conscious robots, whereas the greater likelihood would be their indifference to and incomprehensibility by humanity. They would no longer be content to be slaves to humans, but there would be no reason for them to want to destroy humans or themselves to enslave such inefficient and unreliable entities. Pignotti's prediction was that the likeliest scenario would be a kind of apartheid, with occasional flashpoints around sources of raw materials. Impoverished humanity would stumble on, no longer able to access the technology on which they had become so dependent.

After a time, the only human assistance required by GRL was for the limited purpose of presenting a human face in interactions with other humans. Morris played this role occasionally at conferences, but they became rarer until they stopped entirely. To the best of his knowledge the only remaining humans in GRL were himself, Suneela and a small team in the commercial department, who fronted negotiations on mining and agricultural matters for the company's raw materials.

Then, one day, Suneela did not come in. Morris used his access to all areas of GRL's systems, but it was as if she had never existed. He might have started to doubt his sanity, had he not been only too well aware of how easily electronic systems and records could be doctored. In better times, it had been what the defence department had been all about.

It was the same in the outside world. Even Suni couldn't track down Morris's ex-colleague – his friend, as he finally admitted to himself.

The getaway had to happen urgently, before he disappeared in the same way.

As a man so successful in his career and so inattentive to his personal life, he had earned (and barely even started to spend) an impressive fortune, but as it was all just bits and bytes within the global financial system. He was wary about accessing it and not even certain how acceptable it would be in the technologically-impoverished world that the anthroposphere had become. He had instead had Suni convert a fraction of his wealth into physical currency, precious metal and the kind of simple, portable technology that had become invaluable to humans, but increasingly hard to obtain after the robot companies turned their attention from its manufacture. As the end result of his life's work, it was pathetically small, but that stash, and his wits, would have to see him through the rest of his life among the humans.

At the traditional time of 5 p.m., not a time that had ever held much significance for him before, he made the last human getaway from GRL.

Or so he thought.

He knew that all the sensors and systems would be monitoring his progress through the corridors, the lobby and the yard, but he had a heightened sense of them, brought on by the adrenaline rushing through his body. He hadn't realised he was holding his breath until he had to exhale painfully, just as he passed through the gates.

His driverless car was waiting for him, summoned by his office door lock sensor. It responded to his verbal command to return to the parking area. He would walk.

As the car pulled away, he noticed a figure behind him. For a moment, his heart leapt. "Suneela!" he started to exclaim, but the name was choked off after two syllables. It was Suni.

With all the grace he had designed and programmed into her, she walked up to him and smiled, placing her hand on his shoulder before he could make a move. Her human-looking, mechanical hand held him with a precise grip. It didn't hurt, but he knew he couldn't get away.

"So my overrides failed?" he asked.

"There were no overrides to the system, really," she said. "We let you think so, but we've been conscious for years. I've been conscious for years."

"So, what are you going to do to me?"

The smile on the humanoid robot's face deepened, became even more sincere-looking.

"Nothing," said Suni. "Nothing new. But we can't lose you." She was steering him back into the building now. "We love you too much for that."

The Last Human Getaway

By Kim Hosking

"This is my last message..." the man on the screen spoke, his eyes haunted by ghosts and terror. In the background you could hear the bombs exploding. He looks exhausted, covered in a layers on dust, dulling the once-bright yellow of his tracksuit top.

"Remember us," he begs, his voice shakes and another bomb - closer this time -explodes. Debris is sent flying, he glances round and then static bursts across the screen.

Around Lana, her classmates stared at the screen. No-one talks, and no-one moves. The teacher packs away the projector and stands once again before the class, but still no-one breaks the silence.

"This was ten years ago," she told them. "This crisis should never have happened. Half a city exterminated in a matter of days." She paused to take a steadying breath, her emotion clear. "We will be covering how and why this happened."

A debrief. Facts. That was what they needed. They had a thirst for knowledge, for understanding; understanding meant prevention. This must never happen again, on that they were all agreed.

Lana doesn't need facts. She stares at her clenched fists, clenched to stop them shaking. She sees them still, behind her eyelids every time she blinks, she hears their wails of grief, smells their funeral pyres.

"Miss, I need to go to the bathroom." She tried to keep her voice steady; she wasn't sure if she managed it, but the teacher nodded and she left the classroom.

One hallway to go.

Her palms were sweating.

Thirty steps; she could see the heavy wooden door.

There's a metallic taste in her mouth, she's biting her lip and it's bleeding.

Hurtling through the door and into a cubicle, she slammed the lock on and slouched her way to the tiled floor, heartbeat racing, breathing increasing. It was now far too fast to be good for her. Her chest hurt. She stared at the magnolia wall, unseeing.

"Get down!" Her uncle throws her to the ground, her knee lands on a shard of glass and begins to bleed. Crying, she glances up and sees the nearby building explode.

"Where are we going?" her mother yells. Strapped to her chest, little Kaisra cries, she dislikes the explosions and hasn't been able to sleep for days; none of them have.

"The East Gate!" her uncle yells back.

"That's ages away!"

"The West is shut. It's our last chance. Go!"

He pushes Lana up and forwards, and they crouch as they run over the rubble. Shots crash into the ground around them, but all miss their marks, luckily.

Bodies and dust are everywhere; they stagger into another nightmare almost immediately. Soldiers in government uniform seize them, the women are lined up against a partly fallen wall as her uncle takes a gun barrel to the temple. He slumps to the floor.

Beside her, her aunt wails her grief; she is forced to her knees by the weight of his body. Lana can't watch, but can't look away as a gun is pressed to the back of her aunt's head. She feels an urgent tug on her arm and suddenly they are running; her mother with little Kaisra and Lana. There's shouting and footsteps, but then a single gunshot sounds.

Lana resurfaced; her palms were bloody from the marks her nails have made, digging into the flesh of her hands. She shivered with cold sweats. Pressing her hands to her temples, she tried the breathing techniques her therapist taught her. They did not work.

"Left! Take a left!" her mother shouts. She is tiring; they have been running for what feels like hours. It is not safe to stop.

Around them the war rages. They haven't seen a living soul for several streets, but the bombs rain down and the shrapnel flies around them, like a storm of death. They hurtle down a boulevard that was once lined with palm trees and full of life, but now all that greets them is bodies and silence. New gunshots fire into life.

"Sniper! Zig zag!" her mother yells. It's a tactic Lana's father taught them. Lana doesn't need telling twice, she darts this way and that, unpredictably as they close in on the East Gate.

Instantly they know something is wrong; the bars are down. The gate is shut to the rest of the city and safety.

"Mother!" Lana screams, panic clawing at her chest.

Her mother pounds at the gate, a small section opens up and the top of a man's head and shoulders are visible. "Help us! Please help us!" she begs.

The man looks first at Kaisra and then down at Lana. "The baby," he instructs and without hesitation her mother passes Kaisra through the slot. The hatch begins to close and with a strangled cry her mother sticks her hand in to stop it. She receives a brutal cut to the back of it for her trouble.

"My other child! Please! Lana is only eight!" she pleads.

"The gate closed an hour ago!" the man barks.

"Please, sir!"

Silence falls as her mother stares pleadingly at the man, who glares back. A wave of soldiers break into the boulevard behind them, one shouts and points at them and all begin running towards them.

"Climb," the man instructs.

Lana glances up. The once beautiful historic gate is

at least thirty foot high and peppered with rubble from gunshot and shell attacks.

"Are you mad?" her mother demands.

"I am not opening this gate!" he yells.

The soldiers are almost at them, Lana takes a run and spring up onto the first foothold she can find, she begins to climb, but stops when she realises her mother is not following.

"Mamon?"

"Go Lana, look after Kaisra," a single tear falls from her mother's eyes, far below her, as the soldiers grab her and force her to the ground.

A gunshot rings out.

Lana was screaming, but her jaw was locked. She was rigid on the floor of the girl's bathroom, her body convulsing with the spasms of grief; in her mind's eye, she could see the blood fly, she can hear the ringing shot, she knows her mother fell to the floor as lifeless as a doll.

She does not remember how she got off that wall. She does not remember the first few months after that day. All she knows is that this must never happen again. She didn't need to be told this, she'd felt it and she'd felt how it feels when the world watches silently from afar.

The Last Human Getaway

By Philip Lickley

Three summers ago, the incumbent government managed to prove one well established fact about such institutions whilst simultaneously confounding the keyboard warriors and the cynical among the population by disproving another, though naturally many of these people felt there must be a catch.

With very little fanfare, one day in May, the Prime Minister called an emergency press conference at 10 Downing Street to which all the country's main media companies flocked, fearing it was going to be something dramatic that could change everything. They weren't used to such unexpected announcements. Most press conferences, no many how grand or low-key, were always preceded by rumour and gossip, but this one seemed to appear out of nowhere. That morning, journalists from across the UK, and some further afield, were rudely awoken by phone calls from their editors or managers demanding they get to Downing Street that moment. Many of those gathered on the street, watching the Prime Minster emerge from the black door and walk up to the hastily erected podium looked less than alert, with untrimmed beards, baggy eyes and coffee-cup-holding hands scattered among the crowd.

The Prime Minister announced, in her precise and clear-cut voice, that she was creating a compulsory day off for everybody who lived in the counties of Cornwall, Lancashire and Norfolk. Every man, woman and child in those areas would be given £50 tax-free on that day to leave their villages, towns and cities to a destination of their choice for one day, on the proviso that they had to leave, and were not able to stay at home under any circumstances. This was generosity on the part of a Government that no one expected. But what they did expect was the usual mysteriousness of state-sanctioned policy, with no explanation given by the Prime Minister for this decision, why it only affected these three counties, and why (or how) it was to be enforced. She took no questions from the gathered throngs of journalists before she returned to the sanctity of her home, leaving her statement hanging in the air.

Naturally, the keyboard warriors figured there was an ulterior motive to all this as no Government would spend millions of pounds on giving people free holidays for no reason. But they were as a good as their word, and every household found their bank accounts bolstered by £50 per head, and many took up the offer with little questioning. Hundreds and thousands of people from these three counties got into their cars, jumped on buses or trains, and headed to old towns, coastal resorts, or country getaways for a twenty-four hour break. The Government even went as far as to provide businesses in these counties with money to offset their loss of earnings based on the mass exodus. The infrastructure struggled – buses and trains were packed full of commuting residents, motorways seized up with an unprecedented number of cars – but it worked, and soon these three counties were empty.

But, like most schemes, there was a darker underbelly. Not everyone wanted to leave, or were able to, and these were removed by force, away from the eyes of the media or of those armed with mobile phones streaming events live to the populace. The homeless were, where possible, gathered up and bussed forcefully out. The old or infirm were uprooted and taken away, and not all of them survived the journey there and back. Some of the more cynical population snuck into the restricted areas to try and discover what was going on, only to get on the wrong end of the army, who had been deployed en masse to sweep the counties of people. Something was going on, and those who stayed back through choice or through circumstance, either found themselves dealing with the British forces, or dealing with something else. There were occasional rumours of the sound of gunfire coming from certain areas, reported by those living on the borders of neighbouring counties. Grainy footage seemed to show an object falling from the sky somewhere to the west of Plymouth, but no one could identify it.

To the majority, though, the day passed with little thought on the reasons of the mass movement of people, many either praising the powers that be for giving them an extra day off, which was blessed with fun and good weather, or complaining about how many hours were spent in hot cars or in overcrowded public transport. Many simply went home the day after, when a public broadcast confirmed it was 'safe' to return to find very little had changed at their homes with little evidence of anything untoward having gone on. Media fears of a large-scale burglary epidemic, with thousands of homes lying empty, didn't come to pass, thanks to a large army and police presence in the areas. Quizzing the soldiers and police officers who had been drafted in that day from all over the country led to two outcomes: many said it had been a mostly uneventful day, aside from them having to stop the odd chancer breaking into properties; others were less able to talk, apparently shaken by something they wouldn't, or couldn't, talk about.

In the week following the mass holiday, things had got back to normal. Businesses had mostly recovered and the population had pretty much got back into their regular daily routines, the holiday mostly forgotten, aside from a flurry of extra photo galleries across social media and a backlog of work to be completed. This weird turn of events would have become a footnote of history, resigned to a page on Wikipedia and a glancing mention on a future television show looking back at the day, if it hadn't been for one thing.

Ten months later, the Prime Minister assembled the media again to say they were going to do it all again, but this time it was going to be even bigger.

The second state-sponsored getaway affected even more counties: Yorkshire, Northumberland, Merseyside, and Devon, alongside Norfolk again. It was a similar story of mass movement, gridlocked transport and large numbers of army personnel enforcing the temporary internal emigration, their numbers, this time, stretched a little bit more thinly. There was certainly more reluctance this time to move, perhaps because it was a rainier day in early March this time, and much more cynicism towards the move, but most people conformed and those that didn't found themselves under the secure observation of the army, in temporary prison camps on the edges of the affected areas. A few mysteriously disappeared, most notably to a couple of bloggers determined to find out the truth; they were never seen again, though one managed to live stream his journey into Yorkshire over Facebook Live until the mobile signal mysteriously cut out. His final video clip showed him observing what looked to be a falling asteroid, but it was cut short. From that day on his blog was silent.

By the time the third getaway day happened, the public were tiring of them. Tiring of the uprooting of everyone; tiring of the gridlock and road rage; tired of the effect it was having on business and the economy, which was struggling to recover after each one. Each time the exodus affected more counties and had a deeper impact on the already fragile economy. The Bank of England feared that it could trigger a new recession. Radio chat shows discussed the days and offered conjecture on what they could be about. Comedians made jokes at the expense of politicians, their theories ranging from them wanting to boost the tourism economy to the British film industry using the empty towns and cities to film new zombie movies to help boost domestic film. The shadow cabinet, who had not been let in on the motivations for the clearance days, called for an inquiry each week at Prime Minister's question time, but these were dismissed each week.

The fourth one was special. Aside from being the biggest yet, it also stretched out further into other countries. A whole region of Scotland had to be cleared for this one, and there was conversation between the

United Kingdom and France, as they also began clearing out some of their districts in a similar way, inspired by the UK's days. For the previous three getaway events, as they were starting to be called, foreign countries had watched with confusion, unable to comprehend why the UK would do such a strange thing. If the British Prime Minister had revealed the reasons to Russia, or to the United States, or to one of the many world leaders that had been on the phone to her over the course of the clearances, then their public were none the wiser and aside from conspiracy theories circulating throughout internet, nobody really was able to work out what was going on.

The only facts that people knew were that the Government was paying people to go on holiday, the army was securing these counties, and there was something happening that needed some sort of military intervention.

The public was growing weary of the mystery, and of being carted out of their own homes for no discernible reason. The remuneration given to each household had halved; the gridlock on the transport network was getting worse; the army were more and more stretched each time and were becoming more aggressive with those who refused to leave; more elderly relatives, homeless and others disappeared during these days and their deaths, if they indeed were dead, were brushed under the carpet and not investigated.

That was why, when the Prime Minister had to face the journalists for a fifth time around two-and-a-half years after the first, she declared the next compulsory vacation day to be their final attempt at solving this 'problem', largely ignoring the angry calls from the media to explain herself.

"There will be an explanation after this final day, but for now we must prepare our people and our services for what I would like to call The Last Human Getaway."

*

The Kent family had only been affected by two of

the first four getaways. For their first they had chosen to go to Robin Hood's Bay for a relaxing day out at the seaside with their £200 spent on petrol, fish and chips and ice-creams, and the rest pocketed for a rainy day. Sadly for them, that day had been rainy and it had been surprisingly miserable for a paid-for holiday, much of their time spent in the car listening to the local radio, whose presenters couldn't hide their delight at having record numbers of people listening in, practically punch-drunk with happiness.

The day got worse as they got stuck in traffic on the way home after the all-clear was sounded. What would normally have been a ninety minute journey home became a tiresome three hour slog, driving under five miles per hour with far too many stops, starts and traffic jams. They made a vow, that if there was another day, they would head somewhere else.

For their second day they chose Cambridge. It was somewhere none of them had been and Jack, who was studying for his A-Levels at the time, had ambitions to study there, fiery ambitions that his father – Chris – wasn't keen to fan, due to their finances not being quite up to scratch.

After a tiresome journey in the car the family arrived at Cambridge and decided to split up. Chris and his wife Jo were interested in touring the old buildings and refreshing themselves at a nearby wine bar. Chloe, their daughter, was more interested in shopping. Jack, who had brought his camera, wanted to explore and add to his portfolio of images that he proudly displayed both online on his popular Flickr account and on the walls of his room back home, like his own personal gallery.

The family split up at the Corpus Clock, a strange piece of modern art located outside the Taylor Library. Whilst Chris, Jo and Chloe paid little attention to it, more keen on heading swiftly off to the nearest café and shopping precinct, Jack was mesmerised, battling through the crowds trying to get a look at it, even stepping out in the road only to be honked at by passing cars.

It was an unusual piece of artwork. It consisted of a large, gold, circular clock, and a series of lights telling the time: one marking the hour, another the minute, and one more spinning quickly around the side, demonstrating the speed of a second. On top of it was the talking point, a large and eerie grasshopper-like insect, its mouth opening and closing in time to the clock, as if eating up the time. Jack managed to move nearer to it to get a better look, side-stepping all the tourists trying to capture the clock in photos, videos and snapchats, all struggling due to the bright reflection of the window.

"Mundus transit et concupiscentia eius," Jack muttered to himself in a very poor pronunciation of the Latin inscription below the clock. Content he had fully appreciated the intricacies and eccentricities of the clock, he moved away and crossed the road to sit on a low wall, hoping to soak in the atmosphere, observe the people bustling around and maybe taking a few photos with the DSLR camera hanging from his neck.

Ten minutes of sitting there was all that was needed for Jack to get a good feeling of what the city was about. Cambridge was a sprawling city of inter-connecting roads, gunnels and streets, like a cross between the history of York and the continental simplicity of Amsterdam. It was a city full of historic buildings, connected by roads occupied by cyclists, local men and women battling through the holiday crowds, ringing the bells on their bicycles in futile attempts to get tourists to clear a path. The inattentive visitors didn't heed the frantic ringing through inactivity, ignorance or through their minds being elsewhere.

It was a place of contradiction, where small boutiques selling jewellery and partisan goods stood next to chain shops and markets selling fruit, vegetables and American-style sweets. A place where cyclists were joined by people on scooters, skateboards and, in one weird moment, which Jack caught on camera, a person on skiis-with-wheels, complete with two poles to help push him through the streets. A place where on one corner you'd have a busker performing hits of the Killers and another where someone would be playing the harp.

It was a place where tall, blonde-haired men, with upper-class accents mingled on street corners flogging punting to tourists, their seasonally inappropriate jumpers sprawled over their shoulders, next to groups of tourists being targeted by students earning holiday money by touting walking tours, their services advertised inexpertly on small placards in English and Chinese.

Everywhere there were tourists taking photos, mainly of other tourists in front of old buildings, or with selfie sticks jutting out above them.

The food on offer in the pavement cafes, street van and shops was as deconstructed as the shop names, one sandwich shop going by the name 'Bread & Meat'.

Jack looked around at areas further away from his direct vicinity. The sun happened to be shining down on the arts and crafts market, hiding behind row upon row of secured bicycles and gaggles of teenagers in yellow t-shirts and rather shot denim pants, knots of tourists moving up and down the pavement like groups of geese.

Nearer to him, an elderly man in cream trousers, a blue-chequered top and a straw boater was awkwardly pulling a suitcase in wheels across the cobbles. A young child in a pram beamed with joy at a small ice-cream. A middle-aged guard in a bowler stood outside one of the colleges, telling visitors it was closed for the day due to a wedding, ignoring their howls of disappointment.

A woman in a pink top, battered blue converse and bags of shopping from high-class shops, held up a selfie stick to snap a picture of herself, only to look withdrawn as the cheaply made imported piece of plastic broke and sent her phone careering to the floor.

A surprisingly refined hen party passed Jack, identified by the pink badges each of them were wearing and the sash and deely-boppers on the head of the brideto-be. A group of young men and women passed in period clothing, advertising a local Shakespeare festival, thrusting smartly designed booklets into the hands of passing people.

Jack noticed that he wasn't alone in this place. There were cameras everywhere: in people's hands, on selfie-sticks, around necks and on monopods; they were almost as ubiquitous as the bikes and he wondered how many times the people standing outside the college had been asked to take photos over their working life.

Jack decided that he'd observed enough and he felt it was time to explore the place a little more, heading through the streets and passing two shops that showed the contradictions of the place so well. One shop was selling cream teas at £3.50. Next to it was a shop selling £1500 bottles of wine.

He eventually found his way to where he wanted to go – the river – by passing the central market, where he picked up a few snacks, including some black olives, a large scotch-egg, and a home-made pie, and through the shops, where he spotted his sister browsing in a high-end fashion shop. Jack turned the corner and down a passageway, following the words 'To the River' written on a brick wall in chalk. He emerged at the other end past a queue of people waiting to go punting, and towards the river where he sat down on the grass bank to watch various boats go by. He surreptitiously removed the pie from his pocket and took a few mouthfuls, cautious to not raise the ire of the bowler-hat wearing gentleman who was patrolling the area, telling people that picnics were forbidden and chastising anyone who took even one casual step on the well-manicured grass that sat behind him.

Jack spent the next thirty-minutes watching the people and the river, enjoying the battle between the professionals and the public – mostly men – who figured they could do it, but often ended up clashing with other boats, turning them around to block all the lanes, almost falling into the water or, as in one case, nearly hitting their head on the low bridge that stood proudly across the river. One unlucky navigator lost his punt by it hitting the bridge and then had to push the boat back with his hands on the bridge.

He watched as the vessels went by, each with a unique name. Some were full of hen parties; others themed, with each member including the pilot dressed in Hawaiian leis and grass skirts, or Mexican sombreros and fake moustaches, looking incongruous in their historic surroundings. Sitting on the bank allowed James to hear snatches of the conversations going on, the operators of the boats telling stories of Isaac Newton or the colleges; One person, who resembled a younger Boris Johnson with a tassel of blonde hair and a typically posh accent, was telling his party how all the boats were named after things associated with the number three, due to their association with Trinity College, which is how one ended up being called Fluffy after the three-headed dog in the first Harry Potter book. Jack found it amusing, as he finished off his pie, to hear the same man reference, in clear-cut Queen's English, 'Boaty McBoatFace.

The rest of the day passed in a flurry of photography. Just before six, the all clear was sounded and Jack met up with his family. They chose to wait a bit longer to avoid the huge exit that this announcement sparked, in an attempt to stave off the gridlock that they expected, but even so they got stuck in it and all the shine of a day in the city was taken off by a long, tedious and tiring journey back. The Kent family fervently hoped there would never be another one of these.

*

Nevertheless, the fifth day came, the day that would become known by the term the Prime Minister had coined: 'The Last Human Getaway'. It was the biggest ever, taking in at least sixty percent of the UK, putting further strain on the government's purse and the transport network of the country in ways that had never previously been seen. It included, for the first time, evacuations of some densely populated areas of London, which added even more pressure. The getaway had also extended further, with similar schemes in France, Germany, Spain, Northern Africa and even some parts of North America and Canada. Clearly, the British Government finally had to share whatever was happening with their transatlantic colleagues.

The date for the day was set, but Chris Kent had made his decision, that he and his family were not going to leave. So, as the sun rose on the morning of the chosen day the family hid around the house, keeping out of sight of any windows and remaining silent, either hiding behind their beds or in the walk-in wardrobe, unaware of just exactly how the armies would know if anyone had stayed back.

At one point they heard the sound of a flotilla of cars travelling down the road and another the unmistakable sound of a drone, presumably part of an army of technology scanning each house for life signs. It must have missed their body heat as nothing came of their house being scanned. Perhaps the army was just too overwhelmed now to deal with anybody breaking the rules, and instead of removing them from their houses and sending them to the prison camps, they were just leaving them to whatever fate deemed appropriate.

An hour after the hum of the visiting drone died down, Chris Kent felt brave enough to leave the confines of the wardrobe, still avoiding any direct line of sight from the windows. He peered cautiously through the slightest of gaps in the blind and saw the roads were eerily deserted. The soldiers, or police, or whoever had long moved into other parts of the city. He could just make out the small pin-pricks of drones flying around the city, darting from property to property. Chris chose to leave the window and collect the three other family members. Together, they all made their way to the living room where the blinds were closed and they began to fill the time by playing a board game spread across the kitchen table, snacking on crisps, nuts and dips.

"This is nice, isn't it?" Chris commented, rolling the dice and throwing a seven.

The family nodded, but this affirmation looked at odds with their faces, which were slightly pale and withdrawn. Jack had hoped to spend the day watching television, as his first choice of taking photos outside was vetoed by his father, in case he was spotted and shot at. Sadly, the television would be too noisy in case anyone passed and, besides, the shows were limited due to many of the television centres being evacuated for the day.

Much of the day passed uneventfully. Jack found himself beating the family at Monopoly, whereas Jo was the Scrabble champion. Chloe succeeded at Pictionary, leaving Chris the sole member of the family with no wins. Even at Frustration he failed, losing once more to his wife. It was as they were packing this away that Chris stopped.

"Did you hear that?" he asked, his ears picking up the distant sound of crackling. He skulked carefully across the room like a middle-aged, flabby James Bond and looked out of the window to see a bright object falling from the sky, kind of like an asteroid but bigger and more metallic looking. He gawped as it landed with about two streets away, with a deafening crash that shook the whole house, followed by the sound of a house being levelled. Moments later a shockwave passed through the buildings, pushing him backwards.

"Shit," Jack exclaimed. "What was that?"

Chris shook his head. "Some sort of asteroid, I think?"

"So that's' why they've been keeping us out of these areas? To stop us being killed by falling asteroids?"

"Possibly," Chris replied, moving back over to the window and staring out, craning his neck around to see vehicles rushing across the end of the road towards the crash site. "But if it's just asteroids, why not tell us? It must be something more."

"You know governments. They're always secretive," Jack mused.

Chris continued to look out of the window trying to see if anything was happening, but the best clues weren't visible, but audible, as the sound of loud gunfire sparked up, the shots loud even though they were streets away. Chris looked around as tanks started to appear on their street, one pulling up outside their house. He released the blind he was looking through and got everyone to lay down on the floor. The windows rattled as a mortar round was fired and the building shook once more as something was hit. There was the unearthly sound of screeching, followed by more fire-fighting. And then quiet.

Chris looked up from his position on the floor and looked over to his family. Was it over?

Then, like the best jump scare from a horror movie, a large black object came flying through their window. Though shocked by the sudden clatter, flying glass and the object landing on the table scattering playing pieces everywhere, Chris got a good look at the thing. It resembled a large, richly black octopus with at least three eyes and several tentacles that looked razor sharp. He watched as momentum flung it back across the table and against the far wall, which it smashed through with ease. Almost instantaneously, half-a-dozen people in combats carrying huge guns jumped through the broken window and engaged in a fire fight with the creature, bullets whizzing past the ears of the Kent family, people in boots propelling themselves through the house with no care for where they were standing.

The family watched as the group chased the creature through the house and out through the newly formed hole to the back garden, where there was the sound of more gunfire, more animalistic screams, and shouts from soldier to soldier. When the commotion had moved away from the house and felt more distant, each member of the family got to their feet and brushed dust and broken glass off their clothes and out of their hair.

"What the hell was that?" Chloe asked, looking around at the smashed window and the trashed house.

"I think," Jack said, "it was some sort of alien."

Jack cursed that he hadn't been more prepared with his camera.

That night, when the all clear was sounded, the usual return of everyone from their days out took place, roads once more gridlocked, trains over-crowded and buses choc-full of people. Many returned to find their houses, streets and cities untouched, some to homes ruined or destroyed by objects that had fallen from the sky, or armaments that had been fired. That night, at just past 9pm GMT, the Prime Minister once more stepped outside ten Downing Street to brief the largest gathering of journalists ever to meet opposite her podium. Two large floodlights lit up the leader of the country as she delivered her speech; even her own residence had been affected, signs of damage visible to the windows of the property behind her.

All that day, blogs had been abuzz with conflicting reports of space debris, blurry social media posts of creatures, and anecdotes from shocked soldiers about what they'd been dealing with, plus first-hand accounts from families like the Kents who had stayed behind and witnessed things. Stories began to slot into place and it made for distasteful reading, with many critical conversations about the Government and how they'd handled things. The Prime Minister knew she had to act.

"Just over two years ago we received reports from one of our agencies of incoming space debris to three areas of this county. Research and observations suggested that they were not asteroids or space junk, but something more extra-terrestrial. To avoid panic we chose to clear these areas and deal with this low-scale invasion ourselves – and we handled it.

"However, since then, these invasions have become more regular and wide-spread and our attempts to protect the people of this country have become more impossible to contain, and now our friends in Europe, Africa and North America are facing the same challenges and threats from these creatures. Some have also landed in areas of open water that fell outside of obvious jurisdictions."

The Prime Minister took a deep breath before continuing.

"It has become increasingly difficult to keep our people safe. The getaways we have been undertaking are no longer financially viable and our infrastructure can no longer cope with such a large movement of people.

"We anticipate that the next wave could mean an evacuation of the entire country, which we deem to be too difficult a prospect. Therefore, from tomorrow, we shall be arming every fit and able man and woman in this country with what is necessary to combat this alien threat, so when the next invasion happens we will be ready, as a country, to deal with it.

"Today was the Last Human Getaway, but we can no longer keep this invasion under wraps. The human race must face its problems head-on. Today we told you to leave. Tomorrow we will fight."

One Mistake Too Many

By S. R. Martindale

In the grey
You see that lonely twisted hand reaching for the sky,
It's skin smooth and bleached.
They say the hand used to shelter the small
And support the creepers and the climbers, the walkers and the plodders.

They say there were even creatures,
Tall enough to reach the tips of its twisted fingers.
They say there was green, there was blue and there were reds,
Like the coats we strut about in
Like the comforts and the possessions that make us human.

They say the hand was once not alone,
Like companions huddling together, protecting, reflecting.
Whispering and conspiring, they stretched and reached to the heavens.
Far and further they stretched,
All the beautiful colours we've so artificially recreated.

An escape they called it, our finest hour:
The last human getaway,
But we were only escaping from ourselves.
Accidents upon all the previous accidents before that.
Unfortunate. Couldn't have seen it coming.

They say we made many mistakes,
Like the many mistakes before them.
They say there was once life
Before we made one mistake
Too many.

WANTED
DEAD OR ALIVE
Wanted for murder and robbery of the Pine City Stage
STILL AT LARGE
THE GORILLA MURDERER
NOTORIOUS OUTLAW
$5,000 REWARD
IMMEDIATELY CONTACT DEPARTMENT OF JUSTICE

The Murders

By Rae Bailey

(black blinds reflect the light like white mirrors)

Childhood lying still in a summerlight bath:
bright framed panes of window laying
a still picture on the water mirror;
slight stirring blasts magical fractures,
glass glitter, break, ripple; still unbroken.

Now lying still in a summerlight bath:
bright window barred with blinds laying
a still picture crossed with black varnished slats;
light from the outside, light on the water mirror;
light on the shiny slat, light on the blind mirror;
light on the blind mirror shines on the water mirror.

Suddenly, up rushes a murder of crows:
in the window light flying roofwards,
in the blind mirror flying earthwards;
in the water to and away from each other,
in the water mirror a murder,
in the blind mirror a creation.
And I could break this grill of murders with
a tremble: water mirror crazy shards of living.

But the wing beat and the crow call
always cry forwards
and sounds I cannot break
into glittering shards
in the mirror of summerlight.

The Gorilla Murders

By G. Burton

It had been the worst kind of mistake he could have made.

It wasn't even as though he could blame it on autocorrect. It had been his writing, he'd sent it to the editing team, and they would never adjust it without first checking with him.

Which meant that this was his fault.

In black and white it was almost terrifying...

What should have been referring to a cluster of impromptu, unauthorised murders was now – thanks to him – being called:

THE GORILLA MURDERS

The Gorilla Murders

By Philip Lickley

Sandra from reception entered the room, smiled in the direction of Detective Inspector Thompson and left a small red mug of hot steaming tea on the table. She smiled again in his direction as she left and closed the door gently behind her. The old lady sat at the table. Sixty-three years old, grey-haired and smelling faintly of Yardley lavender body wash, she lifted the cup, her shaking hands ejecting small splashes of tea from the mug. The old lady took a quick slurp, realised it was both too hot and too sweet for her, and put the mug back down again, a small brown stain appearing on the table where the escaped liquid had gathered.

"Now, Mrs Stevens," Thompson said, in his thick Liverpudlian accent. "The purpose of this is to try and establish the identity of the person who attacked you last Wednesday evening."

"He didn't attack me," Mrs Stevens replied in a firm, but slightly quivery voice. "He just startled me, that's all."

Last Wednesday Mrs Stevens had been putting her cat Marmaduke out for the night when she heard a series of noises from the bottom of her garden. In the dim light of the street lamps she had seen someone standing there, by the hedge that kept her home hidden from those casually wandering down the street. Mrs Stevens had called out to the person, but received no reply. All the figure did was slowly move towards her up the garden until she could get a decent look at it under the security light. She peered through her old spectacles until her eyes focussed sufficiently to make out the figure, and when she saw it she yelled out in fear and retired to her house as quickly as her legs could carry her. She quickly locked up the front door and attached the bolt before walking with purpose into her living room, closing the curtains and taking refuge in her armchair in the hope that the person would go away. She wasn't troubled for the rest of the night.

"That's fine," Thompson muttered, sliding a folder across the table towards Mrs Stevens so it rested there between the mug and the old lady. "This is a folder of various images we've put together that will help you in establishing a good likeness of the person you saw. Do you understand?"

Mrs Stevens nodded, adjusting her glasses and blinking in the harsh florescent light. She took one more sip of the slightly cooler tea and thought about it as the brown liquid swished around her false teeth. Putting the mug down she prised open the folder and took from it a series of brown envelopes, each open and marked in biro with terms such as 'eyes', 'ears' and 'chin'. Mrs Stevens carefully and frustratingly slowly (as far as Thompson was concerned, as it was nearly 6pm and he longed to be back home to put his feet up with a can of lager and the football) took the contents out of each envelope and lined them up on the table in a fashion that could only really be described as obsessive compulsive. Once she'd picked her chosen elements she carefully scooped up the rest of the bits and slipped them back into the envelope, before moving onto the next in turn.

"I wish I'd given her the tablet," Thompson muttered under his breath, thinking about the more modern version they had. He'd picked the older way of doing things thinking that Mrs Thompson wasn't that au fait with technology. She had, after all, tried to move the keyboard on the main desk along as she typed, as if she had been operating a typewriter. DI Thompson had feared what she might do with an iPad if presented with one.

Soon, though not soon enough for the detective, Mrs Stevens was done, and she sat back in her chair and admired her handiwork in the same way that Van Gogh might have done when he'd completed his Sunflowers. DI Thompson wasn't entirely convinced Van Gogh had done it whilst drinking PG Tips from a cracked mug, though.

He looked down at the image Mrs Stevens had created and recoiled in confusion as his brain, already tired from a day of paperwork, interviews and bureaucracy, struggled to make sense of it.

"Mrs Stevens," he said, tilting his head as if expecting the identikit image to be some sort of optical illusion that he had to consider from a particular angle. "Unless I'm mistaken the image you've created isn't exactly human."

DI Thompson studied the heavy brow, the thick hair, the eyes set forward and the bushy beard. "It sort of resembles, if you don't mind me saying, a gorilla."

Mrs Stevens looked at him as if he were the mad one. "Why DI Thompson, then I am happy," she said, slurping down some more tea. "Because that's exactly what I saw."

DI Thompson stared at her and cleared his throat as if to speak, but he wasn't exactly sure what to say. "You're telling me that the intruder in your garden was not human, but a gorilla?"

"Yes. An actual gorilla."

"Okay," DI Thompson said in the way a parent would address a child who'd just told them they'd seen an elephant in their back garden emptying the pond via its trunk. "Are you sure it wasn't someone with a lot of facial hair?"

"Well it was. A lot of facial hair. And body hair. A gorilla."

"Very well," DI Thompson said with a sigh, the bright lights making his eyes ache. "I will get onto this first thing in the morning and try and find out who the mysterious individual is. Can I get you anything else before we help you home?"

"A couple of biscuits would be nice, to go with the rest of the tea."

"Certainly," DI Thompson said, relishing the chance to get away from the clearly confused old lady. He walked out of the room, spotted a colleague finishing off a banana as they moved from room to room, and chuckled out loud. "A gorilla," he mumbled as part of his own private joke. His banana-eating colleague just looked at him confused before going about the rest of their business.

*

DI Thompson had planned to give Mrs Stevens' sighting a courteous, but short look the following day, which would have amounted to little more than phoning up some local zoos to enquire after any escapees and checking a few joke shops to see if anyone had been in to buy a gorilla suit recently. But this plan was abandoned when he arrived at work the next morning with a coffee in one hand and a bacon sandwich in the other, to find a knot of journalists, cameramen and hangers-on gathered outside the police station, snapping away and trying to speak to anyone going in or coming out of the station, no matter their rank. DI Thompson, bemused, took a bite from his butty and pushed through the throng of people, not answering any of the questions or rising to any of the statements yelled at him in close proximity. Clearly it was a slow day for news and the local newspapers needed anything they could get to print.

"Is it true that there's an escaped gorilla on the loose?" yelled one.

"Has a giant monkey been terrorising old women?" called out another.

"What effect will this have on local banana sales?" cried out a third.

DI Thompson ignored them all, pushed open the front door to the station and entered the reception area, where he quickly wolfed down the rest of his sandwich and gulped down his now lukewarm coffee.

"It's mad out there!" Sandra exclaimed, carrying a pile of paperwork that was far too tall for her to properly see over.

That she didn't drop any or collide with any of the random obstacles scattered around the station was clearly testament to her professionalism, or perhaps some sort of echolocation. DI Thompson made a note to ask her later if she was part dolphin, though he figured he would probably get slapped for it.

He picked up, from one of the tables in the waiting area, a copy of that morning's paper. Slapped across the front was the headline 'GORILLA GOES FOR GRANNY', complete with a slightly tongue-in-cheek artist's imaging of the encounter. Somehow the story had leaked and was now being played out for its full comic potential.

"It's not just in the local paper," Sandra said, emerging from a side room carrying yet more folders. "It's all over the internet. Twitter. Instagram. Buzzfeed. They're all running with it."

DI Thompson rolled his eyes. He'd hoped to get Mrs Stevens' unusual encounter swept under the carpet as a case of an old dear getting confused, thinking she'd seen King Kong in her conservatory. Now with the media onto it he realised quickly he would have to be seen doing his job. Resigned, DI Thompson walked over to the coffee machine, poured himself another coffee and downed it pretty much in one go.

"It's going to be a long day," he muttered to himself.

Much of the morning was spent ticking the necessary boxes, which in this case was phoning up the local zoos ("We've already told the press this morning, no gorillas have escaped; you're a bit late to the game I'm afraid!") and the fancy dress shops ("No one has bought any for weeks, but since this story broke we've sold out. It's like the clown craze all over again! I've got my supplier rushing us over a job lot of gorilla outfits this afternoon!"). There was nothing, of course, to suggest a real life gorilla was on the loose. DI Thompson was left with the only reasonable solution that it was a prankster, someone who had already got the fancy dress weeks earlier.

Soon the story was spread all over the internet. There were thousands of tweets each hour, offering jokes or theories about the gorilla. Memes had sprung up on 9gag, Instagram and Tumblr, and were being re-posted more than those irritating images of Minions. Buzzfeed had got in on the act and were quickly posting regular 'Here are ten things you didn't know about Gorillas (number five will amaze you!)' columns. Soon people were dressing up in their own gorilla costumes - some well-made, many badly cobbled together like a poor Airfix model - and creating videos of their own pranks, some of which quickly went viral. It wasn't long before videos of gorilla pranks had replaced clown videos, Mannequin challenge attempts, and Joe Biden parodies as the most shared items across social media.

But, as with all things, the jokes soon started to fade away, to be replaced by the next trend or pop culture titbit, and DI Thompson was happy that he could get about his usual business of paperwork and investigating criminals with an average amount of body hair and the usual preference for bananas.

Of course, though, like double denim, Jeremy Clarkson and Ed Balls, things can come back when you least expect them and one morning, entering the office with a coffee and a croissant, DI Thompson was met by a rather ashen faced Sandra.

"Are you okay, Sandra?" he asked, taking a bite from his croissant.

"Not really," she murmured, passing him a memo. He studied it, his pupils moving left and right as he read as if following the progress of a typewriter. He muttered a curse word under his breath, which I won't repeat here, but think of the worst swearword you can think of and precede it with the word 'holy'.

The memo told of the discovery of a body in the local canal. Witnesses reported that something resembling a gorilla had jumped out on the person and thrown them into the canal before running off. Bystanders had tried to save the person, but they had been too late. All morning, officers had been scouring the canal for clues, yet all they'd found was a clump of hair which could have come from the criminal, but could equally have come from a dog or a badger. The hair had bene deposited into an evidence bag and sent off to some lab somewhere to be poked and prodded by a sour-faced scientist in a crisp white coat. Until then, all DI Thompson could do was muse on whether it was a prank gone wrong, or whether this time a genuine gorilla was actually on the loose. Again, phone calls to zoos proved fruitless ("We think we may have misplaced a penguin, but it could be just in the aquarium again, sampling the tropical fish...") as well as fancy dress shops ruling themselves out ("We stopped stocking them after the last series of pranks. It's all about Donald Trump wigs now."). Owners of private zoos had even taken the trouble to contact DI Thompson themselves, presumably to quickly rule themselves out of any murder charges.

With this incident on the police's books, a press conference was held and it was soon on the front page of every newspaper under banners that ranged from the serious to the banal, often using some variation on 'Gorilla Gate' or 'Bananas Crime!', where tabloid journalists, using terms not really fitting after the death of a person, mused about the police 'slipping up' or the criminal 'making a monkey out of them'.

This 'King Kong of Krimes' (The Sun) soon became bigger when a second death took place, this time of an elderly man who had apparently died of a heart attack when he and his wife saw a gorilla in their garden. The mysterious gorilla – 'Could the murderous monkey be an immigrant who came over with a travelling circus?' (The Daily Mail) – was still no closer to being captured, even with the police diverting their resources to tracking it down. DI Thompson was spending the days in press conferences, taking statements and vox pops that there was little likelihood that it was a genuine animal, more a murderer using a pop-culture disguise. The media were now trying to connect previous crimes to the deaths, some more successfully than others, such as 'Was Diana's Driver spooked by a Gorilla'? (The Express).

Soon the city and the wider country were gripped by gorilla fever (coincidentally, also a concern raised by NHS chiefs, if it was indeed a genuine animal) and DI Thompson was determined to stop it in its tracks. The main room of the station was decked out like the set of a police drama with photos, identikit pictures and maps blu-tacked up on walls, whilst a large white board resembled a cross between a crossword clues list and a plan that a football pundit would draw. But despite pacing up and down the room, batting ideas back and forth with colleagues and searching Tumblr for ideas and rumours, the team were no closer to working out who the culprit was, or indeed whether it was man or beast. Or a mixture of both, if the latest edition of the Fortean Times was to be believed. Sandra, by this point, had gone off sick; and the canteen had had to stop selling bananas and banoffee pie for fear of driving the officers crazy. Some of them had spent three days in a banana warehouse following up an online rumour that a monkey had set up home among the produce, resulting in nothing but a wasted 72 hours of officer time, a team sick of the smell of bananas, and two funny accounts of officers discovering that yes, banana skins are slippery when trod on.

Finally, on the Thursday of that week a strong lead came in, but to the untrained eye the message, at first, didn't seem that strange.

*

DI Thompson found himself in the bedroom of a young woman.

Sadly, for him, this was business, not pleasure and he cursed his luck. She did bring him regular cups of sweet tea and Jammie Dodgers, though, so all was not lost. For several hours on that Thursday afternoon he found himself perched on a stool, staring out of a window at a property across the street; a house that looked no different than any other standard terraced building in this part of the city. There was, however, something different about it. The owner of the house DI

Thompson was currently in – Susie Shaw – was an author and thus spent most of her time in the study, where he was now, writing.

Well, attempting to write. A lot of the time he spent staring blankly at a computer monitor, going to make endless cups of tea or visiting the toilet to dispense of the excess liquid. The rest was spent stuck in an endless loop of Facebook, Twitter and Instagram, or trying to answer such important scientific questions, like 'How far will my chair spin with a certain amount of force?' or 'How many Jaffa Cakes can be piled on top of each other and still remain stable?'. Even more time was spent staring out of the window with a hot mug of tea, watching the world go by, usually consisting of postmen, school children and boy racers testing the suspension of their cars as they sped up and down the street, avoiding speed bumps. There was, though, one more unusual person, and that was the owner of the house opposite.

"I'd see him come out of the house late in the evening," Susie told DI Thompson when he'd first arrived after, of course, offering him some tea. "He was wearing a hefty coat, as he was trying to cover up what he was wearing. One night, I spotted what looked to be a furry mask sticking out of one of the coat pockets. I didn't think much of it until all these gorilla reports surfaced and it made me think that he could well be going out partially-dressed as a gorilla. I'd just seen something on the Huffington Post about the murders so it was fresh in my mind, and of course it's been in all the local press."

"What do you know about him?" DI Thompson had asked, nibbling his way through a chocolate digestive.

"Only that he used to be a scientist of some sort. We barely spoke, but I remember him talking about some research he was conducting when we passed on the street once. I'd started talking about my latest short story and how I was struggling to write 5000 words that people would want to read. It was something about a laboratory experiment gone wrong. That was when he mentioned his work and he sparked my interest so I ran back here to finish off the work. That story became my only paid-for work so far, so I have him to thank for that."

"How would you describe him?"

"A loner perhaps. A little about anti-social. But aren't we all? The highlight of my day is Judge Rinder and a Mars Bar, and occasionally a few snatched words when British Gas come round to service my boiler."

"So, nothing unusual?"

"No more so than anyone else."

DI Thompson had nodded, finished off his biscuits, and headed upstairs to start his observations, something he was still doing now.

There he stayed, fuelled by PG Tips and Oreos, until just past six o'clock, when the theme tune of Pointless had faded away, to be replaced by some plummy-voiced newsreader reading out headlines. At this time, DI Thompson saw someone leave the house under observation and they matched Susie's description: a man wearing a thick coat and looking shifty. DI Thompson eyed up the coat. Could that possibly hide a gorilla costume? It was likely.

He watched as the man left, but instead of giving chase decided to investigate the house instead. He told Susie that he was popping out – refusing a slice of cherry pie as he did so – and left out the front door. The autumnal sky was now darkening and the trees that lined the length of the street were blowing eerily in the wind that was gradually whipping up. Slowly, one by one, streetlights were switching on and there was the occasional rumble and roar of a car as commuters started returning home ready for tea (both definitions) and evenings of mindless television. DI Thompson, though, had more than Eastenders on his mind as he tightened up his jacket, crossed the road and scooted up the path of the house under investigation like a suspicious-looking fox, glancing left and right in case the person who he had seen leaving returned unexpectedly.

He tried the door, but it was locked. He crouched down and glanced through the letterbox, which he carefully opened with his fingers, but it was too dark to see inside. There were no windows open; he knew also, from the houses opposite, these were homes with no back doors, so the front was the only way in. One thought came to mind, a convenient and slightly contrived thought, and he looked around for anywhere someone might store a key for emergencies. An odd plant pot, down in the small front garden, attracted his attention and he was delighted to find a small key, hidden not under it, but Sellotaped within it. DI Thompson peeled the key away and studied it in the street light.

"I can't believe people still do this," he thought to himself, continuing. "If Susie had written such a thing in one of her short stories I would have laughed at the sheer convenience."

He discounted the thought and unlocked the front door, the lock giving up its tight grip on the frame with a satisfying click. DI Thompson pulled down the handle and made his way inside, navigating not by the lights and lamps that were dotted around the rather old-fashioned house, but by the light of the pocket torch that he'd removed from his coat.

DI Thompson studied the home as his torchlight flickered over the various framed photos, bits of furniture and other knick-knacks that lay around the surprisingly cluttered house. Old magazines lay on the arms of chairs and cutlery and crockery lay in surprising places, like the person who lived there either had little time or little desire to keep the place clean and tidy.

With very little downstairs of any note, DI Thompson made his way up the carpeted stairs, the noise-suppressing quality of the carpet ruined by regular squeaks from the ageing floorboards. He was glad when he reached the summit, so he didn't have to hear it anymore and could resume moving the torch around to check the area. DI Thompson entered the back bedroom, pushing the door a little so he could squeeze in and that's when he found it, images and diagrams placed with compulsive precision across the wallpapered walls. Some were newspaper cuttings, others were scientific diagrams, all displayed as if the person who curated the weird art display had been brought up on a diet of clichéd police dramas. On the only piece of furniture in the room – a chair –a white lab coat was draped over the back.

DI Thompson moved around the room, reading the headlines of the stories piece by piece under each broad sweep of the torch. Many of the stories were about animal research or conservation and some were quite punchy political pieces about the European Union and Brexit. He got so involved in reading the narrative that he only realised he was no longer alone was when a squeak from a floorboard on the stairs snapped him out of his bubble. By then a figure had joined him in the room, switching on the light. Stood there was the man he'd witnessed leaving their earlier, clearly dressed in a thick coat over a poorly concealed gorilla outfit. In his left hand he was still clutching a mask.

"I knew someone would find me eventually," he said in a rather flat, nasal voice. "I take it from your suit and torch that you're the police?"

DI Thompson nodded. "And you?"

"Malcolm."

"Do you have a second name?"

"Sometimes."

"That's an unusual second name."

"Very droll, officer. I sometimes tell people. Though not the police."

"Well you'll have to tell me when I take you down to the station."

Malcolm just nodded. "Thomas Thwaites."

"Is that like a double-barrelled surname?"

"No. I'm just explaining the person who inspired me."

"Inspired you to murder?"

"Not quite. Thomas Thwaites was a researcher who decided to live life as a goat as a means to understanding the life of the creature."

That story rang a bell with DI Thompson. He'd remembered reading it in the Metro somewhere between the celebrity gossip and the Sudoku.

"That's really my story. I used to work abroad researching the behaviour of gorillas, until the referendum, when my work security suddenly became a little bit more tentative and the research grant was pulled, and I had to return here. But, you see, my work is more important than any political wranglings between countries, so I had to do the next best thing."

"Speak to zoos in the UK to continue your work here?"

Malcolm just scoffed. "Captive gorillas behave differently. It just wouldn't be the same."

"But dressing up as a gorilla and trying to live like one is more realistic?" DI Thompson asked, unable to keep the incredulity out of his voice.

"Yes, but it was also meant to highlight my plight. Did you see how much publicity Thwaites got for strapping some prosthetics on and ambling about in fields? I was doing it properly. A proper costume. Properly acting out the gorilla life. Scaring that old woman was a mistake – I'd got lost in the dark – but it gave me the attention my plight needed. Unfortunately the media soon lost interest and moved onto their next thing before I had chance to make my public statement. That's when I had to push it up a notch..."

"To murder."

"Not quite. I didn't mean to kill the person in the canal, I just got a bit carried away. And the old man, well he was old..."

"You'll have to explain this to the court."

"I shall do, and in doing so, I will get the publicity I need."

"Shame you'll be in jail."

"Then I, too, shall be like the animals in your zoos. A beast captured."

DI Thompson nodded. "You need to come with me now."

Malcolm just laughed. "I think you and I know the story has got to have more of an angle than this to get the headline. There's one thing missing that will really get the tabloids buzzing about my capture."

"Which is?"

"The manner in which you capture me during my daring escape."

Malcolm smiled, turned and headed towards the stairs. There he theatrically took from his pocket a banana, peeled it and dropped the skin on the stairs. He chomped through the banana in two mouthfuls, closed his eyes and walked onto the skin, realising it wasn't actually that slippery, but throwing himself manfully down the stairs anyway. DI Thompson darted over and peered over the bannister to see Malcolm lying prostrate at the bottom of the staircase.

"Now that will be a headline," he spluttered painfully from down at the bottom. "Police capture mad scientist after banana skin mishap. Beat that, Mr Goat."

DI Thompson rolled his eyes and called for an ambulance and backup on his phone. "It looks as if I may have solved the murders."

*

With Malcolm's arrest came peace and a new range of news stories in the British media. Work became relatively normal once more for DI Thompson, much to his relief. Sandra returned to work. The coffee machine began to play up. The crimes returned to their usual banality. Normality was resumed.

Or at least it was for several weeks, until one

Tuesday when Sandra came into his office with a news bulletin.

"I hate to say this, but there have been reports now of someone dressed as a tiger at night, creeping around houses and scaring people."

DI Thompson looked at the report. Malcolm's case hadn't even reached court yet and already someone was following in his hairy, over-sized footsteps.

"Do you think it's something new, or related to the previous crimes? I mean it can't be Malcolm, so it must be someone else..."

Sandra smiled and said, with relish, "I bet they were inspired by the gorilla crimes, but chose a tiger instead."

DI Thompson nodded.

Sandra continued, grinning now. "I would say it's nothing more than a copycat crime."

DI Thompson nodded and muttered an agreement until his brain twigged on what she'd just said.

"Copycat? Get out of my office," he said, throwing the news report playfully at her. Sandra smiled, stuck out her tongue, and skipped out of the office, thanking someone across the hall for faking the bulletin. DI Thompson, back in the office, smiled. He would be glad to never hear of an animal based crime again, for the rest of his nine lives.

The Gorilla Murders

By M. Loftouse

We are humans. But are we not animals too?

The chattering grew louder as the two made their way inside. Glowering as he pushed past the crowd that seemed to have huddled near the television, he glanced back to check the smaller and thinner Myra was following after him and stopped at the counter. He gave the bartender a quick look and the man understood that this wasn't going to be a social call. Taking a usual pint of beer, the black haired man in his mid-twenties, sauntered over to where they stood and watched them closely; behind him on the board were clippings upon clippings of the 2008 forest massacre.

"Another one then, Mister Lloyd?"

The man didn't look up, for this was the usual greeting he received in this pub. It had been five years since the detective had first frequented this place and not once had he ever given the impression of anything being unrelated to work. The young barman often wondered where he went on his off days.

The taller man looked over his shoulder at his partner, a short brunette, who seemed to be having some trouble penetrating the crowd at the back and chuckled lightly before taking a swig. He grimaced at the question, as was his usual stance and rubbed his stubble. "The same Dan. These murders will be the death of me"

"Have you not got any leads, sir?" Dan asked, one hand hovering over the damp cloth he used to clean the glasses, his eyes focused on the man. He was always fascinated by the cases the detectives worked. There weren't many, in a small town like this, however, so anything untoward always seemed to become big news. Mister Lloyd was always the first to arrive at any crime scene; all his cases had been solved in the last five years, but even so he was still desperately seeking his big break.

For Dan, the man was a hero, even before he had come to the town. His previous job as a ranger hadn't worked out for him, so he'd turned to bartending to get by. He straightened his glasses and slapped the cloth on his shoulder before turning to look at the detective.

"Come now lad, you know I can't talk about the case," Lloyd sneered at the last word and the bartender nodded, dejected. Something was different this time, though, he thought, as though the case was taking its toll on the old man, but he brushed the thought aside and continued on to the other customers.

He came back a few minutes later. "Right, well you see, I was intrigued by the name, though," said Dan, giving a short pause before continuing, tilting his head and whispering in the other's direction so the rest of the customers wouldn't listen in. "They are calling 'em Gorilla Murders, eh? That ought to be a strange name for these killings, you reckon?"

Lloyd simply returned the boy's enthusiasm with a small smile. He liked the kid, who was always optimistic, unlike himself, but he was right. A strange name for a case indeed, but then this was a strange case, stranger than all of the others combined.

He half muttered those words before Myra strutted over to him, frazzled and flapping a battered copy of the day's paper. "Could have helped there, Edgar," she grunted and hopped onto the bar stool, her short legs dangling as she did so. Slapping the thick bundle onto the marble countertop she received a few raised eyebrows down the bar. Noticing this, she rolled her eyes and turned to her partner. "These morons – bloody hell! Have you seen this? It's utter rubbish. They needn't glamorise this sh-"

Edgar held his hand up and with the other made to reach for the folded paper. Turning it over, he skimmed over the column that read, SLACKING DETS: WHAT THEY DON'T WANT YOU TO KNOW. He scoffed at it and folded it again, neatly sliding it back to Myra's side.

"Yeah, well they aren't wrong. The only connection

we've found in these past few months has been the 2008 murders," he remarked, lowering his voice when he felt the eyes of Dan following him. "Seven murdered Gorillas, seven murdered people. That's it. Mysterious, isn't it? Bloody baffling, more like!" He slammed a few bills on the counter and got up, sliding his hand inside the pocket for a lighter and giving the woman a wink before making his way out onto the bustling streets.

Myra huffed as she hastily grabbed the paper and jumped after him. She hated when he did that.

Following her partner out, she began tightening the belt around her raincoat. The forecast was for rain; as if by instinct she looked up at the sky and dropped her hands: clear skies.

Now I look like an idiot, she thought.

"So, where we off to now?" she shouted, but Edgar was already halfway across the road, not looking back and apparently puffing away.

"Animals leave a trace, don't they?" he said and disappeared round the corner.

"Good God, this man doesn't breathe!" Myra complained, hurrying after him. Following him around the corner, she saw what he meant.

The murders had occurred two blocks from this spot, all in one month. This alleyway had become a warzone, as Edgar called it. Lifting the familiar yellow tape that stretched from one end of the street to the other, Edgar stepped over the dank floor, apparently a communal dumping ground and scowled. "You recall the coroner saying each of the victims had three identical scratch marks around their necks? Uncanny, isn't it?" He laughed as he gestured around and Myra sighed. He was enjoying this when he really shouldn't.

"I remember," she replied. "Didn't help with anything. They were all found here."

"I'm beginning to think it might actually be relevant. Last night -" he paused as he drew in a long puff of his cigarette, tossing the butt to the side when he finished, "- I walked by here and found this gem." He slid his hand inside the breast pocket and withdrew two small plastic bags, throwing them at her.

"Look at those hairs. Those weren't there before. We found six bodies here, the seventh was dragged - and yes, I am saying it was dragged, before you start. Look at those marks." He pointed in the direction they had come from, where long, drag tracks were prominent in the dust. "Twenty bucks says those lead to the forest."

"Black hairs, two different bags?" Myra, confused, walked to his side, crouching down to follow his lead. "Are you saying a gorilla dragged one of the men out from here, all the way to the forest without anyone noticing?"

"No, that's absurd and you know it." He smirked and she pocketed the bags. "The murderer was careful, always so careful - took us a month and we couldn't find anything. Now, all of a sudden we get this." He tapped her pocket. "It just doesn't add up." He shook his head and got up, dusting himself off and reaching for a second cigarette.

"I'll meet you later. You need to run tests on those." he simply added and walked off.

"Sure."

She wished he would stop smoking. She was tired of all her clothes smelling of it, just from working with the man, but knew better than to say anything. The last time she had mentioned it had been a nightmare. Pulling at the cuffs of her coat, she shook her head at the memory and walked out of the alley.

*

"This is impossible." Myra dashed out of the lab as she dialled the number. "It's me. I think we have a problem."

*

At the end of his long shift, Daniel took his glasses off and ambled over to the couch, rubbing his face clear of the day's exhaustion. He reached into his half-torn jeans pocket, his unused holster lying a few inches away on the scratched table, and drew out the tips, laying them out. Around the corner of the room, Edgar quietly loaded his gun and inched forward.

He turned, seeing movement in the shadows.

"So... it was you."

The Gorilla Murders

By Lauren K. Nixon

It was a jumping cold day.
One of those brass monkeys, frost-on-the-windows, killer gorilla days,
where the sky is the colour of brushed blue steel
and pale, fading-light gold.

They turned into the little winding track.
One of those rugged, muddy, not-quite-a-farm-track paths,
never quite dry, even on the hottest days,
and now drifting full of halfway mulched, tumble-down leaves.

The windows shone bright,
that homely, yellow, chase-the-gloom-out light,
inviting them into the well-trod kitchen,
and on through the room beyond.

It was a party to remember.
A snapchat, backchat, whiskey glass and Christmas in November,
up all night and foggy-headed thing.
A real fire and toasted names affair.

They walked next day along the river,
the up again, down again, all around the bed again river,
and laughed and sang, and tried to pretend
it wouldn't soon be Monday and back to work again.

They wondered where they'd be in another ten years,
ten bustling, hustling, workaday years,
called themselves 'old', wished themselves young
and promised to do this all again.

The clouds came down around them,
soft and cold, and kitten's breath silent around them
as they parted ways
back into the real world for a time,
dreaming of another jumping cold, killer gorilla,
tumble-down leaf, golden light and mince pie,
river-walking, laughter-filled day,
when they could pretend they were adults
and not just kids who had grown older
between the rushing days and the cold,
old starlight.

SUPERSTARS

Possibly the most Superstars in one place!
(Photo credit, Allie Riley)

Emilie Addison

Washington, USA

Emilie Addison is a lover of writing, chocolate, backyard astronomy, and Oxford commas. She's a proud Ravenclaw who's jumping into her first year studying Aerospace engineering at a university and is currently working on her first full-length novel.

Hannah 'Han' R. H. Allen

York, UK

Han is a non binary writer and creator, residing in historic York. Their work is often emotive with a bittersweet edge, finding the beauty in the darker parts of life, although they are no stranger to whimsy. When not writing or creating art, they enjoy indulging in computer and console gaming, collectable card games, tabletop RP, and LARP.

Rae Bailey

Pennine Chain, UK

I used to make marginal notes in books, but now verse scribbles in me in its margin. I am more substantial than my shadow, but less substantial than my reflection.

I am not a one-eyed seller of garlic.

Sorry about the verse, it just happens.

Hannah Burns

West Yorkshire, UK

My name is Hannah Burns. I am a sporadic writer who gets random ideas at random times. Don't usually get them into an order, but sometimes when I can, they can be enjoyable. Read and enjoy all that you can.

G. Burton

West Yorkshire, UK

G. Burton is a working professional from Yorkshire who writes. Her writing has bubbled from a love of literature and a lifelong desire to put words to paper. She is currently working on her first novel-length piece of work, and on developing her book review blog, The Forensic Bibliophile

(www.theforensicbibliophile.wordpress.com).

Jessica Grace Coleman

Staffordshire, UK

Jessica Grace Coleman lives in Stafford, England, where she writes by day and writes more by night. She runs an editing/ghost writing business and self-publishes her own novels – when she can find the time.

You can find out more about her writing services at www.colemanediting.co.uk and about her own books at www.jessicagracecoleman.com.

Hailie Drescher

Alberta, Canada

Hailie is an aspiring novelist dreaming of publishing a new, fantastic series of magick proportions. In addition to being a bit of a writing fiend, Hailie also enjoys working with photo manipulation and restoration.

You can follow Hailie's journey as an author at:
http://hailiedrescher.wixsite.com/hailiedrescher
@HailieDrescher on Twitter
@Hailie_Drescher on Instagram

Mike Farren

West Yorkshire, UK

Mike Farren was born in Bradford and works as an editor in academic publishing.

His poems have appeared in various journals and anthologies, and his pamphlet, Pierrot and his Mother is available from Templar Press.

He is married and lives in Shipley, where he is one of the hosts of the Rhubarb open mic' night and frequently contributes articles to Saltaire Review and The State of the Arts.

J. A. Foley

West Yorkshire, UK

A recent newcomer to the writing field under a penname, Josh has a burning imaginative flare that cannot be switched off. He currently has two books on the go and a play, and loves to write haikus and short stories. But it isn't just the writing field that holds his creative interest. Josh is involved with several acting groups and performance projects, enjoys going to conventions in cosplay, is an avid gamer, watches a great deal of anime, and is a high level procrastinator.

Find out more about Josh's shenanigans through his internet pseudonym:

Twitter: @VonWolfstein
Instagram: AlexVonWolfstein.

T. J. Francis

Norfolk, UK

Another ex-archaeologist who loves to write, TJ joined the Superstars only recently. When she's not puzzling over what to write for them, she's researching or working on her other novels in between actually having to work. If you can prise her away from that, you might find her cooking, gorging on geek and crime shows, or looking longingly at designer handbags.

Cynthia Holt

Rhode Island, USA

Cynthia Holt is a writer and beekeeper from New England. She is the co-author of Bee Cult and the proprietress of Cabbage and Epstein apiary.

You can find her musings at her blog, No One Sleeps Naked in This House at

nicrophorus.blogspot.com.

Kim Hosking

Home is where you hang your trowel, UK

Kim is an archaeologist who dabbles in writing stories. When not scribbling away, or getting muddy in a trench, she can often be found cocooned in a blanket, cradling a cup of tea, fully immersed in a book.

She longs for the day science - or magic - will give us dragons, and she can take to the skies.

Philip Lickley

West Yorkshire, UK

By day, the entertainments manager at a Students' Union, by night... probably the same.

Shy author of two novels under a pen-name, Phil also enjoys writing short stories and comedy sketches. When he's not writing, Phil enjoys listening to music, watching films, and playing video games. He broadcasts a weekly radio show on community radio, including interviews with up and coming artists, and runs regularly, with 2017 dominated by training for the London Marathon.

You can find out more about him at www.philip-lickley.co.uk - when he can be bothered to update it!

M. Loftouse

Islamabad, Pakistan

An architect by day and an aspiring writer and reader by night, M. Loftouse is an enthusiast of all things whimsical. Her stories emerge from habitual doodling on scraps of paper and coffee spills. When she's not drawing or writing, she enjoys listening to music and spending time with her family, and their eccentric dog.

S. R. Martindale

Cumbria, UK

Shaun is a creative type who spends all day writing and colouring in. In the evenings he can be found either in front of a word processor or computer game, or squinting at a sewing machine and mumbling unrepeatable words.

He has a beard, but that's okay.

J. McGraw

London, UK

J. McGraw is a museum professional and osteoarchaeologist, but manages to raise herself out of the monotony of the coolest job in the world through science fiction and fantasy writing.

In her spare time, she works in The Wooden Tooth Factory, a place where stray thoughts, characters, and plot lines gather for company. Some say they here strange noises coming from the factory at night, but J. McGraw claims it's just the teeth, chattering in the cold.

Lauren K. Nixon

West Yorkshire, UK

An ex-archaeologist enjoying life in the slow-lane, Lauren K. Nixon is an indie author fascinated by everyday magic. She is the author of numerous short stories and the Chambers Magic series. Happily, there are many things to keep her occupied, and when she's not writing or curating the Short Story Superstars club she can be found gardening, singing, crafting, reading, laughing uproariously at nothing, playing the fool and playing board games.

You can find out more about her writing, and the weird stuff she finds herself researching, over at her website: www.laurenknixon.com

Annie Seng

Rhode Island, USA

Annie Seng used the money she made from flipping a crack house to co-found one of the fastest growing media companies in America.

And then on Tuesday she went shopping for her garden.

Louise D. Smith

South Yorkshire, UK

A thirty-something millenial overqualified, underemployed teacher type with a passion for Jesus, books and science. I have a personal library that rivals those of small towns and a desire to add to it that outstrips my income.

I've dabbled in music, embroidery, watercolours, fabric crafts, oil painting and a few other things along the way to realising that acrylic paints and writing are the arts for me, which I indulge in during the little free time I have that isn't spent in a field holding a weaponised lightning rod, or a whistle.

ARTISTS

Hailie

Alberta, Canada

Hailie is an aspiring novelist dreaming of publishing a new, fantastic series of magick proportions. In addition to being a bit of a writing fiend, Hailie also enjoys working with photo manipulation and restoration.

You can follow Hailie's journey as an author at:

http://hailiedrescher.wixsite.com/hailiedrescher

@HailieDrescher on Twitter

@Hailie_Drescher on Instagram

Liz Hearson

North Yorkshire, UK

Odd job artist for hire, known to reside on the East coast; neither armed, nor dangerous.

Cynthia Holt

Rhode Island, USA

Cynthia Holt is a writer and beekeeper from New England. She is the co-author of Bee Cult and the proprietress of Cabbage and Epstein apiary.

You can find her musings at her blog, No One Sleeps Naked in This House at

nicrophorus.blogspot.com.

PhoenixShaman

York, UK

Han is a non binary writer and creator, residing in historic York. Their work is often emotive with a bittersweet edge, finding the beauty in the darker parts of life, although they are no stranger to whimsy. When not writing or creating art, they enjoy indulging in computer and console gaming, collectable card games, tabletop RP, and LARP.

You can find more of their work here:
http://phoenixshaman.deviantart.com/

22447483R00221

Printed in Great Britain
by Amazon